CASEY E. BERGER

FIRST LIGHT

aethonbooks.com

FIRST LIGHT
©2021 CASEY BERGER

ACKNOWLEDGMENTS

This book was almost a decade in the making, and so many people contributed in that time to my growth as a writer and as a person. I will do my very best to acknowledge them all here, but if you played a role in my life in the last ten years, you left your mark in some way or another.

Huge thanks to my earliest readers: Justin, Michael, Alannah, Larkin, and Mary Beth. You took a book that was raw and mostly unformed and helped me see what it could become. Through your enthusiasm and support, I started to believe that this story could be more than a fun hobby, and that I could be more than a dabbler.

I've been fortunate to be supported by two different writing groups, who contributed in entirely different ways to this work. First was the little informal enclave formed by friends and colleagues working in LA back in 2011-2012, who nurtured the earliest seeds of this idea — back before Jaya was even called Jaya and when the big bad was a civilization of galaxy-invading aliens. Special thanks to Joe and Jenna, whose support and feedback continued long after the group itself went its separate ways. Second was the Durham Writers Group's SFF chapter, whose detailed and thoughtful feed-back helped me clean up the draft of this book that would eventually get an offer of publication. Thank you for your detailed critiques, and for celebrating with me when I signed the contract. Community is everything, and all of you are a part of this work.

It was just a few people who really cut into what this book was and helped me see what it could become. My later readers: Ryann, Jonathan, Baxter, Joseph, and Dave. And my critique partners, who are far more precious than gold. Michelle, thank you for sticking your fingers into every plot hole and pulling until it was a giant rip I could no longer justify ignoring. Your insights and perspective made this book so much stronger, and our many talks about craft and language and story and love and life enhance my days and my words in equal measure. This wouldn't exist without you: I would have trashed it long ago, but instead it became something better. Alannah, your thoughtful reflections on character and language helped me see my book in new ways, showing me places where I could dig deeper and give more to the characters and the world. Our lengthy discussions about art and worldbuilding and psychology and the business of being a creator have enriched my life as an author in ways I never even imagined.

To all the people who helped me in so many ways as I tried to get this book published, thank you for your willingness to provide a glimpse into your path, for the phone calls and emails and retweets and all the other little ways you supported me. To Michael Mammay and Hayley Stone, for your unflinching honesty about this process and your patience with my anxious questions. To Rachel Griffin, for your open-armed welcome into the world of the online writing community and your feedback on everything from query letters to release parties. To Cassandra Clarke and the SWFA mentorship program, for all you gave of yourself in time and effort and honesty. To the 2020 and 2021 debut groups, for giving me a home and a space to let all the scary, ugly, and fearful parts of this process out (and to celebrate the giddy highs as much as the desperate lows). Through all your efforts, you peeled aside the veil and let me not just see into the world of publishing, but take that first step on my own.

So many people outside of publishing contributed as well. To Uncle Mike, for your insights and legal expertise. To Mary Beth, for answering all my ridiculous questions about protocol and trauma care and science fiction medicine with infinite patience. To Larkin, Mary Beth, and Kate together, for enduring many floods of anxieties in the group text and always encouraging me to speak up for myself. To Leticia, for always having an open seat waiting for me at Kafe Kerouac and keeping the coffee flowing and my spirits high. To the teachers who read my middling adolescent words and saw something worth praising and encouraging and shaping. All of you kept me going in ways that are hard to tease apart: thank you.

Thank you to Aethon Books — and Rhett and Steve in particular — for giving me a chance to get my words out into the world, and for believing in me enough to ask for two sequels. Everyone involved in the publishing process works so hard, and while I don't know everyone who was involved in prepping my book at some point, I'm grateful for all your work. To my editor, James, thank you for the time you spent making the text stronger and helping me tie together all the pieces that are so easy to lose as an author. You pushed the prose and asked the tough questions and as a result, this book came out much stronger.

Finally, I owe so much to my family, both of the blood and found variety. For cultivating a love of books and stories. For encouraging curiosity and questioning. For tolerating and maybe even joining in my philosophical meanderings. And for always, always keeping my feet firmly on the ground even while my mind roamed this universe and others.

And to Justin, who appeared in my life on the very day I finished the first draft of this book. Whose entrance in my world signaled both an ending and a beginning. If I believed in signs, you would be one. But I don't believe in signs: I believe in you, and I believe in us. Thank you for being there for all the parts of me. The elation and the heartache. The anxieties and the hopes. The scientist and the artist. You see me, and I can't begin to find the words for what that means to me.

I could only dream when I started this novel that it would be out there in the world. I never could have imagined that would grow into the story that it is today. Thank you, readers, for letting me share this world with you. I hope it brings you as much joy and catharsis as it has brought me.

Dedication:

To Justin,
For believing in this long before I did.

ALSO IN SERIES

FIRST LIGHT
URSA MAJOR
DARK STARS

"The gates of hell are open night and day;
Smooth the descent, and easy is the way:
But to return, and view the cheerful skies,
In this the task and mighty labor lies."
- Virgil, the *Aeneid*

1

It was just behind her sternum, in that part of her chest that felt the most sheltered, where she could fold in on herself if she needed to. That was where she neatly wrapped the images of gore, the coppery smell of blood, the sensation of stepping on lifeless limbs. That was where she pictured storing it all away when her job demanded it.

Lieutenant Commander Jaya Mill had seen enough violence and bloodshed in her fourteen years of service that this part of her was carefully cultivated. It was a place of darkness, sealed away behind a will stronger than the alloys of the armor they wore into the field. Rarely did the door crack open and let the darkness out to sicken her. And it wasn't the destruction around her that left the way open today, that allowed the clammy tendril of fear to wrap around her insides. It wasn't the bodies strewn across the colony. It wasn't the smell of their rotting flesh, ghostly and faint and perhaps only a trick of the mind after her suit's filters had scrubbed the air.

It was the voice that sent a chill through her.

Beside her, Lieutenant Salman Azima picked his way through the bodies that had piled along the corridor, abandoned there once the gurneys and temporary beds had been packed two people deep.

The emergency lighting still cast a flat light on the carnage. It had happened so fast.

They didn't understand yet what it was. But they understood its purpose. That was clear before Jaya and the rest of the *Avalon*'s company had set foot on this colony. The group that claimed responsibility for this attack called themselves the Sons of Priam. They claimed that only by razing the old could they right the wrongs of the galactic powers and bring about a new world. Their leader—although he kept his name and his image from the propaganda they broadcast to the farthest reaches of Union-controlled space—spoke with a dark power. And his voice...

It wasn't a particularly terrifying voice by most standards. It hadn't been altered to produce any effect. And yet, it haunted her. Slightly breathy, with the rich timbre of the lowest notes of a flute. It made the tiny hairs on her forearms stand on end. Something in his voice tugged at her subconscious and dug into the deepest secrets in her mind and pulled them forward.

Jaya crouched down, removing one of the sterile kits from her pack. This was as good a place as any she had already passed to take samples. The hospital had been the first on this colony to send out the alert, a mere twenty hours ago. The quickest of the victims had come straight here the moment they felt ill. Most had not been so fast to assume the worst, and as Jaya took in the white-walled corridor heaped with putrid corpses, she thought perhaps those who had waited had been better off. It was all over so fast, every human and alien resident on this colony dead before the first relief ship could arrive and the military could quarantine the area. At least those who had not sought medical attention had been able to die at home. Surrounded by loved ones.

Corporal Elias Thompson's voice came over the comms. The implanted communicator in Jaya's ear broadcast his voice crisply, the fidelity so good she could hear the tears in his throat. She closed her eyes, wishing she could grant him some privacy, but they had a job to do. His older brother had been on Yangtze, one of the other colonies hit. Just yesterday Thompson had been bragging about how the wages he sent home had allowed his brother to invest in new equipment for his farm. How bright his future would be.

Jaya understood the loss of a brother. Her own brother's disappearance remained a jagged wound in her heart to this day, more than two decades later. But her family was one of those secrets the voice had stirred up, and they were roiling dangerously at the front of her mind right now. She held them close, her own private grief— and fear.

"No one moving on the third floor," Thompson said. "Infrared says the bodies are all cold here too. There are some offices, though. Thought Sal might want to have a look."

"Good work, Corporal," Jaya replied. "Sending Lieutenant Azima to you now."

She looked back at Sal, who nodded and began to pack up his own testing kits to join Thompson on the third floor.

"Roger, Lieutenant Commander," Thompson said.

"Hey Mill," Rhodes's voice broke through, on a private line. Lieutenant Commander John Rhodes was Jaya's counterpart, leading his own small strike team through the government buildings just a kilometer away.

"I'm listening."

"We're about done over here," he said. "Are you ready for exfil?"

"Not quite," Jaya replied. "Head to the rendezvous point and we'll be there when we're done. Azima is going to hit the hospital computers and see what he can find. You get anything good?"

"Negative. No sign anyone saw this coming. We'll have to have the quants work their magic, but it's like this place was cursed."

"You can say that again."

"Okay, we're headed out. Meet you at the RP."

Rhodes signed off and left Jaya in the silence of her biohazard suit, crouched over a body. A sudden wave of grief rushed up in her, tightening her chest. She swallowed it back down and took a deep breath, closing that door. There would be time later.

She took her last sample and checked her palm drive. The tiny computer, implanted in her skin, was wirelessly connected to a control panel on the wrist of her suit. She brought up a layout of the hospital, displayed as a three-dimensional holographic map. Two dots on the third floor showed her where Sal and Thompson were located. A third dot roamed the outside of the building. That would be Jordan Vargas, completing her perimeter check. The corporal was uncharacteristically quiet today. The team's internal channel was usually raucous with banter between Vargas and Thompson, but today there was only Jaya's own thinking to occupy her mind.

Jaya interrupted the silence. "Alpha team, report."

"On my final sweep." Vargas's voice was still brash, though without her usual swagger.

"I've checked all the floors," Thompson confirmed. "On three now with Azima."

"This hospital's data security is a fucking joke."

Jaya couldn't help a smile. That would be Sal. His sharp edges hadn't softened at all in the ten years she had served with him.

"I take it you'll be done soon, then?" she replied drily.

"Download in progress," Sal said. "We'll have all the automated data, but I'll be shocked if anyone in this hospital made any notes once the crowds rolled in, and considering they were sick, too..."

He paused, and Jaya finished sealing up the sample bag while she waited. Long gaps in the conversation were also typical of Sal. She could picture him now, his dark brown eyes narrowed at the screen in front of him, his previous train of thought suspended indefinitely like a hung code until he finished whatever had distracted him.

"So we won't have much in the way of on-the-ground description, but we should have lots of data to process. Could find a pattern," Sal concluded. "I've got everything I need."

"Time to go, then," Jaya said. "Bravo team is waiting for us." She switched to the master channel. "*Avalon*, this is Alpha One. Mission accomplished, all participants accounted for. Bravo team is at the RP and Alpha team is en route. Requesting exfil."

"Lieutenant Lupo is on her way in the shuttle, Alpha One." The *Avalon*'s captain—Peter Armstrong—replied, his voice warm and determined. "We're expecting you. Come on home."

"Thank you, Captain."

The rendezvous point was half a kilometer outside the capital, but Arcadian Gardens was a tiny agricultural colony, and calling the capital a city would be generous. It spanned less than two kilometers north to south, and was even shorter east to west. Its population was a few thousand, nearly all humans. While other colonies boasted thriving multi-species populations, agricultural colonies like this one weren't a draw for residents from any of the other civilizations of the galaxy. Outside the capital, agricultural compounds swept along the curve of the planet, and the remaining sixty thousand citizens of Arcadian Gardens lived there, managing the crops that they exported to richer colonies and stations in the United Human Nations.

Or used to. Preliminary sweeps showed a cold and desolate countryside. No heat signatures. No living beings, human, alien, or livestock. Not anymore.

It hadn't been all that different from the colony where Jaya had spent her teen years. Her gut tightened, and she had the sudden urge to call her uncles.

They reached the rendezvous point in short time. Bravo team stood in the wheat field, four figures shrouded in bulky suits, stark against the daylight in this empty world.

"Approaching RP," Jaya announced.

"We see you, Alpha team," Rhodes replied. "Ready to go home?"

"Very."

A rush of air buffeted their suits as the shuttle descended. The wheat in the field compressed and rippled—the only motion they had seen in hours—as Lieutenant Linh Lupo brought the shuttle gently down, opening the airlock aperture.

All eight of them filed in and the doors closed. Jaya blinked against the dimness of the airlock after the bright light outside. A gentle hiss announced that the decontamination procedure had begun, and they waited patiently until the warning lights above the door flashed from red to green. Still, they peeled off their external suits in grim silence, turning them inside out and stuffing them in a biohazard box. Rhodes sealed the box and stowed it before anyone even moved toward the door controls.

The faint green glow of the controls shone on Rhodes's dark face, cheekbones and cropped hair sharp against the backlight. His characteristic soberness seemed softer in this close, quiet space, and his strike team—Shea, Werner, and Martel—stood close by his side. Thompson, in contrast, looked queasy and pale in the cool light, and his eyes were bloodshot and hard. He didn't shrug off Vargas's hand on his shoulder when she approached him, but he closed his eyes. A wave of nausea passed over Jaya, the fear and brokenness rising momentarily to the surface. When she looked at Sal, he was already staring back at her, a dark eyebrow quirked up and his curls askew from the suit's helmet.

She took a deep breath. It would do her team no good to see her weakness. She squashed it down and into its box, sealing it as tightly as she could.

Rhodes activated the door controls and they stepped through as the inertia tugged on them. Lupo was taking the shuttle back up to the *Avalon*.

"Locking our approach," Lupo announced, sliding out of her

seat as the automated controls took over. She tossed her long black braid over her shoulder and joined them in the awkward circle they had formed, everyone standing just a little closer than normal, hesitant to break the contact. Lupo reached for Vargas's hand, squeezing it tightly.

"We'll be home soon," Rhodes said.

"Then what?" Shea asked, their dark eyes flitting between Rhodes and Jaya.

"We find a way to help," Jaya replied. "We pick up the pieces."

The conference room of the *Avalon* was barely large enough to hold the two strike teams and their commanding officers. Four naval officers and four marines, and the room still felt small with the eight of them assembled in their service dress grays. They had barely even had time to shower and change once the samples and equipment were properly cleaned, filed, and stowed, and Jaya's still-damp hair was gathered in a low bun.

"This is the single most pointless part of our job," Sal grumbled. He leaned his lanky body back in his chair, shaking unruly dark curls—just barely within regulation length—out of his eyes.

Jaya just chuckled. Back on the *Avalon*, away from the devastation they had seen below, clean and in fresh clothing, the oppressive weight of what had happened was already beginning to lift, and a sense of normalcy was returning. The routine could be both soothing and frustrating. And debriefs could feel stuffy and pointless, for a group of people who preferred working to talking, but she accepted them as an occupational hazard.

"You don't have to pretend to like this," he said, responding to her laugh. "You're Armstrong's golden child even without sucking up."

"If you're any indication, attitude is not what wins promotions around here," she said.

Sal opened his mouth, but before he could respond, Armstrong and Tully entered the room and the small assembly of naval officers and marines stood at attention. All conversation died out instantaneously at the arrival of their commanding officer.

Captain Peter Armstrong had been at the helm of the *Avalon* since before Jaya had graduated from the Naval Academy, and Commander Tully Coolidge had come aboard the ship as his second-in-command just a few months ago. Armstrong surveyed the crew with calm blue eyes shining bright in a weathered brown face, his broad shoulders rising above most of the personnel. Tully strolled behind him, his posture less stately, gray streaking his short, fine hair. He winked at Jaya and Sal when he met their eyes. Jaya suppressed a smile at the small scoffing noise Sal made in response.

Since his arrival, Tully had tried to connect with the crew by putting on a fun-loving uncle persona to undercut the gravitas of Armstrong's steady leadership. It was a frankly feeble attempt. He always seemed to be playing at something, but Jaya could sense a sharp edge behind it. Like Armstrong, Tully didn't miss anything, but unlike the captain, he mimed looking the other way.

But his attitude had a way of boosting the morale of the team. Perhaps she was just too deep in the counterintelligence game to trust easily. So she returned his wink with a mild smile.

Armstrong faced the crowded room, his brow furrowed.

"Preliminary reports from the *Shambhala* on Presnovodnyy and the *Atlantis* on Yangtze put estimated casualties at two-point-two million, but that figure is still rising. The *Kilimanjaro* has been rerouted to Amazonia, but we expect to find the same thing there."

Jaya exchanged a glance with Sal. Valhalla-class frigates like the *Avalon, Atlantis,* and *Shambhala* were crewed with special IRC —Intelligence, Reconnaissance, and Counterterrorism—squads in order to be able to quickly gather information and perform precision strikes. Dispatching an Everest-class cruiser like the *Kilimanjaro* meant they had truly been caught off-guard.

There was a hushed murmur in the room—somewhere between resignation and empathy—and the cold wash of shock began to thaw. A new twinge followed, this one of guilt. There had been so many deaths like this, and each time the news was a blow. But the galaxy always returned to its usual patterns and ways. There was an inevitability to it, and also a pragmatism: life could not continue if it were frozen in perpetual grief. But Jaya wondered how much was lost every time they were able to turn their heads away from the tragedy and toward the daily work.

At least she could say she was working toward the end of this violence.

"I received new orders from Rear Admiral Reid," Armstrong continued. "Now, I know this last assignment was very long, and we are all in need of some shore leave. But the timing is not in our hands, I'm afraid. The *Avalon* and its company has been tasked with investigating this new group responsible for the attacks, the so-called Sons of Priam." He gave a sympathetic smile. "We'll still get our break, but it will be a short one. We dock at Argos Station at oh-seven-hundred hours the day after tomorrow for two days of shore leave. In that time, the *Shambhala, Atlantis,* and *Kilimanjaro* will send their detailed reports from the colonies to HQ and we'll have something to work with. All personnel should be prepared to report back to the ship forty-eight hours after we dock."

He glanced around the room, making eye contact with every one of the officers. Then he nodded to Jaya. "Lieutenant Commander Mill, you will supervise the drills tonight."

"Understood."

"Dismissed," Tully said crisply.

The rustling of starched uniforms and the murmured conversations of the officers dwindled as the room emptied.

"Well, it's nice to know the latest threat to the galaxy is just the stuff of nightmares as usual," Sal said, his expression wry.

"That video was awful," Jaya said. "Something about the voice unsettles me."

"The voice of a psychopathic mass murderer? I can't imagine why that would be unsettling. I, personally, would like to listen to that video before bed every night because it soothes me."

Jaya laughed at his mocking tone. "Okay. Mystery solved."

"What would you do without me?" Sal linked arms with Jaya.

"Oh, that reminds me," she said. "My palm drive is acting up. I was using the heat signature sweep a lot down there, and now I'm getting an alert of some sort."

"What does the alert say?" Sal asked as they veered into the IT office and headed to his desk in the back corner of the room.

"Something something system something," she replied, perching herself on the desk.

"Your attention to detail never ceases to amaze me."

"Oh, you're only pissed 'cause I saved your ass on that recon last week."

He flashed her a wicked grin: "You better watch what you say, or you might find your palm drive starts malfunctioning in... interesting ways."

His threat was hollow, and she returned it with a gentle shove. He pulled out a data pad and connected to the signal from Jaya's palm drive, then gestured for her to enter her passcode. A holographic display rose up over the tablet as his hands danced across the screen, running diagnostics.

Sal was all fine lines, tall and slender. The strength he had built in his military training never outshone the intellectualism he was so proud of. His shoulders rounded as his gaze fixed intently on the task at hand, and if she didn't know him better, she would assume he had already dropped the train of their conversation.

She chuckled. "Okay, truce. I'll keep saving your ass if you keep fixing my gadgets."

"Hey, I've won a few rounds solidly against you in training."

He resumed his focus on the software, flying through various screens she hadn't even known existed in the operations menu of the palm drive.

To her, the palm drive was just a tool she used in combat. To Sal, it was a secret world full of information. She had no idea what was going on in his head when he zoned in like that, but she definitely knew that she didn't speak the same language as Sal and the machines.

"So, what do you think?" he asked.

She didn't have to ask about what.

"It's fucked up," she said. "I want to know who this guy is. He's being cryptic about his agenda. All we have is his proclamations of general corruption and a vague reference to the founding of Rome."

Sal looked up from his work, momentarily distracted. "Wait, what about the founding of Rome? How did I miss that?"

"It's just some things he said in the video. *Fortune befriends the bold*, *To tame the proud, the fetter'd slave to free.* They're quotes from the *Aeneid*. Priam was the king of Troy. They're intentionally referencing the birth of a new empire out of the ashes of this one."

"Oh," Sal said. He lowered his voice, ensuring their words wouldn't carry across the room to the other officers at their desks. "This something you got from your mom?"

"Yeah," Jaya replied, her voice lowered as well. "She said its themes ran deep in human literature. It's part of our culture. It was important to her."

Sal nodded and dropped the subject. It was one of the reasons they got along so well. He was the only person who knew a few details of her childhood, and in exchange for her candor, he gave her privacy. Sal was also the only person she knew aside from herself who could keep a personal secret, if he had motive. In a ship as small as the *Avalon*, gossip was a favorite sport, and Sal a champion competitor, but her secrets traveled from her lips to Sal's ears, where they remained locked inside him.

The ones she told him, at least.

"There," he said, shutting down the data pad and unplugging it from her palm drive. "Good as new until you break it again."

She hopped off his desk in a smooth motion.

"Thanks," she said. "You're right—I don't know what I'd do without you."

"You'd be buried in broken technology with your track record," he laughed. "Please try to remember that it's a scalpel, not a sledgehammer."

"Oh, look at you getting fancy with your words. I'll be careful with it, I promise."

He sighed and shook his head, waving her away. Her palm drive beeped, indicating a new message. She brought up the interface.

You are destined for more.

That was it. Five words. No subject. Sent from an address that appeared to be no more than random numbers.

She stared at the message, suspicion thrumming in her veins. Who would send her this message, and how in the galaxy did it get past the Navy's stringent security protocols?

"What is it?" Sal asked.

She realized that she had stopped in her tracks and was now standing in the middle of the room, interrupting the flow of traffic. For a brief moment, she considered showing the message to Sal, but something made her stop. She closed the palm drive and headed toward the door.

"Training at eighteen hundred ship time," she called over her shoulder. "Don't forget!"

"I never forget," he called back.

2

The grand ballroom of the Arbiter's mansion was iridescent in the evening light of Iralu City. Outside, the glow of the metropolis frosted the large, geometric-latticed windows, which refracted that light into its component parts and scattered it through the room's sparse columns and high arching ceiling.

Displays of opulence were uncommon in szacante culture, but the Arbiter often hosted dignitaries from the larger of the three superpowers, the Nareian Empire and the United Human Nations, so some level of resplendence was expected. Especially if the Szacante Federation wished to secure their tenuous role of third superpower in the galactic political balance.

Tynan Vasuda believed this third spoke was of the highest importance. The szacante could provide the calm, rational voice in the tempestuous discourse between the humans and the nareians. It was this belief that had led him here tonight.

The Arbiter and the Minister of Science were holding a dinner in honor of the accomplishments of the Arbiter's Advisory Committee for Advancement, a group of which Tynan was a proud and vocal member. It was a poorly kept secret that tonight's dinner was the preview to a series of retirement festivities for the current

Minister of Science, and Tynan was determined to secure his position as the likely nominee to replace her. He scanned the room for the Arbiter, hoping to get a word in before the evening was over. Most of the guests tonight were szacante, their slender forms accompanied by holographic projections of their virtual assistants, but a few human and nareian officials were in attendance as well. The newer members of the szacante political establishment were instantly identifiable by the extra distance they put between themselves and the muscular nareians who stood head and shoulders above most of the guests.

"Arbiter Vihica and Minister Harta are approaching," the voice of Min, his Virtual Assistant, said through his implanted earbud. Although she shimmered beside him, a holographic image of a female scazante on long, slim legs, she kept her words private. He appreciated her tact, as always.

Tynan's assistant was not unique—every szacante was implanted with a virtual intelligence when they acquired early language skills. These implanted protocols were free to learn and grow with the child, and they developed traits that complemented their partner's. Some szacantes' VAs had gregarious personalities, and Tynan had witnessed many that would carry on full and animated conversations with their partners' friends and neighbors. He was grateful for Min's quiet presence.

Tynan worked his way through the sea of people and their semi-transparent VAs, careful not to pass through any of the holographic displays. That would be exactly the sort of affront he was trying to avoid tonight. As he reached the Arbiter and Harta, his heart began to pound in his chest. Min's soothing voice again filled his ears, reminding him to count his breaths.

In for four, out for eight. In for four, out for eight. His heart thudded less insistently now. That would do.

"Doctor Vasuda." Minister Harta touched her temple with

silvery-skinned fingers in a traditional Szacante greeting. Beside her, her VA mimicked the gesture.

"Wonderful to see you, Minister," Tynan said. "And Arbiter Vihica, it's an honor." Tynan and Min repeated the greeting, but to the Arbiter they added a small bow. It never hurt to be a little extra accommodating.

"We've met before, Doctor Vasuda, have we not?" the Arbiter asked, his voice thin. Tynan had to strain to hear him in the din of the conversations around them.

"Indeed." Tynan suppressed his thrill of joy. "At last year's cere-mony for the Medal of Virtue. I was asked to assist in the presenta-tion of the medals to the academic recipients."

"Of course," the Arbiter said.

"Doctor Vasuda is a recipient of the medal himself," Harta inter-jected, and when the Arbiter turned an interested face toward Tynan, Harta winked.

"Oh, of course," the Arbiter said. "Such an eminent scientist as yourself. You have contributed much to the advancement of our people. Was it my predecessor who awarded you?"

"It was Arbiter Lika."

"So long ago," the Arbiter exclaimed. "Forgive me for not remembering. You have been such an exemplary figure in your field from such a young age, it is easy to take your success for granted."

"I try not to, Arbiter. I strive every day to continue to bring our people knowledge and—more importantly—the wisdom to use that knowledge properly."

"Sage words," Harta agreed.

"I won't keep you, Arbiter," Tynan said. "I know you have many people who wish to speak with you tonight."

They said polite goodbyes and parted ways, the dreadful thud-ding in Tynan's chest now replaced with a heady buzz. That had gone even better than he had expected. His parents had been polit-ical savants, mastering the art of dialect and the science of networking. That ability had not transferred to their son, who had grown up with a greater love of science and math than schmoozing. But if they were alive today, Tynan thought they would be proud. He was well on his way to becoming the next Minister of Science, where he could guide szacante research practices for the next generation.

He tried not to smile too brightly. No sense in getting ahead of himself, and he certainly couldn't explain his joyous countenance to anyone who might ask. He took a drink from a server and sipped it, letting the sharp spice of it cut through his giddiness.

It was not a moment too soon.

Kujei's voice broke through the murmur of voices around them. He had always spoken at high volume, as if orating from a public auditorium for all to hear. The concept of hushed respect was foreign to him, and just the sound of his voice caused Tynan to cringe at flashes of memories from his first university days.

Kujei Oszca had been Tynan's research mentor on his first doctoral degree. Tynan had been one of the youngest students to pass through the research laboratories of the great Capital University of Dresha, and Kujei had initially been a supportive and encouraging mentor. He had challenged Tynan to learn new methods, to think creatively and pull insights and techniques from other disciplines. It was partly Kujei's early influence that had encouraged Tynan to pursue more doctorates later, while running his own research group at a smaller university.

Every discipline had so much to offer, and Tynan wanted to dive as deeply as he could into all of them, returning with treasures of knowledge he could use to advance his work and help his people maintain their status as the greatest minds of the galaxy.

But after the early days of his first doctorate, as the novelty began to wear off for both of them, Tynan and Kujei's relationship had soured. As Tynan had become more adept at methodology, he began to question Kujei's. His mentor took too many risks, pushed the science in ways that made Tynan uncomfortable. Kujei had the attitude that if he didn't ask permission, he couldn't be denied, and so he followed his own whims. And he always got away with it, because his results were so brilliant.

Tynan understood the value of taking risks, of course. But he worried that Kujei's habits would take him from innovative to unethical.

And then, inevitably, they did.

When Tynan had reported Kujei to the university, they refused to act. Kujei walked the ethical line, but the university failed to see that as dangerous. Or perhaps they didn't want to be the university who let the most famous xenobiologist in the galaxy go.

Kujei still worked there.

The crowd laughed in response to whatever Kujei had just said, bringing Tynan back to the present. He realized this particular swarm of people was a crowd around Kujei. He drew closer and saw the Arbiter standing next to his former mentor, pale face and watery eyes creased with laughter. Laughter at the words of the person Tynan hated most in this galaxy.

Tynan didn't hate a lot of people. Hatred was frankly a difficult emotion. It took a lot of energy to hate a person, and Tynan had never seen it lead to good results. No, hatred was not rational. But he couldn't help the way his every nerve began to buzz at just the mention of Doctor Kujei Oszca. Seeing him was even worse. His formal robe tonight was perfectly tailored, its faint silver sheen the perfect accent to his mauve skin. He had more charisma than any szacante Tynan had ever met, and he wielded his charm like a weapon, cutting down all those who stood in his way.

And ever since their years in the same research lab, back when Tynan had first challenged his research practices, the person in Kujei's way was most often Tynan.

Kujei was a brilliant researcher, but he believed in the utter supremacy of knowledge for knowledge's sake. To Tynan, this was a fundamentally un-szacante perspective. Knowledge was a powerful gift. Through knowledge one could eradicate one form of suffering after another. Through knowledge, they had expanded out into the broader galaxy, and one day—through knowledge—they would surely discover methods that would allow them to reach farther-flung galaxies. Through knowledge, the Szacante Federation could mediate the hot-headed duo of the United Human Nations and Nareian Empire.

But a gift so powerful must be managed properly. A gift so powerful must be cherished and evaluated with great caution before being applied to the problems they faced. Any other way was likely to create more problems than it solved.

"I couldn't believe it either," Kujei was saying. "Here I was surrounded by nareians at a formal reception, and my translator was just returning gibberish. I had to politely excuse myself—word-lessly, might I add—and steal away to a closet to rewire the whole thing. Of course, this was back before we had developed the adapt-ability matrix we use now that allows us to synchronize our transla-tors with our palm drives. I'll tell you, that night was an adventure."

Everyone laughed, and Tynan drew his face into a stony glare. The Arbiter leaned in to Kujei and waggled a finger toward him.

"You have always thought on your feet," he said. "Ever since you were a little sapling of a child. I recall when your father and I were renegotiating the trade agreement with the Nareian Empire…"

Tynan's world shrank in that moment. The room closed in on him, and the Arbiter's story no longer reached his ears. Or if it did, he found he had no will to translate the sound waves into words. After all, he could feel in his gut the inevitable result.

It didn't matter how smart he was. It didn't matter that the current Minister of Science clearly thought he was the best choice. Once again, he was in Kujei's way, and the oncoming charm offen-sive was strong as a shockwave.

In for four, out for eight. In for four, out for eight.

He found himself on the outskirts of the room, having left Kujei and his crowd of adoring followers behind. Min was admonishing him about his adrenaline levels and reminding him to breathe.

In for four, out for eight.

No. No, he was not going to let his oldest rivalry stand in his way. He knew he had the best course of action for the Federation. He had plans, and a comprehensive theory of advancement. And most importantly, he would not compromise the integrity of szacante research. Theirs would not be a nation of quick advances followed by the inevitable crisis and realization that they had played with forces beyond their comprehension. They would comprehend *first*.

He could do this.

The blue light of the youthful twin suns pushed its rays through the windows. The brightness reflected off the sleek metal architecture of Iralu City, summoning all within its reach to the spectacular view of the szacante homeworld's capital city. But Tynan, as was customary, had his attention fixed on the samples before him. He glanced up frequently at the numbers populating the holographic display as he measured viral levels in the tissue. That display spoke his language more than the power of the vista from his neglected windows.

It had been a night of light and fitful sleep, and he had often woken in a cold sweat, seeing his future evaporate before him in nightmares. But when the suns had begun to rise, he reminded himself that his work spoke for itself and he had plenty of it to do today.

He was the first in the lab as usual. Senior scientists such as Tynan rarely performed laboratory work, their time mostly spent on long-term planning and research direction. Most scientists at his level felt they had earned the right to never pull on scratchy synthetic scrubs and experience the claustrophobic respirator and go through two stages of decontamination upon entrance and exit to the lab. But Tynan felt the loss of the *feeling* of science, the hands-on work and mindful repetition. And so he spent quiet mornings in the lab before getting on with his day as the boss.

This was his pet project. Of everything that Tynan's organization had studied, this virus held his fascination. It had appeared relatively recently, with devastating neurological effects on its hosts. About a decade back, it had wiped out a human colony when it managed to jump species. The virus had a complex structure, and its ability to cross from one sentient species to another made it a top priority for all the major funding sources.

And Tynan wanted to be the one to understand it—to wield this knowledge in order to develop vaccines and containment protocols. This knowledge had the potential to help so many.

"Min, can you run the analysis on this set?"

"Of course."

"Thank you," Tynan replied, storing the samples back in the climate-controlled cabinet set to exactly their experiment's settings. He entered the decontamination room and removed his gloves and the specialized suit and respirator once the door had closed again. He breathed deep when he emerged from the room and made his way to a sink, where he washed his hands thoroughly—more a ritual now than something serving any scientific purpose.

He stepped back from the sink, running his spindly fingers over the pale skin of his forehead.

Min materialized beside him, a concerned expression on her face.

"You are worried," she said. She was matter-of-fact. She was always matter-of-fact—he found it soothing.

"We're so close," he said, hearing the strange binary of anticipation and dread twisting around each other in his throat.

"Why are you worried, then?" she asked.

He turned toward the window in the hallway, still blind to the sleek lines of the city below, but the light seemed to impart some of its energy into him. He sighed, feeling an iota of the tension in his neck and shoulders flow out of him with that sigh.

"It's such an enormous possibility," he said. "To find a way to eradicate this virus, to keep it from jumping species again." He sighed at the pleasant sensation that dream evoked in him. "And if I succeed, I can show the Arbiter that my methods work, that my guidance can push our knowledge forward with integrity."

"Perhaps it is the responsibility that is weighing you down?" Min offered.

Although her attention appeared entirely fixed on him, Tynan knew that most of Min's processing capabilities were devoted to running the statistics even as she interacted with him. The abilities of virtual intelligences still filled him with awe, and more than a tinge of envy. He let out another sigh—this one more of a laugh.

"Perhaps," he said, smiling at Min. "But perhaps it's just that we seem to exist constantly on the verge of a breakthrough. Each glimpse of the other side is so thrilling… but at any moment we can slip back down the edge. To failure."

"But this has always been true of science. The old prophets said that the greatest good is to increase the collective wisdom of the people."

"And the greatest evil is to play a part in their destruction," Tynan said, finishing the phrase.

He turned away from the light of the binary stars rising over the false horizon of rooftops and skyways and began the walk to his office.

"The analysis is completed," Min said, "but you have a visitor."

"What?"

"The board wanted you to meet with him, Tynan," Min pushed gently. "You agreed to hear him out."

Tynan recalled dimly that he had committed to a short meeting.

The irritation at his own past decision in light of his current sense of urgency shot down the nerves of his back, leaving a warm flush. Another knot added itself to his tension. He waved his hand, and Min's visual projection vanished. He turned the corner toward his office, where a tall human was waiting for him, pacing outside his door.

The electronic lock flashed from red to green, and Tynan opened the door to his office and motioned for the human to join him as he entered the room.

Tynan expected some sort of greeting or formalities to be exchanged, but the human man pulled a chair out and sat across the desk from Tynan. The unexpected shift in decorum pulled those knots in his back even tighter as he slowly lowered himself into his own chair and stared across the desk at the man.

The man's eyes searched the room rapidly, and Tynan could almost feel the race of thoughts beneath the sunset-colored hair on the man's head, like a radiating heat.

"Doctor Vasuda," the man said. His voice seemed too large for the small office, and Tynan winced.

"Yes," Tynan said.

"I represent a very large business," the man said. "Our research team has been searching for months for a scientific facility with the very expertise that your foundation specializes in. We reached out to your board of directors last month and it seems we have a lot in common."

"I don't understand," Tynan said flatly.

"We'd like to make a deal." The man met his eyes, and Tynan's hands grew clammy. He pressed them against his knees and swallowed. Remembered his breathing.

In for four, out for eight.

"What are you offering?" Tynan asked.

The man stood and turned on the holographic display of his palm drive. He projected an image in front of Tynan. Pages of legal documents floated before his eyes, and Tynan found himself hunching over to read the small type. The man continued to stand, his once-flighty gaze now fixed with intense focus on Tynan.

Min's voice came over the private implant in Tynan's ear: "The agreement is for purchase of the foundation by a group called Calista Holdings," she explained. "It specifies the transfer of shares to a new board to be named by Calista Holdings."

Tynan nodded slightly. His eyes glanced over the document but he wasn't reading. He was listening.

"Research direction will be determined by Calista Holdings," Min continued. "You will no longer be the principal investigator. They propose creating a position above you; a director's position."

Anger bloomed in him, the warmth of it spreading through his limbs. This was exactly the kind of offer Kujei would love. He would gladly hand over his work for the promise of rapid expansion.

"I'm not interested in your offer," Tynan said, waving at the documents in a gesture of disdain. He looked up at the man from within the shadow cast by his tall figure.

"You will still have creative freedom," the man countered coolly. "We're interested in cultivating your talent, not stifling it."

"I will no longer be the head of this organization."

"But you will be the neck—able to turn us toward new horizons. It's a matter of galactic security. You are not the only individual interested in protecting the future of the galaxy. We can offer incentives to your employees, encourage more efficient work, and provide avenues toward clear practical applications. We believe much more can come out of your little research firm with our support and influence behind you."

The warmth of anger expanded into a hot flush. It loosened the knots that had been tightening throughout this conversation. Tynan stood abruptly. "I don't agree that we have much in common. Our values clearly differ."

"Yes," the man said, smiling and remaining composed. He took his seat again and looked up at Tynan. "Let us discuss the question of value. We think your research is *quite* valuable."

"I think you define value differently," Tynan replied shortly. "This meeting is over. I've heard what you have to say and I reject your offer. I'm sorry you wasted your time."

Tynan crossed to the door, showing the way out with his long-fingered hands. The man remained seated a moment longer, contemplating Tynan with an outward coolness, but the szacante felt the fire in his core matched by the man's eyes. He finally stood and exited the room without a word. Tynan closed the door, his arms shaky. His entire body was a live wire.

"The offer was high," Min observed.

"I don't want their money," Tynan said. "I've spent years on this research. This is *my* work."

"Tynan, remember your breathing."

He took a deep breath.

In for four, out for eight.

The tingling of his nerves began to subside as he thought about the years he had poured into this research: developing new methods, new analysis tools, delving deeply into this mystery and pulling its secrets out. Those secrets, like pieces of a puzzle, still needed to be assembled, and some remained hidden. But he would not relinquish control until it was done, or he was dead. Whichever came first.

But he was certain it would not be the latter.

3

The deep, private darkness of FTL travel held the *Nasdenika* gently. Mara checked their course. She would be dropping into sub-luminal speeds shortly, and soon would arrive at Balei's station, which orbited an otherwise satellite-devoid young planet. She didn't like how close they were to Narei, but she reminded herself that this was a simple bounty—she would be out of this corner of the galaxy, well-paid and onto the next job, in no time.

Mara yawned, stretching her body and flexing all her digits—a vestigial motion that would have extended sheathed claws back when the early nareians had ruled the tropical regions of their home-world. She reached for the belt that held her knives at her waist—her own, modern interpretation of her ancestral retractable claws—and checked its various pockets and attachments. This routine, now so embedded in her tissue that it felt like a natural extension of the stretch, pulled the last of the sluggishness of space travel from her mind.

Mara touched the top of the control panel and floated back to her seat, directing herself with the deliberate motions of someone who had grown accustomed to moving in zero-G. She strapped herself into the captain's chair and glanced over at the empty seat beside it, intended for an executive officer.

Of course, Tai had never been her XO. He hadn't been the captain, either—they used to bicker over whichever chair was nearest. Each had held the other's life carefully, each responsible in equal measure for the other. But if she was being honest, she had always been the more serious of the two; she had also been the one less willing to hand over her safety. Tai had managed to coax out the carefree child that she had crumpled and stuffed into a dark, musty corner. To open her up, to know her entire complex history even with its danger.

But she had still always trusted herself just a little more than she trusted him.

The galaxy had a brutal sense of humor. In the end, she had been the one who had endangered them. The oppressive breath of her former life was hot on the back of her neck. It was still pursuing her —of this, she was certain.

Mara flicked a glance at the video screen. Her bounty, Velkar, was still strapped into his chair in the small cell, safely contained. He was barrel-chested for a szacante, but still rather slim compared to most of the other races Mara was in contact with most frequently. He glared at the camera, his VA giving a similar glare through her shimmery holographic projection. Mara had jammed Velkar's personal communication channel, naturally, but there was no way to stop the VA from showing herself. Or talking, aloud or privately to Velkar. But that was all she could do, and for now the two were just glowering. Mara flashed a wicked grin she knew they could not see.

She may not be comfortable with her proximity to Narei, but this job paid well, and every expensive job she pulled brought her a step farther ahead. Widened the gap her pursuers had to cross. Money and power were nothing to them, but they didn't understand the dark underside of the galaxy that Mara now called home. She was earning currency they couldn't spend, and every assignment she took mapped out a new network, expanded her reach into the dark parts of space that most of civilized nareian culture believed to be empty.

"I'll pay you whatever he's paying you," Velkar shouted from the back.

"So you noticed we're getting close."

"I'll double what he's paying," the szacante responded.

"Balei would just hire someone else," she said. "And as much as I would love double pay for less work, I have a reputation to uphold. That's something you should have considered for yourself before you skipped on a job half done."

Velkar muttered what Mara was sure were obscenities, but she couldn't be bothered to listen. His VA flickered away, clearly realizing that the double glower wasn't any more effective than the single one.

Balei's space station was as opulent as one would expect for someone who hired a bounty hunter over a botched job and a stolen down payment. Mara watched its gleaming metal frame grow in the screens as they approached. The structure was far larger than any one individual could possibly need. Of course, it was perhaps a reasonable size for the headquarters of a crime syndicate.

The bounty on Velkar would be pocket change to someone of Balei's standing, but Mara knew it wasn't about the money. It was never really about the money.

They docked, and Velkar squirmed against the firm grip she held on him as she dragged him down the corridor from the shuttle port. The escort Balei had sent to accompany them walked briskly alongside, indifferent to Velkar's struggle, but his weapon was displayed clearly and she knew he would be trained to use it.

When they reached Balei's office, the tall doors swung open. Balei's chair appeared empty behind the heavy metal desk, but Mara approached with a swift determination. She came to a stop a few meters from the desk, jerking the arm of the szacante to bring him up to her side. She looked directly at the chair and spoke:

"I haven't got all day for your magic tricks. Here's your offender. My job is done."

Balei seemed to materialize from the air itself as his skin shifted back to its natural deep purple. He rose from his desk, all four long and slender arms fanning out to frame his bare, narrow torso like wings. He wore no clothing, which would be surprising in the lair of a tycoon of any other race, and even downright scandalous in others. But Balei was krolin, and the krolin didn't care for physical adornments. Their superb camouflaging ability was their crown and scepter.

Every race believed itself to be uniquely gifted, but by the gods of Narei, if the krolin didn't see themselves as the true and destined rulers of the entire fucking galaxy, Mara would eat her own knife.

Balei smiled, an expression that oozed across his face. Mara didn't return it. Instead she tightened her grip on Velkar.

"Twenty percent of what he owed," she reminded Balei. "That was the agreement. In dark credits."

There had been a time when she was a reputable bounty hunter on the payroll of governments across the galaxy. But she had fled the system after the Olean job had robbed her of her partner and what small aura of safety she had wrapped around herself, and now the only jobs available to her were outside of law enforcement. Fortunately, those were also the jobs most willing to pay in the thriving but very illegal dark credit system.

Balei scoffed, and she thought for a moment that he sounded like his feelings had been wounded. She moved her free hand to her hip, cocking her elbow out and fixing Balei with a firm stare. He didn't hire her to entertain his emotional needs, and she sure as hell wasn't going to let that become an implicit part of the deal.

Balei met her stare and waved to a member of his staff behind her. One of the two Krolin guards approached, grabbing Velkar with two arms. He extended one of his remaining arms toward Mara, opening his hand to reveal a small drive. She connected it to her palm drive and ran a scan, the tech checking the credits' encryption and ensuring they weren't traceable.

"You have a magic trick of your own," Balei remarked. "Your own camouflage."

She raised a thick eyebrow at him. He nodded to her arms. Her sleeves were rolled up to above her elbows, tattoos obscuring the natural pattern of her skin. The nareians had lost the dense fur coating of their ancestors long ago, but they retained patterning on their skin. Mara had covered nearly every inch of her skin with patterns of her own. Her arms were sleeved in connected vines, twining across her shoulders in a pattern with no start or end. Hidden on her back, beneath her shirt, was a stylized flame: a nareian counter-culture symbol and her first tattoo, acquired mainly to spite her mother. Even her face, clear of most natural markings, carried two tattoos on each cheek.

"I like how they look," Mara said.

"It only covers who you used to be. It doesn't help you hide."

"I do just fine," she said. Her scan finished, and Balei watched her.

"Acceptable?" he asked, his tone mocking.

"Exactly as agreed. You know how to reach me if you need my services again."

"Unfortunately," Balei said, "I don't think you will be available next time."

Fuck. Mara already had a knife ready in her hand when the second guard raised two guns. Every hair on her body stood on end in the electric thrill of fear and adrenaline.

"I'm not sure what you'll get from killing me," Mara said. "Twenty percent of a down payment?"

"It's not your fee that is valuable," Balei said. "You call yourself Zamya, but since our last meeting, I've learned your true name.

And that you are as much in demand as a bounty as you are as a hunter."

Mara did not miss the look of surprise on Velkar's face. She should have been surprised as well, considering the vastness of the galaxy. The odds that her family would find her through a petty krolin smuggling tyrant were about the same as her ship colliding with one of theirs in deep space. Yet she wasn't surprised—she was always expecting this moment, although she couldn't have anticipated when or where it would occur.

"And what exactly did they offer you?" she asked. She wasn't listening for his answer, she just wanted him to talk. The longer he talked, the more time she had to think. To find a way out of this fucking mess.

The guards would have strict instruction not to kill her. She knew the price of her retrieval would be far surpassed by the punishment for her death. No, she was a bounty he needed alive. But although she was certain they wouldn't kill her, she was less certain about her ability to overpower three krolin with four arms apiece when they tried to stop her from going through that door. And then there was Velkar—right now, he was a wild card.

Balei knew what she was up to, though. The jackass was smarter than he looked. He gave a low chuckle and replied:

"You know your worth. Now I do as well."

"Then you're also aware that by having your bodyguards even point those weapons at me, you risk losing everything. Or should I assume those guns are nonlethal?"

She saw Velkar's face twitch at that—just the slightest shock of recognition. She wondered what his VA was whispering to him in his ear right now. Interesting, she thought. Sometimes, you have to play the wild card.

Mara raised her arms slowly in a gesture of surrender, the knife still clutched in one. She began to lean forward, lowering the knife toward the ground.

"I know when I'm beat," she said, and glanced over at Velkar. He was watching her closely. Good.

With a twist of her torso, she sent the knife spinning from her hand straight into the neck of the krolin with the guns. Her other hand grasped the pistol in her utility belt and pulled it free, sliding it across the room toward Velkar, who twisted out of the grip of the shocked krolin that had been holding him. Mara pulled another knife from her belt and flung it toward the grand desk. It seemed to pause in midair, and then Balei reappeared. The knife was sunk between his eyes.

Velkar grabbed Mara's gun and whirled, shooting the one remaining krolin guard. Three wild shots, but one of them found its target. Sudden silence rang in Mara's ears. It wouldn't be long before more guards arrived.

"Call it even?" she asked.

Velkar's VA flickered back into view, and Mara stepped back. They weren't physical objects, but she still didn't like standing so near to them.

"If you give me a ride back to Aisen," Velkar replied. "You left my ship there."

"I'll do you one better," Mara said. "I'll get you Balei's shuttle and you drive it wherever the fuck you want."

Velkar smiled, a smug and satisfied expression. "Deal."

"Now give me my gun back," Mara said. At the instant flash of protest that erupted on Velkar's face, she gestured at the dead krolin guard. Her knife protruded from his neck. "You can have both of his."

Velkar looked at the dead guard, then his gaze flickered to Mara's belt, where another knife glinted. He swallowed hard, then handed her gun back to her. She replaced it in its holster and retrieved her other two knives from her victims, wiped them clean, and fastened them carefully back in their slots on her belt.

She led Velkar out the door of the office, back toward the small docking bay of the station. His VA floated alongside like a techno-logical ghost. They'd lost the chance to download the station's data by killing Balei and his two henchmen. If there had been more time, she would have been more careful to keep one alive. Their palm drives wouldn't work with the owners no longer breathing, and Mara knew she couldn't risk anything in this station surviving for someone else to find. She didn't know where Balei might have stored the information about her, but he would have been secretive. This was not a reward he'd want to share with anyone else.

Up ahead, Mara heard a chaotic and confused conversation. The voices were around a corner, moving toward them. Mara pressed herself up against the wall, just inside the corner, and waved Velkar to a spot where he would have a good angle. He moved back, keeping his gun raised. His VA disappeared.

When the guards rounded the corner, Velkar fired immediately. The first krolin was hit with a stunning beam and sank to the ground. The two behind him immediately reached for their weapons, fanning out, but Velkar was already shooting at the one on the left, and he crashed to the side, unconscious. Mara grabbed the last krolin. She got her arm around him and pressed her knife solidly against the soft spot on the back of his neck before he real-ized she was there. He stilled, but she could feel the rapid rise and fall of his chest.

"Velkar," she said, and the szacante looked up from the two unconscious bodies he was already rifling through. "Get the security data."

Velkar nodded and approached Mara's prisoner.

The krolin squirmed, and Mara made sure he felt her blade dig in just a little more, releasing a dribble of blood that ran down her knife and dripped onto his arm. He stopped with a harsh intake of breath, then opened his palm drive.

"Take everything," Mara said. "We don't want any surprises."

Velkar completed the transaction, transferring the station's security files to his own drive. There would be layouts, structural notes, and security codes in the data. And, Mara hoped, a way to ensure that this station and everyone on it would be silenced. When the data transfer finished, Velkar shot the krolin, and he slumped over.

Velkar's VA appeared suddenly, and Mara swore and jumped.

"Can't you turn that damned thing off?" she asked. The VA just shot her a cold look.

"Would you like me to set any filters on this data?" Velkar asked.

"No filters, just give me the data."

Velkar shook his head.

Mara closed her hand around the handle of her pistol, but Velkar was still shaking his head.

"You need me now," he said. "You can't kill me."

Mara bit back a growl of rage and let go of the gun. He was right, and she should never have allowed him to make it out of that room. Trust was not a feeling she was comfortable with. But she also knew that without Velkar's help, she wouldn't have been able to capture that krolin alive in the first place.

"You're right," she admitted. "I need you. And you're lucky— you don't know enough for me to kill you when we're done. But I need your help making sure that this station becomes cosmic dust once we get off here. I don't have explosives, but I wager there's enough information in that security data to help us figure out how to do it. We can kill Balei's entire business. Wipe clean your debts. Force anyone who wants to carry on his work to rebuild from the bottom up."

"First you unjam my VA."

"No chance," Mara said. "Not until we leave here."

Velkar weighed her words. His VA stayed motionless, but Mara knew they were having a private conversation, one-sided though it might be. Those machines creeped her out. Finally, Velkar nodded, as though he'd come to a conclusion.

"It wouldn't do to go through all this trouble of escaping just to have some henchman decide to pick up where Balei left off, would it?" he said. "Let's go pick out my new ship, and then we can decide how to make this station go boom."

He turned and continued toward the docks. Mara rolled her eyes mightily, but followed him, pulling her gun out and keeping it ready as they rounded corners. But she didn't need to worry—it was quiet. She imagined most of the remaining personnel were hiding or had gone straight to Balei's study via other routes. They had a few more minutes.

In the hangar bay, Velkar gravitated straight to Balei's nicest ship—a luxury yacht with a small range. It would get him to Aisen, though just barely, but she could see he was entranced by dreams of power and wealth. She was begrudgingly impressed when he tore himself away from the yacht and selected instead a solid, well-armored transport. This szacante might actually make it in the underworld, if he could figure out how to complete the jobs he took.

Mara went to a console in the small security room overlooking the hangar bay and, when Velkar unlocked the terminal for her, started to search through the files. From here, she could cause all the airlocks to open, which would accomplish the goal of silencing anyone Balei might have told about her origins. But what she needed was to remove all evidence—digital or physical—of her existence.

The station orbited a small planet whose molten core was still violently active. The surface of the planet could barely be called solid, its crust constantly roiling and shifting with eruptions from the magma below. If she could destabilize the orbit of the station, and send it decaying down to the planet below, she could guarantee its destruction. And the likelihood of someone risking the expedition to retrieve parts of this station from a dangerous protoplanet… well, she knew the cost-benefit analysis here.

Start from scratch would win out.

So all she needed was to shut down the station's power and generate an explosion violent enough to knock it out of its stable orbit. The power would be no problem. She could manually shut that down. It was the explosion that would be troublesome.

She looked up. Velkar was busy moving expensive furnishings and decor from the yacht into the smuggling ship he had elected to steal. Mara didn't have the technical skills to sabotage the kind of advanced reactor that would be powering an entire station, but a yacht? That she could do.

Mara crossed the hangar bay to the yacht and climbed up the side of the vessel to the opening that allowed for repairs during transit. Velkar unlocked the panel for her, giving her a condescending smile as she controlled her frustration. It only took a few minutes to remove the pieces that would control the heat and pressure, and then she moved to the control room of the yacht and fired up the engines. It would be about thirty minutes, she guessed. That was enough time.

She paused on her way out, ducking into the yacht's galley. The storage area was filled with produce and dry goods. The refrigerated cabinets would no doubt be packed with meat and perishables, but Mara's own ship had no way to preserve food over the trip home. She made a few trips to her ship, bringing whatever she could manage that would not spoil in a two-day journey. She spotted a few bottles of clear liquor and grabbed those as well. Then she returned to the small security room and logged back into the console. With the codes Velkar had provided, it wasn't hard to find Balei's personal correspondence. She downloaded it all to her palm drive and set her mining program to look for one word: her given name, *Marantos*.

"Velkar," she shouted into the hangar bay. "Got everything you need? I'm about to shut off life support."

Velkar replied by scrambling into the yacht and removing one last valuable item. He waved his assent. She watched him carefully, turning the situation over in her head. He knew her identity was valuable, but Balei had never revealed what that identity was. The krolin had been keeping his information carefully guarded so only he could use it. And Mara found it unlikely that Velkar would have the sort of connections that could lead him to that information on his own. The little thief was greedy, yes, but he seemed to understand his place. Small-time crime. And he wasn't even very good at that. There was a chance he would be dead within the year without Mara's intervention.

And still... could she risk it?

She made her decision and punched the instructions into the console, along with the override codes Velkar had sent her to complete this part of their plan. Life support off. Airlocks open, except for the small pocket of the hangar bay. The station was theirs.

Mara stepped outside the console and drew her gun. Velkar was staring up in admiration at his new ship, and he turned toward her as she approached, his mouth open to say something. He paused, his eyes flicking to her gun as she raised it. She shot once, a clean blast into Velkar's head, and then she boarded the *Nasdenika*.

She started the engines and exited at just the speed required to break through the force field that kept the atmosphere inside the hangar bay. Then she accelerated, pushing the *Nasdenika* to its limits. It wasn't long before the glow of the explosion lit her displays, then instantly snuffed when it broke through the seals and released the remaining atmosphere in the hangar bay. For the first time all day, Mara heaved a sigh of relief.

It didn't look like much, but the station had moved as a result of the explosion. Its orbit had changed, and it was accelerating— falling in toward the planet. It would take a few days, but eventually it would be gone. Debris in the molten soup of the planet.

The data mining program chirped and she pulled up the results. Her eyes flicked once over the message, read it through and recognized immediately the sender. It was a fixer; someone who worked for the wealthiest nareians. And she knew this one's employer. She knew her all too intimately. *So it wasn't my family after all.*

It was time to pay her a visit.

Mara rolled her sleeves down over the tattoos on her arms and settled back in her chair. Balei wasn't wrong about her camouflage. She had left her past on Narei behind and become someone new years ago. It was not only right but necessary that she change her literal stripes.

But she also liked how they looked.

Especially the two on her face. Those were the most recent, stylized to match the natural markings on Tai's face in soft, sweeping black lines—like brushstrokes—out from the nose toward the ears.

Those tattoos were a reminder.

4

Their boots stomped on the floor downstairs. Heavy combat boots like her father still wore even years after leaving the military. Jaya associated that deep, resonant thud with safety and family, but something on the most instinctual level in her knew this dark and thunderous chorus meant trouble.

She had concealed herself in her hiding place: the gap between her parents' bed and the smooth, hard floor. The place Kier always pretended not to know about when they played hide and seek, even though she hid there every time. It was dark and cramped, and now, without the excitement of playing a game with her big brother, it was claustrophobic, menacing. There was no thrill, only fear.

The bed skirt in front of her was flung aside and a hand quickly stifled her shriek. Her eyes adjusted instantly to the bright light, and she calmed when she saw the pale face of her brother.

Kier removed his hand from her mouth and beckoned her out, holding a finger to his own lips to encourage her silence. There was no need—fear had stolen her chattiness.

When he spoke, his voice was barely a whisper.

"Follow me."

Those boots were still stomping in the kitchen, and now there were voices too. Shouting reverberated through the walls, the sound waves spreading so it seemed like it was coming from everywhere at once. She recognized her mother's voice shouting back.

"Kier," she whispered, "I'm going to be sick."

He hushed her softly, guiding her with gentle hands on her shoulders. Only four years her elder, he had always been her protector. Mama said he was becoming a man, but Jaya only saw the same boyish face she had always known.

Her brother poked his head outside their parents' door, then steered Jaya out and down the hall quickly and silently, their bare feet shuffling along the floor. He opened the door to their father's office at the end of the hall and pulled Jaya inside, then shut the door manually so that it would not make a sound when it latched shut.

"Kier," Jaya whispered, careful to keep her voice as hushed as his. "We're not allowed in here. Father said..."

"Hush, Jaya." Kier's voice was suddenly sharp. If Jaya had been older, perhaps she would have recognized fear at the edges of his tone.

He approached a keypad and rapidly typed in a code. A panel in the wall slid open. Jaya watched it, eyes wide. Behind it was a tiny space, barely large enough for a few people to stand closely packed.

"In there," Kier said. "We have to hide."

"What about Mama?" Jaya heard her own voice rise in pitch, terror constricting her throat.

"Mama said to hide. Please, Jaya."

She complied, squeezing into the tiny space and nestling into Kier as he joined her. Her legs shook and she tried to steady herself against him. He reached up, about to type a code into the interior panel, when they heard their mother scream from downstairs. Kier stiffened, and Jaya looked up at him. His hazel eyes flicked back and forth, and Jaya's own heart beat to the same fearful rhythm. His hand wavered, then dropped.

"Stay here," he said, hurrying out of the little room and running to the desk. He dug out a pistol—the one their father always kept, just in case. They weren't supposed to know about it, but Jaya had seen him take it out from time to time, as if to reassure himself of something. Kier held it now, knuckles white.

"Kier..." Jaya whimpered. She didn't want him to leave her alone in here with those terrible noises downstairs.

"Jaya," he said firmly, returning to her and crouching. "I need you to promise me something."

She nodded.

"Stay hidden," he said, meeting her eyes. She was starting to understand what her mother meant when she said Kier was becoming a man.

She nodded again.

"Promise me," Kier demanded. Jaya heard the strain in his voice. "Promise me you will stay hidden. No matter what happens."

"I promise," she said with all the voice she could manage.

"Good." He pulled her into a tight hug. "I love you, little bear." His breath rustled in her hair.

"I love you, big bear." She didn't understand why they were saying this now, but she was glad to have his protective arms around her.

And then he let go and was across the room before she could say anything. He typed the code back into the keypad and the panel in the wall slid shut again. The last she saw of him was his hair, as red as her own and mussed from their embrace, as he walked out the door.

Jaya stared up at the darkened ceiling of her pod. It was the dead of shipboard night. How late, exactly, she didn't know. She had been like this for a while, lying awake, her thoughts strange and unsettled. What little sleep she had gotten was filled with restless dreams. She checked the time on her palm drive—still about two hours until reveille, and then the day would begin in earnest and the skeleton crew that ran the night shift would return to their pods to sleep.

She closed her eyes for one last attempt at getting some rest before the day. Another day of travel, and then tomorrow they would arrive at Argos. The silence pushed in around her, and she tried to settle into the peace of it, but her mind would not quiet down. There was an unending refrain going through her thoughts, stirring up long-dormant anxieties.

Fortune befriends the bold.

With a heavy sigh, she sat up, flipping her blankets aside and swinging her legs over the side of her bed. She got up and opened the small storage space beneath the mattress, removing her data pad and uniform. She briefly ran her fingers along the smooth edge of a violin case tucked behind her clothes.

She dressed in the tiny space beside her bed and sat back down, folding her legs under her, the screen of her data pad casting a low light over the darkness around her. Her data pad greeted her with a few messages, mostly routine memos. She opened again the strange message from the day before: *You are destined for more.*

Was it some sort of junk message that had made it through the military filters? Viral advertising, the meaning of which would not be apparent until later parts of the campaign appeared in her inbox? She stared at the words, hoping they would rearrange and reveal a meaning behind them—something more substantial than the sort of vague and curt messages one tended to find in the fortune cookies given out at old Earth-themed restaurants on Argos.

She ran a search on the address, but it turned up nothing. It was, indeed, a string of random numbers. Perhaps she could ask Sal if he knew how someone might get a message like this through the military's firewalls.

Not right now, she thought. She wanted to think about it some more, and part of her still wondered if it was no more than one of life's bizarre occurrences, no different from encountering a babbling stranger in the corridors outside a bar on Argos late at night. No, she couldn't let this unsettle her.

She filed the message away in a password-protected folder, and began to sift through the contents of the folder. She had read each and every file, message, and note in here dozens of times, but every time she hoped she'd catch something new.

Ever since that day over twenty years ago—the day her parents died and her brother disappeared—she had been looking for Kier. At first, when she emerged from the panic room hours after the last sound of boots on the floor had wilted away on the summer air, she had thought Kier was dead, too. That day was filed away in her mind as evidence. Blood on the floor, but no bodies. Drag marks in the dirt outside her home. Smoke rising from her father's lab. News reports exclaimed about the powerful explosion that had killed her father and his small team of researchers. And a report of a suicide— her mother's body had been found beneath a bridge in a riverbed one town over.

There were no reports about her brother. Only silence. Until a few years later, when she received a message from Kier. She opened that message now, the words familiar to her eyes:

Little bear. I just wanted you to know I'm alive. Stay safe, and don't try to contact me. They are watching. Big bear.

She had, of course, tried to contact him, only to have her message returned with an error from the server.

That was the last she had heard of him, but it hadn't stopped her from looking. Her uncles had taken her in, and she had continued her life far from the place she had grown up, in her mother's home colony. At sixteen, she joined the military and left the small and remote world where she had spent her adolescence. She put all the energy she had into finding her brother, but the trail stopped with that message.

And she had stayed hidden. While she had no reason to assume Kier meant anything beyond staying in that panic room until the immediate danger had passed, she still held his words in the back of her mind. They grew there into a sort of religion: *Stay hidden, no matter what happens. Promise me.*

Hiding had become easy for her. She had a face she presented to the world, a thick shell of competence and rigor. She was careful to perform well, but never to stand out, holding back in sparring matches if she had already won too many. Over the years, she had developed a keen sense for the moment people were starting to talk and choosing exactly that moment to fade into the background.

And locked inside, the ache of everything she had experienced.

But that was normal, wasn't it? The IRC was not a career for the faint-hearted. Just because she had one extra tragedy to lock away with the rest didn't make her that unusual. And the trade-off for the trauma was a close-knit team of people she trusted. People she even loved. And money to send home to her uncles—more than she could have ever earned as a farmhand.

She had wanted more for her life, but so had others.

And still, as long as she knew Kier might still be alive and out there somewhere, something was missing. Until she found him, a piece of her would always be tethered elsewhere, with her missing family.

Jaya heard footsteps approaching from outside her pod. She closed the folder quickly and navigated back to her messages before the knocking came on the exterior. She flipped the pod door up and saw Sal, his eyes wild with excitement.

"I found something," he said. "Armstrong is calling an emergency meeting. We're going after the fuckers."

Soft blue light teased at the horizon as Jaya set the charges. The compound bulged from the surface of the rocky moon, and somewhere far above them in the dark sky, the *Avalon* sat in passive orbit waiting for their job to be finished. Sal had found a suspicious money trail that led to the four colonies hit and was able to trace its pattern back to this blocky compound. Hired nareian mercenaries provided protection, but it appeared to be mostly humans coming and going. Its proximity to Arcadian Gardens gave the *Avalon* a chance that Armstrong was not going to pass up.

After a careful assessment from high orbit, he ordered them in.

"Alpha One, this is Bravo One," Rhodes said through Jaya's implanted earpiece. "We're in position at the rear of the compound."

"Hang tight, Bravo One," Jaya replied. "We're almost ready."

"Copy. I've got some marines itching for a fight."

Jaya chuckled. Behind her, Vargas and Thompson held their weapons at the ready, scanning the area. Thompson had gotten some of the light back in his eyes at the opportunity to get on the ground. They were all excited to have a chance to strike back at the people who had destroyed so many lives.

Sal crouched nearby, draped over his rifle. He gave her a thumbs up, calm as always. It was his good work that had led them here, and he was ready to follow through.

"They won't have to wait long," Jaya assured Rhodes, setting the last charge on the door.

She backed up and shouldered her rifle. A premonitory shiver ran down her spine, and she scanned the area with her palm drive—the images became superimposed over the clear panel of her helmet. Inside the compound, a few red and orange humanoid blurs moved around. Most appeared to be prone, likely still asleep. But outside, the patrols were creeping around the building.

"We've got kitty cats," Thompson announced over Alpha team's channel. The corporal had his weapon pointed around the left side of the compound, where the catlike figures of the nareian mercenaries were approaching. It wouldn't be long before Jaya and her strike team were in their line of sight, and she didn't like their odds with half a dozen nareians bearing down on them on all four legs.

"I see them," Jaya said. "It's time."

She waved the team back, and they crouched behind a rocky outcropping half a kilometer from the compound's entrance. If she timed it right, they could take out a handful of the guards with the blast and catch the rest before they knew to look on their heat scopes. She attached a scope to her rifle. The others did the same, the rhythm smooth and satisfying.

Bravo team was in position. She sent the command.

The quiet backdrop of black sky thick with stars vanished against the blinding white of the explosion. Jaya flipped off the infrared scan, no longer useful with the radiating heat of scattered shrapnel muddying the image. She relied on her own eyes and the magnification of her scope and called out her shots as she took them.

A nareian guard who rounded the corner toward the blast. Another one.

Shots rang out behind her like echoes, mercenaries dropping to the ground when the accelerated particle beams found their targets.

"Incoming," Jaya announced. The remaining nareians had located the source of the rain of energy blasts and turned toward the team. They shifted from bipedal movement to quadrupedal, swift as cavalry, the muscular curves of their backs flowing like water over rocks.

Jaya shuddered. "Don't let them engage hand to hand!"

Her instructions rang out as she took down one of the oncoming assailants. The intensity of her team's fire increased, and the air crackled with energy as the onslaught started to fall.

One of the nareians, wounded but still fiercely quick, leapt over the boulder nearest to Thompson. He tried to shoot, but his unwieldy rifle was not built for close quarters. The nareian already had the advantage. She attacked, knocking the gun away. Jaya swung her rifle over her shoulder on its strap, grabbing a light pistol as she rolled from her spot. She let her momentum carry her forward, stunning the nareian from behind with her palm drive's EMP. Thompson scrambled for his gun as Jaya delivered a precise shot just behind the nareian's ear.

Jaya crouched beside Thompson. "You okay?"

"I'm fine," he replied, resuming his position and bringing his gun back up to ready. He was breathing hard, but his hands were steady.

The area around the compound was still now, debris scattered and cooling alongside nareian bodies as Alpha team made their way toward the door. The blast had rocked the compound, and Jaya knew the scramble of just-woken humans would become more lucid as the minutes passed. They had to move quickly, or lose their advantage.

"Bravo One, we've cleared the front of the building and breached the entrance. Alpha team is moving inside."

"Roger," Rhodes replied. "Bravo team will clean up the remaining combatants outside and meet you at the RP."

Jaya leveled her pistol in front of her.

"Take cover," she warned her team as they approached the door. They fanned to the sides, pressing against the warped structure just as a stream of particle beams burst through the opening. At a break in the fire, Vargas leaned out and took a few well-placed shots.

"That's five for me," Vargas crowed, and Jaya could almost hear her cheeky grin. "You better catch up, Thompson. I'm smokin' your ass."

"I'm just waiting for you to get overconfident," Thompson said. "Then things will turn my way."

"She's not overconfident yet?" came Sal's wry voice.

"Fuck you, Azima," said Vargas.

Jaya broke in, preventing Sal's response. She was glad to have her team's energy back, but they needed to focus.

"We need to push in," she said. "I'll take point—cover me."

Her team acknowledged, and Jaya risked a quick glance into the dark interior. She pressed back against the wall. A deep breath in, then out. She waited for another break in the fire. When it came, she ducked down and moved inside, rolling quickly to hide behind a heavy metal shelving unit that had been thrown down by their breaching charges. From behind the shelf, she had a better angle, and scanned the room quickly. It was empty.

She crouched behind the cold metal as her team joined her, taking a moment to check their weapons and do a quick scan of their armor. The memory of particle beam fire still thrummed in her ears and tainted the air. It tasted bitter in her mouth. Any moment now they would hear the drum beat of boots on the floors and the high whine of particle beam rifles, and she didn't like their chances of holding off another attack. Not from this position.

"We've got to move now," she said. Outside, there was still silence.

Sweat pooled at the nape of her neck in an uncomfortable trickle. She didn't explain why she felt they should move now, when it seemed in this moment of quiet that they had all the time in the world to complete their objective and get to the rendezvous point.

"Mill, where are you?" Rhodes called over the comms. Despite the sound-cancelling technology of the military communications system, Jaya could hear crackling static when the frantic pitch of the particle beams overwhelmed the tech.

"Just inside the main entrance," Jaya replied. "Pushing farther in now—looking for the communications center. What's your status?"

"We got runners out the back," Rhodes replied. "Lots of them."

"Can you handle them?" Jaya asked.

The silence over the line lasted just a little too long, and fear twisted like a knife in her gut. But finally Rhodes's voice broke into the stale quiet once again.

"We've got them for now," he said. "Proceed to objective."

Jaya motioned for her team to follow, and she began to creep through the narrow hallways of the compound. They cleared each room as they passed. It was mostly empty sleeping quarters, bed covers thrown onto the floor in the haste to respond to the attack. The walls of the compound were the same gray stone of the moon itself, cool and damp in the early morning air.

Sal nudged a door open with his shoulder and waved Jaya over.

"This looks like their central comms room," he said.

She led the way in, gun forward, but the room was empty. Her team followed.

"What do you need?" Jaya asked.

"I just need a second," Sal replied, sliding across the command console with cavalier grace and immediately settling in as if he had been there all day, his fingers flying across the console and bringing up holographic screens in rapid succession. She couldn't see his face beneath his tinted helmet, but she knew his dark-eyed gaze would be snapping back and forth from screen to screen. She had watched him hack before, his body eerily still and only his hands and eyes moving with a sharp purpose.

She signaled Vargas and Thompson to follow her as she crept along the side of the room. They spread out, in position to cover Sal if the doors were breached, as he retrieved the intel they had come for. Jaya brought up the holographic display of her palm drive and reviewed the layout of the compound they had constructed from scans and best guesses. She marked her location and sent the details to Rhodes.

Outside the room, she heard the powerful, rapid tread of encroaching forces. The hairs rose up on the back of her neck.

Jaya opened a private comm line. "I hope you were being literal, Sal."

He seemed to ignore her barb, but the pace of his typing increased. Then, he rolled his shoulders and leaned back.

"The encryption is tough," he said as he removed a data drive from the console and sealed it in a metal box. It was a small Faraday cage designed to protect electronics from the radiation of the particle beams. "I'll see what I can do when we get back." Sal grinned. She could see the flash of white teeth even through his tinted helmet. "I was afraid this would be too easy, anyway."

"Be careful what you wish for."

The footsteps were outside the door already, and Vargas and Thompson began to fire preemptively through the opening. The constant pressure kept the assailants from breaching. It seemed they would be able to hold them off until Bravo team arrived, but then a movement in the doorframe caught her eye.

"Grenade!" she shouted.

Vargas and Thompson dove. The detonation rocked the room, throwing twisted shrapnel from a destroyed desk in all directions. Jaya's position was shielded from the debris path, but she couldn't see Thompson or Vargas. She peeked out over the overturned desk.

Two humans in full chrome armor and carrying shotguns were closing in fast, and three more with pistols were pushing through the door. She still couldn't see Thompson or Vargas, and Sal was protected behind the console. Meanwhile, the space between her team and the two combatants with their destructive short-ranged weapons diminished.

Jaya holstered her pistol and steadied herself, then vaulted up and over the desk, sprinting at the two with shotguns.

The faster she moved, the more the world around her seemed to slow. She could see them up ahead, moving toward her as though through water, their motions fluid and sluggish. She launched herself from an overturned table, her outstretched hands connecting with two sternums. An electromagnetic pulse from her palm drive temporarily interrupted their armor's circuitry, stunning them.

As they staggered back, her fingers were already closing around the handle of her gun. She took two deliberate shots, puncturing their armor in the weak spot where the helmet connected to the neck. They dropped. The loud clanging of their suits on the ground was masked by the auditory fog of combat. Nobody else would hear them, but she heard the reverberations. She felt them in her chest. Jaya was exposed in this position, but it also gave her higher ground. She swiveled, taking a deep breath as she did. Before she exhaled, she lined up three shots and executed them, registering each fatal blow as they landed. The three remaining soldiers crumpled to the floor, one by one. She dropped back down behind the overturned table and let the heavy air escape her chest.

The pace of life returned to normal. Her heartbeat was quick and strong, already returning to its regular beat in her chest—a reassuring rhythm.

The room around her was still now. She closed her eyes for a brief moment. The seconds ticked away percussively. She stood and crossed the room, dragging a heavy desk and throwing it against the door. It would buy them a minute.

She scanned the room. From her higher vantage point, she saw Thompson huddled over Vargas. In an instant, she was kneeling beside the two, blood pooling slick against her armor. The grenade had ripped away a section of Vargas's suit, and the leg beneath was shredded by shrapnel, white bone showing beneath the pulverized muscle. Thompson had already activated the tourniquet built into Vargas's armor. That would at least stem the blood flow. Vargas squeezed Jaya's hand and Jaya squeezed back.

"Alpha One, this is Bravo One. We're outside your position. Building is cleared, and we have a prisoner."

Rhodes's voice spread warm relief through Jaya's body. Thompson stood and cleared away Jaya's makeshift barricade so Rhodes and his team could enter the room.

Martel and Shea dragged with them a man whose hands were bound behind him. The Sons of Priam they had encountered thus far were all in chrome armor, and this man was no different. But his armor bore an insignia of some sort—an image of the Coliseum from old Earth. He must've been some sort of leader, perhaps the commander of this compound.

"Get anything from him?" she asked.

"No," Rhodes said. "But he was making a call to someone when we got there. They'll know we're here."

"Boss?" Vargas asked, her voice strained.

Jaya put a hand on Vargas's shoulder: "We'll get you to the doc right away." She opened a connection to the ship. "*Avalon,* this is Alpha One," she said. "We have a marine down. I repeat, marine down. We need immediate exfil."

"Acknowledged," Armstrong replied. "Shuttle on the way."

"Did you get it?" Rhodes asked behind her.

Sal pulled the small metal box from his kit, holding it up.

"Nice work, Lieutenant," Rhodes said, clapping Sal on the shoulder.

The man they had captured began to shake, and then he crashed to the ground.

"What the hell is happening?" Rhodes shouted. Shea crouched down to roll the man over. They checked his vitals and scanned him with their palm drive.

"He's dead," Shea said. "He just... he just died."

"Was he wounded?"

"No," they said, turning a blank expression on Rhodes. "Seems... unharmed. He just died."

"There are sterile bags on the shuttle," Jaya said. "Bring him back with us and see if the doc can figure out what happened to him."

Vargas groaned, and Jaya gripped her hand tighter as the marine took shallow, shaky breaths.

"Help is on the way," Jaya promised. "We'll get you out of here."

5

Jaya grabbed a meal bar from the mess hall as soon as the post-mission briefing ended and headed for the med bay, eating as she walked. When she arrived, she saw Armstrong standing at the doctor's desk, a serious expression on his face. Both turned as Jaya walked through the door, and a bright grin spread across the face of Doctor Sun-mi Choi. Jaya swallowed her bite half-chewed and stood in a smart salute, but Armstrong waved off the formality. She joined the two, storing the empty wrapper in her pocket as quietly as she could.

Doctor Choi was fairly new on the *Avalon,* but what Jaya had seen of the doctor in the busy first few months onboard had impressed her. She never seemed to tire, always ready with that same bright smile. Jaya had already heard some of the junior officers calling her by a nickname: Sunny. It certainly fit.

"Doctor Choi was just updating me on Corporal Vargas," Armstrong said.

"That's why I'm here," Jaya replied.

"She's stable," Sunny replied, the previous joyous expression on her face transitioning smoothly to one of earnest concern. "But the damage was severe. There's not much more I can do here—she will need to lose the leg, and with a cybernetic replacement and extensive rehabilitation, she can have a normal life again. But I can't guarantee that she'll be anywhere near her current capabilities."

Jaya crossed her arms against the pit forming in her stomach.

Armstrong worked his jaw as he listened to the news, and his eyes darkly reflected the blue-tinted light of the med bay. Blue eyes had become less and less common over the dozens of generations since humans left Earth, but Armstrong's bright-hued irises were among the few that still appeared from time to time. His face bore the weathered skin and wrinkles of hard years, but when the harsh lines softened into a smile, those blue eyes sparkled with the energy of a much younger man.

Jaya had found as a young and anxious recruit that those smiles gave her a view of the man Armstrong was behind his duties. In the stress of her first years in the military, those moments were like a glimpse into her own future: a private promise that the job did not rob its vessels of their humanity.

"I haven't told her yet," the doctor said. "She's been sleeping since the medication kicked in, and I wanted to speak to both of you first, and, well... I was waiting for her to have some company."

"I understand," Armstrong replied. He glanced at Jaya, who read the question in his face.

"We shouldn't delay," Jaya said. "She knows it's severe. It's better that she just know now so she can start to reckon with it."

Sunny nodded and led them back to a curtained-off bed. She peeked inside the curtain and there was a murmured conversation. Then she drew the curtain back. Vargas's skin was ashy, dull in comparison to the usual warm, bronze tone, and there was a pinched look around her dark eyes. Sunny pulled over a second chair and both Jaya and Armstrong took a seat.

"Hey, marine," Armstrong said. "How's the leg?"

"The doc gave me some good drugs," Vargas replied with a strained grin. "Don't feel a thing."

Armstrong returned Vargas's smile with one of his own, and Jaya saw the corporal relax just a little.

"You did well today," Jaya said to Vargas.

"Thanks, boss."

"Doctor Choi has some news for you," Armstrong said. "About your leg. Are you ready to hear it?"

Vargas swallowed, and Jaya thought she saw her face grow even paler.

"I guess... now's as good a time as any," Vargas said. She began to pick at the edge of the blanket with her hands, the motion betraying her nerves even as she set her jaw.

"The injury is quite serious," Sunny said. "We did everything we could to minimize the effects and to localize the damage. But I'm afraid the damage was too severe at the injury site. We have to amputate."

Jaya saw Vargas's grip on her blanket tighten, but her face remained fixed in its previous expression.

"There's some excellent new cybernetics technology coming out of TA Tech," the doctor concluded. "It will be a very long recovery, but you could have full functionality. Maybe even stay in the military in some other capacity, if it's your wish..."

She trailed off, realizing that Vargas was no longer listening. Vargas was staring down at her leg, as if she could see straight through the hospital blankets covering it.

"I can recommend you for a position at HQ on Argos," Armstrong said. "And the Navy will pay you a disability stipend through your recovery. After that, you'll have to see what it is you want, and what the military can accommodate."

Vargas turned away for a moment. When she looked back at them, her dark eyes burned with a determined blaze.

"I can push myself," she said. "Return to full strength, full speed. I can still be an asset here."

"The technology is advanced, but the Navy has very high standards for physical fitness for this level of work," Sunny said, her voice cautious. "It's extremely unlikely you will be able to return to the field. Not at this level."

"I didn't sign up to do a desk job!"

Anger and misery battled in Vargas's face. Jaya swallowed, allowing the buzz of tension thrumming through her muscles to soften.

"You don't have to make a decision about any of this now," Jaya said. "You can take your time. Talk to me, talk to Captain Armstrong, talk to your friends."

Vargas nodded, silent.

"We'll let you rest," Armstrong said. "I'm sure you'll be swarmed by visitors in no time."

"Yes, Captain." Vargas's reply was flat and cold.

Sunny drew the curtain closed again behind her as she and Jaya walked back to her desk.

"How long?" Armstrong asked the doctor.

"It depends on how well her body accepts the cybernetics. Could be months to full functionality, could be a year. But it's unlikely she will ever be able to pass the physical tests to return to IRC."

"She's not going to like that," Jaya said, the weariness in her body creeping into her voice.

The doors behind them opened, and Jaya turned to see Lupo. The navigator stopped in her tracks and saluted.

"At ease, Lieutenant." Armstrong smiled, with a meaningful glance toward the back of the room. "She's back there."

Lupo nodded and headed toward Vargas's bed. Jaya saw the first smile brighten the marine's face as the navigator sat down beside the bed and took Vargas's hand in both of hers.

Armstrong and Jaya said their goodbyes to Sunny and left the medical bay. As the doors whirred shut behind them, Armstrong stopped.

"Commander, I was hoping to have a word with you," he said. "My office?"

"Yes, Captain," Jaya replied.

The captain's quarters were modest, by the standards of anyone who had grown up planetside. But aboard a frigate like the *Avalon*, where expensive life support systems were carefully calibrated to every centimeter cubed of open air, the private room alone was a luxury. The tiny nook with its solid desk was a sanctuary of quiet for work and strategizing, and the small window above the desk was a rapture of thick stars smattered across the velvety black of space.

Jaya's eyes were always drawn to the window in the infrequent occasions she visited Armstrong's office. Her gaze was pulled toward that infinity outside their small metal shell as he sat down at his desk.

"It will not be an easy transition for her," Armstrong said, motioning for Jaya to sit.

She did, smoothing the stiff fabric of her uniform. "Vargas had promise and passion. That's what I'm most worried about—she wanted this work and this work alone."

Armstrong let out a breath, the sound heavy and dark.

"With an injury like that, even with the best cybernetics and extensive therapy, it's unlikely she'll qualify for IRC again," he said. "Is there someone she can talk to?"

"She's close with Lieutenant Lupo," Jaya said. "But I think she should also speak with someone on Argos when we dock. Someone who has experience with reassignments and can help her through the process. Someone who won't be leaving with the *Avalon* on our next departure."

Armstrong ran his weathered hands over his face. "Of course. It's standard procedure after an injury like this, but I will make a note on her file to recommend continued support as she begins physical therapy."

"Thank you," Jaya said. She let her posture loosen, her shoulders fall a little less squarely. "I've grown very fond of her."

She confessed it softly, still anxious after all these years that these attachments and expressions of emotion would be perceived as weakness. Armstrong's reaction seemed to confirm her fears. He frowned, and steepled his fingers beneath his chin.

"That brings us to the subject I wanted to address," Armstrong said. He stood and paced to the opposite side of the office. Jaya's chest constricted, her private box of fears rattling louder inside. She pushed it down.

"What is it?" she asked, when the silence had stretched too long for her to bear.

"You are perhaps the most talented officer to have ever passed through my ship," he said. "I knew the day I saw you in training that you had potential to be a great combatant, and over the years that you have served under me, I have learned that your skills in observation are remarkably keen. You are an impressive officer."

She said nothing, her heart pounding in her chest. These were not words of admonishment, but she heard the note of criticism in his voice. She waited.

"But those are not the only skills you need if you want to progress father. You're my second officer, and I would like to see you one day command your own ship. To do that, you have to learn to connect with your team."

He turned back around to face her.

"I know you care about the people who serve with you. I'm not doubting that. I also know you're capable of forming strong bonds with your peers. Your friendship with Lieutenant Azima has been a constant in your time here. But in general your demeanor is cold and aloof. Leadership is not about holding yourself above your subordinates."

He returned to his desk and sat. Jaya stared at the smooth surface of the desk, a dark metal alloy that approximated wood in its coloring and texture. She didn't think she could speak if she tried. In the silence, she forced herself to look up and meet Armstrong's eyes.

His face had softened, the intense blue of his eyes somehow less piercing now as he watched her with concern. When she had been a small child, she had lived for the rare expressions not unlike this from her own father.

"You've learned much in the ten years you've been a part of my crew," Armstrong said. "But you still have lessons to learn about leadership."

His face darkened slightly and his forehead creased.

"The burdens I believe you understand. There are choices that you alone will have to make that your team may not ever comprehend. You must be ready to shoulder the consequences of those choices yourself. And there are choices you may have to make that go against your training—against the chain of command. And again, you must be ready to face those consequences yourself.

"But the thing I don't believe you understand yet is that your team must be willing to follow you, even when you make a decision that doesn't look like the right one. They have to trust you enough to follow you into anything, and they will never trust you if you don't let them close to you."

Jaya swallowed, a deep ache beginning behind her sternum. The idea of releasing even a tiny amount of all that she held inside sent a rush through her, and a cold sweat beaded on her neck. Vulnerability was something she avoided. Vulnerability could get her killed.

But here was Armstrong telling her it was necessary, if she wanted to be the leader her team would need.

She had always seen Armstrong as tough, but as she turned over that image of him in her mind, she realized his strength was more complex. It was the moments where he let down his guard and showed his weakness that made Jaya and her fellow officers trust his judgment. They never doubted that he carried his choices with him long after they were made, and for that reason, they knew he would never take their safety lightly.

And still, it was one thing to admire that quality in Armstrong. It was another thing entirely to find it in herself.

"Thank you for the advice," she said. Her mouth was dry, and she swallowed again. "I'll work on that."

Cold. Armstrong's choice of word cut deeper than she wanted to admit. She chewed it over in the mess hall the next morning as Sal flipped through the Navy's latest round of briefings, making annoyed sounds in his throat. His breakfast sat mostly abandoned next to him.

"Sal, do I come across as cold?" Jaya asked.

He closed the screen at her words, turning to her with his matter-of-fact expression. "I mean, the marines all think you have no soul."

"Jesus, Sal. You didn't even try to sugar coat that."

He shrugged. "You don't keep me around because I'm nice."

"Why do I keep you around?" she asked.

"Because I'm relentlessly charming."

"You're one of those things, that's for sure."

He flashed her a smile.

She chewed on her lower lip and crossed her arms. "No soul? Really?"

Sal leaned back in his chair, settling into the conversation as if it were any other chat. His body expressed nonchalance, but his brow furrowed earnestly and he held her gaze firmly.

"Look, I know that inside you're all emotional and touchy-feely," he said. "And I know that you had a lot of shit in your life that made you prickly on the outside. I'm a big fan of prickly on the outside. But yeah, that makes it hard for people to get close to you."

Across the mess hall, Rhodes stood with his empty tray. Though he had five years on Jaya's thirty-one, he had been promoted to strike team leader a few months after Jaya had. The first year that they served together had been rocky. He had considered himself a superior officer, and her higher rank bruised.

He met Jaya's gaze across the shifting lines and gave her a subtle thumbs-up. His begrudging friendship was hard-won. It had required more than a few narrow escapes together to soften his stiff attitude to something approaching friendship. And now, with Armstrong's admonishment still rattling around in her head, she wondered if Rhodes had been right to think he deserved the higher rank.

After all, he had an easy rapport with his strike team. They knew when to joke around with him and when it was time to shut up and listen. They smiled when they saw him, and looked to him first whenever there was trouble. Jaya's team was close-knit, but she had always been on the outside. Even Sal managed to worm his way into the team. Jaya used to think that being a leader meant having this chasm between them—at least on the field. She used to think that was what would keep her team safe.

"You put up barriers, Jaya," Sal continued. "You know this. I know this. I may have come crashing through those barriers, but not everyone will do that"—he held up a hand to keep her from inter-jecting—"and they shouldn't, I know. I'm not really sure how I made it in, but frankly, it wouldn't hurt you to open the door for everyone else."

She tightened up, as if her entire body wanted to fold inward, to seal up that box with all her secrets and her history and the fears she took out to examine when it was only her and the silence.

"At least crack a window," Sal said. "You know it's not as scary in there as you seem to think."

Jaya would have given everything she had for that statement to be true. She shifted uncomfortably.

"Or you could just do nothing," Sal said. "It's not going to get you promoted, but in my opinion, leadership is overrated. Too much responsibility, not nearly enough fun."

Jaya laughed, feeling the tension start to ease as Sal leaned forward and took a last bite of his breakfast, grimacing.

"Anyway, we dock at Argos in two hours," Sal said. "First thing I'm going to do is get food that wasn't reconstituted from dust using water filtered from our own piss."

"Sal, where do you think Argos's water comes from? Natural springs?"

He made a face. "That's different. Argos's water filtration plant is the best in the galaxy. It infuses the water with minerals just like you'd get on any planet."

Jaya rolled her eyes as they stood to clear their trays. Sal had grown up on Argos and you couldn't pay him to say a bad word about the station. But he had a point—the food was better—and Jaya was looking forward to finding a few moments of quiet.

6

Mara had no trouble tracking Yanula down. After all, she had spent more than half her life hunting hardened criminals, assassins, and corporate spies. Tracking down the rich niece of the second-most powerful woman in Narei was almost offensively simple. Yanu was a member of the Hydean clan, and a minor celebrity these days. Ten years Mara's senior, she was in her prime, and she had transitioned from little-known minor nobility to a member of the nareian glitterati.

The Hydean family had split off from the royal family seven generations ago, but that didn't stop them from nestling their way as close to the throne as they could manage. In the light of the public eye, they were charming foils to the Empress's stiffness, affable and popular and regulars at every official event. In private, their matriarch Palva pried into every fine crack in the royal family's structure. It was Yanu, her least favorite niece, who had provided Palva with her greatest victory in decades, and that had won Yanu a leading role in nearly every public spectacle.

Yanu was expected to be the guest of honor at a formal dinner on one of Narei's outer colonies. The royal family rarely extended itself beyond the inner colonies, and social engagements on the wealthier and more valuable of the outer colonies were one of the Empress's favorite bones to throw to the scheming Hydeans in an attempt to keep them occupied and their thirst for power slaked.

This was only one of the things about her mother that disgusted Mara.

It had been more than two decades, and though Mara was certain the Imperial Guard had updated its training and techniques in that time, the hired security for the Hydean clan were former Imperial Guards, still conditioned in the old ways. The Imperial Guards had trained Mara in self-defense as a child, in case of assassination attempts. And Mara had memorized their patterns and had kept up with the weaponry since she had left. The black market lagged behind the most cutting-edge technology by mere weeks, and Mara made sure to never miss an update.

And so, with weaponry that matched their own and intimate knowledge of the instincts that guided them, Mara had found it almost laughably simple to cut through each and every guard stationed in the opulent guesthouse in which Yanu slept soundly that night.

Mara kept a wire wrapped around her hand as she clung to the ornate carvings of the ceiling, approaching the door to Yanu's room. She stopped above the guard stationed there, arms burning. She released one hand to shift the wire into her palm, and then she dropped down, the garrote around the guard's neck before he could make a sound. She laid him down gently, pressed up against the wall, where his shape melted into the shadow.

Outside the guesthouse, waves crashed against steep cliffs. The sound muted Mara's footfalls, already kitten-soft against the floor in her sleekest boots, as she nudged the door open. Her knife replaced the wire in her hand in a swift motion. There was much to recommend about the latest technologies, but Mara found that very little surpassed the cruel curve of a blade when it came to setting the mood.

The faint light of the stars cast a watery sheen over the still form in the bed. Mara watched as the slow rise and fall of Yanu's chest paused, then resumed, its rhythm altered. Yanu's eyes fluttered open, their amber irises fixing immediately on Mara.

"I thought I might see you," Yanu said, her voice still as rich and throaty as Mara remembered. That quality that was imbued in Yanu's voice in her memories never came through in the newsfeeds.

"I can tell when you're lying now," Mara said. "Don't bother."

Mara sat on a low bench across from the bed. Yanu pushed herself up on her forearms, the starlight spilling over the curve of her shoulders.

"Are you here to threaten me?" she purred. "That's almost sweet. I'm flattered to still rank so highly on your list of enemies."

Mara leaned forward, the flat of her knife against her palm as she rested her elbows on her knees.

"You're the one who's been following me, Yanu. I'm almost impressed. How many bounty hunters like me did you need to hire to track me down?"

Yanu formed her mouth into a little moue. Fifteen years ago, that pout might have tugged on Mara's heart. Instead, she rotated the knife slowly in her hand, letting the light glimmer off its sharp edges. She saw Yanu's eyes lower from Mara's face to her hands.

"So you figured out my latest identity," Mara said. "Congratulations. You win a visit from me."

She kept turning the knife, shifting her grip, strengthening it, then she rose from her seat and crossed to Yanu and the bed. Mara sat gently onto the bed, the knife in her right hand. She trailed the fingers of her left hand slowly up Yanu's arm and over her shoulder, caressing her mane when she reached the nape of her neck. Yanu's breath caught, a small sound against the crashing of the waves.

"Not what you were hoping for?" Mara kept her voice low, the voice she had once reserved for whispering into Yanu's neck, for confessing her secrets into the tangle of their limbs. Yanu held herself still, but Mara felt the rapid pulse of the veins in her neck.

Mara leaned in close, whispered against Yanu's cheek: "It took me less than a day to find you. Less than three hours to kill every guard whose job it was to protect you. And it would take less than a heartbeat for me to gut you now."

She drew the knife forward, watched as Yanu's eyes followed its motion.

"Remember that, next time you want to waste your money hunting me down."

Mara stood, releasing her grip on Yanu's mane. She stopped in the doorway, taking in the dark, quiet room and Yanu's rapid breathing.

"I'm not a naive little princess anymore," Mara said. "This was your warning."

Mara brought her ship into Uduak, displacing air and sending gritty sand into the sky, where it settled slowly in a fine layer over the *Nasdenika.* She opened the airlock. The hot, dry atmosphere pushed into her ship and hit her like a dense wall. As she walked out into the sunlight, she looked back, scanning the small interior of her ship. A familiar feeling disturbed her thoughts and sent a bitter rush through her body. Death hung over her shoulder, like a physical presence, its cold hands on the vulnerable curve of her neck. She brushed the thick mane back, covering her nape, without awareness of her own gesture.

The empty ship stared back at her, at once the dependable structure she relied upon without a second thought and a strange and haunted space.

This is it now, she reminded herself. *It's just you.*

It had been over half a decade, and she still wondered when this sense that she was forgetting something would finally fade away. She feared its loss as much as she hated the dull ache it revived in her chest.

She turned away, and the door closed behind her, locking to all but her own biometric signature, then stepped out into the sunshine. The afternoons on Uduak were hot and dry. Mara tried to stay inside as much as she could—her people had evolved for the damp jungle heat of Narei, and the parched desert air sucked away her energy.

The hami wore pale robes to deflect the sunlight and protect their sensitive skin, and they extended the offer of these robes to visitors of their planets. They were a generous people, known as the caregivers of the galaxy. They were not officially aligned with any of the three most influential races, but they provided the majority of the relief efforts for every kind of disaster. Their colonies were invariably service-oriented: orphanages, hospitals and clinics, refugee camps. During the more than hundred years of war between nareians and humans, the hami had taken in displaced persons from both sides, and hami refugee camps were perhaps the only places human and nareian had lived side-by-side in those times without violence.

Uduak was an orphanage colony. A sturdy clay-brick series of buildings rested within the walls ahead, where lost children from neighboring planets and space stations found a new home for themselves. They grew up well-fed, well-loved, and well-taught by the scholarly monks.

When Mara arrived at the gates, Bay, one of the senior monks, greeted her and ushered her out of the blistering sun and into his office. She towered over him; the two were a vision of opposites. Mara was tall and muscular, as most nareians were, with a thick mane of hair on her head and the curved and catlike limbs characteristic of her people. Bay was as short and round as a hami could be, his bald head shining in the afternoon light as he dropped his hood back on his plump shoulders. He blinked his one, large eye at her benevolently.

"We are glad to have you back, Zamya," he said. "Would you like some tea?"

"Thank you, yes," she said, perching somewhat precariously on a low chair.

Bay filled two clay mugs with hot tea and took a seat across a short table from her. Mara took a sip of her tea—it was spicy and sweet, just as she remembered it.

"It's time for me to move on," Mara said. "The stars are getting too crowded this side of the galaxy."

Bay nodded solemnly, but refrained from criticizing. Mara had wondered how a peace-loving people would accept the regular presence of a bounty hunter, but they never tried to steer her away. They were lovers of the outcasts and the destitute, and while Mara hated to think any part of her spoke of desperation, she knew they were a perceptive people.

"We have been thankful for your presence," Bay said. "You are always welcome here."

Mara gave a grim smile and took another sip of her tea. The quiet of Uduak was so different from the noise and chaos of her life after she left. It always took her a few days to adjust, but once she did, the peace sank into her bones and carried away the darkness of her life.

She had gotten too used to peace, and it had caught up to her, as it always did.

"I have one last donation," she said. "Produce and grain— already unloaded at the port, and I believe Sola will be sorting through it in the kitchens as we speak."

Every time she came back, she brought what she could afford, knowing the monks were struggling to feed themselves and the children here on this remote world. Perhaps it revealed her cynicism— that she was implicitly buying their silence and their protection—

but she was uneasy taking their help without offering something in return.

"Your generosity humbles us," Bay said, bowing his head.

"It's hardly generosity when it feeds me, too."

The tiny monk took her hand with what she had come to interpret as a beatific smile, though their faces were so foreign to nareian eyes that their expressions had no evident translation. Bay rose from his chair, though he was barely taller standing than sitting.

"Go in peace, Zamya. We will not forget our time with you."

She thought it might be better if they did.

Mara drew in a gasping breath as she woke, her sheets twisted wildly around her legs. She untangled herself and leapt from her bed, bending over near the window and letting the cool desert night dry her sweat-damp mane. The pit in her stomach slowly unwound, settled by the herbal scent of the monastery's gardens wafting in the open windows. Sleep would not return tonight.

Her one-room hut was quiet. Her belongings were scattered about, divided into what she would bring with her and what would remain behind. The former items were mostly crammed into durable magnetic crates, the latter in piles to be collected in the morning.

She wondered if leaving Yanu alive had been a mistake. She told herself that such a high-profile killing would only close the net around her. After all, it was not just the Hydeans looking for her, but her own family as well. Sparing Yanu had been the wiser choice.

That was how she sold it to herself, at least.

Mara pressed a small button on her wrist, activating her palm drive. The holographic screen appeared, hovering above her upturned forearm.

Four standard hours past midnight, and here on Uduak it meant day would not break for another six hours. Long days and long nights—they made her itch with restless energy. She shivered. The night air brought a chill in with it, but she could not close the window just yet. The chill was a welcome relief against the cramped and sweaty confines of her nightmares.

She sighed. If she was going to start her day now, she didn't want to stay cooped up in this room for the first six shitty hours of it. She pulled on simple leggings and a loose shirt and fastened her utility belt around her hips, checking that her gun and the sharp, curved knives were properly holstered before leaving.

Even here, on this tiny, remote planet populated only by the peaceful hami and their good-works orphanages and hospitals, she always carried those weapons with her.

In these dark hours before the sun rose, the desert was chilly and flat beneath the night. She ran along the dunes, stretching her limbs and bringing blood to her cold extremities. The vast sky, its profound black expanse spanned by the smear of the galactic core, pulled her the rest of the way from the haze she had inhabited since she left Balei's lifeless station to fall slowly into the planet it once orbited. Under those stars, each point of light so sharp it seemed artificial, she felt suddenly overwhelmed.

While the immediate danger of Balei turning her over to become a pawn in her mother's power struggle had passed, it left her rattled. The understanding that they were still pursuing her after all these years was a constant background noise in her mind, but this was the first time in six years that they had come close enough to disrupt her life. Was their powerful reach extending deep into the underworld now? Had they expanded their network, its branches now tangling with Mara's own? Or had Yanu just caught a lucky break—a fluke that would not repeat itself?

Mara's limbs were heavy and tired, as though they had already accepted what her mind had not yet: the gap was narrowing, and her days of freedom were numbered. She pushed through, not allowing her fatigue to stop her run, and when she finally circled back to her little home, sweat and exertion left her shaky and flushed.

In about three hours, the hami monks would wake and begin their morning vigil—hours of prayer and meditation in the bleak desert to welcome the rising of the sun. Despite her natural inclinations against religion and—even more—tradition, the sight of their small round bodies sitting peacefully in meditation and the low sounds of their rhythmic chanting had become familiar and almost dear to her.

Uduak was more home to her now than Narei, she realized. The taste of the thought was both sweet and bitter. She returned to Uduak when there was a break in work, a brief pause in the influx of jobs—she felt safe here, as if the peaceful presence of the monks provided a shield from the dangers of the galaxy beyond their little planet. There were billions of beings in this galaxy who were hiding, and billions more who wanted the hidden ones found. She just had to be better at finding than whoever might be looking for her.

She had not felt this fragile in a long time. Like the beams that supported this latest iteration of her life were rotting, and she was only now seeing the depth of the damage. She had been working hard, each job followed by another, the savings carefully stowed away, until she had to move again and spend her hard-earned future to reinvent herself. Every time, she thought this would be the last transformation.

She was bone tired. But she would begin again.

7

The entrance to Tynan's apartment opened at the touch of his hand, his biometric data unlocking the door without so much as a chirp of acknowledgement. The smooth metal plates slid open silently, and Tynan made his way straight to the kitchen, not even glancing behind him as the door closed just as quietly as it had opened.

He liked the hush of his apartment. Too often, the galaxy seemed designed for distraction. There were moving images on nearly every external surface—advertisements and news and the reality shows the szacante media had recently adopted from the humans. He scoffed at those aloud, the sound of his disgust settling into the surfaces of his kitchen. In here, Tynan thought as he sat at his small round table, he had a sanctuary of quiet. Everything was smooth lines and simple designs. The colors of his home were silver and white and pale blue, and the surfaces were pristine and undisturbed. Here, no one watched him, no one looked to him for leadership. No one questioned him or challenged him.

Min appeared, as though she could read his thoughts. She could not, although she had access to all his vitals and the result was that her predictive algorithms sometimes appeared to approximate clairvoyance.

"Do you want me to start the convection oven?" she asked. "Your food is likely to be growing cold, based on the time we spent in traffic on the route home."

Tynan opened the compostable container he was still clutching and set it on the table in front of him. He held his hand above the open box and a gentle push of air flushed against his skin.

"No, Min," he said. "It's fine."

He began to eat, the comfort of his nightly routine soothing his racing mind. Work, as it often did, occupied the bulk of his thoughts just beneath the surface. Viruses that could cross the boundaries between species had decimated entire colonies in earlier years. Humans and nareians had not advanced their xenobiological research far enough to model and predict these events, and with interactions among the species growing more and more common, it was a primary interest of all three major powers to understand the vectors for diseases that could hop across the boundaries and wreak havoc on unprepared communities.

Thanks to Tynan's work, they were crossing beyond a boundary of knowledge and into something new. And even with this vast expanse of new possibilities these viruses provided, he marveled in a sort of familiar amazement at the way life seemed to always take the same pathways. Those reactive, opportunistic, and unconscious developments of evolution still spoke a language that his scientific tools could interpret.

More than a decade before the szacante would make first contact, back when they still believed themselves to be alone in the galaxy, the humans and nareians had been at war with each other. A brief lull in the conflict led to the first joint settlement, and soon the first epidemic, and then the second.

Relations between the nareians and the humans had again soured. The humans demanded reparations for the lives caused by a nareian virus and the supposed carelessness of the nareian people. The Nareian Empire refused, and withheld technological advances they had promised to sell to the humans. Tensions rose until a colony dispute sparked an all-out war. But after the decades of infighting and the devastation brought by illness, both races had grown tired. After six more years of war, the humans and nareians finally signed a peace treaty, though relations remained cold to this day.

It was in this chilly political environment that the szacante arrived on the galactic stage. They immediately found a comfortable role in the galactic economy, researching as much as possible, soaking up the massive opportunity for scientific advancement at the nexus of these three great civilizations.

Tynan had been making strides in understanding this neurological virus—so much so, in fact, that some members of his board had suggested the military might be interested in the technology. After all, if the szacante wanted to protect themselves from their more militarily inclined neighbors, their best weapon was their skill in science.

He had drawn the line at that. The szacante may have been slower to emerge on the galactic stage, but the relative remoteness of their homeworld and the corresponding lack of urgency had allowed them to remain safely cocooned on Dresha, developing their technologies and their knowledge with caution and great attention to detail. Their first interstellar ships had already been refined, balanced, even beautiful. Not like the slapdash hunks of welded-together metal he saw in encyclopedia entries about the first human ships.

Tynan scoffed again as he finished his dinner and fastidiously wrapped the crumbs in the packaging and placed it in the tube that led to the building's compost center. Tynan couldn't help but feel that the humans had just found themselves in the right place at the right time. While the szacante were developing tools to improve the lives of their people and protect the tranquil beauty of their homeworld, the humans were carving deep scars into their home and exploiting their own people. They had destroyed Earth and left out of necessity; it was pure curiosity that pushed the szacante out of their star system and into the path of the nareian-human conflict.

Although they were approximately the same evolutionary age, the szacante were already composing music and modifying crops to feed millions while humans were still hitting rocks with other rocks in order to make sharper rocks to hunt their prey. The humans may have pushed out into the wider galaxy first, but they had done so with mediocre machines and a thirst for conquest—a combination which left them always scrambling for a foothold as they expanded outward. The szacante way had been much more elegant, and in Tynan's view, it was better to be right than to be first.

Tynan checked the time on his palm drive. There were still a few hours left in the day before he should go to bed. He brought the holographic screen up in front of him and logged in to the virtual community for Sequence, a strategy game that was nearly as old as the first szacante civilization. He chose a game setup and awaited an opponent.

It was many hours before he finally pulled himself away and retired to his room, even after Min's repeated warnings about the time. But when he did finally climb into his narrow bed and pull the light blankets up to his chin, he felt a warm cheer that had been absent for most of the day now pulsing through his limbs. He yawned once, gave a long and sleepy stretch, and fell immediately to sleep.

The pleasant anticipation of a day of work lay ahead as Tynan entered his building. The morning was bright and clear, and he'd had a good night of sleep. Even the constant, irritating reminder that he had a meeting with his board first thing failed to rattle him.

He took the lift up to the top level of the building. The board met in the large conference room looking out over Iralu City's bay. As he approached the room, he saw the other eleven members of the board seated around the table. They seemed to know he was coming, all turning to watch his arrival through the transparent wall.

"Doctor Vasuda," the chairwoman—an older szacante with graying skin and very pale yellow eyes—said, standing as Tynan entered the room.

"Let's get started," Tynan said brusquely, taking his seat at the table. "I have a lot to do today. Big advances ahead."

"I'm glad to hear that, Doctor Vasuda."

Tynan froze in his seat. At the corner of the table, Tynan noticed with a slowly creeping fear, a human was seated. The same man that had come to Tynan's office with an offer of a buyout now rested his chin on steepled fingers in the conference room. Sharp, cold eyes were fixed on Tynan.

"What's happening?" the doctor asked, his voice shaking despite his best efforts. "Why is this human in our board meeting?"

"We accepted his offer," the chairwoman said.

"I'm the principal investigator," Tynan objected. "I founded this research organization."

"You aren't the majority shareholder," the human said, a smile growing slowly behind those steepled fingers.

"No one is!" Tynan's voice rose. "That's not how business is done here."

"Perhaps that is a flaw in the system," the human replied, his voice calm.

Tynan spluttered, his mind racing too fast to connect the thoughts in a logical order.

"It's meant to prevent the sort of self-interested monopolies you human organizations fall prey to," he argued. "You need consensus and agreement—the sort of agreement that comes from excellent reasoning and long debate."

The chairwoman made a sort of half-polite coughing noise from behind Tynan. He turned, watching in bewilderment as she gestured to the remaining board members.

"The rest of the board thinks the offer is fair," the chairwoman said. "Calista Holdings can provide us with assets, with influence… we could make a name for ourselves. Hire more scientists—"

"We don't need more scientists," Tynan insisted. "Not at the expense of our freedom. We have a research goal, and we are making progress toward it. We *are* making a name for ourselves."

The silence that responded to his plea told him everything. The decision had been made, and it would not be unmade. For the first time since he had founded this research organization, his voice was silenced.

How had he gotten here? How had his reputation—his vision— eroded so far? And how had he failed to see it happening?

The human stood, and Tynan was again darkened by the shadow of this tall, broad-shouldered man. He was steered out of the conference room by the man's steely frame, and when the door shut behind the two of them, Tynan looked up at his adversary—the victor in a war Tynan had not even known he was a combatant in.

The man's eyes, no longer cold, blazed golden with the light of his triumph. For the first time, Tynan felt the energy radiating off the man. Underneath the tightly coiled indifference of his expression, there was a deep and savage vein of power. It was raw and explosive, and for a moment, Tynan thought this must be what it was like to stare into the volcanoes of Mitania—one of the Szacante Federation's first and famously failed planetary engineering projects.

And then, the moment he recognized it, the heat was gone from the man's eyes.

"You were correct before, doctor," the man said quietly. "We define value differently. It is clear that despite your talent, you will not fit with our new research direction. I took the liberty of having your office cleaned out for you. An aircar is waiting for you at the twentieth-floor landing deck with all the personal effects we have permitted to be removed. You understand the security precaution we need to take."

Tynan could only gape as he fumbled his way uneasily toward the lift, his feet seeming to forget their way. He glanced back as the man returned to the doorway, his shoulders beneath a tailored shirt relaxed and his expression cool and composed. But Tynan could not unsee what he had found boiling beneath an exterior that was as calm as the dark, sleek contours of a volcano.

───────

Tynan sat in the main room of his apartment. The bright afternoon light through the windows had begun to soften into a warm evening glow, and the shadows cast their lengths farther across the room.

Min had long since left him to his mood, after hours of prodding him to try to take his mind off his situation. With no work left to pull his focus away, how was he supposed to stop these ruminations from drawing all his attention? She eventually ceased her attempts, only occasionally piping in to remind him of his breathing.

His legs were drawn up under him, and though he sat in stillness, there was an energy buzzing through his body. An anxious hum of adrenaline; fear clutching at him. He could not still the reeling of his thoughts any more than he could stop the gusts of wind announcing the arrival of winter in Iralu City. One idea rose to the front and was immediately swept away by another, too tenuous to grasp with his attention.

The absence of his work was a cavity inside him. He looked around his home; the ascetic emptiness of the space struck him. A chair, a small table for consuming the food he usually purchased pre-cooked, and one holographic plant that he had been given by his staff on the occasion of their first publication.

His staff had long since given up on adding any warmth to

Tynan's life. He had considered it clutter once, but now he felt the loss as the shadows stretched into the bare corners of his apartment. The long, straight, and uninterrupted lines of perspective seemed to point him in one direction, but when he tried to follow the call with his mind, he saw only the aching, hollow nothing he felt within. What just a day ago was a peaceful openness now felt lonely and barren.

Tynan was used to isolation. He had Min, of course, and he always told himself his mind and his VA were enough to make a kind of home for himself. He had never really had friends, not the way they were described to him. As the only child of the szacante ambassador to the human agricultural colony of New Denmark, he had not endeared himself to his classmates—the human children of farmers and agricultural technicians.

When his parents had hosted gatherings with the local leaders— all botanists and biologists and animal physiologists—he begged to be allowed to stay and be a part of the scientific conversations. But even when he was permitted to stay and talk with the adults, he had been relegated to a curiosity: the oddly precocious alien child.

When he was nearing adolescence, he had applied to all the prestigious boarding schools in Iralu City. When the acceptances flooded in, he forwarded each one to his parents, and filled their formerly quiet morning breakfasts with pleas and arguments to let him attend. He finally wore them down, and his mother accompanied him to the small colony's port to be transported on a diplomatic vessel to Iralu City. She rode silently beside him in the aircar. Now, so many years later, Tynan finally recognized her silence as the dying breath of her political aspirations for her young and headstrong son. He recalled the look of quiet resignation in her pale green eyes as she embraced him a final time at the station. She promised they would meet in a few months, when the annual State Dinner called all the ambassadors home to honor their work.

His parents were indeed honored at the State Dinner that year.

Tynan recalled his hazy memories of that night, sitting shell-shocked in the seat next to the Arbiter. He was the guest of honor, clothed in stiff and spotless mourning white—the event that was meant to be a reunion of his family instead became his final good-bye. A mob of colonists, unhappy with the new restrictions on soybeans imported from the United Human Nations, had attacked the diplomatic residence on New Denmark. Tynan's parents had been killed in the attack. Now their only son sat in a room full of the most important people on Dresha, a tiny figure with a pale and pinched face.

By then, Tynan had already distinguished himself as the top student in his school. Even then, he'd known he was on the course he had been dreaming for himself—access to the best universities in the galaxy, advanced degrees, and research freedom. The pristine expanse of things in the universe still not understood was open to him to discover. And since he would never follow in his parents' footsteps, he instead forged a new path in their name. He became the best-known scientist of his time: a rising star, still young and capable, with his own foundation and an embarrassment of riches flowing into his research coffers from human and nareian security organizations alike.

Everything that had been important to him—the only thing left that had enriched his life—was now gone. Swept away as thoroughly as if it had never existed. He wanted to hold onto it, wanted to grasp tightly to any piece of his work that he could summon out of the depths of his mind and hang on to it. He needed to regain his name, his reputation, his life. Beneath the anxious hum these thoughts created, a vigorous pulse was beginning to make its strength known. The pulse drew his thoughts together, consolidated them into one focused beam.

"I need to fix this," he said, more to himself than to Min. "I need to get my life back."

8

When they docked at Argos Station, the officers followed Armstrong and Tully to headquarters. Sal had grown up on Argos, and his family had an apartment there, but for those not fortunate enough to have family or the means to own their own home on Argos, HQ was where most stayed when on the station.

As Jaya passed through the docking bay, the noise and organized chaos of the station surrounded her. Argos was the capital of the Union and had been since they left Earth over two hundred years ago, having chosen not to settle their diplomatic and military headquarters on any particular planet. Perhaps there was a sentimentality to it—they had not found a world capable of replacing Earth. But the reality of it was more likely that the space station afforded a control and security that a planet could not. It was too large to be maneuverable, but still small enough to secure each sector individually. Most importantly, it was easy to evacuate in an emergency.

The station was the size of a large but compact city, with millions of citizens. It was the headquarters for the political, diplomatic, economic, and military powers of the human race. The main atrium just beyond the docks welcomed visitors passing through customs. Large screens covered entire walls. Polished news anchors delivered the most exciting stories to the population of the station as advertisements blared, calling attention from even the most centered of citizens passing by. Jaya's focus was pulled to the catchy music and garish colors of a home-protection service ad before she drew it back. Then, the audio from a news sequence one screen over drew her attention.

"The head of a galaxy-renowned szacante research firm, Tynan Vasuda, has been forced out of his foundation in an apparent board coup," said one of the anchors, her stylized dyed hair and iridescent white teeth shining out from the screen. "Sources inside the company say that new leadership is taking a more ambitious direction with the firm's mission."

"Unusual, isn't it?" Armstrong said.

Jaya glanced at him and realized he'd caught her deep in thought, his keen eyes missing nothing of what flickered across her face.

"What is?" she asked.

"That there would be any news coming out of a szacante research firm other than dry press releases about their discoveries. Makes you wonder if this is really the galaxy you grew up in."

"We live in unusual times, Captain."

Armstrong chuckled. "My father used to say that when I was a kid. It seems every generation has lived in unusual times."

"I guess we just keep adapting."

"That's the idea," he said.

They reached the elevator and Armstrong sent an encrypted request through his palm drive for special access to the Diplomatic Level. The elevator arrived quickly, sliding smoothly open for their entrance. The Diplomatic Level was where the crew spent most of their time on Argos, at least when they weren't in the Forum for their rest and recreation time. They piled into the large elevator and the door began to slide closed when a szacante approached. Her suit was professional but ill-fitting, and she had the glazed-over eyes of a new arrival to this buzzing and compact metropolis. Armstrong stepped casually into the open space at the front of the elevator, halting her entrance.

"The Szacante Embassy?" he asked.

The szacante woman nodded. "I need to file a claim. What level is it on?"

"You'll need to take the other elevator."

He gestured around the corner, where the public-access elevator for the various embassies was located. His voice was gentle but firm as he gave instructions. "The Szacante Embassy is marked on the display inside the elevator. It's on the fourth level, but it's very clearly marked once you get inside."

The woman gave a nonverbal reply that was half assent and half bafflement, but she turned and made her way toward the other elevator. Armstrong chuckled quietly as he stepped back inside and allowed the elevator doors to close.

"Every damn time," Sal muttered under his breath, and Jaya elbowed him in rebuke.

To Sal, she knew every lost newcomer to Argos looked like a colonial bumpkin too stupid to follow the basic instructions clearly displayed on every screen in the station. But Jaya's first weeks on the station years ago had been consumed by a haze of excess and commotion, and she saw echoes of her own past in the eyes of so many of the faces that wandered the corridors of Argos today.

"Not everyone is born and bred Argos elite like you," she retorted quietly.

Sal elbowed her back gently, a contrite acknowledgement.

The elevator doors opened again, and Jaya was greeted by the quiet energy of the government wing of the Diplomatic Level. While this area was just as bustling—if not more so—than the rest of Argos station, it operated under a hush. Heads were bent over desks as they passed through the corridors. Jaya made eye contact with two uniformed officers who were deep in conversation. Though their words were too low to reach her ears, they stopped speaking when they locked eyes with her, and watched her until she rounded a corner.

The election was imminent, and Jaya could feel the anxiety emanating from the Parliamentary Quarters, where the Legislative Chamber met and the Chancellor and the Cabinet had their offices. Many of the government officials were up for re-election, and the current Chancellor had personally endorsed her party's choice to replace her.

This candidate was Richard Emory, the founder and CEO of TA Tech, more formally known as Terra Aeterna Technology. TA Tech was the largest conglomerate of military and civilian technology corporations in the Union and arguably in the galaxy. They developed and distributed weapons, telecommunications, medical equipment, and nanotechnology. The scope of their interests was far-flung, and their products were ubiquitous. Emory was quite possibly the wealthiest human in the Milky Way—Jaya did not believe the wild rumors of his fortune surpassing even that of the Nareian Empress, but she did find herself wondering idly what freedom wealth of that magnitude must bring.

It wasn't a long walk to Jaya's base apartment. The spartan room was significantly larger than her tiny pod on the *Avalon*, with its own desk and dresser, but still had little room for furnishings or possessions to sprawl out. Jaya removed the violin from her bag and set it on a shelf, where it stayed while she was on the station. She placed her folded uniforms in a drawer and opened the one above it, where her civilian clothes were stored. She changed into a dark green sweater and gray pants, splashed some water on her face, and tucked the fine coppery wisps of hair that had slipped out of her braid behind her ears.

Back in the main room, she stuffed her bag into a storage space near the door and looked around. It wasn't much, but at least it was hers.

She closed the door behind her, and it locked automatically as she headed down the corridor toward the elevator to the Forum.

The Forum was the hub of Argos. While there were restaurants and shops across every level of the station, this was the most trafficked and popular area. Jaya tried to spend as little time here as she could, but she always stopped to buy a meal from her favorite vendor. She took the spit-roasted meat, doused in szacante hot sauce and wrapped in flatbread, and ate it as she retreated from the noise and chaos to one of the quieter neighborhoods of Argos.

It was a pleasant corner of the station—residential apartments and small shops. The denizens of Argos station were mainly wealthy, affording them luxuries like the boutique clothing stores and antiques shops she passed. Small cafés boasted fusion menus— the haute cuisines of Argos that showcased traditional human flavors with an exotic, alien spin taken mostly from szacante cooking.

This quarter was more modest, and relatively neglected by the flashy targeted advertising that was omnipresent on the rest of the station. A military lifestyle precluded the sort of freedom to acquire *things* the conglomerates counted on for their profits, and shipboard life was a restful oasis in this respect at least: there were no ads to distract, to tug at secret desires, to play on insecurities. Here on Argos, it was nearly impossible to open one's eyes without being assaulted by color and block text, and always in the background were conflicting murmurs—some enticing with promises of improved lives, others cautioning against the world outside with chilling news of colony skirmishes and terrorist attacks.

Jaya stopped in front of a small antiques shop. In the display, a black grand piano cast elegant shadows on the store walls. The interior of the lid was as smooth and glossy as the curved box itself, its surface reflecting the metallic lines of the hammers and strings. The burgundy of the velvet-upholstered bench drank in the light of the display, its tone rich and soft, and the shadows cast by the lid on the keys beckoned to her even through the artificiality of the screen.

The digital display in front of the store read: CLOSED. She sighed, turning to leave, when the door opened.

"Can I help you?"

She turned back around. A man stood in the open door, watching her with dark eyes framed by thick lashes. Smooth black hair fell loose over his shoulders, and the expression on his bronze face was open and curious.

"I was admiring the piano," she said.

"Would you like to see it?" he asked.

"Oh, no," she replied. "You're closed—I don't want to keep you late."

"Not at all. Come on in." He waved her in and stepped back to give her room to enter the shop.

She could have just explained that she couldn't buy the instrument and stopped wasting his time, but she followed him into the shop, and he closed the door to the quiet street behind them. The shop was cozy, its color palette soft and deep at the same time, with none of the harsh metallic hues of Argos's corridors. Old lamps gave the room a golden glow, and the citrus smell of wood polish mingled with the earthy scent of paper.

Her eyes were immediately drawn to the piano. The instrument sat in the corner, its lines as graceful as it looked on the screen, the soft light painting it hazy like a memory. Jaya moved toward it.

"I just got it in," he continued, leaning against the payment console. His posture was relaxed and confident, his sleeves rolled up to his elbows. He was around her own age, but he carried years in his posture, in the way he looked over the space around him like he was seeing it from a great height.

"It's restored," he added.

"It's gorgeous," Jaya said, and when she heard the note of awe in her tone, she flushed. Here, in front of her, a deeply buried piece of her life was calling out to her, trying to rise to the surface. She looked back at him and saw a slight frown of concentration creasing the bridge of his nose.

"Here on shore leave?" he asked.

For a moment, she forgot the piano. "Yes," she replied. "How did you know?"

"I can smell military training."

"It must stink like hell on Argos, then," she said.

He shrugged. "Yeah, lots of military folks around here. I don't usually get them in my store, though. What brings you to an antiques shop?"

Jaya looked over at the piano.

"We used to have a piano," she said. "Nothing as beautiful as this, but I loved it. I'm sure I would have worn the keys down to nubs if I'd had the chance."

"You play?" he asked.

"Not for a long time."

There was something in his smile that released a little of the ache in her chest. Something wistful in his eyes.

"That's not something you lose." His voice was quiet. "Not really."

She struggled to find words, but found that his echoed in her mind instead. His smile remained, creasing the corners of his dark eyes and yet still heavy with some deep understanding. Loss. And also permanence. How some things could still linger, even when there was no longer space for them.

"Go ahead," he said, gesturing to the piano.

"I can't buy it," she told him, the words bursting out of her guiltily. "Shipboard assignment, nowhere to put it."

He nodded. "I know. You don't have to buy it. Just play it."

She raised an eyebrow at him, taking in the earnestness in his expression. He leaned forward, his forearms resting on the console.

He half-smiled and tucked his hair behind his ears as he watched her. Jaya sensed he was reading her, facial tics and posture like a language she suddenly realized he spoke. She shifted, abruptly aware of the space between them.

"I have a theory," he said, "that works of art like this lose their power when they aren't appreciated. What's the purpose of a piano like this if it just sits growing dust in an antiques shop?"

"I guess you have a point," she said.

"Besides." His grin flashed, wickedly sly. "I love music."

She took a seat on that velvet-lined bench. With one finger, she gently depressed one of the keys, hearing the pure and resonant middle C emerge from the box as the hammer struck the steel string.

"It's tuned and restored—I had a guy in here yesterday to get it ready to sell," he said. "You should have heard it before. Even I knew it sounded wrong."

Jaya played a few more notes, their frequencies matching the tones forming in her head before she summoned them from the piano.

"It sounds good now," she said.

She met his eyes, and he stepped back, as if he had just become aware of the moment he was intruding on.

"I'll just be doing inventory at the console. Go ahead and play as much as you want." He extended his hand. "I'm Luka, by the way."

"Jaya," she said, shaking the offered hand. His grip was warm and strong.

"Nice to meet you, Jaya."

She smiled at him, and he returned it before taking a seat behind his console. He secured his hair back from his face and his fingers began to tap away at the screen. Even that corner of his shop, intended just for conducting the details of the business, was decorated warmly. Books lined a shelf over his head, their spines alternating warm ochre and deep green and night sky blue. Luka's posture expressed all the comfort and ease of this space of his, leaning slightly forward, wisps of hair already escaping the band that held them back and softening the sharp line of his jaw. He had turned those searching eyes to his console and she saw now how his lashes curled up, dark even in profile.

Jaya realized she was staring, her pulse suddenly pounding in her temples. She turned her attention back to the piano.

She began with a simple piece, letting her fingers remember this kind of motion—nimble and quick, and quite unlike grasping a gun or forming a fist. She wondered if Sal felt the switch the way she did. His music was in the keys of a console. He drew information out of the ether as Jaya drew a melody. Her fingers adjusted quickly, the tiny muscles of her hand loosening and stretching. She transitioned into a more complex composition, testing her flexibility, letting her pinkies reach notes far removed from her thumbs.

As the piece came to a close, she closed her eyes, letting her hands find their way across the keys themselves. It had been so long since she had played on an actual piano—the holographic keyboards had no aesthetics; their sound was hollow and her fingers flew over empty space instead of smooth, cool ivory. She played the final note, and though the sound faded from the air quickly, its shadow hung in the silence.

She opened her eyes.

For a moment, nothing disturbed the quiet. She looked over at Luka, who sat watching her, eyes dark in the amber light of the room, his work quite forgotten. "You're very good," he said.

"Thanks," she replied.

Carefully, she closed the lid over the keys of the piano. The hush of the room felt delicate after the music, like even the air was listening.

"You're welcome to come back," he said. "Any time. Maybe you'll give this piano some life while it waits for a home. And I would love to see you again."

"Thanks," she said, suddenly flushed. "I will."

She had crossed the room by now, and he closed down his console and turned off the lights, one by one. They parted ways in the corridor as he locked up the shop behind him and Jaya made her way to the military barracks. Although the clamor of Argos continued around her, she had sunk deep into another world—one filled once again with music.

Biology was a powerful thing, and while humans had not lived on Earth for generations, the human body still craved Earth's cycles. Argos was structured accordingly, though with the firm rigidity of a carefully designed calendar. There was no changing of seasons, and the artificial lighting rose and set at the same time each day, with a sort of flat predictability.

In the Forum, the high ceiling was smattered with tiny lights, imitating the night sky that their ancestors had looked on from Earth. Although Argos was in an entirely different sector of the galaxy from Earth, the constellations were the same constellations onto which the human people had projected their oldest mythologies, rotating through the hemispheres and the seasons. Jaya's eyes always looked for Ursa Major and Ursa Minor when she walked through—the big bear and the little bear nestled safely together in the Forum's night skies.

Jaya was settled into her bed. Her little room was peaceful and dark, but even in the stillness, she couldn't sleep. It was jarring to not have the constant, low-frequency vibration of the ship's engines. In space, the motion of the ship was invisible so long as it was moving at a constant speed, which it almost always was between FTL jumps. But the thrum of the ship itself was always there, almost alive and breathing as much as the crew.

The quiet of the base at night was stale, in comparison. Music still played in her head, and Luka's words filled whatever silence was left. *That's not something you lose. Not really.*

She rolled over onto her side, staring into the velvety black shadows of the room. Then her palm drive beeped, the sound reaching her ears through the implanted earpiece. She opened the holographic display: it was Rhodes. She answered.

"I need your help. We have a personnel situation. I'll send you the location."

"On my way," Jaya responded.

She threw on the clothing she had worn earlier in the evening and tucked a pistol into a shoulder holster. Covering the whole thing with a jacket, she hurried down to the Forum Level.

The location was a small, unremarkable bar. Drinks were cheap, and the place was packed. She spotted Rhodes right away—in a booth halfway back in the room, struggling with a very large, drunk man.

The man was Thompson, and judging by the smell of him, he had started his drinking long ago. Perhaps as soon as he had set foot on Argos and dropped his belongings in the barracks. His jacket was stained with sweat, liquor, and vomit, and he was shouting at Rhodes, who was trying to remove him from his booth.

Thompson's words were incoherent by now, but when Jaya approached, he mumbled something in her general direction. Rhodes helped steady him as he teetered back, his mouth set in a stern line.

"You could hear him four tables down shouting about the Sons of Priam. He's pissed out of his mind and was drawing a lot of attention."

Jaya glanced around. There were furtive glances cast their way from a number of tables, and others were looking very firmly at anything but Thompson.

"Still is," Jaya said. "We should get him out of here."

"Yeah," Rhodes agreed. "Help me get him upstairs. I already settled the bill."

He maneuvered himself under one of Thompson's arms, and Jaya wedged herself beneath the other and hoisted the large man up.

Together, they carried Thompson out of the bar and toward the elevator. His shouting had turned to nonsensical mumbles and then silence. His head drooped as they carried him through silent hallways into the barracks.

"My apartment," Rhodes said. "I'll keep an eye on him tonight."

"You sure?" Jaya asked. "Shouldn't we take him to the med bay?"

Rhodes shook his head. "Not like this. He's fine, and I've got a few sobriety tabs that should ease him back from the edge. But we should avoid HQ. If they catch him this wasted, he won't be. Shore leave or no."

They got into Rhodes's apartment in a neighborhood not far from the Diplomatic Level's main entrance and hoisted Thompson onto the couch. Jaya helped Rhodes peel off the stained jacket and Jaya rolled it and tucked it under her arm. Rhodes pulled a chair up.

"Thanks, Mill," he said.

She turned to leave, and then paused. "Did Thompson call you?"

Rhodes heard Jaya's other question in the silence that followed. Thompson was on her strike team, but Rhodes had been there before she had even known about it. He sighed, and then he looked at the unconscious man as though he might wake from his stupor and provide an answer. After a moment of silence, with Thompson as still as the dead and not looking likely to offer an explanation, Rhodes spoke:

"This is a tough job. It's a tough life. You know it. I know it."

Jaya nodded her agreement, and Rhodes continued. "Thompson was a private first class in my very first strike team command. He pissed me off even then. I never thought he was serious enough for this job. He was always goofing off, always ignoring regulations and protocol. But people liked him—he lightened the mood. After a rough day, it was Elias Thompson who got everyone together. Got them to laugh, to forget about whatever had happened."

He reached over and pulled the blanket up more snugly. "It took me a long time to realize that was a skill," Rhodes admitted. "It took me a lot longer to learn how to cultivate that skill myself."

Rhodes smiled, his teeth white against the dark brown of his face, even in the dim light of the room. But it was almost a grimace. There was a long silence. They both watched Thompson—his breath was shallow for sleep. His rest would be fitful at best tonight, and he would have a head full of regrets in the morning.

"I don't always like him," Rhodes confessed out of the darkness, "but when it matters most, he pulls it together and does his job. He has a place on the *Avalon*, and like it or not, the company wouldn't be the same without him."

"True," Jaya said.

"I think Thompson knows that I feel that way. He may not realize that you do, too."

Jaya nodded, the words landing hard. They weren't delivered harshly, but she felt the blow all the same.

She shut the door quietly behind herself and took the dirty jacket back to her apartment, doing her best to wash the mess off in the sink. She hung it over her shower door to dry and readied herself for sleep for the second time that night.

In bed, she took in a deep breath, letting the cool sheets settle around her. Fragments of notes and phrases of music stirred in her head, latching on to the quiet and filling it, keeping sleep at bay. She kicked the sheets off.

Sitting up on the edge of the bed, she held her head in her hands, massaging her temples. Her palm drive chimed, and she looked, expecting another update from Rhodes. But the message wasn't from Rhodes.

Don't you understand yet that you're different? Simon and Aman should have kept you better hidden. There's a reason you weren't registered with the Union at birth. You can't trust them.

The second anonymous message flooded her with adrenaline. This one was too specific to be viral marketing: it named the uncles who had raised her, who had spent more money than they could afford buying her black-market citizenship papers when they found out her parents had failed to register her and Kier. She checked the time on New Sheffield—it would be early morning there. She turned on the lights in her room and requested a video connection on her data pad.

After a moment, Uncle Simon's face appeared in the screen, sunburnt and smiling.

"Jaya! What a nice surprise!"

From behind him, she heard Uncle Aman's voice shouting a greeting. A moment later, his face appeared behind Simon. His black hair seemed streaked with more gray every time she saw him. Relief flooded Jaya so suddenly she was speechless for a moment and could only smile at them as her hands trembled.

"We weren't expecting to hear from you," Aman said. "Did you get some shore leave?"

"Yeah," she said, half-laughing and still shaky. "I did. I just missed you. And I was worried."

Simon frowned in confusion. "Everything is fine here."

Jaya nodded. "Of course, just after the attacks…"

"There was nothing on New Sheffield, sweetheart," Aman said. "Everything has been boring and routine here since you last visited."

"You haven't noticed anything unusual?" she asked. "Anything at all?"

They both denied any strange events, their voices overlapping. The furrow in Simon's forehead deepened, though, and he followed their denials with a question.

"Were you there?"

Jaya shook her head in apology. "You know I can't say anything about my work. It's just that," she paused, "they were all agricultural colonies. And I thought of you."

"Don't worry about us," Aman said. "You just take care of yourself. You're the one out there saving the galaxy."

"Hardly." Jaya couldn't help the bitterness in the words. "At least, I'm trying."

She sighed, her uncles' smiling faces finally providing her the reassurance she needed. They were fine. They really were. But still.

"We need to go," Simon said. "Day's just starting and there's lots to do. But we're glad you called."

"I am, too," Jaya said. "Will you do me a favor? If anything out of the ordinary happens, will you tell me? Even if it seems like nothing? I'd just... I'd like to know."

They promised her they would report any strange occurrences, and then closed the connection with air kisses and *I love you*s. And then Jaya was left in the silence of her room again, the fear eased slightly, but still pulsing in her heart.

She opened the password-protected personal directory on her data pad and pulled up an old folder. It was full of pictures—family pictures from when she was young. Near the end of the list of photographs was a video file. She hesitated a moment, then opened it, turning the lights out again and propping the data pad up on its stand and curling back up under her covers.

The soulful sound of a violin filled the tiny room, and Jaya let her head ease onto the pillow. On the screen was the image of her mother, small and delicate in the tiny frame of the data pad. She played with her whole body, her eyes closed and her shoulders swaying into the notes. Her dark red hair brushed her jaw, falling across her face as she played.

Jaya's father had taken the video, and in the background Jaya saw the figures of herself and her brother. She was barely out of her toddler years, and Kier a baby-faced eight-year-old, but they both sat silently, orange shocks of hair bobbing as they rapturously watched their mother play music from a book their father had given her.

The video was a memory from a better time. Before she lost her family. Before she lost her dreams. Before her father stopped giving her mother books with inscriptions that read: *For bringing music into my life—I love you.*

When the video ended, Jaya reached up and started it again. She lay in the dark, letting the music wash over her, hearing in the sweet and rich sound of violin notes the sweet and rich voice of her mother speaking to her. She restarted the video again and again, until she finally drifted into deep sleep and let the video play into silence.

9

The next morning, Jaya knocked on the door of Rhodes's apartment, Thompson's still-damp jacket folded over her arm. After a short pause, Rhodes cracked the door, squinting at the light. She handed him the jacket.

"How's he doing?" she asked.

Rhodes rubbed his hands wearily over his neat buzz cut and waved her in. "He's still out," he replied, speaking softly. "But he seems to be resting well now. It was rough for a while."

Jaya glanced over at the couch, where Thompson was tangled in a blanket. His cheeks looked round and soft in sleep, reminding Jaya that he was barely out of his teens. They were all so young, but especially these marines who put so much faith in her and Rhodes to lead them. The sourness in her stomach intensified.

"I owe you," she said.

"He's all yours next time," Rhodes said, the bags beneath his eyes suggesting he might be regretting his previous night's mercy.

She left, shutting the door gently behind her, and headed to the military hospital. Vargas's room was the last one down the long and narrow hall, and she paused in the door when she saw Vargas already had a visitor. Lupo sat in a chair beside the bed, leaning forward, elbows on knees as they spoke quietly together.

When Jaya appeared in the doorway, both women looked up. Lupo smiled, but Vargas gave a shaky salute, her face pale and tense. Jaya waved off the salute.

"At ease," Jaya said. "How are you feeling?"

"Well enough," Vargas said. "Considering."

Lupo stood, squeezing Vargas's hand before letting it go. "I'll go get some breakfast," she said. "Commander, do you want anything?"

Jaya shook her head and waited for Lupo to leave the room before she took the formerly occupied seat. Vargas shifted, sat up straighter in her bed.

"I just wanted to talk to you about this," Jaya continued. "It's a lot to take in, and I know the chain of command is not always good at answering the questions you want answered."

Vargas gave a small, wry smile at that, but no comment.

Jaya crossed her legs and sat back in the seat. "At least here you have fake sunshine," she noted, looking at the warm light spreading across the walls of the room from the small artificial window.

Vargas still did not respond, but her jaw worked.

"I remember the first time I got stuck on extended stay on Argos," Jaya continued. "A few of us were exposed to some sort of spore on a colony when we were doing recon. Got stuck in quarantine for a month. I'd been on the *Avalon* for less than a year then, but it was still hard to be away."

"It's home," Vargas said.

Jaya murmured an agreement.

A silence fell again. Vargas settled back into her pillow and folded her hands in her lap. She picked at the cuticles of her nails, and the dark curls she usually wrapped in a tight knot spilled over her forehead.

"Can I do anything for you?" Jaya asked.

Vargas shook her head.

"You know TA Tech is the best in the business," Jaya said. "And the military hospital here will know how to get you back to full health."

"Full health," Vargas repeated, her voice harsh. She crossed her arms over her chest. "I'll never really be a hundred percent again."

"I know," Jaya said quietly.

Vargas looked away from her, and Jaya looked down at her own hands, clasped on her knees. Jaya had been lucky to have never landed here herself. The wounds she had received in combat or training were mild and infrequent, and she always healed remarkably quickly. She had never sustained anything as serious as what Vargas was facing, although she'd had what felt like more than her fair share of close calls.

Vargas broke the silence. "This is the only thing I've ever been good at." Her voice was muffled slightly, as she was still looking away.

Jaya raised her eyes and waited for Vargas to continue.

"How would you feel if you lost the chance to do the only thing you ever dreamed of doing with your life?" Vargas asked.

The pit in Jaya's stomach expanded. She remembered late nights studying for the Naval Academy's entrance exam, her mother's violin calling to her. How one night she had shoved it under her bed, swallowing the bitter lump in her throat, so its worn case would cease its torturous reminder of what she had once wished for. But she struggled to find the words to explain this.

Vargas still wouldn't look at her.

"I know you're scared," Jaya tried.

"You have no idea." Vargas's voice was low, bitter. She closed her eyes.

They sat in silence for a moment, Jaya with her arms wrapped around her own torso, Vargas looking darkly away. She felt she should leave. Give Vargas her space.

But she remembered that box in her chest, shut tight against the secrets. She saw Vargas starting to build her own box in that moment, starting to shut herself in.

It's not as scary in there as you think.

She still didn't agree entirely with Sal. She was not ready to pry the lid off and spill her secrets into the daylight, but what would happen if she let a sliver of light in? What if that ache in her chest was worse because she had allowed it to fester?

"It takes a while," Jaya began. "It takes a very long time to start to understand how your life will be different. To understand all the changes. The little ones will be the hardest, because you won't see them coming."

Vargas turned her head back. Jaya unwrapped her arms from around herself and leaned forward. "You'll feel like you're not supposed to grieve as long as you will. Because you survived."

"You're supposed to be grateful, right?"

It was just a whisper, but Jaya heard well enough. She nodded. "It looks different on the outside. But you have to let yourself grieve on the inside. Even if no one else understands."

Vargas turned away again.

"Jordan," Jaya said, shaking off the bitter melody playing in her mind. "Talent isn't everything. You've become one of the best in the company, and not just because you have a natural aptitude. You work harder than anyone else. I see it. You're at the drills day after day. You always do more than you're asked."

Vargas stared sharply down at her hands.

Jaya saw the vulnerable shimmer of tears in her dark eyes, but then Vargas closed her eyes firmly and took a deep breath. The tears never fell.

"You're someone who comes out on top," Jaya said. "I know you'll see to it."

Vargas's face softened, although her voice was strained when she spoke. "Damn right I will."

"Good," Jaya said. "That's what I want to hear."

A soft knock on the door frame drew their attention. Lupo had returned, bringing with her the smell of coffee and hot breakfast. Jaya stood, allowing the diminutive navigator to take back her seat and put the food and hot drinks she had brought with her on the little table. Jaya's palm drive beeped—an urgent message from Armstrong.

"The doctors here are going to keep Doctor Choi in the loop," Jaya said, "and she's promised to keep me updated. I'll come by again."

"Thank you, Commander," Vargas replied.

Jaya left the two to their breakfast, pulling up the message on her palm drive. It was addressed to her, Tully, and Rhodes.

Emergency meeting with Rear Admiral Reid. Report at eleven hundred hours to Diplomatic Level, conference room C.

She checked the time and headed out toward the elevators, her pace brisk. The Forum bustled around her, forcing her to weave through the sluggish crowd of morning commuters and tourists. When she reached the elevator to the Diplomatic Level, she requested a lift with her palm drive and took a moment to straighten her jacket, tugging the braided cuffs to smooth the fabric of the sleeves.

"Lieutenant Commander Mill," a voice behind her said, its tone smooth and strangely familiar. She turned around.

She recognized his face immediately—high cheekbones, slight arc of the nose, smoothness of features just a little too perfect to be natural. But then, so many opted for cosmetic improvements now, especially politicians. Stunning good looks were mandatory for the media blitz accompanying political campaigns, especially for seats as publicized as Chancellor.

"I'm Richard Emory," he said, extending a hand to shake hers.

"I know who you are," she said, shaking his hand firmly and holding eye contact with just as much strength.

His pupils constricted suddenly, but not a wrinkle disturbed his cool and composed expression. He raised an eyebrow that was as white as his short-cropped hair. He had an air of military about him, but Jaya found herself suspicious of his calculated bearing. Military associations, though often exaggerated, were known to sway elections.

"Can I help you, Mr. Emory?" she asked.

"I've been hoping to make your acquaintance, Lieutenant Commander," he said, a cool and indeterminate smile folding creases into his face. "I've heard a lot about you, you see," he continued. "Rising star in your field. Tenacious, talented, driven. I'd love to see where you go."

The elevator doors opened smoothly behind her, and she gestured to them.

"Going up?" she asked.

He nodded, and she motioned for him to enter the elevator first. She followed, pressing the button for the Diplomatic Level and confirming the security check in her palm drive. He stood beside her.

"How long have you been with the Navy?" he asked.

"Just over fourteen years."

"You hardly look old enough," he replied, the smoothness of his tone once again raising the hairs on the back of Jaya's neck.

She didn't respond to this, instead meeting his gaze and waiting for him to continue with whatever he intended to say to her.

"Do you like the Navy?" he asked. "Good career for a capable woman such as yourself?"

"Yes, I like it," she replied.

"I served once," he said, and for the first time, he looked away from her, and she could see the pupils of his hazel eyes constrict once again. "For a very short time. I found it…"

He paused, then turned his gaze back to Jaya. She waited.

"Well, I found it a bit too menial, if I can be frank with you," he said. "Too much drudge work. I wanted to change the world, and I felt quite stifled by the rules and regulations."

Jaya kept her face impassive. "It's not for everyone," she replied evenly, swallowing the rejoinder that not everyone had options, as he must have had. "But clearly you've found success on your own terms."

"Indeed I have," he replied, smiling again. "Lieutenant Commander Mill, have you ever considered working in policy? Our leaders often find themselves in need of advice and perspective from someone with the kind of experience you have. Military consultants."

"Consulting?"

It was not something she had considered. The military had been her only way out fifteen years ago, and she had followed that path blindly to where she was now. But today, with more than a decade of counterintelligence experience, did she have other choices? Opportunities she might enjoy?

But her chest constricted at the thought of leaving the *Avalon*. She tried to picture herself in a government office and felt only a cold indifference.

"I haven't really thought about it," she replied. It was, she supposed, the truth.

The doors opened, and Emory stepped out into the hushed energy of the Diplomatic Level. Jaya followed him.

"Well, maybe you should," he said to her, reaching out to shake her hand firmly.

He began to walk down the corridor toward the legislative offices and stopped to look back at her. "It was lovely to meet you, Lieutenant Commander Mill." He nodded courteously once and turned away.

Jaya headed uneasily down the corridor toward the conference room. When she arrived, she found Rhodes already waiting for her. He had showered and shaved, and in his crisp uniform, he almost looked refreshed. Armstrong and Tully soon appeared, followed by Rear Admiral Henrik Reid and a few officers from the HQ office. Reid strode to his seat, a full head taller than most everyone in the room and as stiff as his pristine uniform.

Reid wasted no time once he had taken his seat: "I received the report last night on the data recovered from the encrypted files."

Jaya smiled. Sal had clearly been more productive last night than the rest of them.

"Yes," Armstrong said. "The compound we invaded was running some sort of weapon and equipment laundering system. They had just sent a shipment of black-market weapons and supplies to a base on a remote colony called Collin's Rock. We recovered the coordinates for the colony and would like to move quickly to send in a strike team."

Rear Admiral Reid exchanged a look with one of the officers who accompanied him. It was a deliberate glance, and the hairs on Jaya's arms rose with a prickle. Rhodes shifted in his seat. Something significant had happened. And in their line of work, significant was usually bad.

"We think there is an avenue of greater urgency than these deliveries to Collin's Rock," Reid said, leaning forward and steepling his fingers. He cleared his throat and looked again at the man sitting to his left—a captain with thinning hair, whose forehead became damp with sweat almost immediately upon speaking.

"Our people intercepted some chatter from New Laredo," the captain said. "The colony has been under a lot of stress since the crop failure last year. Unemployment is up, inflation is running rampant. We've been doing our best to support the development of new technologies to prevent the blight that caused the failure and subsidize the local agricultural—"

Reid cleared his throat, and the captain—whose speech had accelerated once it began rolling off his tongue—took a deep breath, his nostrils flaring, and rerouted his babbling to the main point:

"An insurgency is beginning to take hold there," he said. "Efforts to reinforce local government and business have failed, and the growing unrest makes it the perfect opportunity for the Sons of Priam to gain a foothold. The chatter we intercepted suggests a major event there in the near future. Possibly something on the scale of the recent coordinated biological attacks."

"They seem to be recruiting heavily on New Laredo," Reid broke in, "and we need to crush their roots there before they take hold. In that kind of volatile environment, we have to be proactive. We are sending the *Avalon* in to support our infiltration team in the colony and identify insurgent elements to prevent future violence."

"Admiral," Armstrong began, and though his face was calm and composed, the stiffness of his shoulders betrayed his tension. "I believe that the sale of weapons to Collin's Rock is a timely issue. The stockpiling of weapons may signify that they already have established operations there. If we hit them before they are ready, we could interrupt their operations on a larger scale."

"Understood, Captain Armstrong," Reid replied, his voice as measured as Armstrong's cool expression, "but our intelligence suggests that the loss of human life on New Laredo is imminent, and we want to send the team with the greatest knowledge of the Sons of Priam and their operations to handle de-escalation. We will investigate the feasibility of sending a separate strike team to Collin's Rock to disrupt potential Sons of Priam activities there. Are we understood?"

The silence that passed between the admiral and the captain was tense, and so quiet that Jaya could hear Armstrong's jaw clicking as he worked it. His expression finally softened, and he gave a brief, controlled nod.

"We're understood."

"Good," Reid said.

"Admiral," Armstrong added. "There is the issue of the operative we brought back from the compound. The one who died under mysterious circumstances. I think that warrants—"

Reid cut him off. "Our medical team on Argos has done an autopsy and determined cause of death was a heart attack. It was just bad luck. Sometimes fate isn't on your side, which is why we need to stay ahead of these bastards."

He looked around, meeting the eyes of every person in the room, his expression grave and searching. Jaya matched it.

"Dismissed," Admiral Reid said curtly.

Jaya, Rhodes, Armstrong, and Tully stood, saluted, and turned to file out of the room.

Outside the door, Rhodes and Jaya stood at attention, awaiting specific orders from Armstrong. The door closed behind their commanding officer and he addressed them calmly.

"Mill and Rhodes, step up your training until we hear more. Both of these developments are unsettling, and we want to be prepared for whatever we might find."

He paused, then opened his mouth as if to speak again. He frowned and stopped, looking first at Tully—whose expression was impassive—and then to Jaya and Rhodes.

"I want everyone on their toes," was ultimately all he added. Then he turned on his heel and left.

After Jaya and Rhodes had informed the crew of the *Avalon* that shore leave was being cut short, they'd spent the afternoon carefully selecting their strike teams and crafting an infiltration plan. Drills were planned, schematics were sent to every member of the strike team's palm drives, and a rush order for special equipment was sent to the naval supply office. The *Avalon* was being stocked, and finally Jaya had a few free hours on what was suddenly her last day of shore leave.

She changed into civilian clothing and retreated to a bustling café in the Forum. It was the kind of café frequented by people from every sector on Argos:

There was a small group huddled together over a table in the corner that Jaya could tell was military, despite their civilian clothing. The executive assistant to a diplomat conducted staff interviews at a booth near the door, multiple empty espresso cups still stained with rings of bronze crema marking the hours he had been there before Jaya even arrived—and two more steaming shots had been run to his table between interviews in the past hour. A few wealthy nareian tourists stared down Americanos with uncertain expressions —the beverage was only still served at places like this because of the draw the ancient name of the drink provided for exactly this kind of galactic bon vivant.

Jaya wrapped her hands around the still-warm ceramic mug that held her high-G—a strong-brewed coffee injected with espresso— and pondered the information she had gathered so far from the naval intelligence servers. There was not much, yet, and Jaya struggled to pull disparate pieces together. The only thing she could make out for now was that they seemed primarily focused on the Human Union, although there was nothing in their message that excluded the other major galactic powers. Based on their focus on human colonies and structures and their drawing from ancient Earth literature to form the backbone of their propaganda, Jaya assumed that the highest echelons of the Sons of Priam were inhabited by humans primarily if not exclusively.

And their leader? She assumed he was the one who narrated the video, or at least the one who composed it. He was the one she had begun to call "Augustus" in her mind—the presumed future ruler of this new empire they aspired to create from the corpse of the old Union.

She sighed and drained the rest of her coffee.

HQ had put together a psychological profile for Augustus, but

Jaya barely needed to look at it. He would be from the colonies—from somewhere remote. Jaya had grown up in exactly that kind of place, as had many of the marines on the *Avalon*. The kind of place where people were desperate, where the Union didn't seem so kindly as it did to the denizens of Argos and the other wealthy planets and luxury stations. He would be someone who had been wronged by the Union enough times to decide it was worth risking his humanity to bring them down. Jaya didn't need the psychological workup. She knew the type.

They were always looking for megalomaniac killers from the colonies. It was just that this one seemed much more sophisticated. He had certainly caught them by surprise in a way the Union's naval intelligence hadn't experienced in any of Jaya's years working there.

So Jaya was trying to find out what made Augustus different from the rest. She had been concentrating her search on the colonies in hopes of finding some evidence of who he had been before he helmed the Sons of Priam. Aside from a spreadsheet of political dissidents both wanted and already captured on the colonies, a few records of unusual explosions or other attacks pre-dating the Sons of Priam's attack, and a handful of anomalous shipments of technological equipment, her searching was proving less fruitful than she had hoped.

Jaya saved all the data she had discovered to a private folder in her secure naval account and swiped up on the small holographic terminal to pay for her drink. Perhaps somewhere in that data, she would be able to discern a pattern. Some clue pointing to the beginnings of this group, and perhaps to some extraordinary origin story for its spokesperson.

With her account settled and her data pad folded into its smaller configuration and slipped into a utility pocket of her jacket, Jaya turned toward the residential neighborhood where the promise of music waited in the quiet corner of a shop.

When Jaya opened the door, Luka was speaking with an older couple, his expression as earnest and kind as she remembered it. She paused for a moment as the warmth of the room swept over her, soft cushioned sofas lining the walls, rich wooden end tables bearing amber lamps. In the center of that space the piano waited.

Luka glanced up when she entered, a smile instantly brightening his face. He nodded his head toward the piano, a sly look in his eye, then returned his attention to his customers. They were syncing information from their palm drives, and Jaya saw Luka type a note to himself.

"I'll have it delivered to that address tomorrow between eight and noon," he said. "An excellent choice. I'm sure you will be happy with it."

The older couple agreed, and he shook their hands warmly and held the door for them as they left. Jaya had already crossed the room to the piano and taken a seat on the velvet cushion.

"What did they purchase?" she asked, once the door had shut behind them.

"Not the piano," Luka said, his teeth white against the warm bronze of his skin.

She returned his grin with a sheepish one of her own. "Is it terrible that I was hoping you'd say that?"

"No," he laughed. "They actually purchased a much more expensive piece. A twentieth century lamp—one of only a few of its kind that has survived the exodus."

For a moment, Jaya forgot all about the beautiful ivory keys already beneath her fingers.

"How in the galaxy did you get such a rare piece?" she asked.

"Extraordinary luck," he said, but there was a mysterious twinge to his smile that suggested he was being reticent. "Good connections," he clarified slightly. "It's all about knowing the right people. But you could say that of any job."

"I guess so," Jaya said.

"I'm glad you're back," he said.

She let her fingers finally settle on the keys. "Shore leave was unexpectedly cut short, but I had a little time."

"Some sort of emergency in the Union sphere of influence?" he asked.

"You know I can't say anything about it."

He threw his hands up in defeat. "Couldn't help myself."

She turned back to the piano, drawing out a melody that was half remembered and half invented. Even after only one night, the old connection returned—it was like she was one with the instrument. The music was in her head, but it was the piano that sang it for her.

"What made you decide to sell antiques?" she asked, realizing how abrupt the question was as the last notes died away. He was leaning against the wall, his arms crossed, watching her play. He stood straighter at the question and unfolded his arms.

"I used to spend a lot of time traveling for my job, like you," he said. "Visited more places in the galaxy than most people on Argos would even know exist. Spent some time on Dresha, on Narei, on a narean colony called Nemet. All this studying alien cultures made me curious about my own. About our history. I traveled some more —gathered up artifacts, trinkets. And here I am." He shrugged. "I guess you could say I'm a sort of untrained anthropologist who owns a shop to pay the rent. Not a great business model, but I make do."

"What sort of job brought you to so many different planets?" she asked.

"That's a story for another time."

"How many pieces do I need to play to get it out of you?" she teased.

"Let me think about it." He smiled. "Another one right now would be a good start."

She chuckled and began a new melody—one she had played

often as a child. It had an accompanying violin part, and she could hear the complementary notes in her head as she played the part she had memorized as a child. It stood alone, the piano portion, but she felt the void—brief but haunting pauses and incomplete scales hinted at a missing partner. When she finished, she remained still, listening to the violin's last notes fading out in her mind.

"You played that one last night." This time, it was Luka who interrupted the silence after the song.

"It's always been a favorite of mine," she said.

"It sounds nostalgic," he said. That wistful look was back in his eye, and it resonated in Jaya. She suddenly imagined what it would be like to tell him everything, to open up that box of secrets she had buried so deep and that the music was beginning to chip away at. There was freedom in that thought. Something sparked in her, and that spark was followed by a rush of fear.

So she sealed her lips, turned away from his earnest eyes, and began to play again.

10

Tynan curled up under the covers of his bed, but there was no room for sleep in his frantic mind, which had grown overcrowded with half-formed plans and anxious grasping at memories. He clutched his data pad, trying to recreate the work of so many years. He had been locked out of his own research and he was left with only what he had stored in his brain.

Which, while a lot, was not nearly enough.

It was the culmination of years of work by hundreds of scientists, combining genetics, epidemiological data, statistical modeling, and analysis that covered nearly every branch of science. Tynan may have had more advanced degrees than he could count on his fingers, but he could not have done this work alone, no matter how much time he was given. And now his work was proprietary—belonging not to him, but to the foundation he had once helmed.

Tynan made a fist with his hand, concentrating all his anger—his frustration with his board for their greed, with himself for not anticipating this move—and then he brought his fist down on the mattress beside him. The resulting *whump* and soft cushion of fabric around his fist did not provide him with the cathartic release he had been looking for. He sat up, thrusting the covers aside, and rested his head in his hands.

What did he have? He asked himself this question, then reframed it in his mind. His access to equipment and data had been taken away, but that didn't mean he lacked access to resources. For a decade now, he had been the highest paid individual at his research firm, and his minimalistic lifestyle meant the money had been sitting in a bank, relatively untouched, accumulating interest in dividends according to the ministrations of the very capable financial advisors he had left it with.

Tynan brought his accounts up on a holographic screen in front of him and let out a low whistle when he saw the number he had ignored for years.

"Min," he said. "Contact the best attorney in Iralu City. I want a meeting tomorrow morning."

There was a brief pause—barely a microsecond—and Min replied. "I have scheduled an appointment through the Virtual Assistant of Perit Turay for the third slot in the morning timetable. Ms. Turay is the attorney on retainer for the Ministry of Science and should have the necessary background to handle a case concerning intellectual property in speculative research."

"Thank you, Min." Tynan breathed a sigh of relief. Min's ability to synthesize his scattered requests with the obvious context was a constant, soothing certainty.

Still, he did not try to return to sleep, not just yet. Another thought nagged at him. His bank account had been enriched by the salary he had written into grant proposals from the three major powers. The Szacante Federation, while generous with scientific funding relative to other categories in their budget, had been the smallest contribution. The Human Union and Nareian Empire, on the other hand, had enough wealth—and perhaps more importantly, political anxiety—to spend freely on szacante research.

Was it possible he was not alone in this fight? Could he have the full strength of two galactic superpowers at his back? He couldn't imagine a lone person powerful enough to face down the military strength of the Human Union Navy or the Nareian Imperial Fleet, especially when both superpowers had a stake in the research.

He wasn't used to thinking of his work on this scale. He was used to taking the money of these two governments and leaving their specific interest in his research at the bank. They had been willing—in fact, eager—to fund him in the past. Perhaps they would be willing to wrest his work back from the hands of this callous private corporation and deliver it back to him. After all, they had invested specifically in his leadership, his research directions.

"Min," he said, "please compose one more letter. Send one to the Human Union Office of Science and Technology, and a separate version to the Nareian Imperial Scientific Directorate. Let them know the situation, and that I am requesting their assistance in regaining control over this research."

Min confirmed when the letter was sent, and Tynan breathed a sigh of relief. He would meet with the attorney tomorrow, and with any luck, he would have both legal and political assistance in this fight.

He leaned back down, adjusting the ergonomic pillow beneath his head and closing his eyes. His mind still refused to quiet, but now he could at least lose himself in fantasies of recovering his life's work.

Bright morning light from the twin suns warmed the lobby of the law offices on the penthouse level of one of the tallest buildings in the city. The ceilings arched above him, the lines like the curving branches of treetops coming together in the forest canopy. Plants were clustered in every corner—the most iconic species of Dresha, carefully curated by experts to remain in such beautiful condition in the interior of a tall building rather than sinking their roots into the rich soil of the Dreshan continental plates.

Tynan sat stiffly, his nicest outfit suddenly feeling quite shabby next to the austere but fashionable attire of the many lawyers who buzzed through the lobby. They seemed to draw all the energy of the suns to propel them from what Tynan assumed was one important meeting to the next.

You are the recipient of the Arbiter's Medal of Virtue, Tynan scolded himself internally. *You are the most famous scientist in the system. And you have the money to pay them to fight for your work.*

He counted a few breaths, then straightened slightly, feeling his backbone return with the reminder of the few cards he had to play. This was not his usual environment—this was the world his parents had belonged to, and one which he had never felt a part of despite their efforts. But he was here with a goal in mind, and he was determined to see it through.

The door in front of him opened smoothly.

"Ms. Turay is ready for you," Min announced quietly through Tynan's private earpiece.

He startled nonetheless.

"You can do this," his VA assured him, her sensors no doubt indicating the agitation of his heart rate and the anxious sweat that was beginning to gather at the nape of his neck and threatening to trickle down his back. He breathed—*in for four, out for eight*—swallowed, then stood and entered the doorway.

The office was less grand than the lobby, but still held a richness that spoke of power and influence. The attorney sat calmly at her desk, her long, thin fingers clasped together in front of her.

"Welcome, Doctor Vasuda," Perit Turay said with a broad smile. "I read your Virtual Assistant's summary of your claim, and I must say I am intrigued."

Tynan returned the smile weakly, then swallowed and tried

again. The result was more energetic this time, and he began to relax.

"I really just want to be able to continue my work," he said.

The attorney waved his words away. "This is a question of intellectual property," she said. "This work is the result of your scientific acumen, which is itself a sort of national treasure of the szacante people, if I do say so myself."

The hot flush of nerves in Tynan's body gave away to one of pride.

"Thank you," he said. "I hope there is something you can do. I don't know what I had put in the founding documents for Vasuda Research, but I will have Min send over the complete records from my tenure there."

"I'm sure that, regardless of the founding documents, an argument can be made for the rights to the research based on promises made to your funding sources. Your primary funding came from the Human Union Office of Science and Technology and the Nareian Imperial Scientific Directorate, is that correct?"

"Yes." Tynan nodded. "My research was relevant to the security of both military superpowers."

"That is likely to be a powerful bargaining chip in our arguments," Perit said, her smile reassuring. "Do you have any questions for me?"

Tynan's mind went blank. He wouldn't even know where to begin. That was why he had come here, to speak with the experts. How could he have any questions at all?

She seemed to notice his attention rummaging around in his own mind, because she reached a hand kindly across the table, refraining from making contact, but drawing his focus back to her. "We will take good care of you and your work, Doctor Vasuda. I can assure you of that."

That was good enough for him. He nodded.

"Have your VA send everything over, and we will produce a

contract with our standard rates for you to look over," she said. "Expect that before the first slot in the afternoon timetable. We are looking forward to working with you, Doctor. Protecting szacante research is near to our hearts."

"Thank you," he managed, and a real smile crossed his face for the first time that day.

When the fourth slot after noon on the following day had passed with no word from the law offices, Tynan began to worry. After the meeting, he had been on the verge of giddy. He had even ceased his obsessive reconstruction of his data and instead purchased a nice lunch at a restaurant downtown, then returned home to play Sequence in the virtual community.

Although he had been anxious when night came with no word, he went to bed with hope in his heart, and visions of being reinstated in his office playing across the inside of his eyelids when he closed them.

But when the next morning crept into midday with still no response, the strange silence over his communication channels began to obscure that vision with fears of a future spent in idleness. He checked with Min every few minutes, and her replies became increasingly irritable, at least relative to her usual serenity.

Finally, he asked Min to connect him to Perit's office directly. His call was refused. He tried again. Another refusal.

After the third refused call, a ping notified him of an incoming message. It was brief, and dashed the last of Tynan's short-lived hope.

Dear Dr. Vasuda,

We apologize, but due to an unforeseen conflict of interest, we are unable to take your case. We wish you the best of luck.

Perit Turay and Associates.

Tynan read the message again. And then another time. He called the office again, and this time someone answered.

"Ms. Turay is unable to take your call, Dr. Vasuda," the junior attorney he finally reached said.

"What happened?" Tynan asked. "Yesterday, she was enthusiastic about the case. She was practically gleeful!" His voice rose with the expanding knot of frustration in his chest.

"I can't tell you that, Doctor Vasuda," the attorney said. "I just know that we were told—"

He broke off then, and Tynan could hear a muffled conversation in the background. Min's translucent image blinked consolingly at him. When a voice returned on the line, it was Perit Turay.

"Doctor Vasuda, I am asking you to drop your inquiry." Her voice contained an odd quality he did not immediately recognize. She sounded different from yesterday afternoon, her former exuberance and confidence leeched out of her voice so thoroughly she almost sounded like a different person.

"I don't understand," Tynan said for what felt like the hundredth time. "If you're concerned about my ability to pay, I assure you I have sufficient funds."

Over his private line to Min, he asked her to bring up his balance again. He would negotiate with every last credit he possessed.

"You should not pursue this," the lawyer insisted, and this time Tynan recognized the quaver in her voice. It was fear. At the same moment, his balance appeared in front of him on his screen. His accounts were empty. His mouth went dry, and all the blood seemed to evacuate his extremities at the same time, leaving a tingling in his fingers and toes.

"Doctor Vasuda?" Perit asked.

"Yes, I'm here," he replied.

"Do you understand now?"

He swallowed hard. "Yes, I do."

The air in the park rippled, a surprisingly firm pulse against his skin, as another shuttle lifted off from the nearby port. The twin suns were setting now, but although Tynan's face was turned in their direction, his attention was diffuse, scattered around the metaphysical spaces of his mind.

This park was one of the beloved gathering places of Iralu City. Located high on a hill, the multistoried transport lanes rose up to meet it on one side, and a dramatic drop on the other side revealed stunning views of the gleaming modern spaceport and the vast ocean beyond. Nearby, a family sat with a picnic dinner, and the gleeful shrieks of the children echoed the distant roar of each shuttle that lifted to the skies.

Tynan didn't know how long he had been sitting at the bench in this park, or what had even guided him here. After his case had been rejected, Min had sent out hundreds of further requests. Every law office on Dresha with any experience in intellectual property had received a message from Tynan. And every law office on Dresha had declined his case. The excuses—when provided—varied in phrasing. Some were conflicts of interest. Some claimed the case fell outside their area of expertise. But every vague and generic rejection letter arrived too quickly and read too forcefully to be coincidental. One, perhaps, he could dismiss. A dozen, even. But with every inbox ping adding another data point to his set, the resulting collection was resolving itself into a sharp peak around one likelihood: his case was marked in some way.

He had exhausted his options. The initial rush of hope that had flooded his body with energy now left him shaky and feeling empty, as if the entire ocean had surged through his veins and washed everything out. He had begun pacing his apartment, and then left his building to walk the city. He needed a purpose, a direction. He needed somewhere to go. And so he had gone up, like a plant chasing the light of the suns, to the highest natural point in the city. And now he sat here on this bench in a crowded park, his legs achy and stiff, and his mind still racing.

His life had changed so violently over the course of only a few days that he still felt the itch to work, to return to his data and his samples. He had been making such progress—his entire research firm had. Their discoveries had unfurled one by one from the small initial branch of knowledge they had been given, each new experiment pointing them in a new direction. His foundation had grown exponentially, hiring new scientists and technicians and galactic historians.

For a moment, Tynan went so still it seemed that even the fatigued pulsing of blood and fluid through his stressed muscles had frozen. He breathed in deeply, smelling the conflicting traces of ozone and salt in the air.

There was still the possibility of intervention by the humans or nareians, but he had received no response yet from them, and every hour that passed made him doubt his chances more. He realized they probably would be happy to continue to fund the research with another scientist at the helm. After all, did they really care who was in charge, as long as the work got done? It seemed not.

"Doctor Vasuda?" The voice at his back was warm. Human, he guessed, filtered through a high-quality translator. He turned to look behind him.

The woman *was* human, and very tall. Her skin was dark and her hair fanned out around her face in tight curls, streaks of gray in the black gleaming like precious metal in the setting suns. Two other humans stood next to her. They were all dressed inconspicuously, but there was something so arresting about the way this woman stared him down that Tynan instantly knew she was powerful.

"Yes, that's me," Tynan said. "What—" he stopped. The only

thing he could think to say right now was *what are you doing here?* That, or *who are you?* And neither of those was very polite.

The two people beside her were watchful—Tynan saw the way their glances seemed to scan the park in a constant and repetitive sweep, as if every moment presented a new chance to spot, well... something. Tynan wasn't really sure what they were looking for. They were tall humans as well, but shorter than the woman who had spoken to him. On her left was a man with short black hair and eyes an icy gray, and on her right was a woman with hair almost a blinding white-gold.

"Can I help you with something?" Tynan had finally managed to come up with something that expressed his confusion at their presence without sounding like the humans on New Denmark he'd always mocked. Dull and slow. Rude and thoughtless. Tynan didn't want to be any of those things, but he felt them all right now.

"I think we can help each other," the woman said. "May I join you?"

Tynan nodded, and she took a seat on the bench beside him. Her smile was as warm as her voice, and she looked at him as though she was truly seeing him, not the way he was used to humans treating him. He was used to the duals of scorn and reverence—either the human didn't care who he was, or they wanted something from him.

"My name is Indigo Onyema," the woman said. "I am an investor, chiefly in the science and technology sector. And I have been watching your work for years."

Tynan felt his chest collapse, the faint flicker of anticipation he had embraced at this woman's dynamism and optimism dying out with her words.

"I don't have any research anymore that you can invest in," Tynan said. "Unless you're willing to start from scratch."

She leaned back, her eyes twinkling. "I had heard about your misfortune," she said. "And that's why I'm here."

Tynan's heart surged at that, and then he admonished himself for hoping. Hadn't he already learned?

"I don't understand," he said.

"I have been watching your work for years," Onyema repeated, "and I have also been watching the man who bought your research. Your methods and your skill I very much admire, and I think the galaxy would benefit from more of your influence in its developments."

Tynan was not sure how to respond. He nodded a bewildered thanks, and she continued.

"The man who purchased your company has a very different view of things, I am afraid. I don't trust his leadership or his hands in the kind of sensitive work you were doing."

Tynan said nothing. He didn't understand how her feelings on this matter would change anything. He had already tried to get his work back and no one with the power to help had been willing to do so. Tynan didn't see how this woman's wealth would get him any closer.

"I used to work with this man," she continued. "I understand him. Most people are afraid to cross him. I am not."

"Did the Human Union send you?" he asked suddenly.

She smiled and shook her head. "I'm afraid the Union is likely to turn a blind eye to this. I am an independent entity. I can give you a platform and find allies—other like-minded people who are willing to take him on."

"Yes," Tynan said immediately. "Yes, I would like that."

She chuckled. "You aren't going to ask me what I get out of this?"

Tynan's face grew hot. Of course, she had to have a motive. She had presumably flown halfway across the galaxy to meet with him, and for what? To altruistically help him get his research back? To help a person she had literally never met before this moment?

"Do you want a position on the board?" he asked. "It seems there will be some openings."

She chuckled at that, too. "A board position would be assumed, given that I will be providing the capital to get you back on your feet. But I would like something else from you."

That sour pit of dread formed again, Tynan's heart rate and respiration rising. Before Min could chime in, he began to count his breathing. *In for four, out for eight.*

"What is that?" he answered, after what felt like a lifetime.

"I may ask you, from time to time, to send me reports."

He let out a sigh of relief. "That's routine," he said. "We send out a quarterly review to all our investors with updates on progress, and any time something is published, you will be notified, of course."

She shook her head. "Another kind of report. There is rising interest in your area of research, and there are other people out there trying to use the advances you and other scientists are making to enrich their own power."

He didn't understand what kind of report he could possibly send to help her with this. It seemed much more her area of expertise than his.

"All I will want from you is an in-depth state of the field report. Who is doing research on cross-species disease vectors, and what avenues do they appear to be pursuing? Who are new names in the field, both investors and scientists? And perhaps over time, we will be able to establish patterns, determine who might be using this research for purposes less idealistic than your own." She watched him with a level gaze, and he gaped back.

"That sounds like spy work," he blurted.

"Consider it research of another kind," she replied. "I promise, I won't expect you to break into research labs and steal information. I just want to keep an eye on the field, and it would be much easier with an expert helping me. Think it over."

She sent her contact details to him, and Min acknowledged the transfer politely. Onyema stood, then, her motions smooth and graceful. She touched her temple lightly with her fingers, a smile still playing on her lips.

And then she walked away, her two escorts following her like shadows, leaving Tynan alone in the deepening twilight of the park.

11

The gentle hum of the *Avalon* resonated in the air around Jaya as she walked down the hall, her body carrying her along the routes she knew well. She had worn these paths into the very fiber of her muscles, knew every twist and turn of the ship and every shortcut by heart. The ship was just a thin bubble of metal and air in the vast emptiness of the universe, but the familiarity of it surrounded her like a thick, protective blanket.

She moved a little more freely here on the *Avalon*, the thrum of fear and secrecy diminishing to pianissimo in the background of her mind. She clasped a thermos of tea, the heat of the liquid radiating slowly through the metal to warm her hands pleasantly. The route from the mess to her quarters was quiet this time of the evening; with training completed for the night, most of the officers and marines were still enjoying their dinners and would find their way to the rec room on the other end of the ship in due course. Jaya intended to join them as soon as she finished her daily log.

Her palm drive chimed, and she glanced down at it. A message from Armstrong: *Report to captain's quarters ASAP.*

Jaya pivoted, turning back toward the lift, a small pulse of anxiety beginning in her chest. She squared her shoulders as the lift carried her slowly up to the topmost level of the *Avalon.*

As soon as she stepped out of the lift and into the narrow corridor that led to the quarters of both the captain and the XO, she heard the voices. Armstrong and Tully, arguing.

"—due respect, Captain, but another team can handle this," Tully said. "We have more pressing issues."

"I disagree, *Commander.*"

Jaya could hear the hard, dangerous edge in Armstrong's tone. She wondered if Tully—at whom the vocal blade was pointed—understood what it meant when the captain of the *Avalon* set aside his usual kindly father demeanor and allowed his teeth to show.

"I don't," a third voice broke in—it was Reid, the frustration in his voice only barely audible through the flattening that occurred in secured communications feeds. "This can easily be accomplished by another squadron. We can scramble a reserve frigate from Argos.*"*

"Admiral, this message raised red flags," Armstrong said. "I think the doctor is in more danger than he knows—more danger than anyone could suspect. This is a rescue mission, not a routine civilian pickup. I believe the Sons of Priam will have intercepted this communication. Until we understand how they achieved a coordinated attack of such massive scale without tipping off anyone in intelligence, we have to assume that they have eyes at very high levels in at least one of the three major powers. This doctor's work is dangerous in the wrong hands, and it fits the profile of biological weaponry that we have seen so far from the Sons of Priam. I have more reasons—a list of them long enough to warrant data compression and sensitive enough to require our strongest encryption if I tried to send it to you at HQ. Instead of going to those lengths, I am asking you to trust my crew and my analysts."

The silence dragged out, Jaya's heartbeat thundering against her ribcage as she—and Armstrong—awaited the response of the admiral. She knew she was not supposed to hear this conversation. Not only was it not meant for her ears, but the heavy material of the walls should have diminished the waves of sound to a level too low for the human ear. Jaya felt that familiar creeping sensation up her spine.

Too often, she heard things she was not supposed to.

Finally, she heard Admiral Reid sigh—a solid, percussive sound.

"Alright, Captain Armstrong. I have no more reasons to keep you from pursuing this lead. But I want you back on the New Laredo mission fast. This detour cannot exceed forty-eight hours. If it does, I will abort, and you will be rerouted."

Jaya heard Tully's reaction, a frustrated sound in his throat. She could imagine the steely expression on Armstrong's face as he acknowledged.

"I also want that list," Reid said. "In writing. I trust you, Armstrong, but I'm not taking this risk on good faith alone."

"I understand," he said. His voice had returned to its usual gentle rumble. There was no longer a need for the edge—he had won. "We'll send our updated route within the hour."

There was another pause, as if Reid were reconsidering. Something was left hanging in the air—words that the admiral was biting back. "Forty-eight hours, Armstrong," he repeated.

A shuffling sound, then Tully's voice, strained and unexpectedly angry: "Captain?"

"Dismissed," Armstrong replied calmly.

Jaya quickly opened a file in her palm drive, pretending to read it as the door opened and Tully exited. She glanced up, then stood at attention as her superior officer passed her.

"At ease," Tully said. "Is the captain expecting you?"

Jaya met Tully's eyes. Nearly all the frustration she had heard from him moments ago appeared to have evaporated. It was only visible to her in the slight flare of his nostrils and his dilated pupils.

"Yes, Commander," she replied.

"Go on, then," the XO said, gesturing casually back to Armstrong's door before passing her and pressing the lift button.

Jaya entered Armstrong's room tentatively, knocking softly on the door frame. The captain was hunched over a schematic on the desk, mapping out a route through the stars. When he saw Jaya at the door, he ushered her in and tapped the schematic. The map converted to a three-dimensional projection, a small neighborhood of the galaxy hanging in the air in front of them. Jaya shut the door and walked toward the map.

"We've had a change of orders," Armstrong said, and Jaya sensed the anticipation in his tensed shoulders and the rapid movements of his hands. "We are stopping before New Laredo to extract a szacante scientist from Dresha."

"Extract?" Jaya asked, keeping her expression mild. An uncomfortable feeling bloomed in her from lying so smoothly to someone she trusted so much. But past experience showed that revealing what she had overheard would result in unwanted scrutiny.

"I intercepted a message," Armstrong said. "It was sent to certain members of the Union government as well as their counterparts in the Nareian Empire. The message was from Tynan Vasuda —that szacante researcher whose foundation was just purchased out from under him. He was in shock, and his message made it clear he hoped that one of our governments would be willing and able to pluck his research foundation back from the claws of its new board of directors and place it back under his control."

Armstrong sighed then, a sound that was almost a laugh, and Jaya saw a strangely melancholy smile ghost across his face just before his steely demeanor returned.

"That is not a thing that we can or should do," he continued, "but based on his account of what happened, and what I learned of his research when I began to dig, I think he's in a dangerous position."

"What sort of danger?" Jaya asked.

"He had access to knowledge," Armstrong said. "Knowledge most individuals never even scratch the surface of, concerning disease vectors for the virus that wiped out the foundling colony in Sagittarius about ten years ago. And considering the scale of the biological attack by the Sons of Priam, I think there's a clear link. The corporation that financed the buyout of his research foundation is technically legitimate, but it's young and doesn't appear to have any real purpose. They have all their documents in order, and they have money flowing in and out, but no obvious product or service to offer. Now, they could be just a recent start-up floundering to find their brand, or…"

He met Jaya's eyes as his thought trailed off. She completed it.

"It's a shell corporation," she said. "And I would bet that they have an affiliate or a client on Collin's Rock."

Armstrong's eyes sparkled with a smile, the wrinkles at the corners deepening. "Exactly."

Jaya continued the idea through to its conclusion: "So we have a scientist working with dangerous biological material, whose work was legally stolen from under him by an organization that has ties to the intended destination of the weapons the Sons of Priam were smuggling."

"His work is highly sensitive," Armstrong said. "The Szacante Federation may not understand the stakes involved here, but we can't afford to miss a step on this one."

"And if the nareian government decides they want to protect their investment and get to him first…"

"Then we may lose any chance to learn about what's really going on here before the doctor is sealed behind layers of bureaucratic protection," Armstrong said, finishing her thought.

Jaya nodded. "Protection that is not under our control."

"So, Lieutenant Commander," Armstrong said, smiling at her as he took a seat at his desk and gestured to the open seat across from him. "We are going to need to develop an extraction strategy before our new course brings us to Dresha."

The *Avalon*'s emergency repair request was accepted by the Port Authority of Iralu City, and they were cleared for a twelve-hour stay on the the szacante homeworld. While they waited to dock at the Union base just outside Iralu City, Jaya stood on the observation deck. She gazed out at the planet, serene and marbled with aqua, and shifted the small satchel packed with the nondescript civilian clothing and gear she would need for this extraction. The world seemed suspended gently, far from its binary stars. Aside from the twin suns, she had heard that Dresha looked like Earth, from a distance—blue and green, with white clouds ebbing and mixing together on its surface.

But those similarities were little more than legends now. Few had returned to Earth in nearly two hundred years, and for a hundred before that, it had lost its aquamarine allure. When the last humans had departed for life in the colonies, their original home had been dusty and brown, and supposedly even the oceans were obscured from space by dingy cloud cover.

They docked at the base and submitted the required paperwork. Two sets: one for Union naval intelligence and the other for the Dreshan authorities. Chief Engineer Anaïs Fisher and Armstrong met with the szacante liaison to discuss the—fictional—malfunction in the *Avalon*'s central engine. A minor warning light malfunction, a simple fix, but the kind of fix that must be completed before embarking on a sensitive mission.

After assuring the szacantes that the *Avalon* was a short-term visitor to Dresha, Armstrong returned to the ship and released the company for a brief shore leave.

Jaya, Rhodes, Sal, and Lupo picked up an aircar from the Union base and left together, dressed in casual civilian clothing. They stopped in the tourist information office and purchased a download of the popular sites of Iralu City for their palm drives, then stopped in a café for a lingering dinner. The suns were unobscured by clouds that day, and the four squinted into the brilliant sunset as they left the café, boisterous with lighthearted jokes and plans to visit the Arbiter's Residence before they had to get back to the base. They returned to their aircar and Lupo merged into the packed evening traffic.

They rounded a corner, headed toward the center of the city, and then turned suddenly into a quiet back street. Jaya looked behind them through the aircar's sensors. No one following them, just a normal traffic pattern of businesspeople making their way from dinners or late nights in the office to their homes. Rhodes uploaded their destination to the car's navigation system and Lupo switched to autopilot.

The car took them to a neighborhood filled with tall residential complexes. As they approached their target, Lupo switched back to manual and found a place to park that was away from the main traffic of the road and still half a dozen blocks from the complex itself.

Sal was already fiddling with his palm drive, dropping in on the nearby communications channels. At the same time, Jaya ran a thermal scan of the area and watched the little figures move on the holographic projection. Rhodes watched closely, his eyes narrowed.

"I count nine nareians on the front, some of them probably plainclothes," he said. "Based on their locations, I'd guess at least six of them are hiding. Looks like there might be a few szacante as well, but they may just be building security."

Jaya pointed at the image.

"Two on the roof," she said. "That's our best chance."

"You ready?" Rhodes asked, strapping his gear into his belt and stowing his satchel.

"Ready," she replied.

"Ready," Sal agreed.

They all looked to Lupo.

"I can get us up there," she said, "but we won't have much cover if someone notices us."

"We don't know what the usual behavior in this complex is," Jaya agreed. "We didn't have time to do surveillance before."

"Do we expect the target to resist?" Sal asked.

"I honestly don't know," Jaya said. "But based on Armstrong's intel, he can't really afford to. The doctor's message went to both the human and nareian embassies, and even though the nareians haven't issued any formal response, they're watching him closely. He lit a signal fire over himself and doesn't seem to understand what that will bring on him."

"Poor guy," Rhodes said, shaking his head with a wry smile. "He's in over his head."

"You can say that again," Sal said.

"Okay," Jaya said. "Be ready to move fast once we get up there. Lupo, bring us in."

The pilot nodded and turned back to the controls, biting her bottom lip as she engaged the aircar's engine. As they rose, she hugged close to the buildings to keep them hidden from the view of their destination.

The roof of the building grew nearer, and Jaya saw the nareians pressed up against the wall, hiding from the windows inside the building. She wasn't sure how long they planned to wait, but she didn't want to give them any opportunities.

"Lupo, can you drop us and circle back around?" Jaya asked. "I want to take care of these two before they have time to react."

Lupo frowned. "It's gonna be close."

"That's okay," Jaya said. "Everyone, get ready."

Lupo rolled her shoulders like a boxer before a match, sliding her sleek black braid over her shoulder and down her back with the motion. Rhodes and Sal readied their anti-grav devices, and Jaya removed her own from her belt. Her fingers gripped it firmly as Lupo swung them around, pulling up close to the deck.

"Approach in three," Lupo said.

Jaya's eyes were fixed on the building ahead. She released the door control and it slid open. The air rushed in, its chill stinging her eyes and teasing a strand of hair from the braid that secured it away from her face. The fine red strand flickered in her vision as the wind whipped it around. Jaya crouched like a sprinter, feeling the muscles in her legs already thrumming with adrenaline.

"Two…"

Jaya sensed the crests and falls of the breathing of her team align as they took the same position, ready to jump when the next word came out of Lupo's mouth.

"One!"

They leapt—three bodies springing into action, moving with precision through the doors and plummeting. They activated their anti-grav fields in near-unison, a small tremor rippling through the air at the three simultaneous impulses. Though they were dark, nearly invisible against the heavy night sky, Jaya wanted to make their arrival as quiet as possible.

"Sal," she called over the comm, "You've got one right below you."

"I see him," he replied.

Sure enough, as soon as she saw the crouching being's head tilt up, as if to look at the sky above, he dropped. A moment later, she heard the delayed zap of Sal's particle gun. The roof rose smoothly up to meet them, and Jaya landed firmly on the ground, ducking behind a low utility box immediately. The other two were scattered across the roof, but she saw them take cover as well.

The other nareian had seen them land, and it shot at the retreating aircar. Jaya was tucked away out of the line of sight. She saw Rhodes lean out and take the tall figure out with one shot. The three stood slowly, scanning the roof for motion. Jaya ran a heat scan.

Rhodes approached, his weapon still at the ready. "I'm getting two heat signatures inside."

"Me too," Jaya replied. "The smaller one must be the doctor, but the other one looks like a nareian."

"We've got to get in there," Rhodes said.

Jaya agreed. She motioned to Sal, and the three of them huddled together

"We can drop down to the balcony and get access through the door there—can you crack that lock?" she asked Sal.

"Don't need to," he replied. "Looks like the nareians already got it. I'll take out the comms with an EMP blast, but we won't have long."

"Okay," Jaya said. "On my signal."

12

In the dead of night, Tynan was awakened by an alarm on his internal channel. Min was alerting him, and he shook himself from groggy sleep.

"Tynan," she said. "You are receiving a call."

"I can call them back in the morning," Tynan said.

"It's Indigo Onyema," Min said. "And she's called three times already."

"What?" Tynan asked, sitting up. "Uh. I guess put her through?"

Min connected the call.

"Doctor Vasuda, I'm glad you picked up. You need to leave your apartment immediately." The warmth was gone from Onyema's voice now, but all of the power remained.

Under normal circumstances, Tynan would find a relative stranger telling him what to do in the middle of the night to be an absurd joke. But he didn't get the feeling Onyema was the joking kind, and her voice was edged with steel.

He stammered something unintelligible, and then pulled himself together and concluded with a simple question: "What's going on?"

"That man we talked about," she said. "He sent someone for me.

I was able to escape, but you need to leave now. He's not a person who accepts defeat. He tries again."

A better person would be out of bed by now, Tynan thought, already getting clothed and formulating a plan of some sort. But Tynan instead was frozen in place, the fear now pulsing through his body, keeping him paralyzed as his mind searched about for a reason this must not be true.

"But I barely know him, and he has my research," Tynan said. "What could he want with me?"

"You fought him," Onyema said. "You called the attention of the other galactic powers. He doesn't like loose ends, and you are one now."

Min's voice broke in with alarming statistics about his current heart rate and cortisol levels. He tried to take deep breaths.

In for four, out for—oh damn. In for four… what was that sound? In for four, out for…

"Doctor Vasuda?" Onyema's voice was louder. "Are you there?"

"Yes," he gasped. "Yes, I'm here. Where should I go?"

"Do not go to a friend or relative. Pick the last place you would usually go in a crisis."

Well, that would be easy. He had no real friends, no living relatives. His apartment was where he usually went in a crisis, and right now that was exactly where he could not be. Perhaps a hotel? Pay in anonymous currency? Use a false name?

"Okay," he said. "Okay, I'll think of something."

There was a sound on the other line. A series of loud, high-pitched noises. Particle beam fire—he knew the sound from shows he had watched. Then Onyema's voice came back on.

"I'll contact you when it's safe," she said.

"How will you find me?" he asked, but she was already gone.

He sat on his bed for a moment, his hands trembling, his legs weak, succumbing to the pounding fear in his chest and the helplessness he had felt already for so long. It was amplified now. Min hovered beside him, her projection bright in the darkness of the room.

Am I going to die tonight?

He stood abruptly and grabbed a bag, throwing clothing into it as fast as he could. On his way, he would have to purchase encrypted currency, so they—whoever *they* were—couldn't trace him once he'd left. He had a few open lines of credit—enough to live on for a few weeks under normal circumstances—and he could use those to fund his escape. He just had to hope Onyema could find him before that ran out.

A small, muffled thud from the living room stopped him mid-motion. He exchanged a look with Min and crept quietly to the back corner of his room.

The door opened slowly, and Tynan backed away. He tried to breathe, but his chest was empty. He was growing faint. At least if he passed out, he wouldn't experience the moment of his own death.

A human woman stepped in. Her gun was drawn, but the moment her eyes fell on him, she lowered it. Behind her, a nareian figure was on the ground, face to the floor. There was no blood, but he was motionless.

"Doctor Vasuda," the woman said, her voice soft.

Another surge of adrenaline, this one Tynan was grateful for. He took a heaving breath. She was standing in front of him, and he wasn't dead yet. He hadn't decided if he should be afraid or hopeful.

Tynan instinctively raised his hands above his head—the universal gesture of *I'm not armed*. The human had not raised her weapon, but she held the gun with confidence. He was certain that she could move almost faster than he could think, if it became necessary.

"She's not shooting." Min said, projecting her voice only through the implant in his ear, so the human couldn't hear her.

So? Tynan thought to himself.

"She doesn't seem to want to hurt you," Min said. "Perhaps she is here to help us. Perhaps she knows something."

"I'm here to help, doctor," the woman said, reaching out her hand in a gesture Tynan recognized as indicating friendship. "We're here to answer your request to the United Human Nations."

What do I do? Tynan wondered, feeling the frantic panic creep up his chest. When he had reached out for help, it was for a legal battle with this slippery corporation that had stolen his work out from under him. He hadn't meant for some power broker to find him in a park, offer him all his dreams back, and then flee for her life. He certainly hadn't meant to end up in need of a midnight rescue from his apartment.

He looked over at the dead nareian on the floor. A gun lay at his side. More weaponry and hardware were strapped to his belt and tucked against his leg. Tynan suddenly had the sick feeling that he had joined a game of Sequence that was already halfway over. Only the stakes of this game were more than pride—the winner of this game was the one who didn't end up dead.

Which person wanted him dead, and which wanted to save him?

He turned to Min, looking her directly in the steady, blue image of her face. She nodded almost imperceptibly.

"Our window is closing fast," the woman said again. "We have a transport on the roof."

"The roof?"

The words blurted out of his mouth before he had a chance to collect his thoughts. Despite owning a top-floor apartment, Tynan did not like heights, and somehow the idea of climbing onto the roof scared him more than the gun in this soldier's hand.

"The Union believes you have information that could be essential to stopping violent attacks by the Sons of Priam," she said. "We're here to bring you with us aboard our ship, and eventually to Argos, where you will be granted political asylum."

"In return for what?" he asked, feeling his wits return as the human seemed to be less and less likely to use her weapon.

"We just want to work with you to understand what happened here," she said.

Tynan just stared at her again. He was trying to understand the rules of this new situation, trying to glean any useful information from this strangely calm woman. She returned his stare with one of her own, a tendril of hair gleaming copper as it fell over her eyes and caught the moonlight.

"There's a team of nareian mercenaries surrounding your building," the woman said. "A targeted EMP blast has blinded them to our presence, but they will realize very soon that something is wrong if they haven't already. We need to move *fast*, doctor. If you want to get out of here, you need to come with me now."

The woman moved a step closer, her hand still outstretched.

"Okay. I'll come with you," Tynan said suddenly.

He knew he was out of options on Dresha, and while he didn't know what these humans might want from him, he couldn't really say more for his own government at the moment. And this man, who apparently now wanted him dead. At least going with these humans looked like the best chance at surviving the night. And this might give him a chance to learn more about what had happened, and start to solve the crisis he had found himself in.

He grabbed his data pad from the bed and moved back into the living room. As soon as he exited the bedroom, he was shocked to see that the space he had believed to be empty was full of humans— three of them including the woman, all dressed like tourists except for the rifles in their hands. They must have been there the entire time. A chill went through him.

"Let's move," said the woman.

One of the humans—a man whose black hair was cut so close to his scalp that Tynan could see the dark skin beneath it—spoke into his comm.

"Lupo, we've got the doctor, can you swing back around?"

They made their way onto the balcony, and the woman grasped one of Tynan's arms. The man on the other side of him did the same. He was about to protest the strength of their grips when the air around their feet shimmered and warped, and Tynan felt his own feet rise off the ground. The man was holding a small device—a controller for an anti-gravity field, something he had studied thoroughly in his secondary school years. He knew how simple it was, how effective and stable it was, and yet the sight of the world plummeting around him was enough to make his mouth dry with fear.

"It's alright, doctor," the woman said. He noticed her voice remained gentle even after he had agreed to come with them. Even as she had begun to orchestrate their escape. "We're almost to the car."

They landed lightly on the roof, and the team moved in unison, running toward an aircar that sat waiting for them not far away. The woman pulled Tynan along at a faster clip than he was used to. Before he knew it, he was seated in the car and watching the doors close around him. The driver pulled away from the roof and maneuvered the car down through the buildings.

The man sitting next to Tynan pulled out a small tool kit. He looked up at Tynan, his curly dark hair still wild from the wind. "We need to disable the tracker," he said.

"What?" Tynan asked, and then he realized it: every palm drive was enabled with tracking technology to assist with navigating software and provide the best possible information to the user. But of course, it could also lead people straight to him if they had the technology and the will.

"Yes," he said. "Right. Of course."

He offered his arm out, palm up, and the technician went to work. In moments, the human nodded and put away his kit. "You're all set, doc," he announced.

The woman smiled at him, and Tynan tried to recreate the

expression, but found his face stiff in fear and worry.

"I'm Lieutenant Commander Jaya Mill," she said. "This is Lieutenant Commander John Rhodes and Lieutenant Salman Azima." She pointed in turn to the neat dark-skinned man and the wild-haired one. "And Lieutenant Linh Lupo."

The pilot waved, then returned her focus to her driving.

"Tynan Vasuda," Tynan creaked. "But I guess you already knew that."

"I'm sorry we don't have much time," she said, "but we can explain more once we get back to our ship. Until then, we're going to need you to hide. We have to pass through customs to get back to the Union base. We have a special compartment that will shield you from scans and get you safely through, but I'm sorry—it's not very large."

She tapped a code into the aircar's system and a panel beneath the seat slid open. Reluctantly, Tynan crawled in and curled up into as small a shape as he could manage. The woman was still smiling as she closed the panel again and left him in darkness. He could hear their voices, muted, above him as he blinked against the dark.

He really hoped he hadn't made the wrong decision. But he supposed it was too late now to change his mind.

A knock on the panel startled Tynan out of his nervous thoughts. A voice informed him that they were through to the base, and the door slid open to reveal Rhodes. Tynan crawled out, stifling a yawn. After days of insomnia and the shock he had just been through, the exhaustion was catching up. If only he could make his swirling thoughts settle.

Lupo turned the car into a small port and shut it off. The four humans stepped out, and Jaya offered her hand to help Tynan out. He took it gratefully, still feeling uncertain about his legs. They led him through the wide corridors of the base to the port, stopping in front of a loading platform.

"This is it," Rhodes said. "The *Avalon.*"

It was a simple military frigate. Fairly standard, as far as Tynan was concerned. His own people had engineered marvels of modern science—works of art that adorned the cosmos. Human ships had always had a sense of drab dependability to him. They were functional and reliable, but not much else.

They were granted access to the ship, and he was given a security badge indicating his status as a military consultant. Jaya explained to him that his research was relevant to their search for a terrorist organization, and they would like his assistance in determining how his work might be used by someone with less idealistic goals.

He listened, numb, to their explanations. They sounded a lot like Onyema, which gave him some comfort. *We want to help you. But first we need your help.* He supposed that was better than hiding in his apartment. It was certainly better than whatever had been in store for him had these humans not rescued him.

Finally, Rhodes led him down to the med bay.

The ship's doctor greeted them warmly, insisting that Tynan call her "Sunny." She showed him to a small room just off the med bay.

"I'm sorry, it was the best I could do with short notice," she said, indicating the desk and chair placed inside what was clearly a storage room. "I'll try to clear out the things that I come in here for often, so I'm not barging in and interrupting your focus."

"It's alright," he said, but he couldn't help the sinking feeling in his stomach.

What if this was it? He would spend the rest of his days in makeshift offices, always chasing after his old life and never quite catching up. Or worse, what if he had to stay on the run for the rest of his life? Never able to settle down in a single location, in case the people who wanted him dead caught up to him?

"What is it?" Sunny asked.

He started; he hadn't realized she was so attuned to his expressions. She was looking at him, her head cocked slightly to the side. He found himself at a loss for words—he couldn't tell her what had just been crossing his mind, but he also couldn't find words to explain away the strange emptiness that was settling into his bones.

"Nothing," he finally said. "I'm just thinking."

"Of course," she said. "They brought in a console just for your use—feel free to get set up, and let me know if there's anything you need."

"Thank you," he said.

Min appeared next to him, and Sunny jumped at her sudden presence.

"I'm sorry," Min said. "I didn't mean to startle you."

"No, I'd forgotten about... I'd heard that szacante were paired up with artificial intelligences, I just had never..." Sunny paused and seemed to collect herself. "It's nice to meet you."

There was a note of uncertainty in her voice, as if she wasn't sure if that was how one properly greeted a VA, but Min extended her virtual hand toward the woman and replied:

"Likewise."

Sunny contemplated the extended hand, then reached out her own as if to hold it, but as her hand passed through the holographic image of Min's, she let out a nervous little laugh.

"I think that works better with actual hands," Sunny said.

"I suppose so," Min said, smiling. She touched her fingers to her temple in the traditional szacante greeting. After a moment, Sunny replicated the stance.

Min glanced at Tynan, as if asking, *what now?*

Sunny smiled warmly. "I'll give you a minute. I'll be out here if you need anything."

Tynan followed Min into the small office, giving her an exasperated look. "What was that?" he asked quietly.

"Traditional human greeting," Min said. "They grasp each other's hands and oscillate them once or twice firmly. I didn't realize they wouldn't have an equivalent for Virtual Assistant projections."

"Min, they don't have VA. Of course they don't have an equivalent."

She shrugged. Now that she mentioned it, Tynan had seen a number of humans exchanging exactly such a gesture when he had been present for diplomatic functions with his parents. Min had the processing power to make social observations at the same time as she made intellectual ones. Sometimes he wished for her ability to see these things, but he also knew that social intelligence had never been his forte. And that had always been acceptable to him before.

Aside from recreating all his research of the past few years and finding some way to protect himself from the murderous new chair of his old research foundation's board, he imagined that learning to conform to human social structure would be his biggest challenge. At least he had Min to pick up on details and rules—perhaps together they could learn how to apply them properly.

An alarm blared and Sunny popped her head into the office. "We're departing," she said. "Make sure you're strapped in."

Tynan took a spot in the fold-out seat she was gesturing to, and the safety straps extended automatically and belted him in place. The ship began to vibrate, the waves reverberating up his legs and through his back. A nervous thrill jolted through him and he closed his eyes. A few moments later, the vibrations calmed, though they did not cease, and the alarm blared again. The safety straps automatically released and Tynan stood quickly, ready to be out of its claustrophobic clutches.

A knock at the door told him he wouldn't have much time to prepare before his next challenge. Jaya opened the door and waved him out.

"The captain is ready to see you," she said.

13

The desert wind whipped the pale robe around Mara's legs, the sinking sun cooling the air and setting it to dancing. She stood outside the compound walls, letting the dust coat her skin and sink into her hair. The monks were serving dinner to the children, and the little round huts—the same color as everything else in this desert—were lit up inside, bright white light shining from tiny round windows. Outside the walls, it was quiet.

Mara took a long pull from a nearly empty bottle she had brought with her from Balei's station. It burned and had an oddly sweet aftertaste, but it settled in her belly and dulled the ache.

Silhouetted against the orange horizon, a figure in the distance grew closer. A ship had come into the port not long ago, and now its occupant made its way toward the orphanage. Human or szacante, she guessed. It was hard to tell from this far away and with the figure swathed in desert-friendly clothes.

As he drew nearer, Mara realized it was a human male. The man shielded his face from the winds that threw sand and grit against him as he walked.

Mara drained the bottle and tucked it away. She reached through the long, narrow slits in the folds of her robe, letting her fingers rest against the smooth metal of her gun on one hip and her knives on the other. An uneasy thrill ran through her muscles at the dogged pace of this visitor. He was alone, walking against the falling night on a remote desert world, as if he had a deadline to meet in this place utterly devoid of artificial time constraints.

He finally reached the gate at the front of the compound and looked up, shielding his eyes against the glare of the sun setting behind Mara. They stood level with each other on the dusty road, but his head barely reached her shoulder. She watched him with a natural condescension as the wind whipped his robe against his stocky frame. The fine, gritty sand had already formed a colorless dust on the pallid skin of his face.

"Devi?" he asked.

It was a name she had used once, years ago. That sharp thrill intensified, and her hands gripped the gun in her utility belt more firmly.

"Who's asking?" Mara replied.

"Do you prefer Ausra now?" he asked. "Or perhaps Haiza? Zamya?"

The identities she had assumed over the years reached her ears on the dry wind. He listed them in order, ending on the one she had most recently used—the one she was prepared to burn now that the job for Balei had gone so wrong.

But he didn't use her given name. Her secret name.

"What do you want?" she asked flatly.

"My employer has an assignment for you."

She arched an eyebrow, letting her gray eyes stay fixed, unblinking on him. This unsettled humans—she had noticed that there was something about the way a nareian could stare that made them itch to get away. She watched him shift uneasily beneath her gaze.

"I don't take just any job that comes my way," she said, her voice even.

"My employer is aware of this. Your reputation is well known to him. He thinks you will find his task worthwhile."

"Who is your employer?"

"Like you, he prefers to remain under the radar," the man said. "But he is willing to pay well, and pay under the table."

He held out a small bag for her.

She glanced inside and found lumps of nondescript metals. She ran a scan with her palm drive and suppressed a whistle—these were extremely rare metals, the kinds forged in massive stars and scattered in tiny quantities throughout the galaxy. They were small and insignificant enough individually to render them easy to pawn without drawing attention, and there were enough of them to provide a steady income for a long while.

That, alone, would allow her to buy her own remote planet. Something with atmosphere and water, if not as lush and green as the garden planets popular with wealthy retirees. She glanced up to find the man watching her with a measured look.

"The other half will be given to you upon completion of the job," he said.

"And what is the job?" she asked.

"There is a woman who possesses secrets that my employer would prefer not surface. We think this woman intends to speak publicly about these secrets, and we would prefer she not."

"You're asking me to kill someone. That's not what I do."

"We both know that's not entirely true," the man replied.

"I retrieve people," Mara said. "You decide what to do with them once I bring them back. You want an assassin, then hire a fucking assassin."

"You have a reputation," the man said, "for both skill and subtlety. It took my employer a great deal of effort to find you. He's very impressed by your work."

She stared him down, not yet ready to accept. The metals weighed heavy in her hand—wealth she had not seen in years, and a

155

guarantee for her future. The job weighed equally heavy in her mind. She was a long arm extended out to bring back those who ran away, but it was not her responsibility to mete out justice. She hadn't even killed Yanu, as much as the ugly desires in her heart had pressed the issue. Even as her thoughts raced, she maintained a practiced, blank expression.

"How did you find me here?" she asked.

"My employer is resourceful," he said. "Perhaps as resourceful as you."

"Does anyone else know my location?"

The small, slick smile that spread on the corner of his lips filled her with apprehension.

"Not at the moment," he said.

Instantly, she closed the distance between them, her empty hand shooting out to close around his neck. Their faces only inches apart, she fixed the full intensity of her gaze on him.

"Do not threaten me," she said slowly, her voice low. "I don't give a shit who you work for. But you're right—I am resourceful. And if you push me, you'll find out exactly what I'm capable of."

He quivered beneath her grip. His hood had fallen back, and his hair—the same wan color as the sand—was already accumulating dust. His eyes were wide.

"Do not come here again," she said.

"I won't," he gasped.

She released him with a shove, watching him stagger back. She closed her hands around the metals, considering them carefully. "Where do I find this woman?"

The man exhaled. His previous calm had evaporated the moment Mara had closed the distance between them, and he was struggling to regain it. It didn't matter.

"That is why your skills are so important," he gasped. "My employer has been unable to find her. She disappeared."

"I need everything your employer has on this person. Even

things he believes are irrelevant may have some value. Don't hold anything back."

"So you'll do it?"

"I'll need a line of credit in whatever name your employer wishes to use. This sort of work takes additional resources."

"That can be arranged."

Mara put the metals back in the satchel and tucked it into her robe. This would do.

Her new employer sent her everything he had on her target—a woman called Indigo Onyema. Onyema had made her home on Argos for years before she had vanished, and its status as a hub for galactic travel meant it was as good a place to start as any. Argos was not an overly friendly port for a nareian, but enough diplomacy and galactic commerce was conducted there to make it closer to indifferent than dangerous. And she had a few contacts there that would allow her to purchase whatever she might need for this job once she had completed some reconnaissance.

Mara completed the final pre-flight checks on the *Nasdenika* and strapped her small pack to a cargo panel in the cockpit. Her ship was too small for artificial gravity, and she had been cavalier with standards enough times to know that a few minutes of prep time outweighed the clean-up efforts.

Bay was waiting for her on the small walkway that approximated a port here on Uduak. He held out a small pack with dried fruit and meat—a rite bordering on ceremonial that he had never missed the chance to carry out himself when Mara was preparing to leave for another job. It held new meaning now that this would be her final departure from Uduak.

"May our bounty nourish your body and your soul," he intoned.

"Thank you, Beloved Teacher," Mara replied, knowing the

words of the ritual well enough to recite them back to her benevolent hosts. The dusty air stung her eyes and she blinked, her throat constricted.

"Don't forget that all action comes from our intentions," he said. "Take time to meditate and focus your intention with each new day."

"In my line of work, intentions can change from moment to moment," Mara said, sighing at the naivety that accompanied a life of quiet contemplation instead of one of action.

"All the more reason to take time to meditate," the monk replied, and Mara thought she saw a flicker of amusement disturb his otherwise blank expression.

"Thank you for the food."

"May you always remember the link between all things, and may you recognize the light of the stars in your heart."

Mara just nodded at this final phrase, shrugging off the uneasy feeling inside of her as she turned her back on Uduak and strapped herself into the captain's chair. It certainly didn't feel like starlight.

14

The deep peace of shipboard night seeped in through the walls of Jaya's pod. The small space had become so familiar to her over the years aboard the *Avalon*, and she stretched out her tall frame as far as she could on her bed, pressing her palms against the cool wall behind her.

They were headed to Collin's Rock, a move that Reid had reluctantly approved after Armstrong submitted the report Doctor Vasuda had made of his own work. Armstrong had argued that this virus was being developed on Collin's Rock for use elsewhere in the galaxy. They would arrive in a few hours, and Jaya and Rhodes had spent the rest of the previous day inspecting the weaponry and gear their small task force planned to use when they arrived.

Jaya had been ruminating on that meeting with Doctor Vasuda, her mind trying to wrap itself around the intricacies of the research the doctor described. The jargon had stirred up something in the back of her mind, and now memories knocked around like deep, dark silt on the bottom of a rarely-used channel, the doctor a barge cutting through the sludge and releasing it to muddy the waters.

The science she was accustomed to hearing about these days was always something from engineering or information technology.

Sal nattered on about data science and cryptography when he got tipsy, and she was more than used to relaying messages about broken parts and program malfunctions from the engineering crew. But the doctor had talked about biology and genetics—and his explanations had recalled conversations between Jaya's parents during late, sleepy nights in her childhood.

Jaya had never understood her father's work. She had just been a child when he was killed, after all. But she knew he'd loved his research, and had believed it could change the world someday. She knew it from the way his voice had risen in excitement as he regaled her mother with news from his day, apologizing sheepishly whenever Jaya's mom hushed him for pulling Jaya from her dozing. She knew it from the way his attention had always been directed away from them and toward his lab.

She remembered how her father would carry her off to bed then, her mother leading a sleepy Kier by the hand, until the two were tucked cozily under their blankets. And then she remembered the murmur of her parents' voices in the next room lulling her to sleep.

She also remembered standing in the dusk as the day that had killed her parents slowly bled into darkness. Smoke from her father's lab rose into the heavy clouds in the distance. The glow of the fire merged with the glow of the dying sun, setting even more of the horizon ablaze. She had stayed hidden, like Kier made her promise, until it had been silent so long that she couldn't stand it anymore. And when she ventured outside and saw her father's work burning madly, she finally knew that she was truly alone.

The wind was cold, but she was too afraid to stay in the house. She packed a small bag, taking a few valuables she knew she could use to barter for a ride. As she stood in the doorway, their old piano caught her gaze. She went over to it, reaching out to touch its smooth surface with her dusty fingers. A spatter of blood now decorated the ivory keys and she pulled away in revulsion. The feeling folded in on itself, wrapped tightly in her chest, and her mind slid away from the implications.

The walk to the nearest town was long. The night was inky black on their tiny agricultural colony, and by the time she reached the town, not even a single window was illuminated from within. She slept in the marketplace where the locals traded the small percentage of their harvests that the government permitted them to keep, curled under a stall with her head on her bag. Although the bag was hard and lumpy, the edges of the case that held her mother's cherished violin digging into her cheekbone and her jaw, the exhaustion took her into a deep and dreamless sleep.

When she woke the next day, she found the shuttle port and gave a man her mother's best earrings in exchange for a flight to New Sheffield. For three days, she clutched her bag to her chest, huddled in a corner of the economy shuttle. When she landed, she walked the three miles from the port to her uncles' farm, and stopped short of knocking on the door.

What if something had happened to them, too? What if they feared taking her in and sent her back? What if they just couldn't afford another mouth to feed?

She was frozen there, her hand raised to knock, when one of her uncles, Simon, swung the door wide and nearly knocked her over on his way out to gather eggs.

"Jaya?" he asked. He ran a hand across his forehead, pushing his red hair back. He paused in shock, his fingers still forcing the short hairs up and back so they stuck out from his hand like a rooster's crown.

"What was that?" Jaya heard the voice of his husband behind him.

"It's Abigail's girl," Uncle Simon said, his voice wavering. "Jaya, what happened? How are you here?"

Simon crouched down and reached for one of Jaya's hands,

prying it gently from her travel-worn bag. Uncle Aman emerged from the house as well and stopped short at the sight of her.

"I didn't know where else to go," Jaya explained, her voice breaking.

Uncle Aman folded her into his strong brown arms immediately, and she breathed in the earth and sweat smell of him. She cried into his shoulder, the coarse hairs of his beard tickling her neck. Simon took her bag and held the door as Aman lifted her and carried her into their home.

Her mother's family had nothing, she knew. And she had nothing to offer them either. From that day onwards, her life was no longer filled with lessons in the school her mother ran and music in the evenings with Kier. She no longer had her father's studious care in treating the cuts and scrapes she got from playing on the rough terrain outside their home. She was no longer Jaya Morgan, daughter of Abigail and Andrew—Simon and Aman arranged her citizenship papers and legally adopted her. She was now Jaya Mill.

Now she had the quiet dawns on her uncles' farm, and fresh eggs from the chickens every morning. She had long hours in the sun working the heavy machinery and meager dinners that tasted richer from Uncle Simon's laughter and the heat from Uncle Aman's patch of ghost peppers. She developed strong arms and an explosion of freckles on her pale skin. And she found enough time at night to study from the general curriculum that when she turned sixteen—the year she would have auditioned for the Argos Conservatory if she had been able to keep practicing the piano—she managed to pass the entrance exam for the Naval Academy.

She knew she was lucky. Most people who came from poverty had no choice but to return to it. The military was the only way out, and she was fortunate to have a hidden talent for combat and strategy that she had never had reason to explore as a child.

Jaya still knew she was lucky, but after hearing echoes of her father's words coming from the szacante scientist's mouth, that dark place in the back of her mind turned over again and reminded her of everything she might have had.

And in the midst of the swirl of dark thoughts, something new pushed in. The warm feeling she got in the soft lighting of Luka's shop and the words he had said to her that first night they met:

That's not something you lose. Not really.

Jaya, Rhodes, and the reconnaissance team they had assembled loaded their gear into the shuttle and sealed the airlocks once the *Avalon* had slowed to a gentle thrust. The shuttle brought them to Collin's Rock, the desolate terrain darkening the small shuttle windows as Jaya watched their descent. She had spoken with the szacante doctor before they left, and while he had expressed his willingness to assist them, he had raised his palms in an expression of helplessness until his VA had appeared and assured Jaya that they would be able to consult on whatever the strike teams found below.

Collin's Rock had once been a rocky outer planet of a small star system. A few billion kilometers away, a planetary nebula hung eerily in the vacuum—the colorful remains of what had once been a low-mass star not unlike Sol. The *Avalon* had swung into orbit around the tiny unmoored planet earlier that morning and scanned the surface. Jaya had received the news from Armstrong:

They had found nothing with their optical scan—no objects that looked like they could be buildings against the harsh terrain of the planet. No movement on the planet's surface aside from the currents of wind that swept across the landscape. It was simply, inexplicably, empty.

Armstrong had decided to send Jaya and Rhodes down to the surface with a team to look for evidence that the scanners on the *Avalon* had not been able to pick up. Now, just a few hours later, Lupo set the shuttle down gently and opened the doors. The small, rocky planet was tidally locked with the remains of its star, one side in perpetual twilight lit by the aurora of the nebula and the other in perpetual night. The facility was on the dark side. It was bitterly cold, and the thin wind howled across the valley.

"This is it," Jaya said. "Stay sharp. We don't know what we've got down here, but it could be grim."

Or it could be nothing. She wondered which would be worse.

She gestured for them to fall in line behind her and made her way toward what their intel indicated should have been one of the back entrances to the lab. They made their way up the hill, staying close to the ground, dark even against the black rock. As they reached the top, and the flatlands below became visible, Jaya motioned to her team to stop.

There was truly nothing there. The valley was as empty as the one they had just come from, dust and rubble strewn across barren ground.

"Rhodes," she called over her comm link. "Are you seeing this?"

He was just behind her, and he reached the top of the hill and looked out over the vast emptiness.

"There's really nothing there," he said.

"Maybe they were the wrong coordinates?" Jaya wondered. "The wrong planet entirely?"

Sal pulled up the holographic screen of his palm drive and looked through the data he had decrypted.

"This is it," he said, his voice sharp with frustration. "It was just a simple delivery log. They had an upcoming drop-off here, and they'd been here before, too. Dozens of times. I don't understand."

Rhodes had ventured forward, inspecting the site where the lab was supposed to be. He stopped abruptly and crouched down, reaching toward the ashy soil at his feet.

"What is it?" Jaya asked.

"Look at this." He brushed some dirt aside, revealing a large chunk of something that looked like rock.

Jaya moved forward and knelt beside him. The piece of rock had a sharp corner. A ninety-degree angle. She brushed some more of the debris aside and found another piece with a rectangular edge, this one larger. Jaya pulled a multitool from her kit and used it to blow a gentle stream of compressed air across the object. Dust evacuated a series of small grooves: lettering etched on its surface.

"The laboratory *was* here," she said.

"Damn," Rhodes replied. "That's one hell of an exit strategy."

"Do you think this was it, then?" Sal asked.

"Must have been," Jaya replied. "I'm not sure there's anything left to find, though."

They fanned out around the burned-out foundations, which had before looked only like natural rock formations and silt. In the fierce cold of the tidally locked planet, the ruins had cooled rapidly, leaving no way of knowing how long ago it had been destroyed. But Jaya suspected they had only missed them by a few hours.

Jaya looked around. They had estimated the size of the facility, and their sweep of the area looked likely to confirm that estimate. It had been small.

"Could this have been their only lab?" Rhodes asked as he picked through some rubble.

"We can hope," Jaya said. "But this doesn't seem like enough. If they can pack up an entire research facility, move it in a matter of days, and then utterly destroy whatever is left, they have resources."

She called the *Avalon* over her comm link.

"This is Lieutenant Commander Mill, and I've patched Rhodes in, too. Put Doctor Vasuda on—we need to talk to him."

"Yes, Commander?" the scientist's naturally quiet voice piped up in her ear. "Did you find something?"

"You could say that," she said. "But it's not pretty. It looks like they packed up and destroyed the lab—absolutely obliterated it."

"What?" Jaya could hear the note of discouragement in his voice. "Describe it to me."

"I can do you one better," she said. "Linking video."

She held out her hand, opening her palm drive's holographic projector and scanning the area. Aboard the *Avalon*, the scientist would be seeing the same images she was seeing right now.

"Oh dear," he said, and the tone in his voice made Jaya's stomach sink.

"What?" she asked, hearing the strain in her voice. "'Oh dear' what?"

"Well, I don't really know…" He cut himself off, and Jaya wished she could see him right now. As opaque as szacante expressions were to her, anything was preferable to silence. Confusing expressions she could try to interpret—silence was nothing but a useless void.

After the silence continued to hold far longer than she could stand, Jaya spoke up again: "What, doctor? What are you seeing?"

"Well, you see the way the earth is scattered around you?" he asked. "It looks like the building was destroyed in a fairly even manner. We have similar technology for demolition back home, but regardless they must have used huge amounts of firepower to do this. I'd say they have access to some large weapons."

"God damn," Rhodes exclaimed.

"Just what I like to hear." Jaya's voice was thick with sarcasm, something she realized after the fact might not translate to the szacante. *Damn.* "Sorry," she added. "This just doesn't put me in a great mood."

"Understandable," the scientist replied, his voice surprisingly light. "This is potentially very big news. But certainly not good. I wish there was more evidence for me to go on."

"Trust me," she said. "So do I."

Jaya closed the video link and lowered her arm. She looked out over the sweeping, empty plain with a deep dread sinking into her body.

On the audio channel, the scientist spoke up again: "You brought some testing kits down with you, correct?"

"Yeah, the standard kit. What do you need?"

"Soil samples, atmospheric samples, heat measurements in the site of the former lab and beyond it, the radius of the blast. Debris that managed to not become entirely vaporized. Beyond that, anything you can find."

Anything you can find? mouthed Rhodes with an incredulous expression.

"Can do," Jaya replied. "We'll get started right away."

She closed the audio connection on the comm link and turned to find Sal, Lupo, and Rhodes standing in the rubble behind her.

"Let's get moving," she said. "Spread out, everyone take a kit and start taking soil samples right away. I want to get this done quickly. I'm with you, Rhodes, this place gives me the creeps."

15

Nervous energy rushed through Jaya when they returned to the ship. The *Avalon* was heading to Argos, and would arrive the next day. They had brought more samples back to the *Avalon* than she knew what to do with. Fortunately, they had a brilliant scientist aboard who reveled in exactly that kind of thing. Instead of having to wait to reach Argos to have analysts study the samples and give them a conclusion, it was being taken care of already, and by someone who might have unique insights into exactly what they were looking at.

Jaya had let Sal talk her into a card game when they had finished inhaling their dinners in the mess hall. He had produced a flask of something expensive from Argos and was thoroughly sloshed a few hands in, rattling off a list of the most obnoxious bugs in the standard naval decryption toolkit. One of the other quants, Lieutenant Martel, had joined them for their game and was nodding her head in agreement, although Sal's rapid-fire monologue left no room for her to cut in. Jaya rolled her eyes at her friend and laid down her cards.

"Fuck, Mill, you need to catch up," Sal complained. "I can't play against you when you have a sobriety advantage."

"Then stop giving me the advantage," Jaya cracked, but she took a swig of the offered flask.

She was too edgy right now to do much more—a deep sense of urgency was thrumming inside her that kept drawing her attention away from the game and back toward something she couldn't yet identify. There were threads to this investigation that all tied together somewhere, but Jaya had yet to see the path. She just knew there was some piece of information missing. Perhaps the doctor's tests would turn it up.

And then there was Augustus. She had begun to use this name for him with Armstrong and the rest of the company, and it was catching on. This man who thought it was up to him to start again, to build a new empire for humanity. This man whose psychological profile still failed to match anyone they already had in their system.

Sal dropped his hand unceremoniously, scattering the cards across the table.

"You must be blessed by some long-lost gods, that's all," Sal said. "Everything you touch turns to fucking gold."

Jaya snorted. "I think you're forgetting all the expensive technology I break every time I touch it."

Sal laughed at that. "Oh, right," he said. "Your single Achilles heel."

A clamor of voices at the door announced the arrival of another group, and from the volume and general discord of their discussion, Jaya could tell they had gotten a head start. She watched Thompson bring up the rear of the group with a close eye, and he met hers with a sheepish look. On these long hauls where all there was to do was wait and drink, the second option was often chosen as a distraction from the first. Union naval rules stipulated that blood alcohol content had to be below a strict level for anyone on duty, but the rapid advances in sobriety drugs had quickly made it possible for personnel to acquire a healthy buzz during their off-hours that could be quickly reduced down to functional levels in time to clock in.

The other group sat down nearby and produced their own deck of cards. Thompson dealt and they began to play, but their conversation continued. Jaya was able to pick out their words despite Sal's droning about one of the patches he'd written to overcome the most frustrating bug.

"I heard that he died once."

The voice belonged to Corporal Aki Shea, who had leaned their head conspiratorially forward, short black bob falling across their face.

"Bullshit," Thompson said, but his hands faltered as he dealt the last card out.

"No, really," Shea said. "I heard it from someone in HQ. They caught someone en route to that compound we took and they were interrogated. Augustus died once, and they brought him back."

"It's just a rumor," insisted another corporal, Yusuf Werner, while picking up his cards and sending a stern glance toward Shea.

"You explain it, then," Shea said. "How they've been able to build up so much without anyone noticing? He's a ghost. He doesn't exist anymore—a dead man."

"Or he's multiple people," Werner replied. "How do we know there's actually one leader? Maybe it's a team of leaders, and they just picked one to be the voice."

"Shut the fuck up and just play," Thompson spat.

The group went silent, and for a moment Jaya heard only the sound of cards sliding across the table.

"I fold," Thompson grunted, dropping his cards and taking a long drink.

At her own table, Sal had stopped talking and instead was staring at his hand with intense focus.

"You think you can just will the cards you need to appear?" Jaya asked with a smirk.

"I have rotten luck," Sal replied, and threw his hand down.

The hush that had overtaken the room still felt strained, but as

Jaya gathered up the remains of their hand and began to shuffle, Werner started humming. Jaya smiled.

"What?" Sal asked, as he accepted the cards she was dealing.

"I know this song," Jaya explained. "It's a really old drinking song. The farmers used to sing it after harvest back home. My Uncle Simon would bring out his home-brewed beer and pass it around to celebrate, and by the end of the night everyone was singing."

"You're from Sancus?" Werner stopped humming and leaned over toward Jaya's table. He was young—barely out of training—and he hadn't lost that earnest hope of finding some little piece of home to cling to.

"No," she replied. "New Sheffield. But it was settled by people from Sancus when the old colony started getting crowded."

"We used to sing it in my town on Yangtze, too," Thompson added. There was a strange fragility to the way he said it, and Jaya saw him swallow hard and take another drink from his cup.

The humming resumed, and Thompson joined in with the words on the refrain. By the end of the second verse, there were five people singing, and Jaya felt a warmth rise up in her chest that might have been Sal's high-end booze, or might have been the music. Sal watched out of the corner of his eye, looking out of place for once in his life.

"Come on, Sal," Jaya said. "I can teach you the words."

"I'll sing if you play," Sal retorted.

Jaya looked over at the table next to her. The cards had been abandoned, and they were huddled together throwing out the names of other drinking songs and humming over each other. The harsh lines in Thompson's forehead had smoothed out, and she saw a smile beginning at the corners of his eyes. And she couldn't ignore now the thrill that had arisen at the idea. A door had opened in her, one that she had kept closed for fear it would hurt too much to remember what lay on the other side. But since she had played that piano in Luka's shop, she had felt the soothing balm of music in her life again.

"Okay," she agreed.

Sal gave her a look of genuine shock, but Jaya was already out of the room. She retrieved the violin from under her bed and hurried back to the rec room, where they had already made it halfway through an old folk song, modifying the words to better suit life on a military ship.

Jaya popped the clasps on the violin case and pulled the instrument out. Her time on New Sheffield showed in the fading of the varnish and the wear patterns on the bridge. She'd had it restrung the day she got her first Navy paycheck, but the cosmetic wear was not something she could afford to fix. She wasn't even sure she wanted to—this violin was painted with more than varnish. She took the bow out and turned it lightly between her fingers, then began to tune the strings.

"Where did you get that old thing?" Shea asked.

"Family heirloom," Jaya replied, and a few people laughed.

"Should I get my earplugs?" Thompson heckled.

It was Sal who replied, shaking his head: "No, you won't want to miss a second of this."

Jaya tightened the last string until it sang with exactly the pitch she intended. Then she let the silence settle on the room for a moment before launching into a lively tune that she had heard in some of the less trendy bars on Argos. She saw some heads begin to nod in recognition, and was pleased when people began singing the first verse, mangling only about half of the words.

She ended the song with a flourish once the last refrain had died out, and lowered the violin and the bow. Thompson started a loud, uneven clap, and the rest of the room joined in. She flushed with the excitement of performing again, with the joy she saw in their faces, and took a whimsical bow.

"Damn," Thompson said, when the clapping had quieted. "You sure you're in the right line of work?"

The air left her chest for a moment, and she saw the flicker of sadness in her gut reflected in Sal's face.

"Where I grew up"—she considered the words carefully—"there were two options. Grinding poverty or joining the military. Turns out I have a knack for military work, too."

"Forget that," Shea shouted. "Play something else."

"I take requests," Jaya replied.

To her shock, Sal shouted out a song, and she smiled and pointed the tip of the bow at him.

"Ten years I've known you, and still you're full of surprises," she said.

Sal shrugged, "It's what makes me so popular with the fellas."

Jaya shook her head and started to play.

It was late when Jaya returned to her pod, but the energy of the night was still flowing through her veins, preventing even the will to sleep. She carefully stowed the violin back in the small drawer beneath her bunk and sat down on the edge of the bed.

That uncomfortable nagging feeling returned to her in the quiet of the night. That feeling that something in her subconscious was dragging her in a particular direction—but where? She crossed her legs beneath her and pulled out her data pad. She requested the files on the Sons of Priam from the *Avalon*'s server, and momentarily, they appeared on the screen before her.

The data file was massive—organized chronologically—and pulled from the files they had decrypted from the compound as well as any chatter from before the attacks that was flagged as potentially related. She began to search the intercepted communications, encrypted and then also written in a coded language so strange that even with their entire computational linguistics team on it back at HQ, they had yet to break it. A few were flagged as being likely messages from the leadership. From Augustus.

Jaya read through these flagged messages. They read like a nonsense poem, but always finished with a line from the *Aeneid*.

Our hopes must center on ourselves alone.

That was a favorite of his, appearing more often than most. She rearranged the files, checking for any pattern in their release dates. The first video had only just appeared, but some of these messages reached back two or three years, thick with the same references of the propaganda film. References that repeated in her head. In that voice.

It still grabbed at her insides like a cold, clammy hand.

He never showed himself in the video. The voice was intended to have impact—to leave the listener rapt with attention and feeling danger just over their shoulder. The simplicity of it, the faceless leader. He could represent anyone that way. There was something about it that felt so theatrical, like it was all a piece of performance art. But then there was the very real violence that followed, and that was no performance.

What was it about this man? Everything about him was carefully groomed. Perfectly suited to be the metaphorical—if not literal —face of the movement. He was the star of the show.

But was he the director? The architect? Or just the perfect spokesman?

Augustus, promised oft, and long foretold... born to restore a better age of gold.

Jaya set aside the intel they had collected on known Sons of Priam activity and began to dig deep into her memory. She had read the *Aeneid* in her mother's little schoolroom. It was part of the series of Old Earth Classics that everyone progressed through in their makeshift curriculum.

Her fingers began to tap on the data pad, generating a search cross referencing the text of the *Aeneid* with the massive database of stored communications that the Union Navy kept from any port from which they rented space. Because of the far-flung and generally haphazard state of most of the human colonies, the Union Navy often chose to rent a space in colonial ports, in exchange for permanent security detachments on the colonies. Peacekeepers, they called them. A substitute for local police, in reality.

Of course, for security purposes, the Navy also required that they be granted surveillance privileges to the entire port communications complex.

This was one reason the szacante complained so much about doing business with the humans. But then, the szacante didn't want to be beholden entirely to the Nareian Empire, whose reach was similarly broad, even if their methods differed.

The search was running. Text flitted past her on the screen too fast to read as the algorithm parsed the two massive datasets and ran a neural net, scanning to find patterns with just one button click.

Suffer me to try my force and vent my rage before I die.

The lines rose up in her mind, and she felt a strange, dark connection to the anger contained in them. These powerful sign-offs were about more than ideology to this Augustus, and perhaps to whatever architect had recruited him. These were personal, and perhaps she could pull at this thread until the fabric came undone—back to the very first knot in the cord.

No force, no fortune, shall my vows unbind, or shake the steadfast tenor of my mind.

The words continued to flicker on the screen. She felt the pulsing of them like her own blood in her veins. She shook her head, and that feeling of urgency hummed contentedly inside her. She was certain she was looking in the right direction. All that was left to do was wait.

She set her data pad aside and kicked her legs off the bed. She couldn't just sit around, waiting. Being still was too much for her right now.

Downstairs, in the training rooms, the virtual weapons training stations were all empty. She put on the wraparound eyeglasses and started the program. The artificial weapons were made with the exact same specifications as combat guns—same size, weight, balance, and materials. When she fired off rounds on the virtual training ground, the program generated the right kind of sound, though in reality there was no particle beam for it to fire. Target after target appeared in her vision, and she practiced her speed and accuracy. She was comfortable now with a gun in her hands, though she could remember the days when it was the most foreign thing in the galaxy to her.

She had always been unusually skilled, despite her initial fear of the weapon, and now, more a decade and a half later, it came to her as easily as music always had. She wondered sometimes what she would have become if she hadn't joined the Navy all those years ago.

Her palm drive beeped, and she put down the weapon, switching off the virtual training program. It was another of the cryptic messages, and a chill went through her when she read it:

What happens if the Union finds out who you are?

The next morning, Jaya was still staring at the walls of her pod, a sick terror settled into her belly. It was early, but she knew that to attempt to sleep would be futile. She followed the same routine every morning—quick, precise, and so familiar to her that it was barely more than muscle memory. She ran through it, her mind going through its own routine at the same time. A mixture of the intuition she had learned to trust over the years and a rational cost-benefit assessment.

As she emerged from the showers, hair damp and uniform buttoned, she heard the dawn shift change and wake-up call come over the comms. The night shift was over; the day was beginning. In space, day and night were just conventions, but they stuck to them as much as they could. It made life more manageable.

She went straight to Sal's pod, a few rooms down in the crew quarters. She knew she would catch him before he left for the mess hall. As she expected, she found him tousle-haired and groggy, frowning as he opened the pod to her knock.

"You know it's like thirty seconds after wake-up call, right?" he asked irritably.

"Yeah, yeah, I know," she said. "Not a morning person. I promise we'll get you your coffee, but I need to talk to you first."

He must have picked up on the tone in her voice, because he seemed to wake up more. He invited her in and she joined him on his bed, curling her legs up under her.

"What is it?" Sal asked, rubbing his eyes with the palms of his hands.

"I need you to do something for me," she said. "And I need you to keep it quiet, at least for now."

"That goes without saying," he said. "My lips are sealed."

The pressure in her chest had expanded—she felt the secrets knocking loudly against her ribcage. She had never really expected something external might open a door to her past, as much as she had feared it. Sal was watching her now with tired eyes, and she swallowed that fear and let the beating in her chest become a low background sound.

"I've been getting some strange messages," she started. "And at first I thought maybe it was just some viral marketing campaign or some fucked up case of mistaken identity or something. The first one wasn't exactly... specific."

She trailed off, and Sal waited, uncharacteristically patient. She could see him mentally fidgeting, wanting to ask a million questions, so she leapt in.

"I know this sounds completely crazy," she said. "But now I think this person has been following me somehow. Tracking me. Not physically, here on the *Avalon*, but virtually."

"I believe you," he said. "What's going on, Jaya?"

"I don't know. One of the messages, it said that they knew who I was. And it mentioned my uncles and that they should have kept me hidden."

"What does that mean?" Sal asked.

"I think it means they know something about my parents. There's a reason I don't talk about them much, and it's not just because it's hard. I still don't really know what happened to them."

Sal reached out and took her hand in his, squeezing it. She squeezed it back.

"The day... the day it happened, all I know is that someone broke into our home," she said. "My father was always kind of paranoid, so he had a secret room installed in his study. Kier hid me in there and went downstairs to help my mother. I don't know who they were, but Kier told me I had to stay hidden. I don't know if they even knew I existed. Neither of us was registered with the Union systems when we were born. My uncles had to help me get citizenship when I showed up at their place. I took their last name—my mother's name."

She looked up at Sal's face, his dark brown eyes taking in everything she said. She knew he would believe her—she had never had to lie to him about this. Whenever the subject of her family was raised, she had told him the simplest of details and said she didn't want to talk about it any further, and he had respected that.

"My mother and my father were killed, that I know," she continued. "But Kier—he was taken away. And I heard from him once—just to say he was alive. I haven't heard from him since. I think whoever is messaging me knows where Kier is. Knows where we're from."

"Is that a bad thing?" Sal asked.

"I don't know," she said, raising her free hand in a gesture of defeat. "It depends on who it is, and who took him. I honestly don't know, Sal. I've been hiding my whole life from these people—whoever they are. I was hoping I'd never need the answers."

"What would they want with you?" he asked.

She shook her head: "My father was a scientist, maybe he had some research they wanted. But they could have taken that from his lab, from the office. And maybe they did—maybe they only took Kier because he was in the way."

"Wrong place, wrong time," Sal offered darkly.

She squeezed his hand again, trying to extract some comfort despite the chill she felt inside.

"So can you look at the messages?" she asked. "Maybe try to trace them? There's no way to identify the sender from the address alone."

"Yeah," Sal said. "I'll try."

She handed him her data pad and showed him the folder where she had hidden the messages. Sal took the device, typing the password she gave him. He read the messages, scanning them quickly. Already, Jaya could see the wheels turning. He nodded once, then closed the folder and set the data pad aside.

"We'll figure it out," he said to her. "Whoever it is, they don't know who they're dealing with. We're unstoppable."

She smiled at that.

"Hell yeah, we are," she said. Then, her tone growing more serious: "Thanks, Sal. I'm glad I have you."

"Me, too," he said, returning her smile. "Now, you said something about coffee?"

16

Tynan called a meeting with the officers in their conference room. At first, he had difficulty finding it—he was not used to navigating the cramped, maze-like halls of a space vessel, and he found that he turned down many dead ends. Finally, when he realized just how late he would be to a meeting he had very presumptuously called, he let go of his pride and let Min lead him there.

Then, situated in the conference room with his notes and somewhat flustered from his misadventures in navigating the ship, he prepared to tell them what he had discovered.

"What have you got for us, doctor?" the captain asked.

Min brought up a holographic display on his data pad, showing the results of his tests to the soldiers. Tynan talked them through the numbers.

"The debris from the explosion was scattered evenly, according to the images and video I was sent. The particulate matter was extremely fine, with very few large pieces." The officers exchanged a look among themselves, and Tynan hurried to finish his explanation. It felt like he was already losing their attention. "This suggests some sort of controlled, multi-blast operation. I've seen this before.

In fact, it's a very common demolition strategy in the Szacante Federation."

The officers' expressions shifted, still difficult for Tynan to interpret, but the way they looked at each other spoke of confusion.

"As for the weapons, they were clearly nuclear," Tynan said. "I studied the radiation signature and performed my best calculation of the size of each blast, then cross checked that with your database on known galactic weapons. I can say with high probability that the bombs were from the Union Navy's arsenal."

Now he was certain he could interpret their looks: the stricken expression of a person who was experiencing that heavy, sick sensation that Tynan had been feeling since he began to study the data.

"Do you mean to say that we have someone working with the Sons of Priam?" Armstrong said, his words slow and deliberate and his tone cautiously measured.

Tynan swallowed hard. "I don't know. It's possible there's been some breach of one of your armories or weapons manufacturing facilities. It's also possible they got the weapons from one of the smaller, emerging civilizations that the Union has weapons treaties with."

That didn't appear to make them feel any better.

"I can try to do a more thorough search," Tynan offered. "It will require that I educate myself on a number of topics—physical weaponry is not my area of expertise, but I can determine what I need to know if the Union could get me access to intergovernmental data archives."

There was an uncomfortable shift in the room, as the humans either exchanged glances or attempted to avoid eye contact. Jaya was watching Tully and Armstrong, her eyes flickering from one man's face to the other's. Her face betrayed nothing, but Tynan felt certain he would not want her intense gaze on him that way if he wanted to keep any of his secrets.

"That may be more difficult than it sounds," Armstrong finally said. "We're currently denying to the Nareian Empire that you are our guest."

"They're not thrilled that we retracted the platform from under them," Tully added. "They were planning an extraction of their own, it seems."

"Oh," Tynan said, feeling the situation once again contract around him as he watched his options disappear. His mind reached around for any small grip he could hold tight to, but he was finding it difficult to justify his own involvement in this. It felt like a problem they needed to take up with their own government, and politics was too far out of his comfort zone to even know where to start. "I'll see what I can do with what I have," he finally said.

"That's the best any of us can do," Armstrong said, and while his words were friendly, his mouth was set in a resigned line.

"I do have one possible direction of inquiry, more generally," Tynan added, hesitant.

He didn't know what the Union Navy would consider a useful lead and what they would think was just a fool's errand. The stakes were so high—he was not used to operating under this kind of environment, where both everything and nothing felt critical and urgent all at once. He sat up straighter and continued.

"There is a rare biochemical compound needed for the kind of research I was working on. I can't guarantee that the Sons of Priam are continuing in the same trajectory with bioweaponry in that lab they destroyed, but I know that a fair share of my own research budget was consumed with ordering and shipping this compound. Only a few laboratories produce it, and though it has a few other applications, it is mainly used to protect and amplify delicate biological material. I would say if you can somehow track who is purchasing this compound, any destination that is not a university or an established biological research lab would at least give you a starting point."

Tully leaned forward and rested his chin on his hand, staring at Tynan with a contemplative, but otherwise opaque expression.

Armstrong nodded softly, his blue eyes seeming far away, and then a slow smile crept across his face. He looked up at Jaya and Rhodes.

"Well, officers, it sounds like we officially have a brand-new line of inquiry. Let's get the quants on this right away—I want every shipping route, manufacturing invoice, and chemical order analyzed. There's a signal in the noise, and the doctor just told us what it will look like."

"Yes, Captain," Jaya replied.

Armstrong smiled at Tynan now. "Glad to have you on board, doctor."

Sunny's directions to the mess hall were very clear, but that did not prevent the feeling of panicked disorientation that arose in Tynan shortly after he left the med bay that afternoon. Every so often, a human would emerge into the hall from behind a closed door, the smooth sound of displaced air the only warning before the staccato of boots on the ground and a strange and alien face turned toward him. They nearly all passed him, going the opposite direction, and he stopped more than once, certain that he was going the wrong way in the identical halls with their smooth silver walls and strangely labeled doors.

Finally, the corridor merged with a larger hallway, this one much more trafficked. The stream of bodies was all moving in one direction, and he thought he could smell food wafting through the ventilators. Up until he set foot on the *Avalon,* it had been decades since he had eaten human food, but he recognized the smell from his childhood on New Denmark, and a familiar anxiety welled up in his stomach and stole away his appetite.

He never would have guessed he'd be back with humans—on their ships or their planets, eating their food and drinking their drinks, stumbling through their awkward customs—but here he was. Again, the only szacante in a world that did not belong to them.

Conversation swirled around him as he stood in the line for food. Around a dozen humans pooled together, forming a few groups of two or three, sometimes merging to form larger groups, and always carrying on a conversational tug-of-war too loud for the small room. Tynan shuffled forward in the line, selecting a few items from the buffet whose names were familiar to him, and reaching for a bulb of water at the end of the line. He stopped there and turned to look at the room behind him, that old familiar dread gnawing at his stomach and stealing his hunger away.

The crowd of humans parted around him, the small groups occupying most of the six small tables. Tynan scanned the room and felt a cool surge of relief when he saw that one unoccupied table remained in the corner of the room. He walked there quickly, with purpose, willing the humans around him to ignore that blessedly empty spot.

He sat alone, picking at his plate of food, the clamor of the mess hall becoming a buzzing white noise around him. When his appetite failed him and he couldn't stand the idea of putting another forkful of bland food in his mouth, he placed his dishes in the conveyor and returned to the med bay.

This time, the walk was less foreign, and he found himself back in his little closet office faster than he had expected. He pulled up a holographic screen from his palm drive and entered his login details for the Sequence virtual community.

An error message flashed on the display, informing him that the virtual community was not a secure Union network, then refusing him entry. Tynan sighed and stared blankly at the screen. A deep exhaustion began to well up, seemingly from his very bones.

"Min?" he asked. "Do you want to play Sequence?"

She answered in the affirmative, as he knew she would, and a local copy of the game began on the screen. Playing with Min was a more lonely endeavor, but at least there was something to occupy his mind now and fill the time until he had something he could actually do.

17

Mara slipped off the *Nasdenika* and into the early morning bustle on Argos Station. Her paperwork raised no flags—she had more than enough carefully forged documents to fit nearly any nareian identity she wanted. The humans on Argos had grown accustomed to the relatively large populations of nareian diplomats and businesspeople, and those who betrayed their deep-seated racism mostly only did so through dirty looks and deliberate ignoring of nareian customers.

That suited Mara's purposes—they could pretend she was not there all they wanted. She knew who was willing to do business with her, and she couldn't care less about vendors of cheap trinkets and price-jacked take-out meals in the touristy neighborhoods of the station. She had been on Argos before and knew her way around the back alleys of the city. It was too early for the shops to be open, but what she wanted couldn't be purchased at just any vendor's counter. And anyway, her contact was willing to supply her at any time.

He was called the Fox, though she understood that it was not his real name. The Fox was one of few humans willing to sell to nareians on Argos. He had shown himself to be at least straightforward in his dealings. He offered good merchandise at a fair price, and he sold to those members of the underclasses that most on Argos would report to authorities.

The Fox was a reliable source. At least, until he had a change of heart. For now, it was enough for him to quietly undermine the Union. Payback, he said, for the difficult years he had spent enlisted. And also, Mara thought privately, as a sort of retribution for the things he had no doubt done in the name of the human government.

Mara knew a lot about empires, and the Union certainly was one, despite its name and its claims to democracy. Empires protected what they perceived to be their own property at all costs. The Fox just wanted to spread the wealth, induce some chaos. In Mara's world, that was a damn noble thing. It gave her some cynical pleasure to know that purchasing from him not only brought her the tools she needed to complete her off-the-record jobs, but also made her an invisible thorn in the side of one of the most powerful empires in the galaxy. After all, she had already done her part in undermining the reputation of the Nareian Empress and her royal court.

It was how people like her slept at night. With the faith that they were settling some cosmic score.

The Fox's shop was closed, like all the others on its street, but she knocked on the back door and waited. She shifted her small pack on her shoulder and made sure not to look at the hidden cameras. The cameras and sensors had been there as long as she had been working with the Fox, but she would never tell him she had found them. She understood he had to have confirmation of identity for each and every visitor, and the video feed acted as a sort of mutually assured destruction for the more volatile clients.

After a few moments, the door opened and she stepped inside.

There were two men at the table in the dimly lit room. She smelled the aroma of coffee in the air. The Fox raised his hand in a greeting to her without rising from his seat. He closed the door behind her with a program on his palm drive, his short and stubby fingers flying over the holographic screen.

The Fox was short and built in a way that called to mind the boulders that were strewn across so many arid, lifeless planets. He no longer looked like a soldier, but Mara had spent enough time around mercenaries to recognize his history of military service in the way he moved and spoke, and even in the way he surveyed the room. The man sitting next to him had even less of an air of military about the way he dressed and groomed himself. His dark hair was long and swept across his forehead and brushed his shoulders, undercutting the strength of his features. But Mara saw the same hawk-eyed intensity that marked him as someone who had seen combat.

"Wasn't expecting you back on Argos so soon," the Fox said to her. "What can I help you with?"

"Tech," Mara replied. "I have an unusual assignment. I'm not really sure where it will take me just yet, but I need to start with reconnaissance."

The Fox grunted in displeasure, a cross look settling into the lines of his face. "That's not really my specialty. I don't think I have much, but I'll show you what I've got."

He crossed to the hidden panel on the wall where he kept his illicit merchandise. A biometric scanner ensured that he was the one requesting entry, and then the panel slid aside.

Mara glanced at the other man, who was leaning back in his seat and holding his coffee in one hand. His other arm was slung casually over the seat beside him, but his eyes were still fixed intently on Mara. He smiled, revealing white teeth against his tan face, but his eyes didn't lose their intensity.

As a general rule, she didn't return smiles offered by strangers, so Mara matched his dark gaze with one of her own. His smile changed—not faltering, but instead transitioning from an outward probe to something more thoughtful.

He sipped his coffee.

The Fox's voice broke in as he rummaged through the contents of his hidden storeroom: "You're in luck."

Mara turned her gaze back to her supplier as he brought out a small selection of electronics.

"I still have some of these szacante gadgets a friend brought me." The Fox grumbled and muttered to himself as he sorted through the technology. "What's your bounty this time?" he asked as he returned to the storage area for another look.

She grimaced. "Someone who's already a step ahead, I'm afraid. Standard retrieval otherwise," she lied. She already had the tools she needed to complete the last part of the job.

"Already on the run, huh?" the Fox asked.

Mara did not elaborate, but fortunately for her, the Fox was content enough to listen to himself talk.

"We had a team in here recently tracking down someone who had stolen trade secrets. Some corporate espionage fuckery." He brought another box over and opened it, checking parts and setting aside combinations of gadgets and wires as he spoke. "That shit gets messy," he said, whistling through his teeth. "This was a large team, corporate funded. Money out the ass. Their technician needed some software that's not available outside of military markets. It took me a few days to track down my contact, but I made it work."

He paused and looked up at Mara, wagging one of his stubby fingers at her. "So if I don't have something you need, don't forget I can do special orders. Just might take more than a second to get it in."

"So you've told me," Mara said.

She leaned over the counter where the Fox had strewn the electronics he was now sorting through. She towered over the short man, but he didn't flinch as her shadow fell across him.

He held out a small object in his hand. "This is a new prototype cloaker. Szacante military contract, being tested right now by reconnaissance teams, but not widespread yet. No one will know to be looking for it."

"Sounds useful," Mara said, taking the prototype from him and turning it over in her hand. It was a small, flat disc with a magnetic latch that would allow her to add it to her belt—Union military tech she had scavenged years ago.

"You work alone?"

It was the first time the other man spoke. His smile had been replaced by a serene and unreadable expression, and his voice was as steady and keen as his countenance.

She glared at him. "Not all bounty hunters work in teams," she said coldly, and returned to examining the goods.

"But I'd say nine out of ten do," he replied, his demeanor not shaken in the least by her withering expression. She turned her whole body toward him this time, crossing her arms and flexing the muscles. The dim light still drew out the contrasting patterns of her tattoos.

"I'm faster alone," she answered.

He didn't reply, but he watched her closely, as if she might reveal something in her posture or her expression. She had been doing this long enough to know that her body language remained as cryptic as this man's. They were alien echoes of each other, immovable. Suspicion hung in his eyes, but she didn't need this man to trust her. She just needed to get her gear and leave. She turned back to the Fox.

"Need any survival gear?" The Fox had pulled out a chair and was standing on it, pushing aside items on the top shelf to look behind them.

"Not that I know of yet," she said. "I'll be renting a place on Argos short-term. I could use a referral if you know a guy."

"Do I know a guy?" the Fox said, as if the answer were obvious. She supposed that it was. "I'll send you a contact," he promised, and sure enough, a moment later her palm drive pinged.

"What sort of comms monitoring software you got?" Mara asked. "I think mine might be out of date by now."

"Let me see what I can find," he said, getting down from his perch with a graceless thud and closing the panel in order to open another.

"I should be going," the other man said. "I need to open up the shop." He stood and pulled his hair back into a loose ponytail, wisps of it still falling loose around his face.

The Fox stopped his rummaging to shake his friend's hand, then pull the leaner, taller man into a quick embrace. "Be careful with those wealthy vultures," he said, clapping the man on the shoulder.

"I always am." A cynical half-smile punctuated the remark. He glanced at Mara and nodded once to her in greeting. She ignored him, and the door closed quietly behind him.

The Fox swiveled a console around so Mara could look at his software offerings, and they began the inevitable haggling over his prices. Thirty minutes later, having spent a good deal more than she would have liked, Mara left the store.

The Fox's contact turned out to be the proprietor of a shabby motel in one of the poorest neighborhoods of Argos, where the recycled air was humid and stale. The neighborhood was mostly immigrants, and Mara was pleased to see many nareian faces in the swarms of pedestrians crowding the narrow corridors. Her presence would not make much of an impression in this part of the station.

The room she rented was little more than a converted closet. It had a narrow, hard bed along one wall and a shared bathroom down the hallway. A muted purr of voices and footsteps made its way through the thin walls, but the room was well within the meager budget she had set herself for this job. She wanted to avoid drawing attention.

She set her small pack on the floor beside the bed and took a seat. Her palm drive beeped quietly in her ear, and she found a new message waiting in her inbox. The sender was indicated only by a short string of numbers, but the subject line indicated that this was her new employer. She opened the message, which had securely encrypted files attached to it.

I see you have arrived on Argos. I'm glad you've chosen to take this job. The efficient neutralization of Indigo Onyema is your first priority, but discretion is your second priority. It is of the utmost importance that this does not become a news story. You may keep your advance if you are unable to succeed, but you will only receive the second payment if all the terms of the agreement are met.

There were no salutations, no niceties. The message abruptly ended, and Mara pulled up the files that had been included in the previous message. These files had led her to Argos, the last known location of Indigo Onyema, although Mara was certain she had fled the station by now. Onyema was a woman of means. She had been an early investor in TA Tech, and it had paid off. She owned an expensive home overlooking the Forum—or at least, the property was still in her name, although it was unlikely to still be inhabited. She also owned a cutting-edge racing ship, a standard transport ship, and a luxurious yacht, all of which had departed Argos on the same day just over a week ago, and none of which had arrived at the destinations in their chartered flight plans.

Her employer had also included a list of every flight scheduled to depart Argos the same day that Onyema's ships went missing, including those that were cancelled or delayed. The files included both publicly available data such as filed flight plans and passenger lists as well as the internal notes of the Argos Port Authority. This was information that would be highly regulated.

Mara wondered for a moment if her employer knew how much he had revealed about himself by laying out these cards on the table. He was extraordinarily well-connected, extraordinarily wealthy, or both. And he was desperate for her help.

Mara decided to start with a stroll through Argos's nicer neighborhoods. She would need to purchase something to wear that suggested money and influence rather than her current wardrobe of threats and intimidation. Perhaps if she could explore some of Onyema's old haunts on Argos, she might be able to shake loose some ideas about where Onyema may have gone—or who she may have called on for help.

The shirt Mara bought had sleeves long enough to cover most of her tattoos. It wasn't that tattoos were all that uncommon, especially among the cosmopolitan population of a galactic hub city like Argos, it was the way her tattoos covered her skin thickly, rather than the occasional artful symbol or abstract design. She tugged the tailored pants on, smoothing the fabric at her hip and donning a stylish leather jacket. She would not be able to wear her belt today, a fact that made her distinctly uncomfortable. The face tattoos would be distinctive enough to draw attention, but with the outfit she had put together, they came across as an artful affectation.

She slipped some knives, sheathed in protective guards, into a pocket she had stitched herself into the lining of the jacket. That would have to be enough.

The apartment of Indigo Onyema was thirty levels up from the Forum, its back windows facing the great open atrium. It was one of the most sought-after pieces of real estate on Argos, but as far as Mara could tell, it sat empty.

She found an upscale coffee shop a block down from Onyema's address, ensuring her route would lead her past the apartment on her way. The front steps and grand entryway looked as neat as if they had been tended that morning, but as Mara scanned the neighboring abodes as she passed, she realized they featured identical layouts in slightly varying colors.

Of course, she thought. This area would be managed by some sort of neighborhood association, to ensure the uniform appearance of tranquility and care. Behind the closed curtains, she could see nothing, but her heat scanner revealed the rooms behind the facade to be empty of life.

At her perch in the coffee shop—where she insisted in her most dulcet tones to take her coffee on the terrace overlooking the street —she began to look through the data from the port, keeping an eye out for familiar or suspicious faces in the crowd. She could not rule out that Onyema had been in one of those three ships, but she felt certain that the woman had taken a fourth ship. One not obviously belonging to her. Mara had skimmed the file her employer sent on Onyema, and found that the woman had spent more than two decades in the Union Navy's IRC division. This was a woman who thought at least three steps ahead.

Fortunately, Mara was also adept at seeing many moves ahead and the myriad options that each choice spawned. She would need to expand her search before she could rein it in—she needed more data.

The Port Authority's public records were only available via a written request, and she doubted they would include the depth of information she was seeking. But her employer had already sent her the records from one day, so she closed the records site on her data pad and instead made her request in a message to her employer.

While she waited, she opened the file on Onyema and began to dig more deeply into it. Onyema was a wealthy woman, and a powerful one, in a quiet way. Born on New Hong Kong to middle-class parents who owned a small shipyard that constructed private vessels for the wealthy. Onyema had no siblings, no children, and had never been married, which would make her frustratingly hard to blackmail or coerce.

She had received the best education that could be purchased for a middle-class child, but she was the kind of student who could have earned a scholarship, excelling in her secondary school course-work and athletics. She had competed in an elite intersystem lacrosse league, winning awards and acclaim as a local athletic star. But while she could have taken an academic or athletic scholarship to any university, or even signed with a semi-professional league, she had instead enrolled in the Union Naval Academy and been selected for their elite training.

Mara's employer had her military service records as well, and as Mara paged through them, she raised an eyebrow. There were no redactions, no missing information. The heights of her new employer's reach just continued to extend. It was no wonder this woman had disappeared, if she was trying to blackmail someone with this much power.

But if Mara was going to find her, she would need to find a weakness.

After fifteen years of service, Onyema had been promoted to commander and placed in charge of a nine-person mixed IRC unit based on one of the larger cruisers. She had retired a mere five years later. Mara looked through the records for the names of her team. There had been turnover, of course. But of the nine names on the squadron for their last assignment before she retired, seven of them had been with her for at least three years.

Two of the names—Lieutenant Commanders Anthony Brighton and Tyrone Sloan—were listed in the record as killed in action on that final assignment. They had both been with her for three years, and Mara marked those names off her list. Keith Paakkanen was the highest ranking of the enlisted marines. He had been with her nearly the entire five years between her promotion and her retirement. Mara entered his name into a public records database and it came up immediately: *deceased.*

Interesting. Paakkanen had died a year after Onyema had retired. Mara didn't have access to Paakkanen's military record, but his public obituary said he had died in service to the Union. So another assignment gone wrong? Mara marked his name for follow-up. Juan Burr-Sawyer, Nina Oakes, Devin Fishlock, and Dion

Mustafa were the next most senior members of the team. Burr-Sawyer had served four years with Onyema, and Oakes, Fishlock, and Mustafa just over three. She looked them both up in public records: *Burr-Sawyer, deceased. Oakes, deceased. Fishlock, deceased. Mustafa, deceased.* All killed in service to the United Human Nations. All within a few years of Onyema's retirement.

Mara marked their names as well, and felt a buzz of anticipation as she read the names of the last two members of Onyema's troop: Isao Checiek and Kathleen Manzel, the youngest and least senior members. Unsurprisingly, they were also listed as deceased. Mara didn't need to read more in their obituaries to know they would have also been killed in the line of duty, but she did so anyway.

If these records were to be believed, every member of the team that had survived with Onyema on her final assignment with the Union was then killed in the six years following her retirement. Mara knew that IRC jobs were among the most dangerous in the Union military. She had heard that the training alone was known to kill up to ten percent of those who aspired to these positions, and death was surely ever-present. But for every single person Onyema had led in her final Union days to turn up dead in just a few years... well, Mara was certainly going to look into it in more depth.

Mara's palm drive pinged, bringing her out of her deep focus on Onyema's history. She marked the entry with the final assignment on her data pad before switching over to her messaging system. Her employer already had the port data she had requested. The file was massive, as she had expected. Two weeks of records on every civilian flight into or out of Argos—she would never be able to sort through this on her own. She fed the data into the mining software on her data pad and selected her filters: female travelers, Union citizenship. Onyema had not traveled under her own name, of course, but were there any hints as to what name she might take?

She was too smart to use the name of a loved one or a character from a book or movie. And what about destinations? Unlikely she would go directly to her intended final destination. Instead she would shed identities at multiple ports, taking on new names and paperwork until the trail was too convoluted for anyone to follow. She was both smart enough and connected enough to make that happen.

Mara frowned. She had been given an impossible task. This was a woman who knew how to hide. But she would need help. Just as Mara's employer was connected enough to get Mara classified files and massive dumps of Port Authority data, Onyema would need someone to manage the paperwork, to pilot those three missing ships, perhaps even take her on a fourth ship to whatever her destination was. Some of these things could be accomplished through bribes and third parties, but the paperwork took someone in the government. Mara looked again at her notes on Onyema's deceased squad, and felt a sliver of clarity push through the darkness.

She replied to the message from her employer with an additional request for the personnel files of the seven naval officers and marines who had died in the years after Onyema's retirement. Never mind the flight manifest data for now. The first question wasn't where Onyema had gone; it was who was helping her.

18

The message from Emory arrived in Jaya's inbox as they approached Argos, as if he stood watching for her ship at one of the large observation windows. Sal inquired at the bitter look she threw at her messages when she saw it, and she reluctantly repeated the conversation she'd had with the heir apparent to the leadership of the United Human Nations.

Sal's persuasive skills won out, and Jaya found herself agreeing to a meeting that afternoon. She would give Emory a chance to present his case.

The corridor where Emory lived was an arched, multi-story passageway lined with spotless white townhomes not far from the Diplomatic Level. Their windows gazed pleasantly over the corridor on the front, and at the back they had an expansive view of the central open atrium of Argos and the Forum far below. Jaya had visited Sal's family home before and been awed at their wealth, but next to these homes, his parents' residence looked more like her own childhood cottage than the home of a wealthy couple.

Jaya pressed the button beside the shiny blue-painted metal door to notify Emory's staff that she had arrived, and a moment later the door opened to reveal Emory himself. She stepped back, friendly greeting dying on her lips. She suddenly felt unsure of how to address this man, who carried himself with the assurance of his own power but also invited job candidates to his home and answered his own door when they arrived.

He seemed to read the discomfort on her face and gave her an easy, relaxed smile. "Thank you for meeting me at my home," he said, waving her in. "I prefer to work here when I can. More comfortable."

The foyer opened up into a bright living area with vaulted ceilings. The bustle of Argos moved in silence outside the windows. Chaise lounges the color of titanium stood stark against white floors. It was a well-appointed apartment, and though the decoration was sparse, every item of furniture or decorative accent was a perfectly curated conversation piece. A replica of *La Guernica* took up most of the wall on the right, and on a small end table a carved crystal balance scale caught the light from the window.

"I sent my assistant on an errand," Emory said. "He should be back soon, but in the meantime, can I get you a drink?"

"Just water, thank you," she said. Turning down a drink felt rude, but nerves turned her stomach and she dreaded the thought of putting anything in it.

She stood facing the painting, its stark and jarring lines echoing her own discomfort. In the twisted figures and inky black shadows, the shape of something else called to her. The odd angle of Vargas's leg, the broken bodies on Arcadian Gardens. Years of memories unspooling from their tightly wound place in her chest, all the way back to the screams of her mother and the nightmares of her childhood filling in the parts she didn't witness. A splash of red on the black and white keys of a piano.

But no, there was no red. Only a faint wash of blue over the black and white forms.

Emory emerged from a room behind her, a glass of water in one hand and a cup of coffee in the other. She took the offered glass, which was beaded with condensation. A cold drop ran down her wrist and she wiped it on her pants hurriedly, fixing all her attention on the motion. This was not the time to dredge up the past.

"This has always been my favorite Picasso," Emory said, nodding toward the painting. "The bombing of an innocent town by the forces of Francisco Franco during the first Spanish Civil War. Long before we left Earth, when atrocities like this were newsworthy."

"Scenes like this one are all too common today," Jaya agreed.

Emory nodded, taking a drink from his cup. "Did you know that Franco blamed this bombing on the resistance forces? Claimed his enemies arranged it. It might have worked, too, if Picasso hadn't brought the world's attention to it."

Jaya turned away from the painting, meeting Emory's eyes.

"We all love a hero," she said. "But if I've learned anything in my life, it's that every hero has five or ten people behind them making their actions possible. One person can't save the world. It takes more than that."

His face shifted, a slight curling of the lip ghosting across it before settling into a distant smile. "That's an interesting perspective," he said, "and brings me to the reason I've asked you here."

He gestured to one of the chairs, and she sat. His crisp suit remained smooth as he took a seat across from her.

"About four years ago, my company had a prototype EMP application for the palm drive," he said. "We were developing it as part of an exclusive contract with the Navy, and I received regular reports from the IRC division about its use—redacted, of course." He cut off her interjection with a raised hand. "These reports included use statistics for the most part. Numbers that would be of interest to no one besides the developers. But the final report"—at this his smile sparked across his face, creasing around his eyes— "the final report included a glowing account of how this technology had saved lives one day, in the able hands of one lieutenant."

He arched an eyebrow. The silence hung around them like a structure he had built with his words and his knowing pauses.

Jaya refused to fill it, and instead folded her hands in her lap with an air of patient anticipation.

"Of course, this individual was nameless to me," he said. "I had no way of discovering their identity. But I found myself so compelled by the story that I began to ask around. The more I asked, the more I found one particular officer emerging at the center of the great stories of the IRC's success."

Jaya's heart quickened, and she raised the cold water to her lips to mask the sudden pulse of fear.

"Of course, you know by now who that officer is." Emory smiled at her. Again, the artificial silence. His smile faltered for a moment on his surgically crafted face, a flash of irritation creasing the place between his eyebrows and then vanishing again. He stood.

"You're a rising star in your field," he said to Jaya. "I would say you're a hero, but it's clear you don't particularly like that word. So instead, I'll say you're talented and resourceful, and I am not the sort of person who passes up an opportunity to recruit someone with your level of talent."

"I don't understand what I could do for you," Jaya said. "The skills I use in the field are not the same skills used in politics."

"I disagree." He braced himself on a chair, directing all the lines of his body forward, projecting his strength of will in his stance.

Jaya saw all this, and found it calmed her. He was working hard to recruit her. She began to understand the artificial informality of this meeting, the things he intended her to notice and the effect they were supposed to have. She smiled politely and met his gaze with her own.

"You're able to think on your feet, to see messy situations with a bird's eye view," he insisted. "You don't let adrenaline cloud your thinking, you harness it to your power." He returned to his seat, his breath releasing in a sigh. "You said earlier that one person can't change the world. I know that too well. That's why I need the very best people beside me."

"What is your goal?" Jaya asked.

He considered her for a moment, steepling his fingers and balancing the perfect point of his chin on them. The lines of his face were cold, his white hair crowning his head with an icy finish, but there was warmth somewhere in his eyes. And something more— Jaya felt the force of her own will met with equal force in his eyes. He nodded, as if he finally understood something.

"You don't want the stump speech," he said. It was not a question, but a measured observation. "You truly want to understand the role you would play in the world if you aligned yourself with me and the government I hope to build. You're not looking for words you can use to justify the rewards that come from being connected to power."

He leaned back in his chair, his focus easing some, although to Jaya he still looked coiled, like an animal waiting for its chance to strike. "Lieutenant Commander." He wrapped the words of her title around his mouth as though they were a foreign thing—a barrier. He frowned slightly, the frown of careful thought. "I know that many join the Navy because they have no other choice. I grew up in the colonies myself, and I know the knife's edge of luck that I walked to get where I am today. I have lived the injustices of the Union. My life has been both sides of the very same coin.

"As my business grew, so did my own wealth and my network. With the growth of my wealth and my network came power. Power that one day I realized I wasn't using."

He paused, taking another drink of his coffee. His eyes were focused elsewhere now, their golden intensity frozen in this moment in his own past. He set his cup down, the ceramic ringing against the glass of the table like a bell, and his eyes snapped back to the present, to Jaya.

"What good is power if it lies fallow?" A strange hush had come over his voice, and the question hung in the air both answered and unanswered at the same time. "Don't we owe it to ourselves and to the people around us to use our skills and our opportunities to build a better galaxy? What kind of person would I be if I took my wealth and my influence and I built myself a fortress to hide behind?"

He shook his head, an abrupt and angry motion, and stood again. He crossed to the painting, tilting his head up to take it in. Over his left shoulder, Jaya's eyes were drawn to the figure of a woman, eyes turned up to heaven and wailing, a lifeless child clutched in her arms. Emory stood there, his gray suit and white hair lending him the same monochromatic air of the painting. Small and controlled against the larger-than-life grief displayed before him.

Suddenly a thread of tension loosened in Jaya. She recognized something in Emory, something she shared. He was right—she had joined the Navy out of necessity. But now that she was here, didn't she feel the draw every day of making things better? Of playing her part, using every tool at her disposal, to lessen the suffering that she had witnessed?

Emory sighed and turned back toward Jaya, his smile rueful. It was the most genuine expression she had seen from him yet, and he quickly masked it.

"If I am going to have any hope of making a change when I am elected, I need to surround myself with the right kind of people," he said. "People with integrity and passion. People who care, and who understand how things work in the United Human Nations. And how things fail to work. I can't surround myself with technocrats and career politicians. People who have never left Argos in their life except on an expensive cruise to the resort colonies. I need people like you, Jaya."

She startled at that, the way he used her name. All pretense of formality dropped, and the unexpected closeness tightened around her chest.

"I'm sorry," he said. "That was rude of me. Lieutenant Commander Mill."

"It's fine." she said, waving off his apology, but adrenaline still flooded her veins and thrummed in her mind.

"The way your commanding officer has spoken of you, I feel like I know you already." He smiled. "I met with him last time he was on Argos. He briefed all the candidates on this new threat, and I took the liberty of asking about you. If Peter Armstrong speaks so highly of you, I know you must be a person of integrity.

"You've given him years of loyal service, and he sees your potential. Just like I do."

Jaya looked down at her hands, still gripping the glass and turning pink from the cold. She set the glass down on the table beside her and squeezed her hands into fists, then released them slowly. Her thoughts were thick, moving sluggishly. This was not a path she had envisioned for herself, but then she had never been given the luxury of choosing a path before. Every major choice she had made since she was eight years old was one between life and death, when she thought about it for more than a minute. And now, to think there might be more than one opportunity for her to do something worthwhile with her life? Faced with choices, they felt less like a luxury and more like a test.

Emory was watching her with a controlled patience, all that intensity having returned to his gaze.

She stood, and although she was taller than Emory, something in the way he watched her now—in this first moment of having choices—made her feel young and small and inexperienced.

"What exactly are you offering me?" she asked, her voice more composed than she felt.

"A position in my Cabinet," he said. "Director of Security."

"That's a very large promotion for someone as young as me."

"It's a promotion in direct proportion to your experience and ability," he countered. "But if you feel you need a trial period, I could use you as an advisor on security and counterintelligence. Give you a chance to adjust to the politics before you dive in."

Jaya turned the offers over in her mind, tried to get the feel of them. She would be at the top of the information flow, have access to everything. She could see the galaxy with a long view, maybe help pick out patterns that others missed.

Maybe find Kier.

"I need some time." She masked her sudden breathlessness by straightening her jacket. "It's a lot to think about."

"And you wouldn't be the measured and thoughtful person I know you are if you didn't take some time to consider the options." He smiled warmly.

Jaya extended her hand, and they shook on it.

———

It was a short walk to the hospital from Emory's home, and Jaya traveled most of it still focused on unraveling the dense knot left behind by their conversation.

She had already pivoted once, a move made out of necessity rather than any semblance of career goals, and she had been fortunate enough to have the pieces fall into place one by one: Armstrong taking an interest in her training as a young recruit, the *Avalon*'s assignments bringing her opportunity after opportunity to prove herself and learn new skills, her bond with Sal providing one bright spot of emotional safety, and finally Armstrong again drawing her slowly into the family of the *Avalon* and teaching her how to lead them well. With integrity.

That word. It was a word Emory had used on multiple occasions today. *Integrity.*

Wasn't that the very quality she had been raised to admire? From her mother, the importance of sincerity and fairness. From her father, the value of strong principles followed scrupulously. From her uncles, the incomparability of decency and solidarity. And from Armstrong, righteousness. The pursuit of justice. Weren't these all facets of integrity?

She had never bothered to examine her choices all that closely, believing them to always be choices of necessity. But now, the meandering track of her life seemed to catch the new light of this perspective, setting it aglow.

Wasn't integrity the guiding force behind her behavior? Integrity and a sort of idealism she had always pushed aside, embarrassed at its childish optimism. Wasn't integrity the reason she chose her friends? The reason she trusted Armstrong? The reason she sent money home to her uncles every chance she got? The reason she refused to give up at each and every obstacle in her path?

A job advising the Chancellor of the United Human Nations still felt wrong as she turned it over in her mind. It seemed distant and cold, although she intended to consider it just as she had promised.

Was it the right choice? Or was there a better option out there?

For the first time, she was standing at the edge of a deep chasm of opportunity, and tangled threads of pleasure and dread twisted through her.

Vargas was standing shakily when Jaya entered her room, her hair cascading across the deep line of a frown on her forehead, her eyes fierce and her mouth already forming curses.

"It's like it's not even there," Vargas exhaled sharply and collapsed back down. "I can't tell the fucking thing what to do."

The physical therapist held his hand out and Vargas placed her wrist in the outstretched palm. While he tweaked settings in the palm drive menu, Vargas looked up and saw Jaya in the door. She flushed and looked away with a mumbled hello.

Jaya's confused musings about her future vanished at Vargas's discomfort. "Rough day?" she asked.

Vargas nodded. The physical therapist finished his tweaking and closed the menu. He glanced once at Jaya and then returned his attention to his patient.

"It won't all come at once," he said. "I know it's hard, but you have to be patient. Your brain needs time to adapt to the prosthesis's signals and start to interpret them. The only way to make that adaptation happen properly is to use it."

"How am I supposed to use the thing if I can't even feel it there?" Vargas asked.

"Try directing the rest of your leg. It will be awkward at first, but you'll build up the right neural connections eventually."

Vargas bit her lip, her eyes churning with unspoken bitterness. Her hospital pajamas were rolled up past the knee, and the prosthetic leg extended smoothly from the bandage, the bulge of artificial muscle and the warm bronze of the polymer skin a near-perfect match for Vargas's other leg.

"Try again," the physical therapist urged.

"Would it help if I left?" Jaya asked.

"No." Vargas's reply was swift. "No, I've been alone in this stupid hospital too much lately."

"Her girlfriend was here earlier," the physical therapist said to Jaya. "But she hasn't had visitors this past week."

"We were deployed," Jaya said. "Here, let me help."

The physical therapist stepped aside and allowed Jaya to come forward. She held out an arm to Vargas, who wouldn't meet her eyes, but accepted the offered support. Jaya cupped her elbow as Vargas raised herself up to a stand, the muscles in her jaw tense as she concentrated.

"I've got it," Jaya said to the therapist, who nodded.

"I'll be a few rooms down," he said. "Alert me if you need me back."

When he left, Jaya glanced down at Vargas. Sweat beaded on her forehead and above her lip as she adjusted the weight on her leg.

"So you and Lupo are official now?" Jaya asked.

"Not for long, I'm sure. Being my girlfriend now must be a drag."

"She won't leave you because of this."

"Won't she?" Vargas turned dark eyes on Jaya, the motion causing her to falter on the leg. She gripped Jaya's arm, righting herself carefully. "You know how hard it is, never knowing where you'll be from one day to the next. Now I'll be the one dragging her back to Argos, a dead weight on the relationship. It's impossible to date civilians and that's basically what I'll be."

Jaya did know. It was hard to stay connected to someone whose life was consistent and normal when you were always flying off in the middle of the night. When you couldn't talk about your work with your partner. Sal had gone through a string of boyfriends on Argos a few years ago before giving up. He claimed now that dating bored him, but Jaya had seen the toll those relationships had taken on him, and how the isolation wore at him less than the repeated heartbreak.

And as for herself? Jaya hadn't even tried. It was hard enough to maintain her relationship with her uncles, let alone find enough time to spend with any one person outside of her company to feel anything. She wasn't sure she could even let down her guard enough to get to that point. It was safer to be alone.

But she didn't say all that. Instead, she tightened her grip on Vargas's arm, helping her move steadily back to the bed.

"Maybe you'll be her anchor, instead," Jaya suggested. "Not a dead weight, but something that can connect her back and give her some stability."

"Right. Because I'm so stable right now."

Jaya heard the dark humor in the words. The bitterness wrapped in a joke. Vargas stumbled again and swore. Jaya steadied her with a firm grip, keeping her stumble from escalating to a fall.

Vargas made a frustrated sound—a choked half-laugh. "This is pathetic," she said. "I can't even walk anymore."

"You'll get there," Jaya said. Vargas didn't reply. They took a few more slow and ragged steps to the end of the room and began to turn.

Beneath the hair that had fallen across her face, Vargas's eyes shimmered. One wet track revealed the tear that had fallen, despite the tension in her neck and face that betrayed her effort to hold it in. When they reached the bed again, Jaya helped Vargas sit back down. The prosthetic knee bent, though not as naturally as the other one. It was slow, delayed. It would get better, but Jaya's throat tightened in sympathy.

Jaya sat beside her, releasing the grip on her arm and shoulder. They sat in silence for a moment, Vargas's irregular breathing the only evidence for her continued struggle against tears.

"I'm sorry," Vargas finally said. "This is a weak moment."

"No," Jaya replied. "This is a human moment. This is normal."

Vargas sobbed a laugh at that. "Fuck normal. None of this is normal."

"It's not okay," Jaya agreed. "It sucks that this happened. It sucks to have your dreams ripped away."

Vargas pressed her palms against her eyes, more tears sneaking through her defenses and rolling down her cheeks. She drew a ragged breath.

"When I joined up, I turned in my paperwork at our regional office," Jaya said. "And then I went home and cried."

Jaya paused, giving Vargas room to speak if she needed to. When she didn't, Jaya continued.

"I didn't want to be in the Navy," she said. "I wanted to be a musician. I trained for it. I was good."

"What happened?"

"Something terrible." Jaya picked her words carefully. "My family was killed in the kind of stupid, rotten twist of fate you never dream could happen to you. And then I had nothing. I lived with my uncles. We barely scraped by, and the military was the only chance to earn any money. The only chance to have a future where we weren't all ground into the dust."

"Shit," Vargas said, wiping her face. "I'm sorry."

"My dreams were torn away the day my parents died," Jaya said. "But I didn't believe it until the day I joined up. I didn't grieve until then."

"I get that," Vargas replied. "Easier to survive when you deal with one problem at a time."

"Yeah," Jaya said. "You have the time now to deal with this problem. Use it. You'll be better for it."

Vargas looked away, ran her hand over the mess of tight curls damp with sweat. "Fuck," she muttered. "Fuck it all."

"You can say that again."

Vargas threw her a sly smile. "Fuck!" she yelled, the end of the word breaking into a laugh.

Jaya smiled and nudged her with her shoulder. "That's the Jordan Vargas I'm used to hearing on my comms."

Vargas laughed again at that. "I can be a pain in the ass, can't I?"

"I pity every obstacle in your path," Jaya said. "And I know you'll find a way through this. There will be opportunities you never expected. But you have to get through this first."

Vargas nodded. She massaged her new knee, frowned at it. It flexed, slightly.

Lupo appeared in the door then, and Jaya stood, freeing up the place beside Vargas. The pilot sat beside Vargas, who took her hand and interlaced their fingers. Jaya turned to leave them alone, smiling at the hope she had just seen ignite in Vargas's dark brown eyes.

"Hey, boss?" Vargas said.

Jaya stopped in the doorway and looked back.

"How do you feel about it now?" Vargas asked. "The way things turned out?"

Jaya considered for a moment, taking out the pieces of her life and holding them up to the light. The thrill of adrenaline in combat. The limp exhaustion at the end of a day of hard work. Sal's familiar jokes and Armstrong's hard-earned smiles. The sound of her team bantering in the background. Strength of will arising from the belief that their actions would make a difference—that their risks would give someone else safety.

And the piano in Luka's shop, its presence a song in her mind. Comfort and release in the music, and the warm feeling of pleasant company. The faces of the strike teams as they sang drinking songs along with her violin.

"I took too long to grieve," she finally said. "But I think I'm starting to come out the other side."

19

Mara itched to do something—anything—besides search through records. It had been three days of combing through the military records, the port records, the personnel files, and her employer's own notes on Onyema, and Mara was beginning to regret taking this job. She sat on the hard bed in her rented room while the software sorted through the massive port documents, searching for any flights leaving or arriving to Argos with a company of no more than eight.

The personnel files had been consistent with what Mara had already read—these seven officers and marines had been assigned to Onyema's team for the duration specified in Onyema's files, and afterwards had gone on to serve on other teams until the date of their death in combat. Mara found it far too convenient that every single surviving member of Onyema's last team had been killed in action, all of them in entirely unrelated operations.

The field records from Onyema's last mission with her IRC team were written in dry protocol, with little in the way of details that would help Mara identify the people Onyema had worked with. Mara was certain now that at least some of these people were alive somehow, and that they had covered their tracks by swapping their service records with those of conveniently deceased personnel.

So she had directed her data filtering software to search for flights on personal vessels with a small crew. She hoped a pattern would emerge from the noise, some unusual behavior, anything that might help point her in the right direction.

In the meantime, she was so bored she considered practicing her knife throwing against the wall of this little room, but the desire to not sacrifice any of her precious payment to room destruction charges kept her hands from wandering to the sheaths at her utility belt. She groaned, throwing her head back and stretching out her limbs, wishing to the gods of Narei that she could just *do something*. She had to get out of this room.

She set an alert on her palm drive for the data processing program and threw her jacket on, covering her knives from view, and left. In this corner of Argos, the bars were cheap and filled with nareian immigrants. Mara would be able to get a drink of one of the strong, aged nareian liquors she so rarely found in human and szacante towns, and hone her observational skills on the local population in the meantime. Anything to put some space between herself and that data pad.

The streets were barely more than narrow alleys, corridors where foot traffic dominated and people brushed shoulders as they wove through the crowded space. Mara pushed her way through an alley until she saw a bar, its digital display missing a few pixels, but fluorescing brightly. The cold blue tones were strangely welcoming, and she cut across a slow-moving family to slip through the door and into the dark assembly of bodies drinking and conversing in relative privacy. She selected a booth in the corner and slid into the seat, ordering a double *siltyr* on the built-in terminal, then sat back and crossed her arms comfortably while she waited for the aromatic nareian liquor to arrive.

There were a few humans in this bar, but the majority of the clientele was nareian. A group of three at the table nearest her were drinking in silence, heads bowed and shoulders hunched. Their clothing was shabby and their posture exhausted. Perhaps a rejected claim at the embassy. One of them wiped his eyes, and the woman next to him reached comfortingly for his hand. Maybe a death in the family, then.

Mara looked away.

Near them was a younger couple holding hands over the table; one of them kept glancing at the door nervously. A forbidden tryst, or a sordid affair?

Mara's drink arrived then, and she took a sip. The nostalgia of the flavor hit her more powerfully than she expected. The bleak frugality of her existence faded easily into the background when she was working, and she was nearly always working. Every tiny scrap of cash she could save was set aside, and when she found herself in a bar for work she ordered something she could leave quickly with no regrets—stakeouts in her line of work often turned into opportunities that could not be passed up.

Across the room, she caught the glance of another nareian. She was not much younger than Mara, and she, too sat alone. She watched Mara with honey-colored eyes that caught the dim light radiating out from the bar, and when she saw that Mara was returning her look, she gave a sly smile. Mara's response was slow, measured, but she also smiled.

A commotion at the table with the couple distracted her. The one who had been glancing at the door was standing now, ripping his hand away from his lover's. He stalked out, and the remaining half of the broken couple drained his drink and ordered another. Not a forbidden tryst, then. A breakup.

The woman got up, carrying her drink with her, and moved toward Mara. Mara watched the movement of her body—smooth and easy, no hitch in her step. Most likely unarmed. Mara slid a knife out of its sheath and placed it on her lap anyway. You could never be too safe. The woman reached Mara's booth and leaned gracefully against the support.

"Can I sit here?" she asked, quirking up a golden eyebrow. Her mane was cut short and neat, and she lacked any adornment in the way of tattoos or piercings. Her markings were a tawny brown against a tan backdrop, and she carried herself with confidence. If they had been anywhere but a seedy bar in a poor neighborhood, Mara would have assumed she was an athlete, or perhaps a cop.

Why the hell not? Mara gestured for the woman to take the seat across from her. She sat smoothly and crossed her legs.

"I'm Antza," she said.

"Kala," Mara lied. She took another drink and waited.

"I've never seen you here before," Antza said.

"Really? That's your line?"

"I don't usually need one," Antza replied.

Mara couldn't help herself, she laughed at that. "Yeah, I bet you don't."

It had been a long time, she realized, since she had even let herself consider a physical connection with someone. She could use a distraction from the waiting, which was why she had come to the bar in the first place, and Antza was being anything but coy. Mara brought up a mental picture of her room as she'd left it—she would need to hide the data pad, of course, and Antza leaving her sight for an instant was out of the question. But then, she wasn't planning to let her out of her sight.

Antza was watching her over the rim of her cup, her eyes smiling.

Tai had eyes like that. Big and golden. They smiled at her over the scarf he used to wrap over his nose and mouth when they were working on one of those remote, dusty planets where every breath brought a heavy dose of particulates. *Lot of fucking good that will do you*, she'd tell him. Wearing a scarf when what he needed was a mask. He'd laugh and say *you don't always have to be so self-righteous.*

Mara downed the rest of her drink, letting the sting of the liquid in her throat obliterate the memory. Her eyes watered from it.

"You free tonight?" Antza asked.

The alert on her palm drive pinged, and she pulled up the holo-graphic display to pay for her drink.

"Another time, maybe." Mara sheathed her knife and left.

The walk back to her room was swift with anticipation, compared with the slow drag of her day before the answers lay tantalizingly available on her data pad. She charged into her room and snatched the pad up, projecting the results onto the bare wall so she could see more at once.

The search had isolated nearly two hundred flights, a pronounced decrease from the tens of thousands that had been in the list to begin with. Mara scrolled through the list, looking for patterns. There was a small cargo ship called the *River Teviot,* which made very regular trips with a flight plan to nearby Hadur. They left with more passengers than they returned with each time, but also filled up their holds with building materials from Hadur's mines and smiths. The passengers would simply be a way to minimize their losses on the outward journey. So that was out.

The *Solidarity* had a small, regular crew of three and made frequent trips. Their flight plan was different each time, but the trips were never more than a few days, and each time they returned with an assortment of goods declared as commercial in customs. Some sort of mercantile ship, then, or possibly smugglers with a respectable-looking front operation. Mara flagged them and kept reading.

Another ship that was almost certainly involved in smuggling was the *Aungban,* which also kept an irregular schedule and often filed flight plans at the last moment. But their cargo manifests were always pristine. Their crew switched out regularly, with a few familiar names on each manifest, but a revolving door of passengers and minor crew members. Mara hesitated before letting that one go. It didn't fit Onyema's profile.

She scrolled up and down the list, comparing names and manifests and schedules and flight plans until the buzz from the *siltyr* had been smothered by a single-minded haze of concentration. She kept returning to the *Solidarity*. It was registered to someone called Kai Ahmad, who appeared on every crew manifest as the Master. Also on every manifest were Chief Officer Tetsuo Niegos and Engineer Yuri Kibelstis. That, itself, was not necessarily odd. Their flights, though regularly timed, were never scheduled in advance. Also not terribly odd, so why did Mara feel that twinge of suspicion in her gut?

She sent the names to her employer, asking him to send her any records of those individuals owning a business on Argos, and sat back to take what felt like the first deep breath in an hour. The lines of the manifest list wavered in her vision on the wall as her eyes struggled to readjust after the close scrutiny. She closed them, letting the dark cut through the chatter in her head.

Now was more waiting.

She was starting to regret her abrupt departure from Antza and the bar.

She opened her eyes. While she couldn't access information this detailed from the port authority on her own, she could see what ships were listed as in port at any given time. She opened the main search page for the Argos Port Authority and ran a search for the *Solidarity* for the year prior to Onyema's disappearance.

Nothing. There was nothing.

Mara smiled. She had found her ship.

20

Back in her apartment, Jaya changed out of her service uniform and into civilian clothes. She splashed water on her face in the small bathroom, and then headed for the elevators.

When she arrived at the shop, it was late, and the sign read CLOSED. She raised a hand to knock, then lowered it, suddenly unsure. Why did she feel so entitled to barge in on his time? Surely he had things to do, and letting her use his store as her own personal practice studio was likely not high on his list. She turned away and headed back down the hall.

Behind her, the door opened.

"You're back already?" Luka called.

She turned around. He was leaning out the door of his shop, his dark hair falling to the side.

"Yeah, but I saw that you were closed, so I thought—"

He waved that away: "That sign is for paying customers, not friends." He flashed her a grin, the expression earnest and even hopeful. That smile washed the nerves out of her and she walked back toward him.

"Are you hungry?" he asked. "I was about to order dinner."

"Starving."

He closed the door behind them. "How do you feel about szacante fusion?"

"I'll eat anything," she replied. "But ask for extra hot sauce."

She played a few pieces on the piano as he placed the order on his palm drive and cleaned up the display case, relishing the stretch in her hands and the release in her heart. Here, surrounded by warm lighting and beautiful old furniture, playing with her entire body, the music familiar and joyful in her ears, she was able to cast off that uneasy feeling that was always with her. Here, she felt freedom like she had not in ages. As she transitioned into another piece, Luka came and stood beside the piano, touching the lid lightly, watching her hands dance across the keys. His closeness added a hum to her mind, and Jaya leaned into the music.

When the food arrived, they sat cross-legged on the floor and shared noodles made from a nutty grain and cooked in a sauce of hot peppers.

"I've never seen anyone play like you," Luka said. "It's like you've tuned into something invisible to the rest of us."

"A good piano is…" She stopped, searching for the words. "It's like it can read my mind. I'm not tuning into something else: *it* is. It knows my thoughts before I do, and it expresses them like I never could."

She met his eyes. He was already looking at her with that expression that seemed to read her like one of the books on the shelf behind him. The light from the antique lamps flickered, casting shadows on the strong lines of his face, reflecting from the waves of his hair like streaks of liquid gold. She looked back down at her dinner.

"Where did you learn how to play?" Luka asked.

"My mother taught me," Jaya said. "Her parents had a music school on New Sheffield before the narean cotton embargo crashed the economy. She played piano and violin, and she told me that selling their piano and closing their music school broke her heart. She was fourteen."

Luka watched her, his dark eyes soft with sympathy.

"But they weren't wealthy enough to get out when the economy crashed," Jaya continued. "So they used the money from the school to start a small farm. My uncles still run it, but it's much larger now."

"That's a story I've heard far too often," Luka said. "My parents worked in a manufacturing facility my whole childhood. We didn't lose everything, but we never had much to lose in the first place."

"Are your parents still working there?" Jaya asked.

Luka's eyes lit up with his smile. "I sent them enough money throughout the years that they were able to retire recently. Moved to a small garden planet—not one of those fancy ones, but it's enough."

"I didn't realize the antiques industry paid so well," Jaya teased.

"You'd be surprised how much money the Argos elite have to blow on rarities."

"Maybe not that surprised," Jaya laughed, thinking of Sal's fussing over fashion and his well-decorated apartment. And even with the restraint in Emory's decor, she knew how much he had likely spent to cultivate that air of refinement.

They ate in silence for a moment, the streets outside emptying slowly of people as the artificial twilight settled in.

"So you still haven't really told me how you learned to play," Luka said. "Since your mother had to sell her treasured piano."

Jaya took another bite before she answered.

"My father bought her a piano when they married," she said. "He had a good job, a government job, and he could afford things like that. We could afford things like that for a while when I was a kid. My mom wanted me to be able to go to a conservatory if I wanted to. To have the opportunity she lost."

"And then what happened?"

She met his gaze—his eyes were bright with interest and his smile quirked up to one side.

"There was an accident," she lied, looking back down at her food.

Silence. Luka was still, but she could hear him take a slow, deep breath. "I'm so sorry," he finally said.

"It was a long time ago," Jaya replied quickly. "My uncles raised me after that. I was happy with them, but we were poor. The kind of poor that left me with really just the one option, so I joined up. And here we are today."

He started to reach a hand out toward her, and then pulled it back. "I also enlisted when I was very young," he said. "It was the only way out."

"How long?"

"I honored my first contract," he said tersely. "And then I left."

The rest of the story hung in the air, its details opaque, but its basic form clearer than anything. Jaya reached her hand out now, to where his had retreated. He closed his fingers around hers.

"And look at you now," she said. "You made it out."

"I did." His hand tightened around her fingers, gentle but strong. "Would it be ridiculous if I said I hope the piano never sells?" His voice was hushed.

"I would be lying if I said I didn't hope the same thing," she replied.

They had inched closer, slowly, inexorably, as the evening wound on. The warmth of his body, the strength of his pulse—she could feel it drawing her even closer. His hair fell forward, slipping from behind his shoulder, and she wanted to reach out and tuck it back behind his ear for him.

Her palm drive alerted—the shrill sound broke her attention away, but Luka's eyes caught hers and she hesitated.

Another alert. Urgent. She glanced down: it was from Armstrong.

Report to conference room B immediately.

"I—" She found her voice somehow, despite the adrenaline flooding her brain. "I need to go."

But Luka's palm drive chimed at that moment, and when he looked down at it, all the warmth drained from his face.

Luka leapt up to his console and turned it on, projecting the contents into the air in front of them. It was mid-broadcast. A breaking news alert: *Massive biological attack on New Laredo. The Sons of Priam are claiming responsibility.*

"Shit," Jaya breathed.

A cold, hard pit formed in her stomach. Luka looked back at her, his expression dark. And then her palm drive chimed again. This message was from a sender identified by only a string of random numbers, and it read:

You are more than the Union's pawn. Join us.

Jaya's heart had not stopped racing when she arrived at HQ. The place still had a strange hush to it, but there was an electric energy now as intelligence officers bent their heads low over their consoles and ran from desk to desk, comparing pieces of news and analysis. Jaya moved briskly down the hall to the conference room. Armstrong, Reid, and Tully were already there, clustered in a corner of the room and speaking in low voices. They looked up when she arrived, and Armstrong waved her over.

"What's the status of blue squadron?" Armstrong asked.

"Lost contact about an hour ago," Reid replied. "Last we heard, they were on the ground in New Laredo and getting a lay of the land. No one inside yet."

Armstrong folded his arms tightly, and Tully swore.

"We should have been there." Tully's voice was harsh.

Armstrong flashed him an icy look that should have devastated any junior officer, but to Jaya's surprise, Reid also directed his frustration toward Armstrong.

"Timing was essential on this one," Reid said. "We were late getting into New Laredo and it cost us."

Armstrong considered the two of them, his blue eyes flickering back and forth between his superior officer and his second-in-command. He settled his shoulders back and lifted his chin, then uncrossed his arms calmly. "We don't know enough yet," he said.

Rhodes entered the room then, as stiff and straight as though he were in uniform reporting for a routine drill, though every member of the *Avalon*'s top-ranking officers had not wasted time on changing from their civilian clothing. Only Reid wore his service dress grays, his rank insignia proudly displayed. He had not been on leave when this attack occurred.

Armstrong waved Rhodes over as well, and he joined the circle, his hands clasped behind his back. Sal slid into a spot next to Jaya, his hair mussed and his eyes unfocused. For a moment Jaya thought he might be drunk, but then he looked at her and she realized it wasn't alcohol—it was shock. He looked down at his knees and shut his eyes tight.

She squeezed his hand under the table and he squeezed it back once, then let go and brought his hands to his hair, carefully restoring his rakish image of calm. He sighed, and his eyes were clear when he opened them again.

"The Sons of Priam have released another video," Reid announced when the entire company was assembled.

The video played, and the knot in Jaya's stomach wound tighter with each second. The throaty voice that unsettled her so much claimed this was a homegrown attack, nurtured by the Sons of Priam. As he spoke, Jaya closed her eyes to the images and focused on his voice. She heard for the first time a deep note of sentiment—even pain—in that voice. She opened her eyes again and the pictures flooded her vision: this damaged galaxy, still tearing itself apart even in a supposed time of peace.

Her throat was thick with tears when the video ended, and she swallowed hard.

"Chancellor Lavelle will issue a statement within an hour," Reid said, his voice quiet in the heavy stillness of the room. "Our priorities remain the same for the time being, but the threat alert has been raised to severe, and we expect all personnel at the ready."

Reid dismissed them, and Jaya rose slowly as the room began to empty around her. At the front of the room, Armstrong and Reid stood motionless, facing each other, their faces mirroring each other darkly.

———

There was a knock on Jaya's door the next afternoon. She looked up from where she was sitting on her bed, data pad open in front of her delivering updates on the situation on New Laredo. Sal poked his head in.

"You got a minute?" he asked.

"Sure," she said, patting the bed next to her until he took a seat. "What's up?"

"I ran a trace on the address those messages were sent from," he began.

Jaya's heart began to race. As much as she was focused on the tragedy on New Laredo, she had not been able to shake the message she had received the same night. It read to her like an invitation as much as a threat. It felt like the kind of promise Jaya did not want.

"What did you find?" she asked Sal.

"I was able to pinpoint it to a star cluster, but I couldn't get any more specific without using some protocols that would raise a few red flags with the higher-ups. I can dig deeper, but not without drawing attention."

"Thanks," she said. "This is enough. What cluster?"

"Canis Major," he said. "I couldn't get any closer than that. It looks like it's coming from a router in that system, but beyond that…"

"It could be any satellite, any station, even a ship passing through," she concluded.

"Exactly," he said.

She sighed. "Well, it's a start, at least."

"Anything else happen?"

She hesitated. "I got another one," she confessed. "At the same time news of the New Laredo attack broke."

"What did it say?"

"*Join us.*"

Sal's eyes went wide, and he gave a low whistle. "Well, shit. That's fucked up. We're going to find this person."

Jaya wished for his confidence, but couldn't feel it anywhere inside her. She shook her head, unable to express the strange way it made her twist up inside.

"And whoever it is," he added, "I feel sorry for them when we finally catch them."

She smiled. "Thanks, Sal. I just want to figure this out."

"Me, too."

"How are you doing?" she asked him.

He frowned. "I haven't slept since the attack. I'm trying to keep busy. Every minute I spend searching for them increases the chances that we can get in there and take them down."

She wanted to tell him to take care of himself. As a friend, she should tell him to rest and make sure he wasn't going to run himself into the ground. As a superior officer, she should be more concerned about the dark rings beneath his eyes. But Jaya hadn't been able to bring herself to leave base since the meeting. She had subsisted here on this one floor on protein bars and water and a constant stream of intelligence. So instead she just sighed and said,

"Me, too," and made him promise to eat before he got back to work.

He closed the door behind him when he left, and Jaya returned to her data pad. She logged into the encyclopedia and typed "Canis Major" into the search bar. When the results appeared, she clicked on the first link—a description of the system itself.

Canis Major, one of the nearest clusters to the Sol system, was one of the first to be explored by the fledgling Union Starfleet. It is a small cluster of stars, the most notable of which are Sirius A and B. The Sirius binary system has two planets, both of which are inhospitable to human life and poor candidates for terraforming. Plans to build an orbiting station to serve as the new capital of the United Human Nations in the Sirius system were abandoned when the much younger binary star system in the Ophiuchus cluster was discovered to be suitable for an orbiting station.

Since the 22nd century, numerous small stations have sprung up in the Sirius system and surrounding star systems. Most of these stations are small independent research hubs or fueling depots, and many used to serve as rest stops for galactic travelers. However, since the abandonment of Earth, traffic through Canis Major has abruptly decreased.

That was it. No colonies, no major stations. At least not ones that were known to The Union. Whoever contacted her could have just been passing through, but since all the messages had been routed through the same area, she doubted that.

She frowned. This was unhelpful at best, and frustrating at worst. She turned her data pad off with a discouraged sigh and left her room.

A short walk down the corridor led her to a small room with viewscreens providing the illusion of an overlook onto the Forum. The room was a sort of lounge, with chairs and small tables—a good, quiet place to think. When the doors opened, she realized she had not been the only one with this idea. Armstrong stood at one of the screens, his hands clasped behind his back.

He looked behind him when the doors opened.

"Jaya," he said, his face softening into a smile. He waved her over and she joined him, standing by his side and mirroring his relaxed stance.

"Everything looks so normal down there," he observed. "Life goes on."

"Does it ever change?" she asked. "Does anything shake us out of our routines?"

He gave her a sideways glance. "I think they're shaken more than it would appear. But what can they do, other than just continue to go on with their lives and hope that they aren't next?"

It was a chilling thought—Jaya didn't want to consider it too hard.

"Everything okay?" he asked when she had been silent a moment.

"I've had a lot on my mind lately," she confessed.

"Who hasn't?"

She just shook her head in response, and he looked back at the screens.

"I've been looking into Augustus," she blurted.

Armstrong turned to look at her, an eyebrow arched in interest.

"I haven't found anything definitive yet," she said quickly. "But I have a hunch. I don't think he's the architect."

"A figurehead?" Armstrong asked.

"Yes," she said. "It all feels manufactured. Like we're meant to be looking at him, because he's exactly the man to deliver someone else's message."

"Pay no attention to the man behind the curtain." Armstrong's voice was thoughtful. "That's an interesting theory."

He looked over at her, his blue eyes calm.

"I heard Richard Emory requested a meeting with you," he said. "He's expressed interest in hiring you."

Jaya flushed. "I haven't had any time to think about it," she said. "I never considered leaving."

"But now?"

She shook her head. "Right now, I can't imagine it. But he gave me some things to think about. About how I can make the biggest difference."

"I find it hard to believe you would ever rest on your laurels," Armstrong said. "Wherever you are, you will be working hard. And I have no doubt you will leave your mark. Whatever you choose."

They remained there a while, the peace of the quiet room soothing them, and the motion of the far-below people in the Forum mesmerizing them.

Finally, Armstrong shifted, unclasping his hands. "I should go. And you probably should, too. We need to continue in our routines as well, if we are to have any chance of catching up to the Sons of Priam."

"I will," she said. "I'm just going to stay here a little longer."

"Alright," he said, his expression softening.

When the doors closed behind him, Jaya was left with thoughts that moved like the people below—streams that broke off and reconnected in chaotic whirls. But somewhere behind all that chaos, there was a pattern. She just had to hope she could coax it out.

21

They had assigned Tynan a small guest suite in the Diplomatic Level of Argos while they were on the station, and their instructions were clear enough. He was not to leave the base headquarters for any reason. For his own safety, of course.

Which, in theory, was not a problem. The headquarters had a commissary, medical facilities, a fitness center, entertainment stations, plenty of common areas, and was always bustling with activity. They had even given him a small temporary desk in one of the forensics laboratories.

In practice, the attack on New Laredo injected a layer of panic into the employees on the base, and that frantic pace and laser focus on the problem left Tynan with nothing to do, and worse—no way to be helpful. There was nothing yet to analyze from New Laredo, and he doubted he would be given the opportunity to participate in those analyses without Armstrong personally stepping in.

So when Jaya appeared in the doorway of the laboratory, craning her neck to search the room for his little desk, Tynan felt a rush of joy and gratitude for the familiar face and the promise of activity. He stood and attracted her attention, waving her over to his desk.

"How can I help you, Lieutenant Commander Mill?"

He hoped his smile was appropriate. Despite his rising anxiety at his current lack of purpose, he still feared making a social misstep with the humans.

Jaya smiled as she sat across from him, and the tension in his neck eased a little.

"I've been thinking a lot lately," she began, leaning forward and resting her forearms on the desk. "About this group we're chasing. They're coordinated—much more coordinated than they should be, based on all models of similar groups that have come before them. I know it's a long shot, but you talked to one of them, so it's possible you might have seen or heard something that could help. Do you mind if I ask you a few questions?"

Tynan's mind went blank. "I'm not sure what I could possibly help with. I've already told you everything I could about my research and its implications."

She waved that off. "These aren't research questions. These are questions about your interactions with these people. I understand you met with the person who bought out your board?"

Tynan swallowed, wetting his dry throat. "I'm not very good at describing... well... I mean to say..."

He couldn't bring himself to voice the words: *I have a hard time telling humans apart.* But Jaya continued to smile kindly at him, and so he cleared his throat.

"I'll answer whatever I can," he said.

"Thank you," she replied. "Did the person who met with you make any reference to partners? Or to some hierarchy in his organization?"

Tynan closed his eyes—he brought the scene to his mind. The man in his office, the passion that seemed to radiate off of him. He was powerful. He had an aura of restrained anger. Tynan didn't recall if he'd mentioned anyone else. He opened his eyes.

"I'm sorry," he stammered. "I don't think so. At least, I don't remember. He did say 'we' a lot. 'We are interested in your work,' 'we think your work is worth a great deal,' but he didn't say who the others were."

The frown that came across her face at his words was one he was beginning to understand as *concentration* or perhaps *frustration*. The two were difficult for him to distinguish.

"Okay," she said, drawing the word out. "What about references to the future? Plans for the work, or any hints of it?"

Tynan shook his head. "I'm sorry. I didn't take him very seriously. I found him to be arrogant and I'm afraid I dismissed him out of hand because of that. I didn't expect him to succeed. I certainly didn't expect him to be powerful enough to try to kill both of us. Nareian mercenaries are expensive."

Jaya's eyes widened suddenly. "We thought the nareians at your location were black ops," she said. "Who is this other person? Did they survive?"

"I don't know," Tynan said. "I mean, I know who she is. I don't know if she survived. She showed up after I lost my work. She said she was an investor of some sort, and seemed to have some personal history with the man who bought me out. She was trying to help me —or so I thought. She called me the night—well, the night you rescued me—and said she was being attacked. That he had sent someone, and I needed to run."

"She knew him? Personally?" Jaya was leaning farther forward now, her eyes bright. "Did she ever say a name?"

"No." Tynan wanted to melt in embarrassment. This whole time he had been so focused on getting his work back that he hadn't even tried to learn more about the people involved. He hadn't thought beyond the research, not even for a minute.

Jaya let out a heavy breath. "What about *her* name? Do you know that?"

"Indigo Onyema," Tynan offered, thankful to finally have a question he could answer well. "Her name was Indigo Onyema."

Jaya was nodding. "I'm familiar with Onyema," she said. "Used to be IRC like us. Retired and went on to invest in military tech firms. Did she say anything about this man that might help us identify him?"

"She said he wasn't the kind of person who gives up. She said he tries again."

"Anything else?"

Tynan squeezed his eyes shut again, willing himself to recall details of their conversations. The memories were hazy, the moments of sharp focus always centering around the matter of getting his work back. He cursed his short-sightedness.

"She said she'd been watching him. Watching his work. She said he had a very different philosophy, and she didn't trust him to be a good leader." *Oh!* He opened his eyes. "She said she used to work with him."

He smiled, pleased with himself.

Jaya returned the smile, the corners of her eyes creasing. "I can work with that."

"Glad to help," he replied. "Is there anything else I can do? I'm itching to get my hands on some real work." He nearly choked on the last word, realizing as he spoke it that he had just insinuated that their conversation—clearly important work for her—was not *real work.*

But she didn't seem offended. Instead, she narrowed her eyes, looking slightly away from him. Narrowed eyes usually meant anger, but she seemed instead focused on something inside her own mind. Tynan realized with a thrill that he recognized the expression —it translated to something he felt often. That bolt of realization. The sudden shift in focus to a new theory, a new idea.

"Actually," she said, and his heart jumped. "I do have something you could analyze. Our people have already looked at it, but with your experience..." She trailed off. "We encountered something strange on our last mission before we picked you up. It was a compound run by the Sons of Priam. We captured the person we think was in charge of that branch of the organization and we were ready to bring him back here with us for interrogation when he died."

"Shot?" Tynan asked.

"No," Jaya said, shaking her head. "Just dropped dead. No warning. Autopsy suggested a heart attack, and I don't doubt the ability of our doctors…"

"But you think I might see something they missed."

"Your research probes a very dangerous neurological disease," she said with a shrug. "And the Sons of Priam are interested in it. We have no idea what they're capable of, but their work apparently overlaps with yours somehow, or at least they want it to. Maybe you'll see something we didn't know to look for."

"The virus I study isn't known to cause heart attacks," Tynan replied. "But sure. I would be happy to look into it. I'm not a medical doctor, and even if I were, I have no experience with human anatomy…"

"I'm not looking for a diagnosis," she said. "I'm just looking for evidence of anything unusual."

A complication arose immediately: the body had been taken for disposal.

Under normal circumstances, the family of the dead man would have been identified and his remains returned to them to put to rest. But these were not normal circumstances, the technician explained to him, and while the man had indeed been identified, his family had instead been brought in for questioning and the body disposed of. For security reasons.

Tynan struggled to keep his composure as he explained to the technician that his work was essential to the activities of the *Avalon*'s company and their search for any leads on the Sons of Priam. The technician kept her focus on her console screen throughout the entire conversation, barely acknowledging Tynan's physical presence in front of her, let alone his status as a contributing member of the *Avalon*'s team. Let alone his reputation as a leader in the scientific field.

It was finally when he invoked the name of Peter Armstrong that she let out a long-suffering sigh and brought him to the storage compartment where they kept the samples they had taken during the autopsy. The detailed autopsy report—unredacted, after Tynan's emphatic and repeated insistence—was sent to his palm drive.

Min was already performing a thorough analysis of the report as Tynan made his way back down the hallway, clutching the small metal case containing the samples to his chest as though someone might try to take it from him.

He knew his reaction was extreme. He knew this was a small task he had been given, and his grasping at it as though it were his last chance to redeem his career was utterly absurd. Fortunately, only Min was around to witness his desperation, and she clucked at him over their private connection to remember his breathing.

And so he settled at his desk—counting his breaths in and breaths out—nestled the metal case into an open space on his desk where he could see it, and began to read the autopsy report.

The system the humans used to notate their report was foreign to him. His reading was interrupted by his own questions, and although Min answered them as fast as they left his lips, he began to grow frustrated.

It was like starting over. Normally, he would relish the chance to learn something new. But this felt less like a welcome challenge and more like a rude and abrupt rewriting of the rules. The science was the same, but it was all in a language he didn't speak. He didn't ask for this.

"Tynan," Min interjected before he had time to form his next question about standard hormone levels in the human body and their half-lives. Tynan startled, the question evaporating in his mind. Min took his silence for acknowledgement and continued.

"There's some news," she said. "Before we left Dresha, you had me watching for news of Kujei Oszca. Publications, grant awards, public events."

She paused, and Tynan considered this. He had watched Kujei's career closely, his rival's every step an important motivator. He almost laughed now at the bitter truth that it no longer mattered what Kujei did—at least not to Tynan's career. He had been knocked out of the unfortunate orbit around his former mentor's life.

And still, a nameless emotion tugged at his interest.

"Yes," Tynan replied. "Is there something interesting?"

"He has been named the replacement to Science Minister Harta."

If his mentor's pull had truly been nullified by this drastic change in Tynan's circumstances, why did it feel like the floor had just dropped out from beneath him?

Tynan examined this unusual blankness in his mind. His thoughts grasped around, trying to connect and form a full thesis from the fragments that swirled in him. He drew in a ragged breath, and still found nothing to hold on to.

"This news distressed you," Min commented.

Tynan didn't reply. Min's constant, steady presence had always comforted him in times of stress, but there were moments in his life when—despite her detailed knowledge of his vitals—the gulf between them felt infinite. How could he possibly make her understand right now that moderating his breathing would not be enough to wipe away this sick feeling? Life was full of one-way streets and points of no return, but how was an AI to comprehend the way it felt to know that something was irretrievably lost? That time would move forward, life would continue, without the possibility of righting itself?

"I'm going to take a walk," he announced, as if anyone in this part of the galaxy cared.

No one replied, and he left the laboratory in silence.

The corridors of the naval headquarters swarmed with a hushed excitement. Since the attack on New Laredo, the energy of the entire place had ratcheted up, but without an increase in volume. The military officials wrapped themselves tightly in their secrets, whispering news to each other. Tynan watched the whole thing from the outside, never included.

Even when the humans were attacked by their own kind, they still treated him like the enemy. Or maybe *enemy* was too strong a word. Suspicious outsider. Stranger. Alien.

He had been standing at the window that overlooked the Forum for a long time before he even noticed he had stopped walking. The people moved below, an ecosystem of their own, as he watched. His entire life had been driven by goals and purpose. Plans he had crafted for himself, their endless possibilities spooling out in front of him, providing directions he could choose to pursue. He had never felt so unmoored, shaken loose from his path but given no freedom to move to a new one. He had lost the trail of opportunities, lost even its scent.

At least when his parents died, he'd had his studies to throw himself into. He had directed himself toward something productive, found a way to channel his grief. And now he had nowhere to point himself and too much time on his hands.

Movement at the door behind him caught his attention. It was the tall and lanky lieutenant whose dry expressions left Tynan confused every time he spoke. Salman Azima. He pushed curly dark hair out of his eyes as he leaned against the door frame.

"Hard at work?" Sal asked.

There was that flat expression again. A face that said both *I am very serious right now* and also *I am joking.* Tynan turned away in anger. If they were going to ignore him, why couldn't they at least be consistent about it? Why leave him to his own devices until he wanted quiet and then come trying to make small talk? Humans made no sense.

But Sal didn't leave. He waited. Tynan felt his keen eyes like a heat on his neck. He shrugged his shoulders, as if he could roll the feeling away.

"You're a pretty big fucking deal back home, huh?" Sal finally said.

Not anymore.

"I was," Tynan said curtly. Min flickered into view at his side, her posture defensive.

Sal shifted, and there was another moment of silence.

"I know it doesn't seem like it," he said, "but we need you. These people are not your garden-variety megalomaniacs; at least, they're not following the usual script. We're trying to connect wires here that we've never even seen before, and you're coming at it from a completely different perspective. You might be able to see things we don't."

Tynan turned around, meeting his canny gaze with one of his own. "I have no idea who these people are or what they are doing. How am I supposed to help?"

Sal shrugged, the movement light. He moved closer to Tynan, looked out the window at the station below.

"I wish I had the answer for you, doc," he said. "But this is how it works in our world. Sometimes we have to move forward in the dark. And it's easy to feel like you're being left behind when this happens. But the fact is, everyone is just as clueless."

Tynan thought about Kujei. His former mentor at the apex of his career, looking down over his lifetime of achievements the way Tynan and Sal now looked over the commerce of the Forum. He turned the lieutenant's words over in his head, considering his own position in this new light.

He wished the new perspective was a bright one. But it just made him feel worse, because now he couldn't cast his confusion and frustration as his own struggle. He had to accept that everyone else was suffering as much as he was.

When he looked back at Sal, the human was still watching him.

"What's that game you play all the time?"

Tynan hesitated at the abrupt change of subject. "It's a strategy game. It's called Sequence."

"Ever played poker?"

Tynan made a face. "I've seen it played in movies. I wouldn't like it. I'm terrible at bluffing."

Sal laughed. "You'd be good in this group. Humans can't read you, at least not yet. You're doing yourself a disservice not taking advantage. Plus, it's really about statistics. I think you'd do better than you think."

Despite himself, Tynan smiled.

"Got some time?" Sal said. "I'll teach you. I'd love to see the look on Thompson's face when you take his money."

22

In the midst of the chaos and panic brought by the news of the New Laredo attack, the *Solidarity* filed a new flight plan. It had been a few days since Mara had discovered this anomalous ship, and she had been closely watching for any moves from its mysterious crew. Her employer's search of the three crew members had also turned up no records aside from travel on this ship—no businesses, no residences. Aside from the required birth certificates and Union citizenship registration, these individuals had left no footprints behind them.

That was alright with Mara. She didn't need to know where they had been before if she could track them now.

She didn't trust the flight plan they had filed to tell her their true destination, but it gave her their schedule. She filed a similar flight plan for the *Nasdenika*, ready to abandon it and follow the *Solidarity* wherever it went.

On the afternoon that the *Solidarity* was scheduled to depart Argos, Mara secured her various tools and weapons to her belt and headed straight for the port. The lazy mid-afternoon foot traffic steadily increased to a throng of people as she approached. She fingered the small, round device that she had purchased from the

Fox and considered her options. She glanced up at a narrow stair-
case that lead to the viewing deck, where people congregated to
watch the ships come in. Up the stairs, then.

She found the viewing deck for the appropriate wing and sidled
her way in to face the thick glass of the window. Below, she identified a small, well-worn ship with the name *Solidarity* stenciled on
the side in bright blue lettering. A man was standing at the cargo
bay door, tall with short black hair and gray eyes. He had shrugged
his jumpsuit off his shoulders and it hung loose around his waist,
and he waved his powerful arms as he shouted something at the two
remaining crew members.

One of them, a woman whose pale features gave her a ghost-like
quality, turned around to shout something back at him. The other
shook shoulder-length dark hair out of his face as he hefted a box up
the cargo bay ramp. He handed the box to the shouting man, who
took it and turned back into the ship. The long-haired man turned
around then, an easy smile on his face as he called back to the
woman, and Mara felt a jolt of recognition.

She had met this man just a few days ago. The man who had
been visiting the Fox. Who had watched the Fox sell Mara all the
technological assistance she now had at her disposal.

This complicated matters. Mara had been relying on the equipment the Fox had sold her to help her hack into the *Solidarity*'s
computers and detect their course as they shifted into FTL travel.
This would allow her to follow them to wherever it was they were
hiding Onyema. But now, she had to assume that they would be
equipped with the same technology she was, and that they would
have the capability to block her hack or—worse—detect it and turn
on her.

Mara needed a new plan, and fast. The port agents would be
coming by to do their usual inspection of cargo-carrying ships that
left Argos, and then the *Solidarity* would be gone, beyond her reach.
Their previous excursions had never been longer than a day or two,

so she could probably count on this trip lasting around the same amount of time. That meant they couldn't be going far. But she didn't know when the next opportunity would arise.

She hurried down the stairs and went to the security checkpoint. The Port Authority officer glanced lazily at her expertly forged identification and her filed flight plan, then waved her through. Once inside the *Nasdenika,* Mara snatched some nutrition bars and a few bulbs of water from the emergency stores and stashed them in a light satchel, which she slung across her body.

She already knew she had to keep the *Solidarity* and its crew close. It would just be much closer than she was expecting.

She reached down and triggered the cloaking device, then slipped quietly off her ship and into the crowds. As she walked, she dodged carefully around the travelers heading to and from ships. When she arrived at the dock where the *Solidarity* was awaiting clearance to depart, she pulled herself silently up to perch atop a storage container a few docks down and watch.

Two inspectors were there, speaking with the three crew members. One of them stepped inside the cargo area while the other looked over the manifest. They shouted back and forth a few times. Once they were finished with the inspection, there would be a brief moment of paperwork and signatures before the *Solidarity* was cleared to leave. That was her only opportunity. She ran through her options.

Every ship had various external panels, equipped with sensors to assist the navigator. These panels sometimes needed to be serviced while out in space, and beneath them were narrow crawl spaces that led to the engine and other internal utilities. There was an airlock on the hull near the panels to allow access for repairs. That was where she would have to make her entrance.

She dropped down from the crate and made her way gingerly through the crowd until she was only a few meters from the ship. She could hear the conversation now between the inspectors and the three crew members. The Fox's friend was clearly in charge—he must be the one whose false documents named him as Kai Ahmad —but the other two stayed close to him. The second inspector came out of the cargo bay then and called over: "Everything checks out."

"Great," the other inspector said, and turned his body so that Ahmad could read over some required legal boilerplate before getting clearance to leave.

Mara slipped quietly around to the back of the ship then, tossing a magnetic grappling hook up to the rounded top of the ship. A strong wire connected from the magnet to her belt pulled her up. She removed the hook from the external panels and went toward the airlock nestled among them.

Mara pulled out her tools, quickly and cleanly opening the airlock panel. Once inside, she wound her way through the crawl spaces until she was down on the engineering level of the *Solidarity.* She found herself inside a ventilation duct for the engine, which already hummed in preparation for the trip, giving off waves of heat like the sand on Uduak. Here, in the hot, loud, and cramped vents near the engine, she would be protected from their heat sensors and their physical senses. It was unpleasant, but she was fairly certain it would be a short trip.

She turned the cloaking device off, now that she was securely hidden within the ship. The sounds of the cargo bay hatch closing and shoes clomping on the floor near her announced the imminent departure, and shortly after she felt the inertia of the ship severing its connection to the dock and passing through the atmospheric force field.

There was no turning back now.

Mara had first sensed them about an hour ago. It was the way they kept to the shadows that had struck her nerves. She couldn't know for sure who it was, but in her line of work she couldn't take risks either. She ducked into an alleyway and ran.

The shadows of steel crossbeams flickered as she lowered her shoulders, keeping her body close to the ground, picking up speed. Someone was still following her—she could hear the soft thud of boots on the metal flooring. The sound was muffled, camouflaged. Probably stealth-equipped gear, which made the hair on her nape rise up all the more. She dropped to quadrupedal posture and pushed herself to move faster, all four limbs propelling her ahead, weaving in and out of alleyways and air ducts, the secret world hidden within the station.

If her pursuer were not nareian, this would give her the speed advantage she needed to shake the tail. If it was another nareian... well, she would worry about that if she started to lose ground.

The artificial atmosphere of the space station was dry and thin, the air rushing across her face as she ran. She breathed deeply, absorbing the stale air; it was lower in oxygen than that of her native home. By now, her body was used to adapting to the sudden changes in conditions that came with the life of a bounty hunter, but in moments like these, her lungs longed for the rich air of Narei.

And then, suddenly, the sounds of her pursuer were gone, evaporated from the dry air like dust carried away on a summer wind. She dared not slow too much, but the more ground she gained, the more she was certain of the emptiness behind her.

She slowed. Still she heard nothing.

She drew her gun, rising up on two legs, her hands steady as she waited. Still silence.

Finally, she holstered her weapon, smoothing the sleeves of her jacket down her arms as she returned to the corner of the station she and Tai had been calling home for the past week.

As she walked, stealing through the shadowy neighborhoods and avoiding the central passages of the station, she was already formulating a plan. They would have to leave, immediately. This job was making her uneasy. If she had been discovered and tailed, they would have to move and regroup. She couldn't afford to be caught.

Her anxiety grew as she slipped into the alleyway leading to the cramped and dank apartment they were renting. Its proximity to the humid, noisy life support machinery of the station made it cheap and unpopular and perfect for two headhunters who wanted to remain unnoticed.

The alley was busier than usual; a crowd gathered halfway down the long corridor. The pit in her gut leapt up into her throat, her skin tingling as she picked up her pace.

She ran as fast as she could on two legs, tearing through the crowd with the strength she had built up in twenty years of hard, violent work. As she pushed aside human, szacante, and nareian alike, full-blown nausea erupted at the sight of the open door and thick, sticky purple blood pooling just outside.

Mara woke with a jolt, bathed in the heat still rolling off the *Solidarity's* engine. She was soaked in her own sweat, and how much of that was from the nightmare and how much from the engine's waste heat she couldn't distinguish. She took a long drag from a bulb and unwrapped a nutrition bar.

She ate the chalky bar slowly, her attention on the stretch in her jaw and the bland flavor on her tongue until her heartbeat finally slowed to a normal rhythm. She wondered sometimes: if she had known exactly how ruthless her family and their rivals would be in hunting their favorite pawn down, would she have left the way she did? Then again, it was exactly their ruthless control over her life that had driven her to take the fucking desperate measures she had.

She marveled sometimes that her mother still wanted her back, after what she had become. It would be better for everyone if they just pretended she didn't exist. But choosing the right path wasn't the Empress's way—she needed to win. And, Mara mused, she probably believed that she could tame Mara again. That, after all these years away, she could grind her down into the perfect little figurehead. A flawless carving of nareian ideals, devoid of her own will or spirit.

Or perhaps it wasn't a figurehead she wanted, but simply to remove the threat that her Hydean rival might be able to use Mara against her.

Mara could live with the things she had done in the pursuit of her own freedom. But she wondered sometimes if she could live with what they would do in the name of getting her back.

23

Jaya woke in the middle of the artificial night to an urgent series of pings on her palm drive. She answered the call groggily.

"Sal, is this payback for getting you up so early the other day?"

"I found them," Sal replied. The giddiness in his voice was barely contained.

"Who?" Jaya asked, sitting abruptly and pulling on her uniform as fast as she could. She checked the time—barely after midnight—but the adrenaline was already kicking in, dragging her up from deep sleep to a sort of humming alertness. Had Sal really tracked the Sons of Priam from that tiny kernel of information the szacante doctor had produced? Or had he found more information about those strange messages she was receiving? A sudden twang of tension ran down her back, as though someone had plucked her spinal column like a string instrument.

"The shipments," Sal said. "That compound the doctor told us about. Someone bought some about a week ago. It was scheduled to be delivered to Collin's Rock, but the shipment was rerouted."

"Where is it going now?"

"Are we calling in the boss man, or what?" Sal asked.

"Of course we are," Jaya said. "He'll want to be woken up for this. Meet us in conference room A in half an hour."

"Yes, Lieutenant Commander," Sal said, his mocking only half sincere. "I don't want to speak too soon, but I think we've got these bastards."

"I really hope you're right."

Armstrong's face was haggard as he and Tully entered the conference room thirty minutes later, but when Jaya, Rhodes, and Sal snapped to attention, he returned their salute as crisply as any recent Naval Academy graduate. They took their seats around the conference table, and Armstrong rubbed his eyes wearily.

"What do you have, Lieutenant Azima?" Armstrong asked.

"I followed the tip Doctor Vasuda gave us and wrote an algorithm to mine all records of purchases from the few dozen manufacturers of the compound used in this research. After eliminating any known and reputable purchasers from the base, I was left with only a handful. I then cross-referenced those purchasers with the galactic transit database. Obviously, not all transit is included in this database. Besides the covert military travel, there are always tiny rock hoppers that never make it onto the radar because they avoid ever coming into contact with ports at major transit hubs. But these purchases all came from large industrial colonies, so they would have to leave a trail somewhere."

"Understood, Lieutenant." Armstrong's tone was long-suffering. "Was this cross-referencing fruitful?"

"It was," Sal replied, his feet practically tapping under the table in anticipation. "Most of the remaining purchases I tracked to small start-up biotech companies. They're all worth a second look, in my opinion, since the Sons of Priam seem to be trying to hide their business behind a facade of legitimate commerce. But one of the trails went cold, and that one I think is most interesting."

Some of the heaviness lifted from Armstrong's face, and his blue eyes grew more alert. "Where did you lose the trail?" he asked.

Sal grinned. "I didn't lose it."

He brought up a holographic projection from his data pad. It was a star map, with the route of a small transport freighter tracing a red line through space from a small industrial moon to another small industrial moon.

"They filed a flight plan to Bridgeport, due to arrive yesterday at seven hundred local time. And they did arrive there yesterday"—Sal paused—"at thirteen hundred local time. Their official log— confirmed by local inspection—shows that their cargo was steel alloys for construction, due to be transferred to another ship to be delivered to its final destination on Leander. There was no record or evidence of any biological compounds aboard the ship."

"So where did they go in those missing six hours?" Armstrong was sitting fully forward in his seat now, the fatigue draining from his eyes as the information was revealed.

"That's what I was asking myself," Sal said. He tapped his data pad again, and a new map appeared. It traced out a translucent bubble showing where the ship could have modified its course. "This shows the range they could have traveled within that six-hour window. Now, there is almost nothing in this area. In fact, most people would argue that there is *absolutely* nothing in here. There are no inhabited planets, no registered space stations, not even any asteroids large enough to land on. But there is this."

Sal zoomed the map in, revealing a planetless red dwarf star in the Cygnus arm so insignificant that none of the major galactic governments had even given it a name. It was simply listed in the Union Astronomical Organization's star catalog with an alphanumeric code.

"I'm not sure what we're supposed to be seeing," Tully said. "That system is empty."

"Exactly," Sal said. "Why would anyone look here?"

Armstrong gave him a glance that said he was running short on patience.

"I tracked shipments along routes that passed somewhere near this red dwarf," Sal explained, "going back for the last three years. I flagged anything with a late arrival time, and I checked their cargo logs before departure against their arrival logs. Things have been going missing on this route. First it was metal alloys, prefabbed beams, and glass sheeting. Then air filters, water filters, heating and cooling elements. No one ever complained about these missing shipments."

"It's like they were getting to their destination—that destination just wasn't on any logs," Rhodes said, starting to put together the pieces of the narrative Sal was weaving.

"Yes," Sal said, pointing triumphantly at no one in particular. "I think this system is the most likely destination for the compound. And more than that, I think they're building something here."

"A station?" Armstrong asked.

Sal shrugged. "It's hard to tell exactly what it is. An orbital ship-yard, a small station, some other structure we haven't thought of. But they're building *something.*"

"We should move fast," Rhodes said. "They'll assume we're stretched thin now dealing with the aftermath of New Laredo. And they have no reason to think we know of this location."

"We have the advantage," Armstrong agreed. "I'll get it approved. Prepare to leave Argos this morning."

Nearly twenty hours after the *Avalon* left Argos, they dropped out of FTL into the darkness of a barren patch of space.

Jaya stood on the bridge, watching the approach. They had prepared a boarding force with the knowledge that whatever they found at this red dwarf, they needed to be prepared to act quickly, while they still had the element of surprise. At first, their ultimate destination was unclear. The red dwarf in front of them was dark—

most of its light was emitted as infrared waves, and its orange-red visible hues were weak. It was eerie there, a pulsing sphere of radiation against the black of space.

Then, the faint glint of that red light reflected on metal. A space station on the near side of the star, nearly invisible.

They kept their distance. Jaya looked over at Armstrong.

"Good luck down there, Commander," Armstrong said.

"Thank you, Captain," Jaya replied, standing at attention and raising her hand in salute.

Armstrong returned the gesture, releasing her to her mission.

She headed down to the shuttle bay, where her team and Rhodes's team awaited her.

They left the *Avalon*, the shuttle bringing them quickly and quietly in toward the station, heat shields on to mask their approach from the sensors. The station loomed in front of them, and the shuttle eased in close to the side. Lupo piloted them to a smooth, windowless section of the underside of the station. She brought them in, carefully floating the shuttle alongside the station until they could activate the vacuum seal.

A short rushing sound confirmed that they had soft seal on the station. Jaya opened the shuttle's ventral doors, revealing the smooth sheet metal of the station's hull on the other side. Thompson handed her a targeted particle-beam torch, and she crouched down in front of the door.

She knew what to expect on the other side.

"Cover me," she told her team.

Her team readied their weapons and she burned through the hull, the torch slicing into the thick metal smoothly. She burned a large circle and pushed it through, ducking below the low edge. The immediate pulse above her head told her the guards were taken care of, and when they fell silent, she stood. Four bodies sprawled on the floor of the hallway they had just opened up.

She motioned her team inside. A small contingent remained to guard the shuttle. They split into their two teams: Rhodes leading Bravo team to gather intel, and Jaya leading Alpha team to the most likely location of the Combat Information Center.

It wasn't long before the quiet ended. As they were about to round a corner, Jaya's palm drive picked up heat signatures ahead, and she heard the strum of footfalls on the floors.

"Incoming," she whispered into the comms.

Jaya and the members of Alpha team ducked into a side corridor, out of view of the incoming troops. The soldiers passed by without noticing them, and when it was safe again, Jaya crept out from her position.

"Rhodes, you have a dozen armored Sons heading your way. Try to get out of their path."

"Roger," he said quietly over their shared channel.

Jaya signaled to her team to continue down the corridor the way they had been going. They were moving inwards and upwards, headed toward the most common location of the "brains" in a station like this. With no inside man to give them the layout, it was the best guess.

Up ahead, a control panel blinked red on the closed containment doors blocking their way.

Jaya nodded to Sal, who opened the control panel and began to hack into it. He plugged his data pad into the door, and his fingers flew over the screen, reacting to the system, beating its security protocols.

"There," he said, after what felt like a lifetime in the cold silence. "We're in."

As he said this, the doors parted, sliding on their mechanical frame. The corridor inside was dark, lit only by dim emergency lighting. The team crouched and filed in, staying low to the ground.

"This doesn't seem right," Jaya said to Sal over a private channel. "It's too quiet."

"I know," Sal replied. "This place is giving me the creeps."

"Me too."

Jaya opened the first door to another darkened room. Sal fiddled with the control panel until the lights came on, illuminating a long, white room. High ceilings towered over them. Cells lined a wall; they were large, and the glass that enclosed them was thicker than Jaya's fist. Most likely fortified, shatter proof, and shielded against particle beam fire.

The team immediately fanned out to search the room. The sound of their boots tapping softly on the ground sounded strange in the empty space. Jaya looked around, too, trying to understand the thick glass cages, the scoured and sanitized white floors and walls. She had no idea what it was, but perhaps the scientist would recognize something.

She called up the *Avalon* on her comm link.

"I need Vasuda," she said. "We found something. Looks like a lab of some sort."

Tynan hopped on the line, and she connected him to her video feed again, allowing him to view the room.

"That is most definitely a laboratory," he said. "Do you see any equipment? Pipets? Petri dishes? Solvents?"

"Yes," she replied, opening a cabinet door for him to see. "Anything in particular we should be looking for?"

"I don't know," he said. "Take video of everything. It could all be relevant. Without any experiments in progress, I can't confirm..."

"But do you have a hunch?" Jaya asked.

The doctor made what she could only assume was a sound of annoyance. "I prefer not to go by hunches, Lieutenant Commander Mill. I prefer to use sound evidence and logic to come to my conclusions."

"Humor me," she said. "What evidence do you see here, and what sorts of hunches might it support?"

He sighed. "Well, the cells are the first thing I see. The glass is thick, is it not?"

"Very," Jaya confirmed.

"And they're quite large. They have working spaces within them."

They did. Counters, cabinets, and some sort of closed-off space on top of a counter with another glass door.

"They seem to be small quarantined areas," he continued. "The kind that would be needed for working with sensitive materials and infectious diseases. Or for studying creatures with poor immune systems."

She nodded. She didn't like the sound of that, but it made sense to her.

"And the equipment," the doctor continued. "The lab is clearly not ready yet for whatever project they are conducting, which makes it more difficult to come to a conclusion, but it is clearly a biological laboratory rather than a mechanical one. The micro pipettes, the refrigerators, the petri dishes for cell cultures. They are studying biological specimens, not building weapons."

"Are the two mutually exclusive?" Jaya asked.

There was a pause, and then the doctor replied: "A good point. It seems whatever they were doing, they intended to scale it up fast."

"My thoughts exactly."

"Take video evidence of everything you see. Perhaps I can come to a more sound conclusion then."

"Thanks for your input, doc," Jaya said. "I uploaded that video footage so we can keep it in our files."

"That will be most helpful," Tynan said.

She severed the comm link. "Alright, Alpha team. Let's get all the evidence on vid, and if you see anything that can be sampled, bag and tag it. I get the feeling the doctor is nervous about whatever this place is for, and if he's nervous, we should all be nervous."

"And we've got a deadline, now," Sal said. He had been

searching through one of the consoles, and he turned the screen for Jaya to see.

He had hacked into the security feeds for the station, and it seemed that guards had been alerted to their presence. Video from various areas of the ship showed armed figures moving with purpose down the hallways. A quick glance at the cameras' locations, and Jaya realized they were already close.

"Shit," she muttered. "Okay team, make that double time."

Sal hunched over as he rapidly transferred as much data as he could to his palm drive, seeking out specific drives with some intuition that Jaya could not understand, but seemed clear as starlight to him.

"Bravo team, shuttle team," Jaya called over the comm. "They know we're here. They seem to be headed to us, but we should rendezvous ASAP."

"Roger," Rhodes replied. "No sign of them here yet, but we'll start moving back to the shuttle."

Jaya's team pulled together what evidence they could while Sal retrieved encrypted data files from the console. As quickly as they could, they were out the door and heading back down the hallway.

Jaya opened a private channel to Sal. "Did you get anything interesting?"

Sal replied immediately: "Not sure, but I did insert a virus, which should corrupt their drives. So if we're lucky, we just cost them some valuable information."

"Nice work."

"I know."

The halls remained far too empty. Jaya's unease grew with every deserted corridor they passed. The unit they had seen on the security feeds should have been here by now. She started to have the disturbing sense that the element of surprise had been an illusion— either the Sons of Priam were exceedingly incompetent, or they had a plan that Jaya couldn't begin to fathom.

"Rhodes, what's your ETA?" she asked.

"We're almost at the shuttle," he replied. "So far so good, which means they're probably all headed to your location."

"Shuttle team, get ready," Jaya said. "We're on our way."

She paused, hearing footsteps reverberating ahead. Her infrared scanner alerted her to a number of people just around the corner they were approaching. Jaya raised her weapon, and saw her team follow her lead.

"We'll cover you," Lupo said. "Good luck, Lieutenant Commander."

They rounded a corner into a main corridor. Here, the hall widened, and dozens of large magnetic shipping crates were scattered and piled up in the space. A guard up ahead noticed them and pulled his weapon. Jaya shot him quickly and motioned her team ahead. A door behind them opened and the guards they had seen on the monitor burst in. An alarm began to sound, and blast doors lowered, sealing them into the corridor.

Jaya ducked behind one of the crates and saw her team do the same. She peeked out to take down one of the guards.

"One on your left, Pathak," she called out to the squad mate to her side.

She saw the approaching guard drop as Pathak fired in response. The fire from the opposing side was consistent and powerful—it was a large force for security.

"Cover me," she called, and ducked out of cover, moving up to a closer beam.

One of the guards tossed a grenade their way. Jaya dove, grabbing the grenade as it bounced and lobbing it back to the thrower. He was quick—he managed to move out of the way in time. It detonated, taking down a few of his men, but a portable blast shield went up in time to save most. She saw the man gesturing as he settled behind cover again.

"I miss the days when the terrorists were ragtag outlaws who didn't have access to the best weapons," said Sal.

Jaya didn't reply. She was watching the man who had thrown the grenade. He was targeting the front lines of her team. His aim was good—they narrowly missed one of his well-timed shots.

This man was in charge. The others orbited in his powerful draw, adjusting their movements based on his own. In that chrome armor with an opaque mask, he was a shadow in the room. The power of his presence seemed to warp the movements of the battle.

It was Augustus. It had to be.

As if he heard her thoughts, he turned his head toward her, staring right at her from behind that one-way plexiglass visor.

Jaya rolled behind a new crate and popped out, taking down one of Augustus's men with a shot that punctured his helmet.

Sal took down another of them. Augustus's numbers were wearing thin now. She saw him inching back, preparing to retreat. But they couldn't afford to lose him, not now that he was within their reach.

"Cover me," she said to Sal, and she leapt out, vaulting one of the crates to throw her entire body weight into one of the two remaining men. Out of her peripheral vision, she saw Sal take the other one down. She shot her target at point blank range and then went after Augustus, ready to shoot.

He ducked out of the way, too fast, and took off down the hall. She pursued him, sprinting as fast as her legs could carry her. The blast doors began to rise again, the alarm still blaring.

"Sal," she called over the comm. "Get the team back to the shuttle. I'm going after this guy."

"Jaya, are you sure—"

"Lieutenant, that's an order."

"Understood," he replied.

As they rounded a corner into the station's hangar bay, she used the momentum of the turn to edge a little closer, throwing her weight into a spinning kick toward the retreating man. She caught the edge of his knee, sending him sprawling, his gun clattering away from him. This was her chance. This was not the time to hold back. Weapon drawn, she rounded on him, but he was up faster than she had ever seen anyone move.

He threw out a kick of his own as he hurdled himself up from the ground, knocking Jaya's gun away as well. Jaya watched her gun skid across the floor and drop down below one of the small transport ships. Augustus backed slowly toward the ships, not turning his attention away from Jaya. He stood in front of her, hands up, the sheen of his helmet blocking his expression from her.

She lunged in quickly for a gut punch, but he flew back and out of her grasp as she moved. She sensed his reply punch as he threw it and managed to duck, swinging around behind him. He followed up quickly with a roundhouse kick. She caught his ankle in her hands and twisted. He flipped, his body turning into the forced rotation at his hip.

He landed on his feet, and Jaya moved in again.

Jaya had never fought someone like this. She punched and he blocked, he countered and she was already evading his move. When they connected, they both reacted simultaneously. He matched her every move. Blow for blow, they seemed to be part of the same whole, moving and lunging and countering and spinning away.

Her powerful side kick finally connected with his stomach, propelling him back. He slammed against the wall with a loud impact, like the sound of a heavy hand on a drum.

"Jaya," he gasped.

She froze. For a moment, she lost her focus, thrown by her own name on the lips of the most feared and hated man in the galaxy.

He released the catch of his helmet. The mask slid up, revealing his face for the first time.

"Little bear," he said, and Jaya finally understood why the voice of Augustus held such a familiar timbre.

She saw the broad cheekbones, no longer surrounded by the round baby face of more than two decades ago. She saw the smattering of light freckles on his nose and the layered hazel eyes—gold and green and brown overlaid in the irises. She saw the red hair that curled and pressed flat against his temples with sweat.

"Kier?" she whispered, the fight gone from her fists and her legs. She just stood, her body numb and her mind racing.

Before she could react, he turned on his heel and disappeared into one of the ships as she watched dumbfounded. Then he was gone, his ship breaking through the containment field and vanishing into the dark.

24

The inertial shift tugged gently at Mara's gut as the *Solidarity* began its descent. She waited, her legs cramping painfully underneath her. No matter how much she tried to shift her position, her legs always got the worst of it. She was glad to be landing, although that did raise a new problem:

How the fuck was she going to get off this ship, find Onyema, and do away with her without being discovered?

She had no way of knowing where they were—her entire world at this moment was a meter-by-meter cross-section of venting that was unpleasantly warm and reeked of her own sweat. Despite the discomfort, she gingerly stretched herself out on her stomach and began to edge her body along the vents toward the main living area of the ship. While she had no official layout, it was a fairly standard build for a cargo ship, and she found her instincts served her well as she crept through the ducts.

The main cabin connected to the control room at the fore, the airlock on the port side, and the engine room at the aft. Mara positioned herself near a grate in the duct and peered through the slats. Two of the three crew members were packing up small bags and preparing to leave. Ahmad was missing. Mara didn't like her odds of staying under the radar if she tried to climb down one of the sections of air duct that connected the main level of the ship to the cargo bay below, but she sure hoped that's where he was. This one human was already giving her so much trouble, and he had no idea. She growled.

After a brief and quiet conversation, the man and woman below strapped holsters to their legs and secured pistols there and inside their jackets. The woman tied her pale hair tightly up on the top of her head. Then they shouldered their bags and left through the airlock, closing it securely behind them.

The engine had finally completed its cool down, and the ship sat in uncanny silence. The systems were all powered down, the airlocks sealed. Mara heard the clang of boots on the floor of the cargo bay below her, so they were still unloading supplies, but the main level was deserted. Mara nudged the bottom of the vent grate and it slipped up. She eased herself out, legs first, and clung to the air duct with her hands as she touched her feet to the floor. The rest of her body followed, the silence still undisturbed by her presence.

She crept forward to the control room, her hands a hair's breadth from her knives. The windows in the control room were standard-sized—large enough to see the landing site, but not to provide a glorious view. The thick-paned glass and suite of sensors would be enough to guide the ship in safely, and Mara stayed low so she would remain hidden to those outside.

They had landed in an empty field, tall blue-tinged grass swaying languidly in the breeze. Mara spotted Ahmad standing knee-deep in that grass as the other two humans approached him with their packs. It was unclear if they were on a moon or a planet, but it was some sort of life-supporting natural structure. The source of daylight was too far above for her to see—it could just as easily be a binary system as a single star, and she couldn't make out its life stage by the light it produced. Nearby, another ship waited—a yacht, clearly expensive but not ostentatious—and about half a kilometer in the distance, Mara spied a small structure.

The three humans shaded their eyes with their hands as they looked out toward that structure. Their conversations were blocked from her ears by the ship's thick walls, but she watched them carefully. A smattering of boxes on the ground appeared to be basic essentials like soap and dried goods, and the three crew members stood around the boxes, talking casually as they waited.

Three figures began to grow against the horizon as they approached the group. When they drew close, Mara saw that the one in the center was an older woman with deep brown skin and black curls streaked with gray. Her hair fanned out around her face, and the effect, combined with the regal way she carried herself, gave the appearance of a crown. On either side of her were two men, carrying similar weapons to the man and woman Mara had been watching earlier from her perch. They didn't wear uniforms, but their clothing was utilitarian. Flexible. No loose fabric or restrictive cuts.

Mara understood—she wore the same sort of clothing.

The woman's face creased into a smile and she held out her arms. Ahmad embraced her first, her hand patting his dark ponytail with a casual affection. The other two each hugged her closely, and the five young people each picked up one of the boxes and began to carry them toward the other ship. They loaded them into the cargo bay and then moved toward the structure in the distance. The older woman—Onyema, Mara was certain of that—walked alongside them, and as she turned, Mara caught the unmistakable glint of a gun at her hip. Regal, perhaps. But Mara wouldn't be underestimating her strength or her cunning.

She needed to move. Confined to the *Solidarity*, she would have no way to gather information or formulate any sort of reasonable plan of attack. She scanned the area through the windows as the human forms retreated. It was mostly low meadow, but a few clusters of thick-trunked trees cast deep shade over the grasses. The leaves were dense and lush, and the strength of the lower branches promised safety up high. She watched the humans retreat until they had reached the distant structure, and then she activated both her cloaking devices and the airlock doors. These doors ran on backup power and slid open without a protest. She palmed the controls to close them behind her and sprinted for the nearest cluster of trees, about a hundred meters in the direction the humans had gone.

The bark was rough on her hands as she leapt up and caught hold of the lowest branch. She swung her legs up and rolled onto the supportive branch. She continued like this—reaching up, grasping a branch, pulling herself higher and higher—until she was nestled between large, flat leaves fluttering in the breeze.

From this height she could see more. The structure on the horizon was a temporary housing facility, the kind that could be disassembled and packaged up for easy storage and transportation. The humans were carrying items out of the structure now. Heavy-duty sleeping bags and cooking utensils were piled to the side. Ahmad hoisted a few sleep mats over his shoulder, filled his arms with miscellany, and began to trek back to the yacht.

Mara watched him pass by below the tree, and then the pale woman followed close behind, also heavily burdened with sleeping bags and equipment. The light caught her hair and it flashed gold and white.

She could shoot them from here, Mara knew. She could take out both of them before the others noticed. But then that would leave three heavily armed and very experienced former marines with their brilliant and resourceful leader, whom Mara very much expected to still be sharp with a pistol.

No, that was a bad idea.

As Ahmad and the pale woman disappeared into the cargo bay of Onyema's yacht, the other four continued dismantling the structure. Mara could hear their shouts to each other, instructions called out in a relaxed familiarity. The efficiency with which they tore down and neatly packaged the habitat was impressive.

The blonde woman returned to help them, and Ahmad climbed into the *Solidarity*. The ship's engines woke with a low grumble. Ahmad reappeared and jogged over to the group now gathered around the assortment of items and the packaged habitat. After another round of embraces, Ahmad and the two men who had been with Onyema when the *Solidarity* arrived walked the distance back to the ships again. Onyema, the blonde woman, and the gray-eyed man were still fussing over the boxes at the site of the habitat when the *Solidarity* rose up, pulling in its landing supports and tilting away. It disappeared into the bright blue of the sky.

This improved her odds. But looking over at the group of humans, Mara realized they were also preparing to leave. Which meant her time was now.

They had hoisted up the packed structure and carried it over to the yacht together, three sets of hands balancing the slightly unwieldy package. Mara didn't like the way the leaves muddied her line of sight, and she didn't trust an arcing knife to not glance off one of the twisting branches. It would have to be her gun then, and she would wait until they were just beneath her. She drew the weapon.

They passed nearby, but Onyema's head was blocked by the blonde woman's shoulder. Mara steadied the gun, hoping to get a clear shot. But none came and they were walking too fast for her to consider much longer.

She squeezed the trigger.

The blonde woman's shoulder exploded in red and she gave a strangled cry. The habitat dropped, and Onyema and the other man hit the ground behind it, their guns already out. Just Mara's fucking luck. They opened fire on the tree and Mara dropped to the ground, activating the cloaking device and rolling behind the thick trunk.

"Go!" the blonde woman yelled, and Onyema and the man went

sprinting for the ship, firing behind them. The tree sizzled with the energy of their weapons and Mara kept herself tucked out of the line of their shots. They couldn't see her, but they were damn good at keeping a consistent cover fire that pushed her back against the tree.

She swore and holstered her gun. There was only one last option.

The barrage stopped suddenly, and Mara peeked out. They were boarding the yacht. This was it. She thrust herself forward with her legs, shifting easily into her fast quadrupedal gait. She closed the distance and clambered onto the boarding ramp as it lifted, the front half of her body landing solidly on the corrugated metal as her legs flailed off the edge. Onyema shot in her general direction from the living quarters, and the beam deflected just to the right of Mara's elbow. She swallowed her curse.

Mara swung her legs up and moved down the rapidly closing ramp toward Onyema, who kept shooting. Despite not being able to see her, Onyema seemed to be able to predict Mara's location, keeping Mara from being able to draw her own weapon as she danced away from Onyema's shots. The man shouted from the control room to hang on, and Mara rolled behind a comfortable couch in the living space that was bolted to the floor as Onyema dropped to the ground beneath a table. The ship was accelerating upwards, and Mara hung on to the edge of the couch desperately, praying she would not be flung back against the walls as they broke through the atmosphere.

The muscles in her hands and arms cramped as she gripped the couch, and she saw then the trail of blood from the airlock door. It traveled in a wobbly line and ended beneath her. She glanced down and saw a gash in her leg bleeding profusely. The cloaking device would be useless with her trailing blood behind her. No wonder Onyema had known where to shoot.

The ship leveled off, and the powerful pull of inertia diminished to nothing. Mara ripped the cloaker off in rage and drew two knives.

She remained behind the couch, but she drew her feet up beneath her now, taking deep breaths and listening intently to the room. Onyema was somewhere under the table, but she had to worry about the man, too. She was outnumbered two to one, she was bleeding, and she didn't have eyes on either of her armed and dangerous targets.

No sooner had she thought that than the man appeared in the doorway to the control room. His shot seared through the cushions on the couch and a smell like burnt feathers followed. Mara flung a knife toward him, but he ducked behind the door. The knife clattered off the metal wall. She caught a glimpse of Onyema—on the floor, motionless. Maybe she hadn't fucked everything up, then. She dropped behind the couch again as the man began to shoot. Pain flashed through her side as she went down and the heat of her own blood began to soak her shirt.

Mara switched to her gun and slipped around the side of the room for a better angle, remaining below the furniture. The man popped out again and Mara fired. His reaction was quick, but not quick enough, and she knew at the sound of his shout and the clattering of his gun on the ground that she'd wounded him. She leapt over an end table and kicked his gun farther away.

Onyema stirred, and Mara whirled around to shoot her, but the man was up again faster than she'd expected, and he tackled her. He was tall for a human—at least Mara's own height—and thick with muscle. She was lucky he was unarmed, because all the air was violently expelled from her lungs as she hit the ground with his weight on top of her. She gasped, her head spinning, and tried to throw him off. Every twist sent agony through her wounded side.

"Richard sent you," Onyema said, her voice calm. Mara heaved, trying to reach one of her knives while the man was struggling to capture her arms.

Onyema's gun was nowhere to be seen, and Mara's had skittered under the couch. But she couldn't let the woman move freely for too long, because there was no doubt she was capable of killing Mara if she reached one of the weapons. The man was bleeding on her from a wound in his arm, and Mara jabbed her elbow up right into the open flesh. He flailed his arm, the movement as involuntary as his guttural cry.

It was enough. She got a hand around her knife and swung it around, cleanly slitting the man's throat.

She looked back at Onyema.

The woman's eyes shone, but her posture was calm as she raised her hands slowly. They were surprisingly delicate hands, the fingers long and the palms pale. Her curls seemed to float around her head in the low artificial gravity, following the motions of her head languidly.

"I should have spoken when I had the chance," she said sadly.

"I don't really care what you did or didn't do," Mara said. "This is just a job."

"Is it?" Onyema asked. She was moving very slowly, but Mara saw the subtle shift of her body.

She threw the already-bloodied knife. It sunk to the hilt into Onyema's chest.

It was odd, really. Most people looked surprised when she killed them. But Onyema did not. Her eyes closed slowly, deliberately, and she crumpled to the ground.

Mara followed, her knees giving way under her as the room blurred and refocused and blurred again. This was not how she'd expected to die. Adrift in a luxury yacht, soaked with her blood and the blood of her target. What were the odds she would be found? She had never been one for numbers, and these ones seemed bleak. The room went dark. Time ceased to have meaning.

She woke heaving, vomiting bile into the dark pool of blood on the floor. A sudden burst of clarity, and she clawed her way up a chair and stumbled back into the bowels of the ship. There must be a medical bay. She left bloody handprints on the control panels as she opened door after door. The galley. The head. A bedroom. Another bedroom. And then finally, a room with a large supply cabinet and a gurney strapped to the wall.

She ripped bags of gauze open with her teeth, pressing the absorbent material to her side. Blood was out of the question—they would only have human blood, probably stores of Onyema's and that of her protectors, staying cool and fresh in the refrigerator. She might live without a transfusion, but not if she lost any more.

She tore the cabinet apart until she found a surgical needle and thread. She would give anything for some siltyr right now. Anything to wash the agony into a softer haze. She found some painkillers and dry-swallowed a few. Then she strapped herself into the gurney, bit down on some clean gauze, and stitched up her own side. The leg second, because it was bleeding less. When it was done, her shaking fingers dropped the needle to the floor.

The haze was there now, and the pain felt farther away. Mara lay back on the gurney and watched the ceiling warp and sway through her stupor. Amid the thick, dark fog that was creeping into her periphery, she saw clearly a vision in her mind: The gardens of the Imperial Palace, where she had prowled as a child. Where she had seen Yanu for the first time, framed with bursting white blooms, beautiful and wild. Mara had wanted to be beautiful and wild, too.

She was thirsty.

If she woke up, she would find water.

25

Once Jaya was back aboard the shuttle and flying safely to the *Avalon*, the adrenaline began to clear her system, and she noticed the sharp pain in her side. Her armor had been punctured, blood seeping from the twisted fibers. Rhodes helped her bandage her side with their emergency medical kit.

When they docked, Armstrong was waiting in the shuttle bay. Rhodes offered his arm to Jaya as she disembarked, but she shook her head. The pain was sharp, but she was alert. And she needed the pain—it was a grip, an anchor. She held onto it, gritting her teeth, and walked forward as though nothing were wrong. Armstrong noticed the bloodied bandage as soon as she stepped onto the ground, and he moved toward the oncoming strike team.

"I'm alright," Jaya said. "It's not that bad."

"Doctor Choi will have to agree with that statement," he said sternly. "Med bay. The debriefing can wait."

In the med bay, Sunny carefully removed the hastily applied bandage and revealed a nasty hole in Jaya's side. She cleaned, dressed, and stitched the wound closed carefully and put Jaya in bed.

Jaya refused the stronger painkillers—she wanted to be alert.

Armstrong and Tully arrived not long after, and she was grateful for the clarity of mind.

"How is she?" Armstrong asked Sunny.

"Well enough to speak for myself," Jaya replied.

Tully winked. "You would insist you were fine even if that hole were in your head."

Sunny grimaced at Tully's remark. "It's an ugly cut, but it didn't damage anything important."

"Glad to hear it," Armstrong said, pulling up a chair as Sunny started to clean up the medical supplies still strewn about. "It sounds like you made some interesting discoveries down there."

"Yes, Captain," Jaya said. "The station was nearly deserted, but it didn't look abandoned. Either it was recently evacuated, or they hadn't set up a permanent staff yet."

Armstrong frowned slightly, rubbing his chin as he listened to Jaya's report.

"We found what looks like a massive laboratory compound," she said, sitting up straighter in bed despite the way it made the dull ache in her side sear into a sharp pain. "I sent everything to Doctor Vasuda and our analysts at HQ. Vasuda seems to think it's biological. He wouldn't go into much more detail, but it's his field, so hopefully he can make something out from what we sent him."

Armstrong folded his arms across his chest, his expression darkening and the crease between his eyebrows deepening.

Jaya continued: "If they were able to scale up so fast—not just the laboratory they destroyed, but this one as well—and steal Doctor Vasuda's research from under him, we have to assume they have resources we don't know about. Their reach is much farther than we thought."

"I don't like the sound of that," Tully grunted, his crossed arms mirroring Armstrong's.

"And there's something else," Jaya said. Tully and Armstrong's eyes were fixed on her, and her throat went dry. Armstrong handed her a bulb of water from her bedside table. She drank some, swallowed thickly, and continued:

"We may have found Augustus."

Armstrong's eyebrows rose at that, and Tully uncrossed his arms and leaned forward.

Jaya proceeded: "He was on the station. He's strong. I tried to capture him, but he got away in a shuttle."

"Are you sure?" Armstrong asked.

"The voice was his," Jaya replied.

"He spoke to you?"

"I think he was trying to intimidate me." She continued hastily when it looked like Armstrong might have more questions: "It sounded like Augustus. And he was clearly a leader. Everyone else looked to him for direction."

"Did you see his face?" Tully asked. "Can you identify him?"

She paused. Armstrong and Tully both still fixed her with their attention. Kier's eyes had not left her mind since she had returned to the shuttle—in the hard face, she had still seen those wide young boy eyes. They seemed too bright, as though trapped in another time. And he had looked at her as if not a day had passed and she was still his eight-year-old little sister, stuffed into a hidden room for her own protection.

Had he run because he didn't want to be caught? Or because he didn't want to hurt her, once he saw that she was the one leading the *Avalon*'s forces? After all, *she* had pursued *him*.

He'd had the chance to kill her when he revealed himself. She had been shocked. With shame, she realized that she had frozen, forgetting all her training. She couldn't have reacted fast enough if she'd wanted to.

And she hadn't wanted to.

"He was tall," she said. "Probably two meters, a hundred kilograms, athletic. He wore a tinted mask. It covered his face."

"We'll need you to give a description to HQ when we get back to Argos," Armstrong said.

"Understood," she replied.

"This is good, Mill," Tully said. "We had nothing on this Augustus before. Even just his height and build is a start."

"And we know one of their bases of operations," Armstrong added.

"We need to move quick, though," Jaya said. "We know they're willing to take drastic measures to keep us off their trail."

"I have a call-in to HQ in"—Armstrong checked his palm drive —"twenty. I'll update them with what you told us. Good work, Mill."

"Thank you, Captain."

"Rest up," Armstrong said, reaching over and patting her hand. "We need you back in the field as soon as we can get you."

"Don't rush my patient!" Sunny brandished a packet of gauze at them.

Jaya smiled. "I plan on coming back ASAP," she said, saluting.

Armstrong returned the gesture and left.

Tully lingered for a moment. "You feeling alright, Mill?"

"It's not so bad," she said. "Doctor Choi has a heavy hand with those pain meds. I should be fine."

"Good to hear."

She nodded.

Tully pulled up a chair. "I wanted to ask you about something. A search came up in your log," he said abruptly. "For a star cluster— Canis Major."

Stunned, Jaya found she was unable to do anything but stare at him open-mouthed. She hadn't expected that search to draw any attention, but here was the XO of the ship asking her questions about it. She swallowed, trying to recover.

"A friend was asking me about Sirius," she finally said. "I don't even remember how it came up, but he didn't think anyone lived there anymore. We looked it up. It's a ghost town."

"So there's nothing we need to be aware of there? No intel on Canis Major we should know about?"

"Not that I'm aware of, Commander," she replied. "Just idle curiosity. It can get boring in the in-between."

He scrutinized her for a moment, and the hairs on the back of her neck rose. His gaze pinned her, examined her. She fought the urge to look away, the fear that he might see past her lies. That she might accidentally betray herself and open up that box of secrets. Her neck was damp with sweat.

Finally he chuckled and stood up. "That it can," he said. "Just thought I'd ask. Wondered if maybe you'd heard something—even just a hunch. I'd trust your hunches more than most intel, and any lead into the Sons of Priam is helpful right now."

"Unfortunately, no." She laced her fingers together, hoping the adrenaline would stop tingling through her extremities. "If I had something, I'd tell you. And Armstrong."

"I know," he said, smiling. "Guess I was just hoping… well, get your sleep, kiddo. We'll see you back on duty soon."

"You bet," she said, trying to sound cheerful.

She watched as he left. Sunny bustled over to administer the drugs, and as the pain slowly seeped away, Jaya couldn't ease the lingering fear that kept her from resting her mind.

She woke to the sound of voices in the medical bay. Sunny was talking quietly to the szacante doctor. Her eyelids were heavy, and her mind still raced beneath the drug-induced stupor. She realized her mattress was warped, curving like a gravitational field toward some mass at the edge of the bed. She opened one eye, squinting against the light.

Dark curls backlit by the med bay light swam fuzzily in front of her. She opened the other eye, and Sal turned his head back toward her.

He smiled. "You look like shit," he said.

"Not my best day, Sal," she muttered. "Besides, I'm fine. Just high as a satellite thanks to the good doctor."

Sal chuckled. "Which one?"

"The friendly one," she said, hoisting herself up. Sunny must have given her an extra-strength dose, because her side only protested a little at the motion. The sudden rush of alertness roused the restless thoughts in her mind again. Big hazel eyes pushed into her mind, and the vulnerable dampness of red curls pressed against a freckled forehead. The expression on Kier's face.

Kier. In chrome armor. At the front lines of the Sons of Priam. Killing innocent people. Killing people she loved.

"You're not supposed to get hurt, you know," Sal said. "Drills are an even bigger drag when Rhodes is in charge."

"Sal," she said, and whatever joke he had ready died on his lips.

"What's wrong?" he asked.

She closed her mouth tight, suddenly afraid of what might fly out if she let herself speak. This was not a secret she could share. This was not a secret she could hold, either. Despite all the others she had locked away. Had she really been as safe here as she thought? Could she really trust anyone on the *Avalon*? She used to think she could.

But then, why did she never speak of her parents? Why did no one—save her closest friend—even know she had a brother? Why keep that mask on here, with the people she felt safest with out of everyone in the galaxy besides the uncles who were hundreds of lightyears away?

She sighed deeply, her mind tugging at fragments of theories. If she wanted to understand this, she needed to know more. And the only person who knew even a fragment of her secrets was here in front of her, staring at her with more earnest concern than she had ever seen on his sardonic face before.

"I need another favor," she said, lowering her voice. "I need you to search some service records for me."

"Obviously, I'll do that for you," he said. "But can I ask why you can't just do that on your own account?"

"My search on Canis Major apparently raised some red flags," she replied.

Sal cocked an eyebrow.

"Tully," she said, answering his look.

"Why does he care that you looked up Canis Major?" Sal asked. "It's nothing. Empty space."

"I don't know. But he definitely cared. I want to look into his history. Something's not sitting right with me."

Sal sighed, then pulled out his data pad and brought up the Union's naval records. He searched for Tully, and brought up the holographic display so Jaya could see the list of assignments, transfers, and leaves.

Jaya scrutinized the list, then pointed at an entry.

"Sal," she said, and her voice wavered as she spoke. "He served with my father."

"What?" Sal followed her finger to the date she had identified. "Jaya, there are literally hundreds of millions of service people at any given moment. The chances that they were in the same star system, let alone…"

"No," she interrupted. "They were in the same unit. There were only a few dozen people in their group. They knew each other."

She looked over at Sal, who was staring agape at the display.

"Did Tully ever mention it to you? A 'hey, kid, you take after your father,' or 'your old man would be proud of you'? Or something similarly hokey that Tully would say?"

"No." Jaya chewed on her lower lip, trying to determine

whether this oversight was intentional or accidental. "I mean, I changed my name. He might not have realized I was related."

But doubt grew inside her as Sal scrutinized the page, deep in thought. Tully had been monitoring her, tracking her searches on the naval database. That suggested he had taken some special interest in her—one he had not communicated directly to her.

Tully was secretly watching her. Tully, who had apparently served with her father before he had been discharged.

The same father who had been murdered twenty-three years ago by someone Kier thought was still out there.

26

Her mouth was dry and bitter. Pain burned in her leg and abdomen and pulled her up from the depths of unconsciousness reluctantly. Drugs. She needed more painkillers. And water.

Mara fumbled for the straps of the gurney and unhooked them. She shifted slowly onto her side, easing herself up to sitting. Even her arms hurt, a deep ache that throbbed up her neck to her head. Nausea swept over her at the same time that her vision went black again, and she dropped her head to her knees. She was alive. She wasn't sure if she should be happy about it.

When the sensation of rolling ceased, she raised her head slowly and blinked until her eyes adjusted. The med bay of Onyema's yacht was torn apart. Her blood, now dried and flaking at the edges, smeared the floor and the cabinet. Bloody plastic packages littered the space, and Mara looked down, realizing she hadn't had time to bandage her stitches before she had passed out.

She lowered one foot to the floor, then the other. Drugs first. And water. Fortunately, that bottle of painkillers was on a nearby cart, and she didn't have to stretch much to reach for it. A dozen or so slow, uneasy steps carried her across the room to a small tap. Four empty bulbs were attached to the wall next to the tap, and she removed one and filled it. Small sips accompanied by the pills. She filled the bulb again and carried it with her back to the gurney, stopping at the cabinet along the way for more gauze and tissue repair accelerant. She liberally slathered the latter onto her wounds, and then wrapped the wounds tight with gauze.

There. Now she was alive and bandaged. She stuffed some extra gauze in the pockets of her jacket just in case and took another sip of water.

She supported herself against the narrow walls of the corridor, one hand pressed against each wall, as she staggered toward the fore of the ship. She still had no idea where she was, or where Onyema had been going. But at least she had a ship.

And was alive. She was starting to feel more positive about the alive part.

She stumbled into the living area, the floor still slick with blood. Hers, as well as Onyema's and her protector's. What had happened to the blonde woman? Had she already died before Mara reached the ship? Or would she bleed out slowly, alone in an empty grassland? Mara bent over, vomiting water and yellow bile into the red liquid on the floor.

A glint of chrome caught her eye as she struggled to slow her gasping breath: the cloaking device that she had cast off in her rage. She reached for it, her fingers shaky, and pulled it from the sticky red blood. She wiped it clean on a small scrap of the gauze in her pockets and reattached it to her utility belt. No use throwing away perfectly good technology, and now that she wasn't bleeding freely, perhaps it would be useful.

She glanced across the blood-stained furniture to where Onyema lay.

Except she wasn't there.

Fuck. No, that couldn't be right. Mara staggered over and turned around, her vision following the motion with a sickening delay.

The man was dead. His body lay crumpled on the ground by the control room. But there was no sign of Onyema, aside from the blood streaked on the wall and pooling on the floor.

She was gone. Which meant she wasn't dead, or at least hadn't been dead when Mara had clawed her way to the medical bay to handle her own injuries. Or maybe earlier, when Mara had passed out after the fight. Had there been a body there when Mara had moved to the med bay? She couldn't remember.

She turned to the control room.

It was quietly peaceful when she reached it, lights blinking on the console like familiar starscapes. She dragged herself into a chair and brought up the display. The yacht had a shuttle, but it was gone. The system showed it had detached nearly fifteen hours ago.

Mara swore, letting the sound of the words ring in the empty space.

She brought up the map. They hadn't made it far from that planet, and she was now suspended about a day's journey from Argos in a reeking luxury yacht, her target neither dead nor located. The image distorted in front of her and a heavy darkness snuck into her periphery. She drank another sip of water and put her head down.

After a long moment, she raised her head. She sent a message to the man who had hired her, asking him to meet her at Onyema's yacht when she landed at Argos.

She would have to clean the living area and space the man's body before she started on the path to Argos. The last thing she needed was for a customs official to select her for a random search with a corpse on board. But there would be time for that later. She closed the door to the living area with a command in the console and pulled a nutrition bar from her bloodied jacket pocket. She took a tiny bite and chewed the gritty protein substance until it felt like mud in her mouth. Washed it down with a swig of water.

She would give herself an hour, and perhaps then she would have the strength to hide the mess she had made and figure out what to tell her employer. And even if she didn't have the strength, she would find a way. Until then, she would stay here, slowly restoring herself with food and water. Thoughts—mostly incoherent—swirled around in the back of her mind, menacing her.

This fucking job. Everything about it felt wrong, but it was too late now. She knew that gut-emptying feeling of *too late* far too well by now.

Mara took another bite of the protein bar. Another sip of water.

When she got back to Argos, she would end the contract. As much as it hurt to lose that payout, she was not prepared to pursue Onyema a second time. She was done with this job.

The same man who had brought her the job offer a few weeks ago met her at the dock when she arrived in Onyema's yacht. He looked harder here in the artificial lights of Argos, without the sand and dust coating his hair and face. He was dressed in a smart suit like any other Argos businessman.

She had sent him an account of the job, including her coordinates and the approximate time at which Onyema had fled, as well as the possible remaining woman alive on the unknown planet. When she stepped off the gangplank, he flinched. He tried to cover the involuntary motion with a sidestep, but she didn't miss it, or the way he tried very hard not to meet her eyes.

"Hire someone else," she said. "This woman is too hard for a bounty hunter to kill. Get a proper assassin."

His hesitation hung in the air, a tense silence. "I'm afraid that's not something my employer is willing to do."

"Too fucking bad for him," Mara snapped. "My services are for hire, but I can choose the jobs I take, and I can choose when to leave a job. I'm choosing to leave this one."

The man hesitated again, his mouth half-open to speak, but no sound emerging.

She pushed past him. The *Nasdenika* was in a dock not far from their current location, and she had every intention of filing a flight plan to the farthest outpost she could find and putting as much empty space between herself and this job as she could.

"He thought you might say that," the man said. "Marantos, daughter of her Imperial Majesty Nusantos, most exalted of Narei."

She stopped cold and turned slowly back to face the man. The man had stepped away from her, but he was still in range of her knives. A sudden urge to slit him up the center of his body twitched into her fingers, but she pushed it down. He was watching her, fear evident in his widely dilated pupils. He stepped farther away from her.

Hands grabbed her from behind. A sharp pain in her neck, and then everything went black.

27

Tynan bent over the tiny desk in his cramped makeshift office, watching and re-watching the video feeds the strike teams had sent him and sifting through the messages. He understood most of the video footage—that was as he had expected. It was the messages, the supply ordering, the snippets of notes he could decipher, that had him focused so intensely. Min had shut down for a while, after trying unsuccessfully to talk him out of doing exactly this. She knew as well as he did that this was futile.

He knew what the lab was for. He had known for two full days —since they had left the station—what this lab was for. He was just looking for something that would tell him he was wrong. This process wasn't logical, he knew that. But he needed to look. He needed to find something, *anything*, that could prove him wrong.

The confirmation of his fears had come in one of the notes— studies of the human heart responding to a particular kind of stress. The description of the stress was vague enough to keep their methods mysterious, but their concluding phrase repeated itself in his mind:

Subject adapted normally to the late-term additions. Our

method has been appropriately adjusted to add enhancements in adulthood, with all the same features of previous subjects.

This was something Kujei had been working on years ago when they had parted ways. He believed that there was a way to use the same technology that seamlessly fused VAs with szacante bodies to do more than just provide a constant medical monitor. The technology could be adapted to enhance the body.

The humans and the nareians will be doing this, Kujei had argued at the time. *We don't want to remain weak while they improve their already significant biological advantages.*

Tynan had thought that was a coward's argument. But now?

What if Kujei had been right all along?

There was a soft knock on the door, and Doctor Choi—Sunny—peeked inside.

"I made some coffee," she said. "Do you want some?" And then a thought seemed to hit her, and she followed up: "Have you ever had coffee before?"

Tynan shook his head. "I haven't."

She smiled and came inside, carrying two cups with handles. Fragrant steam rose from the top of the cups.

"I take mine black," she said. "But I have cream and sugar if you want it."

"I have no idea what that means," Tynan confessed.

He took the cup from her—the surface was warm, the heat of the liquid transferring to the material. It was soothing in his hands. He took a sip, and from Sunny's laugh, he knew the face he made must have been rather surprised.

"It's… interesting," he said.

"Too bitter?" she asked.

He nodded, and she got up. She returned a moment later with a white opaque liquid in a bottle and a crystalline substance in a small bowl. She put them on the table.

"Lots of people add these," she said. "It changes the flavor. Give it a try."

Tentatively, Tynan added a few crystals of the strange white substance to his drink and went to take another sip.

"You'll probably want more than that," Sunny said.

He added more and took another sip, and was pleasantly surprised by the change in flavor. It was still bitter, but now there was a sweet side to the bitterness. He added some of the white liquid, pouring until the black beverage had turned a rich brown color. Another sip, and he found the bitterness was nearly gone.

"Better?" she asked. She had been watching him this whole time, and he realized that his reaction to this new experience might be as interesting to her as the experience itself was to him.

"Yes," he said. "What is the substance that makes it sweet?"

"Sugar," she said. "The other one is cream. Or milk—some people use milk. It's pretty much the same thing."

"I like it," he said.

She smiled and took a sip of her own drink. "What're you working on?" she asked, looking up and meeting his eyes.

He looked away, all of a sudden feeling very rude. Everything with humans was an unfamiliar experience for him, and he felt he was always staring at them. "I'm trying to figure out what this laboratory they found was intended to do."

"Any luck?"

"Maybe," he said, the stubborn need to find an alternate explanation colliding uncomfortably with his scientist's desire for truth and reason. He should have told her *yes* but he was not ready yet to admit it.

"Can I help with anything?" she asked.

The small metal case he had brought in the rush to leave Argos sat on his desk. Inside were the samples from the dead man that he was supposed to be working on. He could use Sunny's medical expertise, but he also knew that the task Jaya had set for him was not meant to supersede this more important work. This work that made him feel sick to think about.

"I don't think so," he said. "I have all the data, I just need to keep looking over it until something stands out."

"Should I leave you to it?"

"No," he said, and he was surprised that he meant it. "I think I needed a break. Thank you for the…"

"Coffee," she said.

"Right."

"It'll help you think," she said. "Always works for me. I spent many nights trying to crack a tough diagnosis, fueled by coffee."

"I think I know the feeling."

"You think?" she asked, a smile teasing at the corners of her lips. "You don't know?"

"I don't… we're just…" he stammered. "I don't know how it feels to be human."

"I imagine it's not too much different from being szacante," she said. "Our people have more in common than not. I think most sentient life is more similar than they even realize. It takes a certain kind to make their way out into the galaxy. That's something, at least, that we all share."

He had never thought of it that way before. First contact was a powerful and exciting experience, and every race in the galactic community had a first contact event that shaped who they were today.

"Do you miss it?" Sunny asked. "Dresha?"

"Yes," Tynan said. "It was always home, even when my parents were stationed on faraway colonies. I've lived other places, but now, to be unable to go back… it's not really home anymore, but it still feels like it should be."

"Do you still have family there?"

"My aunt moved to a little colony a few years ago, but I…" he trailed off, realizing that as he wracked his mind for friends and family on Dresha, all he could come up with were former coworkers. Fellow scientists who now would not associate with him. "I used to have family there."

She seemed to understand, or at least she didn't pry any further.

"What about you?" he asked. "Where is your family?"

"I don't have much," she said. "My mother passed away a few years ago, and my father is retired out on a garden planet."

"Are you close?"

She shrugged, and he suddenly realized how personal a question that was.

"We get along fine," she said.

"I see," he replied. He took another sip of the coffee and changed the subject: "Is it always this exciting on this ship?"

She smiled. "It can be, but we do have the occasional lull. Since we got the Sons of Priam assignment, it's been exciting more often than not. Not used to this much excitement, huh?"

"A different kind of excitement," he said. "The intellectual kind. I'm not thrilled with the life-threatening kind."

"A friend of mine used to say he always believed in the one, two, three rule: One horrific life-threatening incident is an accident, two are a coincidence, and three means you really need to consider another line of work."

Tynan chuckled. "I guess I've still got two more before I should consider another line of work."

She laughed at that. "I passed my quota long ago. I don't mind. Makes me feel alive."

He shook his head. "I'd rather *stay* alive," he said, eliciting another chuckle from her. She was so curious—her expressions were much broader than other humans—he actually thought he might be learning to interpret them. He was mesmerized by the changes in her face as she spoke.

"Do all human noses do that?" he found himself asking.

"Do what?" She said, tilting her head to the side.

"Get all wrinkled when they laugh. I never noticed that before."

"I don't think so," she said. "Depends on the person."

"Oh." He took another drink, hoping to hide his own expression behind the mug. Perhaps it was the mental strain from going over the tapes in such detail, but his thoughts were muddled and unfocused, wandering from one idea to the next with no clear path. He had never felt so out of his element as on this ship. And here this human was, trying to make him feel welcome, and all he could do was ask pointless and prying questions about her family and her physiology.

All he wanted was to be back to his research. At least there, he knew what he was doing. Or at least, he had thought that once.

Sunny finished her coffee and went to check Jaya's stitches, leaving Tynan to the bittersweet aroma of his drink and his thoughts. Suddenly consumed with the strange desire to throw the cup across the room, he slid it away gently. He had built his entire life so carefully, designed it to be clean and orderly and predictable. But he had ignored problems that grew right under his nose. He thought it would be enough to do his own work with integrity. That he could ignore the way his culture was changing, becoming more reckless.

He had pushed everything messy away, but that hadn't stopped the mess from interfering with his life. His parents had died. His work had been taken from under him. And now, it looked like the entire galaxy was being upended. And all he wanted to do was push it away.

Outside, in the med bay, Sunny was checking Jaya's wound. Tynan rose and stood in the doorway, watching her replace the bandage carefully. He heard her surprised pleasure at how quickly it was healing, and Jaya took the offered pain pill and downed it with a cup of water.

"So I'm free to go?" Jaya asked.

"As long as you see me every day to change the bandage," Sunny replied. "But yes, it must have looked worse than it was. You should be back to normal in no time."

At Jaya's smile, Sunny raised a warning finger. "But no sparring until I've signed off. Give those stitches a chance to work."

Jaya's smile turned sheepish, and she finished her water and tossed the cup in the recycler. She caught Tynan's eye and crossed the room to stand in his doorway.

"How are you doing?" she asked, taking in what he imagined to be his haggard appearance.

He didn't reply right away. Some part of him still felt safer with the truth buried. But if the last few weeks had taught him anything, it was that closing his eyes and willing the problem away did not work.

Jaya took his non-response with a concerned look. She cocked her head to the side. "You making heads or tails of that lab we found?"

He hesitated, then let out a sigh. "I don't like it," he confessed. She frowned, and he continued reluctantly. "The signs all point to this being a multipurpose biological lab. They are clearly pursuing more advances in their bioweapon, but they seem to have another agenda as well. I'm afraid…"

He broke off, and she waited patiently. He looked up and met her eyes.

"I've worked my entire life for the good of my people," he said. "I've always searched for ways to improve our lives and enrich our knowledge. Knowledge is sacred to us, Lieutenant Commander Mill. You humans have all your deities and your myths. We have our knowledge."

"I think you've read too many history books, doctor." She smiled. "But I understand your point. Science isn't just a job to you, it's a higher calling. You live and breathe your work—I can see that. I've seen that since we first brought you aboard."

He nodded, relieved at the understanding in her voice. "Exactly."

"So what's got you so upset?"

"The idea that my people's research could help anyone do evil. To kill. Knowledge can empower us against various threats. But we have to be careful of it. It can turn us into those very threats we are afraid of."

Her eyes widened at that, and she pursed her lips. She scrutinized him for a moment.

"I think they're manipulating human subjects," he said. "Perhaps other species as well, but they are enhancing them somehow. Making them faster, more powerful. They won't need a larger army if they have an army of superior beings."

The weight of that realization sank in as he said it aloud for the first time. To see research he had once been a part of mutilated and contorted into something sick and violent made him second guess every decision that had led him here.

Jaya had gone silent. She stared at him, a sudden and terrible clarity in her eyes. For the first time, he realized there was much more going on behind her outward demeanor. She was lighthearted and fun with her comrades, and strict and demanding when she was training, but for the first time, he saw her just as herself. After her injury in the line of duty just two days ago, and after every hurdle they had encountered trying to stop the Sons of Priam, he imagined she had no energy left to play a part.

"Damn," she said, crossing her arms. She looked back at him, and the furrow in her forehead softened slightly. She nodded once, more to herself than to him. "We're going to stop them, doc. And your help is the only reason we even know about this. We couldn't do this without you."

"Thank you," he said.

"I'll let Armstrong know about this." She stood to leave.

"Lieutenant Commander Mill?" She stopped in the doorway and looked back at him. He continued: "Do you really think we can stop them?"

Her expression was unreadable. "If anyone can," she said, "it's us."

28

It wasn't long after they docked at Argos before a briefing meeting was called. Jaya sat down in the large conference room with the szacante doctor and the officers who had been working most closely on this project: Rhodes, Sal, Armstrong, and Tully. Armstrong sat, folding his fingers together as he rested his hands on the table. After a moment, Rear Admiral Reid entered the room and the officers stood at attention, Tynan rising just a second after them, his posture uncertain. Jaya met his eyes and gave him what she hoped was an encouraging smile.

Reid gestured, and they all sat again.

"What's the update?" Reid asked.

Sal spoke immediately. "That lab we stumbled on is about to go live," he said, bringing up a list of the data he'd compiled from the computer on the ship. "They've got shipments of chemicals coming in, and all sorts of biological matter. They use coded phrases in their messages, which I've passed on to the analysts at HQ to see if they can make sense of them, but whatever they're working on in that lab is big. They think it's their key to getting the upper hand permanently."

"Who are their suppliers?" Reid asked.

"It's all in the report," Sal said. "It's a very long list."

"I don't want to give them the chance," Armstrong said. "I think we should get back to the station right away and take that lab down."

"The lab was roughly in the center of the station," Jaya offered. "If we could get a team in there and plant explosives, we could take the whole thing down."

"It would be a huge win for us," Armstrong said. "We haven't been able to hit them squarely yet."

"Why go to the trouble to board the station again?" Tully chimed in. "Let's just shoot them down. Drop into the system, get rid of the station, and jump back out."

Jaya opened her mouth to reply, then swallowed her words. Kier was on that station. Or, he had been. She met Armstrong's eyes—he was watching her as she formulated her reply.

"Augustus may be on that station," Jaya said. "We have an opportunity to capture him."

"Even more reason to just destroy the thing," Tully said.

"I agree with Commander Coolidge," Reid said. "If we have a chance to take out the leader of the Sons of Priam, we should do it."

Reid was also watching her now, his brown eyes narrowed slightly. Tully, too, scrutinized her in that way that had recently begun to set her on edge. Jaya realized her hands had clenched into fists, and every muscle in her body felt tensed. She took a deep breath and slowly relaxed her arms, withdrawing her hands to rest on her knees below the table. Blood pounded in her ears, her own heartbeat like a drum.

"Actually," Armstrong said, his voice calm, "we don't believe Augustus is the leader of this organization."

Reid and Tully's heads both whipped from Jaya to Armstrong. From the surprise on Tully's face, Armstrong had not told him of Jaya's theory. Armstrong's face was impassive; his eyes remained on Jaya for a moment before he turned his attention to his second-in-command and his superior.

"We've come across a number of internal communications that indicate a more complicated chain of command within the Sons of Priam. It seems that Augustus is a figurehead—he's the one we're all meant to be looking at while the organization puts down deep roots elsewhere."

Reid didn't move—didn't even shift his weight in the chair—but Jaya saw the anger in the set of his jaw. It sent a chill down her neck.

"This is the first I'm hearing of this," Reid said.

"It's in my latest report," Armstrong countered. "I was intending to submit it after this briefing."

Reid and Tully exchanged a look. Armstrong sat calmly between them, a hard glint in his eyes.

"I want that report now, Captain." Reid's voice was chilly.

"Understood, Admiral," Armstrong replied. He opened his data pad and sent the briefing to Reid, who began to page through it immediately.

An odd silence hung in the room. Beside Jaya, Sal shifted in his seat. She met his eyes, and he quirked an eyebrow up. She shook her head—just barely—in response.

"Can we confirm this is the only laboratory they have left?" Tully asked, breaking the silence.

"There's no evidence of any others in the messages," Sal said. "I can't say for sure, but it looks like this is where they were focusing their attention. At least for now."

Reid suddenly looked up from the report on his data pad. "Is this everything you've got?"

"Yes, Admiral," Armstrong replied. "It's all on there."

Reid looked to Sal next.

"Yes, Admiral," Sal said. "I included everything in the appendices that didn't make it into the main report."

Reid looked back down at the data pad and seemed to consider it closely for a moment. Then he looked back up. "Hit the station," he said. "But this op stays quiet. This intel goes nowhere, understood?"

Jaya saw the questions on all their faces, but no one asked. Reid was the superior officer here—he knew more than the rest of them combined.

"Let's hit them hard," Reid said. "Stop this operation. Try to capture Augustus. I'll handle the rest."

"Yes, Admiral," Armstrong replied.

"And if you are unable to capture Augustus," Reid said, "make sure nothing of that station survives. Better that he goes down with it."

"Of course."

"I'll authorize the armory to release two nukes to the *Avalon*. I'll try to fast-track the requisition for the nukes, but it may take up to twenty-four hours. Make 'em count." He stood and left the room.

"Be ready to leave at a moment's notice," Armstrong said. "Before they get a chance to pull another disappearing act."

The team stood up and filed out of the room. Jaya lingered, slowing her movements just enough to not be conspicuous. Out of the corner of her eye, she caught Tully's look to Reid, who gave a subtle nod.

She left the room with the others, but couldn't help the sense of apprehension growing in her. There was more going on than she was aware of—this was always the case. In the intelligence community, there was always someone who knew more. Classified information was everywhere, often dangling tantalizingly out of reach. But when she could sense the tendrils of dangerous information, that reality was brought to the front of her mind.

She wondered what Reid and Tully knew that she didn't. And perhaps that even Armstrong didn't.

That thought unsettled her most of all.

After the briefing, Jaya headed straight for the antiques shop. When she arrived, Luka was bent over the console at the front, his head in his hands. She stopped short in the doorway, but the door chime had already alerted him to her presence.

He looked up, his hair mussed from his hands. His eyes met hers, and his expression sent a sympathetic jolt through her. His usual warmth was gone, that wistfulness she had seen under the surface now a deep well of anguish. She felt an urge to move toward him, but he closed his eyes for a brief moment, and when he reopened them, the expression was gone.

He half-smiled, and somehow that was even worse.

"Are you okay?" she asked.

There was a long pause, then he shook his head. "It's been a rough few days."

He stood, and his posture loosened, but Jaya felt something still seething below the surface. He held out a hand, and she took it, drawing closer as he stepped out from behind his console. "How have you been?"

Her mind filled suddenly with Kier's eyes. She tensed. "Also a rough few days," she admitted.

His eyes searched her face, and she felt herself harden against his questions, closing him out. He gave a curt nod, as if he understood, and stepped back. He squeezed her hands and then released them, gesturing to the piano. "Maybe music will soothe both our souls," he said quietly.

She tried to ignore the way her heart sank. "I'll do what I can."

She settled down on the piano bench, opened the lid that protected the ivory keys, and took a moment to savor the smoothness of the keys beneath her fingers. Then, she gently compressed the keys, slowly building a sweet melody, letting the piano feel what she needed and convert it to music.

Luka sat down at the chair behind the console. He closed his eyes for a moment to listen, and Jaya saw some of the darkness return in the rounding of his shoulders. His palm drive beeped, and his attention was drawn to something on his screen. After a few moments, he stood and apologized before retreating to the storeroom in the back.

She waited a moment after he left. Everything was just a little unstable in her world right now, and she found herself bracing against the piano. She closed her eyes and replaced her hands on the keys.

This instrument was sure beneath her fingers, responding to her mood, interpreting the tangle of her thoughts without hesitation. As her body began to move, to lean into the music, she began to release, allowing her fear and her sorrow to find its voice in a minor key, in dissonance without resolution.

"I thought I'd find you here."

The familiar voice broke through her focus and sent chills down her spine. Her fingers stilled on the keys.

"You've been watching me?" She kept her tone even. She resumed playing, but her focus had snapped away from the music and to Kier's presence at her back. Every breath he took, every soft murmur of cloth as he shifted his weight, every creak of the floor as he drew closer—she heard it all.

"You come here a lot lately," he said. "I had wondered why."

She took a moment before she responded. "It's peaceful."

He stilled. His breath remained steady behind her. She found herself at the end of a piece, her fingers already searching out the next one. Something their mother had played often in their childhood. After a moment, she heard his breath hitch, and he moved closer.

"You could have killed me," he said. "You didn't."

"I could say the same about you."

"You've been looking for me," he said, and it sounded like an accusation.

She didn't reply.

His breathing was erratic now, and his voice wavered. His footsteps paced behind her, her thoughts treading the same path. This was Kier. This was Augustus. He was her brother. He was dangerous.

He stopped pacing. She kept playing.

"We used to have music every night," he said thoughtfully. "I've missed it."

Her reply ached in her throat, but she kept her tone steady. "I have too."

Kier took a step closer. She tensed, longing for the feeling of her pistol solid against her hip, ready to pull at any point. He stopped. "Jaya," he said. "I'm not going to hurt you."

"You're right." She stilled her hands, the music ending abruptly. "You're not."

"Keep playing," he urged, and suddenly his voice sounded so young, as it had when they had played together as children. The voice struck a chord in her, and she translated that chord into the instrument, into another piece she had played often as a child.

Kier sat gently on the bench beside her, watching her hands thoughtfully, then raising his own to the keys. She made room for him. They had played duets as children, side by side on the bench, Kier always to her right, just as he was now. But he pulled his hands away before he touched the keys.

"I can't anymore," he said. "I've lost it."

That's not something you lose. Not really.

She stopped, turning to look at him for the first time. He stared miserably at the instrument, his sharp profile backlit, square jaw in shadow. The shop's warm light glowed in his copper hair and illuminated the green in his eyes. He was large now, but he had always been her big brother, and his broad shoulders and long limbs had grown in proportion to her own. He still felt familiar, beside her. And distant at the same time.

"I don't think you really have," she whispered.

He shook his head, not meeting her eyes. "You were always better than me anyway."

He stood and began to pace the room. She followed him.

"Who are you now?" she asked. "What happened to you in the twenty years that I haven't heard from you?"

He laughed, the sound bitter.

Jaya glanced at the storeroom door, but there was no sign of Luka. When she looked back at Kier, he was watching her closely.

"I've learned a lot," he said, "since they took me away. I've learned how dark the galaxy truly is. I've learned how few can be trusted."

"Why didn't you come back for me?" She fought the tears in her throat, the fear that had begun to creep into her body. Something in her wished for a place to hide, and for Kier to be the confident and protective force he had always been. Until he was gone.

Instead he stood, half-leaning away from her, his eyes accusing her of something. Then that look of anger and judgment fled his face, leaving a haggard exhaustion. "It was too dangerous."

"*Dangerous*?" she asked, keeping her voice low. "At least we would have been together."

"We can be together now," he said. "I've made such progress, and it's safe for you now. To join us."

"You're the one who's been sending me messages."

He nodded, a smile beginning to clear the storm in his eyes. "I wanted you to understand. You belong with us, not them."

She laughed at that, but the sound was more angry than amused. She stepped closer and lowered her voice more. Luka was still in the back room of the shop, and she didn't want him to hear anything if he ventured out. "You want to talk to me about dangerous? You're *Augustus.*"

"Augustus?" he echoed. His eyes grew distant, and a hesitant smile played at his lips. "I had heard that you were using that name. I like it."

"Kieran, how can you live with what you do?"

His eyes snapped back, her words stoking the fire in them. "How can *you* live with what *you* do? You work for the people who killed mother, who took me away. They studied me, tested me, and threw me away when they were done with me. They would have taken you, too, if they'd known about you. But I never told them."

"I don't understand," she pleaded. "Why did they take you? Why would they want me?"

"You're special," he said. "And so am I. We are capable of great things. People like us scare them."

"People like us?"

"You have to trust me, little bear. It's me. Do you really think I'd be doing this if it wasn't right? The Union has gotten very good at hiding their dirty secrets."

She crossed her arms, searching his face. His expression was earnest, his eyes fixed confidently on her.

"They have to be stopped," Kier said. "Someone needs to do it. Someone needs to step in. He only wants to make the galaxy a better place."

"Who does?" she asked.

"We are restoring the foundations. Think about it, Jaya. Somewhere inside, you know I'm right. You know that the government serves no one but itself."

"No, Kier," she said. "I don't. We work to *stop* terrible things from happening. We work to keep innocent people from dying. Even if you truly believe the Union is corrupt, there are better ways."

"*Tu ne cede malis*," he snapped. The little furrow between his brows seemed immensely deep. He paled, freckles stark against his skin, and the fragility of his expression pierced her with a strange guilt. "Jaya, I need you. You don't understand what they're capable of. What we're doing is nothing in comparison. We're hitting back the only way we can. If there were another way—"

"There is another way!"

He recoiled at the sharpness of her tone. She reached out to touch his arm, but he stepped back.

"Big bear," she said, and this time it was her turn to plead. "Please listen to me. You are so much better than this. I can help you, but not the way you're asking for."

"You don't understand," he whispered. "He said you wouldn't. He said my messages were wasted effort and he was right."

"Who did?" she asked. This man Kier kept referring to—he had to be the architect she had postulated. If Kier would just give her a hint, a piece of his identity…

A slight sound from the back room, and their attentions snapped to the storeroom door as Luka emerged. Kier stiffened, drawing back toward the shop's main door.

"Can I help you?" Luka asked.

"I was actually on my way out," Kier said, his demeanor suddenly smooth and calm, his face a polite mask. He had already crossed the room and was at the door.

Jaya wanted to run after him, but Luka stepped into the space between them and she froze.

Kier vanished, the door closing behind him, and Luka turned back to Jaya.

"Are you okay?" he asked, his eyes going to her hands. She realized they were trembling and she clasped them tightly together, willing them to stop. He turned that searching gaze on her face now, and she felt her darkest secrets written all over her, spilling out for him to see. "Who was that?"

She found her voice somehow. "I'm sorry. I need to go."

He called after her, his voice nearly lost on her as she closed the door behind her. The corridor was empty—no sign of which way Kier had gone.

She headed for the Diplomatic Level immediately and signed in to an open console. She searched the dock records, scouring every ship that had come in within hours of the *Avalon*. One caught her attention, and she sent the record to her palm drive and brought up a holographic image of a shuttle. It was a sleek model—a modified human-style ship, clearly customized. Dark, smooth lines. She had seen it aboard the station, just before Augustus—*Kier*—slipped away. It had docked at Argos that morning and just left. He would already have jumped to FTL speeds—it was too late.

She saved the record to her personal file and contacted Armstrong.

"Lieutenant Commander Mill," he said. "What is it?"

"I need to speak with you, Captain. Immediately."

There was a brief pause before his response. "I'm in my quarters."

She was already halfway to the elevator, her insides in a knot. Something was wrong—she could sense in Kier a twisted, dark pain. She wondered if what he had said was true, and then chastised herself both for believing him and for doubting him.

He had changed, but she had to wonder if the very world she had learned to embrace was what had really changed him. The reality was that she knew that lines were crossed all the time. Stories of torture done off the record, of secret experiments, of people who vanished when they started to push too deep. None of these were far-fetched in her field, but the details had always been hazy.

She knew that some part of her had dismissed the stories—the idea was too ugly to think about and too distant to fear. But now, her every assumption rose up in her as she re-examined the world she thought she knew.

And she still saw his eyes in front of her—at one moment hauntingly sad, at the next burning with rage. She saw the moments when he had been the brother she used to know. Kier had been in there. She wondered if there was any way to bring him out.

The frown began to form in the lines of Armstrong's face only moments into her story. It grew deeper as she relayed her encounter with Kier in the antiques shop. He sat calmly at his desk as she paced the room. Beyond consternation, she could not read his expression.

"Sit down, Jaya," he finally said.

She obeyed, watching as he rubbed his forehead with one hand. He sighed. "He's already gone?"

"Yes," she said.

"What was he doing? Was he threatening you?"

"No," she replied. "He was—"

She paused, wishing she were still standing so she could exorcise some of this dark energy inside her by pacing again. Instead, her hands fidgeted, picking at the edges of her uniform. She stopped herself.

"He all but confirmed that there's someone else running the Sons of Priam," she said. "He kept referring to someone else, but he wouldn't give me any details. Not yet. He—he wanted me to join him, Captain. And there's something I haven't told you yet."

Armstrong's eyebrows shot up at that, deepening the wrinkles in his forehead. Those wrinkles hadn't been there when she had first joined the crew of the *Avalon*. They had grown into him as she had grown with the ship, but this was the first time she really noticed them.

"I saw his face before," she confessed. "I know who he is. And he knows me."

"He knows you?"

She nodded. "I think he may have known I was aboard the *Avalon* all along," she said. "He's my brother."

She took in the slight tug at his eyebrows, and the faint narrowing of his eyes, which he never took off her own.

"Your records list no immediate family," Armstrong said finally. "Just your uncles."

"I know," she replied. "My brother and I were born on a remote colony. I didn't know it then, but we weren't registered with the Union at our birth. When my parents were killed—and I presumed my brother was killed, too—my uncles took me in and helped me become a citizen. I didn't know who he was. Until I saw his face again."

"In an antiques shop on Argos," he said, and the corners of his lips twitched up ironically.

"Yes," she said. It was close enough to the truth. "He seemed to think I could be persuaded to be an ally to him. Converted to his cause."

"Which is?"

"Exactly what the Sons of Priam are saying: cleaning up the Union, airing its dirty secrets, and bringing forth a kingdom of peace."

"You don't sound convinced," Armstrong said, "that he is wrong."

"I understand the goal, but not the means. Murdering innocents in the name of peace is still murder."

He nodded at that, and she saw the narrowing of his eyes soften. He brought a hand to his face, rubbing wearily at his temples. "Thank you for telling me this."

"What should we do?"

Armstrong didn't respond. He folded his hands in his lap, and for a long moment, he stared down at them. Then he stood, crossing to the window in his small apartment that looked out over the jagged architecture of Argos's lower levels.

"Are you still willing to capture him?" he finally said.

"Yes," Jaya said. "I believe we can turn him. He's confused, but he kept referring to someone else. The person in charge."

"You believe we could get him to tell us this person's identity?"

"I do."

"You understand his relationship to you will likely come out once we've captured him?"

"I understand that," she said. "I've only ever been loyal to the Union. And I think eventually he will listen to me."

Armstrong sighed. He closed his eyes for a moment, rubbing at the lines in his forehead.

"I don't see what good it would do to report this up the chain just yet," Armstrong said. "We have a chance to capture him. Let's see where that leads us."

Relief flooded her, releasing the tension in her legs. She relaxed into the chair, suddenly aware of the stiffness of her posture. "Thank you, Captain."

"Lieutenant Commander Mill," Armstrong said, turning away from the window to face her, "you trusted me with this. Now I am trusting you to do what is necessary. Are we clear?"

"We're clear," she replied. "My loyalty has not changed."

He nodded. "Dismissed, Lieutenant Commander."

She stood and saluted before leaving, taking the long way down to soothe her nerves.

29

It was noisy aboard the *Avalon* that night after they departed Argos. The rec room clamored with voices and laughter, and Jaya sat unnaturally still in the middle of it.

"You should have seen his face," Thompson was saying. "He thought I was dead, but I came barreling out of that settlement and it was like he saw a ghost. I still don't know how I survived."

"The average terrorist is too dumb to know to shoot you," Shea snorted, their dark eyes bright from liquor and laughter.

Thompson poured whiskey from his own flask into Shea's cup, then raised his flask in a toast. "To the dumbest assholes in the galaxy—may they all be on the other team."

Sal rolled his eyes and refused to drink to Thompson's toast. He dealt out another hand of cards. "You want to talk about some narrow escapes," he said. "One time I swear Jaya was toe-to-toe with an insurgent with a shotgun, no way he wasn't going to pull the trigger."

Jaya snapped her head up at that and sent Sal a withering look.

"What?" he asked. "You moved so fast. I've never seen anyone jump so high in my life."

"Less talk, more cards," Jaya insisted. She dealt out another round and examined her hand with deliberate focus.

Sal caught her eye over the table as they played. He mouthed a question to her: *are you okay?*

She waved it off: *I'm fine.*

Too fine, in fact. The wound in her side had stopped hurting entirely. Though Sunny had told her not to expect improvement for a few days, her strength had already returned. The doctor would give her one last examination before the mission to determine if she was healthy enough to go, and Jaya had a suspicion that under the gauze there might be little more than an ugly pink mark.

She wasn't entirely sure why that scared her more than the idea of being grounded for this mission.

Sal caught her eye again and mouthed something else: *I'm sorry.*

She softened a little and smiled an apology back to him. She had been too harsh. But in reality, she was distracted, still reeling from the events of the past few days. Keir's words hadn't left her mind, weaving themselves in among her other thoughts, becoming a subtle counterpoint to the melody of her stream of consciousness. *The Union has gotten very good at hiding their dirty secrets.* All governments kept secrets, but Kier was angry, very deep down. She had seen it in the tautness of his face, had heard notes of anguish in his voice. *You're special, and so am I. People like us scare them.* People like us.

That was the phrase that sat the most uneasily in the back of her mind. The strange, nagging sense that something had always been wrong with her—that her skill on the battlefield was not just unusual, but unnatural. Could Keir's claim to greatness be more than just an indication that he had lost his mind?

As soon as she could, she excused herself from the card game and headed for the med bay. She walked to Tynan's makeshift office and poked her head in.

He was deep in conversation with Sunny, and they both turned back to look at her as she knocked on the door frame.

"Sorry to interrupt," Jaya said. "Do you have a minute, Doctor Vasuda?"

"Of course," he said.

Sunny stood and left, giving Jaya a smile as she passed. Jaya closed the door behind her and took a seat.

"I need to talk to you about something," she said. "And I need you to promise you won't repeat it to anyone."

"You have my word. What is it?"

"Something's been bothering me," she said. "About myself, about my strength, my reflexes. They've always been significantly better than they should be. I was a musician before I joined the military, a scared little girl who had barely seen a gun, let alone fired one. But when I got to training, everything was easy. Without realizing I was even doing it, I would react to things. It seemed like once adrenaline kicked in, I was unstoppable."

Tynan was watching her with wide, earnest eyes. He looked intrigued, so she continued.

"I recently ran into someone who knew me in my childhood—knew my family. He said I was different. Special. Could there be anything to that?"

"People say that all the time about their friends and family."

"No, this was different."

"What do you mean?"

"My father was a scientist," she said. "Could he have... changed me somehow? Made me stronger and faster than others? Improved my senses?"

He thought for a moment, frowning slightly.

"I wouldn't say it's impossible," he said. "It would have to be very high-quality work for the military to have not detected it."

"Could you, I don't know, run some tests? Check for it? What would you even be looking for?"

"I could take blood and tissue samples, look closely for nanotechnology in the bloodstream or implants that mimic human tissue. There is also the potential for genetic engineering. I could compare your DNA to that of your parents to check for anomalies."

She shook her head. "My parents both died years ago."

"One moment," he said. He stood and left the room.

Jaya tried to focus the thoughts whirling through her mind. The thought of possibly finally having an explanation for the chronic weirdness of the last decade and a half was a relief. But she still felt that strange tugging in her chest—the feeling that things weren't quite right. If her body—perhaps even her mind—had been designed, engineered, what did that make her? What if everything she had believed to be essential to her was just part of her father's plan, whatever that had been?

He had been deeply unhappy, her father, always pulled between his ideals and the reality of his life. Mother said he had seen dark things during his time in the military, and they had never spoken about why he was discharged. All Jaya knew was that for her entire childhood, she was certain that the world would never be enough for her father. And she was a part of that world.

Had he failed even with her and Kier? Had he somehow built them to be the perfect children and found he just had ordinary kids with ordinary problems? Children who might be able to run a little faster and beat up the other kids if they wanted to, but were still human. Flawed.

The doctor returned, his arms full of equipment, and shut the door again. He set everything on the table and sat down, sorting through it. There were quite a few needles, Jaya noticed. He connected several of the needles to vials, and set another, larger one aside. Then he looked up.

"Do you want me to test for this?" he asked.

She swallowed. The results might not be good, she knew. She might be facing something terrifying, unknown, and life altering.

"Yes," she said finally. "I do."

He took blood samples and set them aside, then picked up the larger needle for a muscle biopsy. That pinched, and Jaya gritted her teeth as the doctor removed a tiny slice of her bicep.

"Hope you don't need that," he said with a twinkle in his eye.

"Did you just make a joke?" Jaya asked, a shocked laugh escaping.

He just smiled and set aside the needles. "I can test all of these in private. I have access to the necessary equipment here in the med bay, and I will be sure that Doctor Choi is not made aware, unless you want her to be."

"Not yet," Jaya said. "Possibly not ever."

He nodded. "I understand. I'll let you know as soon as I have the results."

"Thank you." Jaya stood. "I really appreciate it."

"I'm glad to help, Lieutenant Commander Mill. You've done so much for me."

She nodded, and started to leave the room. She stopped in the doorway. "Doctor? You can really just call me Jaya."

"Very well. You may call me Tynan."

She gave him a smile, and then left.

Jaya threw another punch, connecting squarely with the bag. After a fitful night, she had passed her health examination with flying colors and was cleared to go on the mission. But nerves still ate at her. She hadn't been able to quell the uncomfortable fluttering of her stomach, so instead she clenched her fists and tried to be thankful for the absence of pain in her side.

As the bag spun back toward her, she let loose with a round-house kick that impacted with all the force of her frustration. A little of the anxiety flowed out of her and into the reeling bag, but it was quickly replaced by new tremors.

"You know, even Armstrong might be a little pissed with you if you break our nice gym equipment."

It was Sal's voice. Cool and calm, as usual, but there was a gentler tone to it than his usual thick layer of sarcasm.

"That's absurd," she said. "These bags are too strong for that."

But she relaxed a little and instead of hitting the bag on its next return swing, she caught it, slowing it to a stop. She looked back at Sal.

He just stared at her.

"Can I help you, Sal?" she asked.

He held up his hands. "I come in peace."

She gave him a weak smile, then turned away, focusing her attention on unwrapping her hands. The regular motion was like a salve on her nerves.

"You okay?" Sal asked. "You took off pretty fast from our game last night. I wasn't playing *that* badly."

"Sal," she said, but once she had begun, she realized she had no idea how to finish. For a moment, he just watched her, his eyebrows raised expectantly. Jaya looked away, fixing her eyes on her hands instead as she removed the wrap. "I don't want to talk about this one. Not yet. I need to figure some things out first."

The soft sound of boots on the mats of the gym floor pulled her attention away. Sal followed her gaze: Captain Armstrong was entering the room.

"Lieutenant Azima," Armstrong said as he approached the two. "I would like to speak with Lieutenant Commander Mill."

Sal winked at Jaya and whispered, "Told you to take it easy on the equipment."

She rolled her eyes at him, and he grinned in reply. Then, he turned to Armstrong and saluted.

Armstrong watched as Sal left the room, then turned his gaze to

Jaya, who stuffed the knot of hand wrap in her pocket and saluted as well.

"At ease," Armstrong said.

Jaya relaxed her stance. "What brings you to the training gym?"

"I wanted to continue our conversation," he said, his voice quiet. "At least part of it."

She clasped her hands behind her back to keep from crossing her arms and betraying the spike of fear that lanced through her. She chose her words carefully and delivered them with as much calm as she could muster. "Which part of the conversation?"

Armstrong's eyes softened. "Not that part," he said. "I want to ask you about something you said. You said you've only ever been loyal to the Union."

"I have," Jaya began to protest, but Armstrong waved his hand.

"I'm not questioning you," he said. "It's just a matter that has been weighing on me." Armstrong turned away, looking over at the heavy bag, which still swayed very slightly. He reached out, his fingers brushing the bag and slowing its movement. "Something is brewing. Something I wish I could say I had seen coming sooner."

Jaya pressed her lips together to keep from talking. She felt the tension in Armstrong's shoulders as if they were her own. He kept his voice low, even though the gym was empty.

He drew himself up straighter and looked back at Jaya. "It's become clear to me that loyalty to the Union means something different to each person. That some only serve those at the top. They think the Union is the handful of people whose faces we see in the feeds every day, whose names everyone knows. I worry that even within the Navy, many of us have forgotten that the Union we serve is the people who make it up, not the people who would rule it."

Jaya nodded. He was opening a door for her—giving her a glimpse into whatever it was that had passed between him and Tully and Reid in the briefing.

"I may not have grown up in a poor colony," Armstrong said.

"But I've tried to understand every person who has come through my ship. I've seen enough to recognize there's a fracture in the Union, and the cracks expand every day."

Something passed over his face, and he rubbed at his jaw with his hand. There was that weariness in his blue eyes again. The lack of sleep had left dark bruises beneath his eyes and leached the warmth from his brown skin, but his eyes were still bright with determination.

"I trust you, Lieutenant Commander. You have proven yourself to be a leader, on the field and on the ship. And you think for yourself. We need more of that—people have stopped asking the tough questions, even in the intelligence community. We're all too willing to blindly follow orders. But you don't wait to be told. You trust your instincts, and you keep your eyes open."

She nodded. "Yes, Captain. You taught me that."

"I also have no doubt," he said, "that if you had to show where your loyalties lie, you would make the right choice. That you wouldn't forget who we serve."

"The people," Jaya murmured. "Who else?"

The lines of his face softened briefly. But then he sighed, heavily. "I have some information. It's vital that it not fall into anyone else's hands. That means the people whose orders we follow."

"Understood," she said, but there was a question in her tone.

"This information I mentioned is stored in my palm drive. I have the only copy. And I have taken steps to ensure that it does not fall into the wrong hands."

"Why are you telling me this?" Jaya said. "I'm not your first officer."

He didn't reply for a long while. Then he sighed again. "When we return to Argos, I am planning to request a transfer. And a promotion. I need a first officer whose desire to serve is grounded in the right things."

Jaya nodded. The door was opening wider. That meeting with

Reid had not sat well with Armstrong either. Tully had been overeager to agree with Reid, something Jaya had already overheard although she was not ready to admit that to Armstrong yet. But she also sensed there was still more to his decision—perhaps a change in the dynamics between the two top-ranking officers on the *Avalon*. A conversation she had not yet been privy to. Or maybe his instincts were telling him something the evidence could not yet confirm.

"Thank you, Captain," she said, standing straighter and saluting.

"Lieutenant Commander, I feel confident about this mission with you heading the strike teams. When we dock and the transfer is completed, we will find a secure meeting place, and I will tell you my concerns. Until we return to Argos, I need your silence on this matter. And I need your trust."

"You have that. In the ten years I've worked for you, you have never let your crew down."

Armstrong made a sound not unlike a laugh, but its tone was dark and bitter. She looked up at him again, and his eyes shone pale and hard in his dark face.

"I hope that is true," he said. "I really do."

Jaya's palm drive beeped—they were approaching the station. She glanced up at Armstrong, who nodded.

"Ready your team, Commander," he said.

"Yes, Captain." She saluted before she left. As she walked out the door, she looked back. Armstrong remained still, surveying the equipment in the training gym, the slight rounding of his shoulders the only indication of the weight of their conversation.

30

Mara and her captors dropped out of FTL into the eerie glow of a red giant. She couldn't be sure how long the journey had taken, as she had woken heavily drugged and bound to a seat on a passenger craft not much larger than her own. In her hazy state, it was hard to track the passage of time. When she was coherent enough to remember what had happened, she glared at the man guarding her from his seat nearby, but she spent most of the flight with her eyes half-closed, lost in feverish memories of white marble halls and gardens spilling greenery over stone walls and dirty corridors packed with the galaxy's outcasts and sticky webs of congealing blood.

Her captors spoke to each other, their voices reaching her warped and incoherent. How many were there? It seemed that every time she looked toward them their number changed. Their features blurred and melded together. She forced her eyes to focus on one of the nearby viewscreens, battling the nausea that swam just beneath the surface of her consciousness. A station loomed ahead, and the ship's autopilot was already tracking them in toward it. A cold thrill ran down her back, freezing the nausea into an icy grip of fear.

For a brief moment, she regretted not killing Onyema. But it was not *that* failure that had landed her here. And besides, she'd built up a lifetime of regrets. What was one more or less?

The ship passed smoothly into the docking bay. The opening widened around them like the maw of some creature swallowing her whole. Mara pressed herself against her seat, trying to settle her breath into something approaching normalcy. A slight shudder, and the ship was nestled into its dock.

Someone leaned over her and released her bonds. Too late, she thought *this is your chance*. Too late because by the time her sluggish thoughts had reached the muscles of her arms and legs, she had already been yanked up, off-balance, and then she forgot that she had intended to fight them, to free herself. Her mind lost itself in trying to hold her body upright as they dragged her through a maze of identical silver-walled corridors.

And then she was pulled back into the awareness of pain, which alternated between throbbing listlessly and searing through her body. She looked around her gray surroundings. Her left side felt cold and—oh, that's where the pain was. Localized in her leg and her side. She blinked and realized she was lying on the floor of a flat gray room.

Mara pushed with her hands on the cold floor, rolling her body to face the ceiling. Now she could tilt her head to see most of the room. It was small. Thick shatterproof glass on one side and dull brushed chrome on the other three.

On her back, the pain in her still-healing wounds subsided until it was just a dull ache diffusing across her entire body with each beat of her heart. The cold floor soothed the heat in her abdomen. Fuck, was the wound infected? She had used the antiseptics on Onyema's ship, but human medicine was never strong enough for nareian bodies. Nausea washed over her and she rolled to her uninjured side to heave. Nothing came out.

She collapsed back down and stared at the ceiling until it stopped undulating. There was some comfort in its stark lines— perfect right angles in the corners. Her world was starting to come back into focus, all eight meters squared of it.

A voice came through the sound system.

"Feeling better, your royal highness?"

"Fuck you." The words came out on a thin breath, but she injected as much venom into them as had been roiling in her blood not long ago.

The voice laughed, unbothered by her anger. That was fine, *she* appreciated the anger. Felt it bubbling up in her blood, enriching it like oxygen. She tapped into the vein, drawing that anger into her heart, into her mind. She breathed it like a drug, clearing away the last of the sedative's fog. She closed her eyes and lost herself in the feeling for a moment.

The voice returned again. It was a strangely pleasant voice, musical in its expression. This was a voice with power.

"You won't be here for long," it soothed her. "Don't worry. An old friend is on her way already to pick you up."

Mara groaned. She should have killed Yanu when she had the chance. Add that to her list of regrets. The cold certainty that her life of freedom was at an end drew the euphoria of rage down, sucking it from her brain, leaving only smoldering coals. Mara searched for ideas, any breath of air that could fan those coals back into their flame, that could rekindle her chance at freedom.

"I'm much more useful without petty narean politics getting in my way," she said. "You could use someone like me. I'm resourceful."

That laugh again. This time, less pleasant to Mara's ears. "I see that. Very resourceful of you to have penetrated our station. I'm sure you're right where you want to be."

Mara's mind was starting to warm up, turning over every possibility. What if his sarcastic jab actually held a grain of truth? Was there some way Mara could use this to her advantage? What information could she glean if they thought she was a helpless prisoner, a failed bounty hunter, not even capable of killing an old woman? When they turned her over to the Hydeans, what could she use against them to regain her freedom?

She needed information. As much of it as she could get.

"The money you'll get for my bounty is nothing next to the services I could provide," she said.

"You have no idea," the voice replied. "You're irreplaceable, Marantos."

Mara closed her eyes again. How much time did she have to gather information, to formulate her plan? Not long, according to this man. But he was being careful not to reveal any details.

The voice did not return again. Mara's eyes traced the lines where the blank ceiling met the flat walls, breathing as deeply as she could. With every breath, with every minute that passed, her mind grew clearer. She began to recognize the sounds outside her cell—the scuffle of boots on the floor, hushed conversations between humans.

She wanted to pull herself up to a seated position, but resisted the urge. It was better if they thought she was still drugged, still feeble. The wound in her side had weakened her, but Mara still had reserves of strength to call on. So instead of wasting that strength on sitting up, she turned her head and watched the rushed interactions outside.

A man stood at a console, typing. His hands flew frantically over the keys, then paused. He watched the screen, none of the anxiety leaving his body, and then his fingers raced again.

Was he deleting files?

"Hey you," Mara shouted. The man jumped and looked back over his shoulder at her. There was no mistaking the panic in his eyes. "When does my ride get here?"

"What?" His eyes were glassy, his mind focused still on his task. "What do you mean?"

"My ride," she growled. "Her most honorable ladyship Yanula of clan Hydea is coming to pick me up. Seems like it might need to be soon."

His look morphed into one of anger, and then disdain. He turned away without replying.

Well. She closed her eyes. She might need that reserve of strength sooner than she thought.

Yanu couldn't help but gloat when she arrived. She stood on the other side of the glass, two bodyguards flanking her, and looked over Mara's prone figure.

"Oh, Mara," she said, a cruel smile revealing pointed teeth. "Look at where your choices brought you. Alone in a prison cell, bloodied and drugged silly, with no friends to help. Not much without your weapons, are you?"

"You never could stop your mouth," Mara replied, making the words come out sluggish and slurred. She winced as she pulled herself up.

"I recall you used to like that."

One of the humans stepped forward. He was tall for a human, his shirt cut close to his broad shoulders and trim waist. His hair blazed like a flame on his head, and the moment he spoke Mara recognized his voice as the one that had spoken to her before.

"You'll have plenty of time to taunt her on your way home," he said.

Yanu narrowed her amber eyes to slits and showed her teeth. The man was unmoved, his expression almost a mirror of hers.

"What's the rush?" Yanu asked. "We only just got here."

The man's face warped into a grimace. "The Union is sending a strike team for us," he said. "You'll want to be out of here before they arrive."

Yanu stepped forward, snarling her response: "I thought you had the Union under your thumb. What happened to your admirals, your civil servants?"

"It's under control," the man said, his voice soft and dangerous. "Just a small hitch, which we are handling. Part of the process. Our plans are still underway, and we will have the Union's head and its sword in a matter of days. Then we will discuss the rest."

Mara watched the exchange, saw Yanu's certainty flicker. She always had been a coward. Yanu stepped back.

"Fine," she said. "We'll take her off your hands."

The man smiled, a surprisingly charming expression. He typed a command into his palm drive and Mara's door opened.

She let Yanu's thugs drag her up, relaxing her muscles so that her entire weight was supported by their grips on her arms. She shot a glare at Yanu as they passed by her before letting her head loll back down. Had to keep the charade realistic, and Yanu knew Mara would never pass up a chance to sneer.

The man led the way, his motions swift.

As they carried her through the corridors, the chaos of the station bloomed around her. Humans in chrome body armor streamed alongside them and announcements blared over the intercoms, directing different teams to their positions. Most were being called to the hangar bay. Mara made herself as much of an impediment as she could, noticing how the man glanced back impatiently. She stumbled and hissed, pulling Yanu's attention back to her.

"Yanu." Mara let a hint of a whimper through in her voice. "I know you're a bitch, but do you have to kill me?"

Yanu frowned, a mixture of pity and anger on her face. "How bad is her wound?" She turned back to the man, whose frustration was growing, bringing a light of rage into his gold-ringed eyes.

"She's fine," he said.

"I can't risk her being hurt worse," Yanu snapped. "You couldn't get her a doctor?"

"I don't exactly have nareian specialists on this station. She's fine—she's just being a pain."

"Of course, it's in her nature," Yanu sneered. "But I have more riding on her health than you."

"We don't have time for this."

"Do you have somewhere to be?"

"Yes, actually," he said, crossing his arms. "The timing of my departure is crucial. You're risking the entire collaboration. If I'm not in position when they arrive…"

"Leave us, then," Yanu said. "What, do you think we'll steal something on our way out?"

"I'm better at retrieving things than taking them," Mara said, letting her last word sputter out in a gasp. The effect on Yanu's face was satisfying.

"Fine," the man said. "Coddle your delicate princess. You have one hour before you need to be out of this system. See that you make the deadline."

Yanu nodded. When the man turned to leave, she returned her attention to Mara, her expression cold. "Are you currently bleeding out?"

Mara made a face.

"Then we don't stop moving," Yanu said. "We can go slowly, but we keep moving."

"Fine," Mara spat. "Don't let me slow you down."

Yanu resisted the retort, which Mara could see written in the tense lines of her shoulders, and turned away. They made slow progress as the corridors began to empty around them. The soldiers in their body armor had made their ways to the various ships and internal positions. The announcements ceased, and the station quieted around them.

In the new hush of the hall, Mara breathed heavily, theatrically, exhaling with ragged gasps. Every minute that they supported her weight was another minute of rest. Another minute to pull on the last of her strength. But also another minute closer to the ship that would make her a prisoner again. She had no idea how far the hangar bay was, and the minutes brought her strength and bled time away.

Fuck it, she thought. *Now is as good a time as any.*

She threw a foot forward and staggered, using her weight and the strength of her muscles to pull sharply to the right. She cried out in pain, both real and exaggerated at the same time. The bodyguard gripping her left arm lost his balance, pulled along with Mara toward his companion. His hands came free from her arm. At the same moment, Yanu swung her head around to see what was wrong. Concern was written on her face as she took in Mara's grimace.

Perfect.

Ignoring the way the pain seared in her belly, she threw her right leg up in a powerful kick, connecting with Yanu's face. The motion loosened her right arm from the other guard's grip, and he caught his companion with his outstretched hands. Mara slipped away and took off the way they had come, dropping into quadrupedal motion and ignoring the way her leg and side screamed at her choices.

She turned at random. Left, right, right, straight past a few open hallways, then left again.

First priority, make it as hard as possible for them to find her. Second priority, figure out where the fuck she was and how she was going to get out before Union strike teams were crawling all over the place.

But her body had other ideas. Her leg collapsed beneath her as she took a sharp left and she slammed into the wall. Nauseating pain burst through her shoulder and she curled up for a moment, reduced to yawning in silent agony.

When her vision cleared and she was finally able to draw in a deep breath, she pushed herself up on her knees. Her ragged breaths scraped along her airways. Every muscle in her body was raw.

The corridor around her was empty and silent. No sign of life— no clomping of heavy human feet or even the soft padding of her light-footed nareian pursuers. No voices arguing.

Still, she needed to put more distance between them. She crawled along the floor, leaving bloody streaks beneath her left knee. A few dark red-purple drops splatted below her as she pushed herself faster. She was leaving a trail again. Damn Onyema's companions and their skill with weapons.

She might as well move that second priority up. At this point, once they found her trail, they would find her.

Mara clawed her way to a stand in the next doorframe she passed. She staggered to a console just inside the room and opened it.

She was able to pull up a map of the station. Her location was highlighted with a red dot, and she scrolled through the floor plan and cursed herself. She had fled deeper and deeper into the center of the station. She was in some sort of laboratory. Nearby were more laboratories and offices, and both the armory and the hangar were far enough away to make her groan in anticipatory agony at the distance she would have to cover.

She sank down to the floor, resting her back against the base of the console, her thoughts a stream of invective directed at Yanu, Onyema, the man who had hired her and then fucked her over—and herself. She had put herself squarely in this mess. She had let herself get desperate, and desperation bred stupidity.

The tears shocked her. How many years had it been since she had cried? The last bitter tears had been over Tai's body before she had put steel in her spine and swore to herself that she would never be in that position again. And here she was, crumpled in a bloody, sweaty pile on a strange station.

And Yanu. Yanu would win again. Mara would be returned home less than what she was when she left. Broken. A pawn now for Palva's side of the cold war.

Would it break her mother? Would it be enough to shift the power? The balance between the two families had been pulled tight to the point of snapping, and Mara's return could be the hammer that shattered it once and for all. And what of Narei? Would her homeland survive the fallout?

Mara had never wanted to be Empress. In fact, she'd thought her flight would leave both herself and her people better off. A reluctant ruler would do Narei no good. Besides, she had believed her mother would find another way. That was what she did.

The shuffling of soft nareian footwear spread through the corridor and reached her ears. Her heart sank. It was truly over now.

She looked up. The station's occupants had emptied out most of the laboratory's supplies, but not all the equipment had been taken. Glass beakers overturned on a drying rack sparkled in the light.

Maybe if she hurt them enough, they would decide she wasn't worth it. Maybe one last attempt…

Mara knew she might never be free again, but at least she could make it hurt. One more regret.

She pulled herself up, the blood fleeing her head. She pushed against the spots in her vision and braced herself on the countertop where the beakers were displayed. She grabbed one and smashed it against the side of the counter, leaving a ring of ugly shards at the end. That would do.

She heard Yanu's voice. They had found the trail of blood. Mara pressed herself against the wall beside the door and waited.

Their voices silenced as they approached, but Mara could see them in her mind. They would be following the path around the corner now. They would be approaching the door. She kept her eyes fixed on the entrance, swallowed against the rapid pulse in her throat.

One of Yanu's goons entered first, and she thrust the broken glass into his throat. He collapsed onto her, his blood warm on her face. The fall robbed her of her breath, and she lay stunned as Yanu and her other guard came screaming in. The guard pointed his gun at Mara's head.

Mara groped around the body that weighed her down and found his gun. She fired wildly at them—both shots missing—and shoved the body off, clambering behind the nearest cabinet.

"You fucking idiot!" Yanu screamed. "You can't shoot her!"

Mara steadied her shaking hands and pushed herself onto her right side. She pointed the gun around the corner and fired again. Desperation tasted acidic in her mouth. She just wanted them to know she wouldn't go quietly. Yanu screamed at her lackey again, the words slurring in Mara's head.

Someone slammed into her from the other side of the cabinet. She had misjudged their positions, and now she watched her stolen gun clatter out of her hand and across the floor, where Yanu picked it up and pointed it at her.

She wouldn't shoot. Mara wished she would, as the bodyguard's strong arms hauled her up.

At least she'd gotten one of them.

"Stop," a voice bellowed from the door.

Yanu froze and turned. With great effort, Mara raised her head to see four humans in full armor in the doorway. Three of them fanned out behind the one in front, a woman who called in a clear and musical voice, "Who are you? What's going on here?"

And Yanu, stupid Yanu, fired in panic at the humans.

It was over in a microsecond. Yanu crumpled to the ground and Mara fell hard with the guard who held her up. She landed on top of him, turning her head to see the neat hole in his eye. She tried to raise her head and groaned.

The woman appeared in Mara's vision, and through the clear visor of the helmet, Mara saw the concerned expression on a strangely familiar face. Broad cheekbones painted with freckles and warm hazel eyes, and at the edges of the visor, little wisps of red hair.

She looked just like the man who had imprisoned her on this station.

31

The red giant loomed darkly in the shuttle's observation window, the glass filtering out the harmful radiation, but leaving the sinister glow. The trip had passed quickly—Jaya had kept her thoughts trained on the mission ahead, and that singular focus seemed to bring them closer and closer to their goal, increasing the rate at which the shuttle moved.

The minutes raced by like seconds. Soon the shuttle was sealed to the station, and once again Jaya found herself cutting through the hull. They had chosen their entrance more strategically this time, selecting an area near the location of the central lab so they could get in and out quicker.

The piece of the hull that she was cutting finally came loose, and she pushed it so that it fell into the station. The corridor was silent. The two teams filed in and started down the hall toward the lab.

The hairs on the back of Jaya's neck rose up—something wasn't right. She scanned the area for heat and motion and found nothing, and yet something in her still screamed danger.

She opened her mouth to say so, but was halted by a loud bang.

Then came the rush of dozens of boots on the ground just behind them.

"Run!" she called over the comms. "Straight ahead or they'll surround us. Go go go!"

They ran down the hall as the enemy forces started to pour in behind them. Jaya cleared a room to the left and Rhodes took one to the right. Both were empty, and the two strike teams ducked behind the doorways, taking turns putting pressure on the Sons of Priam forces.

Augustus's men filled the corridor in front of them, their particle beams streaking through the air. Jaya took one down and ducked behind the doorframe again. She saw Thompson poke his head around and take another out. Across the way, Rhodes was changing out the heat sink in his gun. He caught her glance and gave her a nod. Sal was assembling his rifle—it looked like they would be holding out at this spot for a while. He snapped the last piece into place and grabbed a magnetic shipping crate.

"Give me a hand?" he asked Jaya.

Jaya retreated into the room with him and helped him haul the crate to the door. Thompson and Shea moved aside and they shoved the crate down. It crashed into the hallway, providing a short barrier that they could crouch behind. Sal crawled over and propped the muzzle of his rifle on the edge.

Bam-BAM—he took down one of the men at the back.

Jaya and Rhodes crawled toward each other at the center of the crate. They poked their heads above cover, aimed, and each took down another Son of Priam. The enemy forces were going down quickly, but reappearing even more quickly. It seemed the entire station had been on alert, waiting for their arrival. They were cut off from their shuttle now, pinned down in this hallway, halfway to their objective. And although Jaya looked, there was no sign of Augustus.

And none of these combatants had appeared on the scans.

Jaya's dread grew. The technology that hid the IRC strike teams from enemy scans was military tech. It wasn't supposed to be on the black market yet, although that technological cold war was inevitable.

Jaya radioed the *Avalon*.

"Captain Armstrong, Alpha team is in. We've encountered heavy fire, and possible stolen Navy tech. It looks like they knew we were coming."

There was silence on the other end.

"Captain Armstrong, come in," she called again, casting a worried glance over at Rhodes. "Captain?"

Still nothing.

"Damn!" She whipped out of cover, shooting to her right over the overturned cabinet. Again, she heard the loud *bam-BAM* of Sal's rifle.

He was dropping the people at the back as they came in, allowing the rest of the team to focus on those in front.

"Alpha One to *Avalon*, come in," she called. "Anyone, respond!"

A small, frightened voice crackled over the line. It was Tynan.

"The bridge went silent a few minutes ago," he said. "They're on the ship."

Shit. "How did they get on?"

"I don't know. There are a few of us in the med bay. Security has gone upstairs, but we haven't heard from them in a few minutes."

"Keep us updated, Tynan," she said. "We'll come back as soon as we can."

She closed the comm link and took a minute to think. They were near the lab—she just needed to get someone in there with the bombs. If they could keep the Sons of Priam occupied and sneak someone out, they might be able to get the bombs planted. Their second objective of capturing leadership would have to be shelved. Then there was the issue of getting out.

Particle beam fire sizzled in the air above her head.

"Rhodes," she said. "Change of plans. I need you to oversee a team here. Keep them occupied and see if you can thin the ranks. I'll go in with a small team and plant the bombs. When I give the signal, pull back. They've blocked the path to our shuttle, so we'll have to take one of theirs."

"Understood," he said.

Then a realization hit her like a flashbang and she swore.

"The nukes," she said. "Sal, who checked them before we left?"

"I checked them yesterday when we got them in Argos. I took them to the armory when I was done."

"Check them again."

"Now?" Sal asked, as particle beam fire sang across the top of the metal cabinet.

"Yes, now."

Sal crawled back into the room they had initially hidden in and opened the cover of the first bomb, checking the wiring on the timer. He stopped suddenly and looked up at Jaya, his mouth gaping. Then he checked the second bomb.

"The power supply is disconnected," he said. "Both of them. The wire is just gone. They're duds."

"Thought so," Jaya said grimly.

"I can fix it," Sal said. "Just give me a minute."

He pulled a container from his belt and opened it, yanking some wires out and getting to work reconnecting the break in the circuit.

Jaya popped up to thin the front lines of the approaching armored forces, then lowered herself back down. Her back pressed against the metal door of the cabinet, and she tucked her knees up to her side. She watched Sal, willing him to go faster.

After a moment, he closed both cases, pressed a few buttons on the timer, and then nodded, satisfied. "It's not pretty, but it'll work."

"I can't think of a time a nuke has ever been pretty," she replied. "Glad I have you around for fixing gadgets."

"Glad to have you around for your sixth sense," he said, smiling.

She nodded, then turned to the corporals crouched to her left. "Shea, Thompson, you're with me. Each of you grab a nuke—I'll take point. Rhodes, I need your team to provide heavy cover fire so we can get the bombs around the corner. This will only work if they think we're all still over here fighting them."

Thompson and Shea crawled into the room with Sal, and each picked up one of the small bombs and inched their way against the doorframe.

Rhodes held up a grenade. "Flashbang," he said. "On my mark."

He tossed the grenade over the makeshift wall, and the team looked away as Rhodes detonated it remotely through his palm drive.

"Now!" Rhodes shouted. "Get out of here!"

They moved quickly, ducking out of sight around the corner before Augustus's men could see or hear again. The pure note of particle beam fire continued steadily—their team was pressing hard, trying to do as much damage as they could to the incoming hordes. This hallway was quiet, and Jaya, Shea, and Thompson pushed their pace, running toward the laboratory.

Up ahead, two hallways met. A tremor tingled up her legs, and Jaya slowed to a stop and motioned for Shea and Thompson to do the same. She prepared to scan the area ahead.

Then they heard the shouting. Jaya and Sal exchanged a glance.

"Let's go." Jaya broke into a run, pushing the team forward. They stopped, weapons raised, in the door of one of the laboratories.

The scene inside was gruesome—dark, purple blood spattered against the walls, and the large body of a dead nareian in light armor sprawled on the floor. Three more nareians stood, very much alive, staring at the humans in shock. Well, two of them stood. One was dressed far too elegantly for whatever this was, and she leveled her gun shakily at Jaya's team. The second, in light armor like his dead companion, held a very bloodied and very disoriented-looking third nareian by her right arm. He, too, pointed a gun at Jaya.

"Stop!" Jaya commanded. "Who are you? What's going on here?"

Panic widened the eyes of the elegantly dressed one, and time stilled as Jaya watched her finger compress the trigger. Jaya shot before the nareians could, first at the one who presented the most danger, and then at the one holding the hostage. They dropped.

"What the hell?" Thompson exclaimed.

"Check out the woman," Jaya said. "See if there's anything on her that might explain what the hell this was."

She crossed to the crumpled heap of two nareians on the far side of the room and crouched down. The male one was dead, but the woman was drawing in heaving breaths. Jaya did a visual check. While the nareian woman was covered in blood, it didn't seem to all be her own. She opened her eyes then—she had gray irises nearly swallowed by the black of her pupils. Jaya reached for her emergency first aid kit. There wouldn't be large enough doses for a nareian, but she could at least start to ease the pain.

"The fuck?" the nareian said. "Are you with them?"

"Hell, no," Thompson blurted behind her.

Jaya shot him a warning look. "I'm with the Union Navy. I'm going to give you some meds," she said, holding the needle where the nareian could see it. "Can I look at your injuries?"

The nareian nodded, still gasping for breath.

Jaya peeled the woman's shirt up from her abdomen and injected the painkillers. There was a recent wound in the woman's side that had been stitched up—rather clumsily, it appeared. The stitches had ripped at one end and the wound was seeping thick blood. Jaya took a field suture from her kit and closed the wound back up.

"Is that it?" Jaya asked.

"My leg. That's it. I think."

Jaya nodded and moved her inspection lower. Another set of old stitches, these ones stronger, had held in her leg. Her breathing was becoming steadier, less ragged. Jaya waved Thompson over to get extra meds.

"Holy shit," Sal shouted, crouched over the other body. "Is that Yanula Hydea? Fuck."

Shea leaned over the body as well, then straightened with a look of shock. "What is a nareian duchess doing with the Sons of Priam?"

"She's not a duchess." The nareian's voice cracked and she swallowed. "She's just a viscountess."

Jaya turned back to the injured nareian. "Who are you, and why are you here?"

The nareian tried to raise herself up, but grimaced and faltered. Jaya grasped her shoulders and helped her to a slightly more upright position.

Thompson handed over another syringe, and Jaya injected a second dose.

"Call me Zamya," the nareian said, the lines of pain in her face already starting to ease. "I'm here because I was abducted. I was supposed to be a trade. Something Yanu over there wanted in exchange for... well, I never really found out what their half of the deal was."

Sal crossed the space and crouched beside Jaya. "Why you?"

Zamya laughed, a bitter sound. "I'm kind of a big deal," she said drily. "But it's really none of your business."

Sal rolled his eyes.

"So the Sons of Priam were trading you for some favors from lesser nareian nobility?" Jaya pressed.

Zamya swallowed. "She has—had—some political ambitions. Thought she could use me to hurt someone. To climb the ladder. Help me up?"

"I don't think you're ready," Jaya said.

Zamya shot her an icy look and repeated herself. "Help. Me. Up."

Jaya gave Sal an exasperated look, but they both reached out to steady the nareian as she clutched her way up the cabinetry to a standing position. She sighed heavily, then waved them off.

A familiar voice crackled in over the comms—Armstrong.

"Lieutenant Commander Mill," he said. "Can you hear me?"

"Captain Armstrong," she said. "Yes, I can hear you."

The cacophony of conflict surged over the comm—Armstrong's voice was barely audible through it, but she recognized it anyway. Shea and Thompson glanced up at her.

"This is a secure line," Armstrong said. "We've been boarded by the Sons of Priam. Commander Coolidge is working with them."

Jaya found herself too sick to speak. Her instincts, the little chill that had been running up her neck lately when Tully spoke with her… She hadn't let herself imagine it was an imminent threat.

Armstrong sighed, the weight of regret making the sound heavy and thick. "Mill, I need you back on the *Avalon*."

"We're planting the nukes now," she said, waving at Thompson and Shea. They immediately leapt to work, setting up the bombs on opposite corners of the room and entering the sequence to arm them.

"Bravo team is under heavy fire," she continued. "And we're cut off. We'll have to commandeer a shuttle to get back to you."

"Then do it," he said, the strain in his voice breaking something inside Jaya.

Her chest constricted.

He was silent for a moment, and Jaya heard the sound of gunfire in the background rise to a terrible roar. It quieted briefly, and his voice returned.

"They've breached the bridge," he said. "Get back here as soon as you can. And Jaya?"

"Yes?"

"Whatever happens, remember that I trust you."

"Captain?"

And then he was gone.

Jaya looked over as Shea and Thompson finished their work. Identical red lights began to blink on each metal canister.

She looked back at Zamya. The nareian woman was as covered in tattoos as blood, the effect ferocious and chilling.

She blinked her gray eyes. "I can get you a ship," she said. "Yanu's will still be here. I'll fly you back to your ship, but then you let me go. With the ship." She grimaced. "And maybe an extra dose of painkillers."

Jaya nodded. "Agreed."

The nareian looked her over. Jaya struggled to read her expression, but it sent a sudden jolt of fear through her. Zamya nodded back, finally. "Okay."

"Alright." Jaya turned back to her team. "Now let's get the hell out of here. Rhodes," she called into her comm link. "Bombs are set. Are you guys ready to run?"

"I think we can get away, but hurry." Rhodes's voice cracked.

The ache in her chest flared, and fear and dread settled heavy on her shoulders.

"We'll meet you at the docking bay," Jaya said. "If you head down that corridor behind you, there's an alternate path that will bring you around to the bay. I'm uploading the coordinates to everyone's palm drives. Stay safe."

"You, too," he replied.

"Lupo," she called the small team still waiting in the shuttle they could no longer reach. "We got cut off, but found another way home. Meet us back at the *Avalon*."

"Understood, Lieutenant Commander," Lupo replied, her voice tight. "We'll be waiting for you back home."

Jaya looked back at Shea and Thompson and saw the same pinched look around their eyes. But right now, they couldn't waste energy on worry. All they could do was move forward.

"Let's go," she said. "Thompson and Shea, I want you ready to help Zamya if she needs it. We need to get all five of us out of here."

They nodded and took position behind Zamya, who eyed them warily. The corridors remained quiet as they followed the winding path to the hangar bay.

32

The machines were processing the blood and tissue samples he had taken from Jaya. There was not much else for him to do—his analysis of the lab was complete, and he had briefed the teams on what to expect. Now all that was left was to wait until they arrived at the station and could destroy the facilities. Tynan sighed and stretched his arms, the tight muscles in his torso expanding painfully after hours of hunching. Restless, he pushed open the door and entered the med bay proper.

Sunny was sitting at her computer, looking through files. She hadn't asked him what new tests he was running in his office, no doubt assuming he was verifying his assumptions about the lab's purpose. Assuming he was making a valuable contribution to the team. That realization dawned warm and pleasant in his mind.

He took a seat near Sunny, and she glanced up and gave him a smile.

"You busy?" he asked.

"Actually, not at all," she said. "Just trying to keep occupied."

"Me, too."

"The quiet is almost as tough as the action, isn't it?" she asked.

"It might actually be tougher," he replied. Then he laughed. "I never thought I'd actually say that. I dated someone for a while who used to say that I could give our entire race its reputation for cowardice."

Sunny didn't reply, and when he looked back up at her, she had fixed him with a look of such compassion that his chest ached as though her look had pierced right through it. She reached out and placed her hand over his.

"I don't think you're a coward," she said. "Not everyone needs to be ready to rush into battle. We need other skills, too."

"I only have one, really," he admitted. "I'm not brave, I'm not much of a leader. I can barely interact with my peers, let alone inspire them."

"Relationships are messy."

Tynan nodded. "But we still seek them out." He became aware of his incredulous tone as he spoke.

"Of course we do," she said with a smile, as if she hadn't heard the darkness in his voice. "Messy isn't always bad. In fact, it can be quite good."

"I guess."

Her hand was still on his. He decided he liked it—it was warm and soothing. She seemed to be giving him her energy, through the contact and through the insistence of her gaze. It unsettled him, the way she seemed to see right through him, and it thrilled him, too. She saw who he truly was, and accepted it anyway. Despite the late nights and the single-minded focus, and maybe even because of it.

He had grown to enjoy her company. He couldn't say that for many people in his life, and he wondered what that said about him.

"You want a drink?" she asked suddenly.

"Coffee?"

She smiled, pulling a bottle out of her desk drawer. The liquid sloshed in it, a rich golden tone. "No, something a little stronger."

"Are you supposed to have that on board?" he asked.

"It's allowed. And"—she checked the clock on her palm drive—"I'm technically off duty."

"Then, yes," he said. "I could use a drink."

She poured the liquid into a small glass and slid it across the desk to him. He smelled it and winced. The szacante had their own fermented and distilled drinks, of course, and Tynan had partaken of them at various socially acceptable times. He had even tried the human and nareian versions of these drinks at formal celebrations where board members threw liquor around like money. But he still always found himself shocked at the raw strength of the alien brews.

Szacante drinks were much more tame.

Sunny was watching him, the corner of her mouth quirked up.

He drank, a quick gulp, to wipe the beginnings of that grin off her face. But he nearly choked on the fire in his throat and his plan failed.

She laughed and threw her drink back. "What do you think?" she asked.

Tynan practically squirmed beneath the humor in her smile. He chose his words carefully.

"It's strong."

She laughed and poured one more swallow for each of them, then stored the bottle back in its drawer.

"Yes," she said. "That's usually the point."

Tynan drank the next one more slowly, and despite the way it burned his mouth, he imagined some notes of sweetness and spice in the liquid. Or maybe that was just the warmth in his belly talking.

"You've been working pretty hard in there," she said. "Anything we should worry about?"

Tynan felt a sudden urge to tell her everything. To spill it all out as she watched him with those dark eyes. He swallowed.

"Just running some tests," he said. It wasn't technically a lie, but he couldn't meet her eyes.

She made a sound somewhere between acknowledgement and questioning, and out of his periphery he saw her lift her glass to her lips. "They killed my mother, you know."

When Tynan looked up, she was staring into the golden liquid in her glass.

"What?" he asked.

"Not the Sons of Priam, but another group like them. They blew up a station she was on. She was a scientist, working for the Union."

He didn't know what to say.

She drained her glass and set it down on the table with a firm hand.

"My parents were killed in a rebellion," he offered.

She looked up at him. "Is there anyone in this galaxy who hasn't been fucked over by it?"

"By what?" He regretted the words and how naive they sounded the moment they fell in the stillness of the medical bay. Of course he knew what she meant. It seemed that not a day went by that some tragedy wasn't being reported on the news. Tynan had been able to ignore it in his years on Dresha. Had told himself that his own losses were enough—he didn't need to be burdened by the losses of the rest of the galaxy, too. But now that he was sitting here in this quiet room, choking down this fiery drink that warmed him to his fingers and toes, he suddenly regretted how little he knew about the rest of the galaxy.

In Sunny's eyes he saw it: they were all suffering. No one was untouched.

Mercifully, she didn't answer his stupid question. She just sighed and took his now-empty glass in the same hand that held her own. Her chair squeaked as she stood, then she washed the glasses in the sink and returned them to the drawer.

"You're not a coward," she said again when she returned to her seat.

A chime in his makeshift office drew his attention. He stood.

"I need to get that," he said.

She nodded and turned away, pulling up some paperwork on her data pad.

The warmth in his stomach warped, soured. He went into the office. The machines were still whirring, but one of them blinked at him in the dim light of the room. He bent over it and looked through the scope.

That didn't look right at all.

He blinked back the fog of eye strain and replaced his face over the eyepiece once more. He adjusted the magnification again, rolling the dial through from blurry to sharp clarity and back to blurry, fine-tuning it until he was confident the blood sample was correctly resolved. He blinked again.

These cells had been damaged the last time he had looked at them. He'd been certain of it when he saw them shredded a few hours ago in this same dish, their ragged edges swirling languorously in the fluid. He was still sure of it, despite the plump, healthy, red cells that swam happily now in the microscope, because he had thrown as much destructive radiation at them as Sunny would allow in her medical bay—a not inconsiderable amount. And they had shredded, forming a murky cloud of poison in their dish, just as predicted.

And yet, the blood he was looking at now seemed to be coming from an athlete in peak physical condition, with no history of even mild radiation exposure.

He checked another machine.

The muscle biopsy he had taken raised even more questions. The fibers were natural, yes, but they were unusual. They bore absolutely none of the usual signs of the illegal genetic engineering that emerged from time to time, despite how simple it was to identify the modifications. And yet, these fibers were extraordinarily strong and responsive to electrical stimulus.

It was uncanny. These samples would appear to be completely unaltered when subjected to normal testing. And it was nearly impossible to understand how they had been modified.

Was this the kind of enhancement the Sons of Priam had referenced in their notes? They had mentioned previous subjects—had Tynan just stumbled on one?

The thought stopped him cold. This was evidence of everything he fought against. Every moral code, every ethical standard, each one violated by the very existence of someone whose cells could do something like this. What kind of person was living with them right now on this ship? What kind of person was leading the strike team to take down the very labs that might be producing more people like her?

But she had volunteered. She had asked him to run the tests.

And over the weeks he had spent with the company of the *Avalon,* he had always found himself agreeing with Jaya Mill. He had been grateful for her support, for her encouragement. What was her connection to all this? Was she a victim? Had she always known?

He looked closer at the raw cellular material. Time wavered, melted into a haze of concentration as he studied the materials.

Tynan was just starting a new analysis of the blood sample when a red light began flashing on the wall of his tiny office. Its blinking rhythm drew his attention away from his work for a moment and he watched it. It continued, its pulse insistent, and then suddenly stopped.

He was about to return to his analysis when Sunny's voice broke through his focus again.

"Medical bay to bridge, report."

There was an edge to her voice that ended any hope of Tynan's thoughts returning to the work.

"Medical bay to bridge, report," she repeated, and the calmness of her tone felt deliberate.

His mouth was suddenly dry. He swallowed and pushed the door open.

Sunny looked over at him, and he saw something in her face he had never seen before. Her eyes seemed larger, the lines of her face narrower. She met his eyes—her irises were nearly swallowed up by the black of her dilated pupils. She turned her eyes to the duo working medical bay security. The shorter of the two spoke into his own palm drive, repeating Sunny's request for a report from the bridge.

The silence closed around them like a heavy cloak. Tynan could hear his heart pounding in his ears, and the sound of his own breathing, shallow and rapid.

When their call remained unanswered after what felt like an eternity, the shorter guard raised a hand, signaling to the other. "Opening a private channel," he said to Sunny. "Find cover and wait for us to come back. We'll stay in communication."

"Understood," she replied.

"Engineering, this is medical bay," Sunny spoke. "Any contact from the bridge since the distress signal?"

This time, the reply was immediate. A woman's voice, low and hoarse, came over the medical bay's communications system.

"Negative, Doctor Choi. I was about to call you. We've been unable to raise the bridge."

"Medical security team is moving to investigate," Sunny said. "Engineering security, you stay put."

"Acknowledged," another voice chirped. "We're prepared for contact."

"Let's hope this is just a malfunction," she said.

The security team left, sealing the blast panel over the medical bay doors. A hand grasped Tynan's elbow firmly, and he realized with a start that Sunny had crossed the room and was moving him.

She pulled him behind her desk, which shielded them from the door, and they crouched behind it together.

He realized with a slowly awakening dread that she had taken out her pistol, and her face was set in hard lines.

But when she looked at him, he saw those lines soften.

"We'll be okay," she assured him, although the words felt false and empty. "Just stay here with me."

Tynan could not even summon the will to shake his head. Her words washed over him, but he felt nothing.

A sudden, staccato sound burst over the private link the security team had opened. And then silence again.

"Mehdi, status?" Sunny asked. "Contact?"

Dead airwaves were the only response. Tynan struggled to find his voice.

"The mission," he croaked. "We should tell them."

Sunny nodded, and Tynan opened up a connection to Jaya, somewhere out in the blackness of space. Perhaps already on the station. He feared discovering that same ominous silence from the strike team as well when he tried to contact them, but Jaya's voice suddenly rang out strong in his ear.

"Alpha One to *Avalon*, come in. Anyone, respond!"

The relief that suddenly flooded him set his whole body shaking. Maybe there was still a chance. He told Jaya of the silence from the bridge, the eerie ambush they had been caught up in, and when the connection closed, he released a heavy breath.

It made him feel a tiny bit better to know that Jaya Mill was out there, determined to storm back and save them all. A twinge of shame sullied that feeling—a part of him wished he had those same instincts. But all he wanted to do was hide.

The med bay was far from the bridge, even for a small ship like the *Avalon*. Tynan and Sunny huddled behind her desk, waiting for the inevitable sound of soldiers storming in, with nothing but Sunny's pistol to protect them.

He knew Sunny was a woman who was not afraid to fire it. Determination glinted in her eyes, and he knew she would have been trained extensively for a post like this. But he also knew they must be outnumbered. And he was afraid.

"You okay?" she whispered.

They were sitting shoulder to shoulder, keeping their bodies hidden from the door. Sunny peeked around from time to time, although they would both know from the sound of it whether someone had broken in yet. The med bay doors were locked—it would take a code on the door pad or forcible entry to get inside.

He just shook his head in response to her question. He was not one for bravado. He was afraid, and he knew it. And she knew it— he could tell from the way she looked at him with concern.

Even with everything she had to worry about, she was thinking of him.

"I'm glad you're here, though," he said. Something still sat funny with him, after they had talked earlier. Something about the way she had turned away from him when he had gone back to work.

But she smiled and moved her hand to his, interlacing their fingers together. His hands were cold, the blood having fled his extremities. Hers were warmer, and the heat radiated up through his arm.

"How did this happen?" he asked.

Sunny shook her head.

"I mean, how could they have gotten to us so fast?" he continued. "We just arrived at this station. Our team had barely left when we lost the bridge."

"They knew we were coming," Sunny said. "They must have."

"But how could they know? We hardly even knew where we were going until the last minute."

Sunny just looked at him, and the hand not holding his shifted its grip on the gun. Her fingers squeezed his hand with a firm resolve, and he was astonished at how soft and dry her hand felt in his.

"They have someone," she said simply, her voice surprisingly calm.

"One of us?" Tynan asked. "One of *us* is working with *them?*"

His insides went cold as he realized what it meant for the most elite counterterrorism unit in the galaxy to have a Sons of Priam sympathizer buried deep within the heart of its operations. Or perhaps it was more than just this unit—could there be someone higher up in the Union Navy whose goal it was to undermine everything they were doing?

"I can't imagine anyone on our team would…" He broke off, the words eluding him.

Sunny was smiling at him—an expression entirely inappropriate, in his opinion, given that they could die at any moment.

"What?" he asked.

"Do you hear what you're saying?"

"What?"

"*Us. We. Our team.*" She spoke the words softly.

He met her gaze, and saw the way her smile softened the creases in her forehead and deepened the ones around her eyes. Her face was illuminated by the low blue emergency lighting, and she seemed to radiate peace despite everything about this situation screaming danger. The knot inside him softened.

"You're a good man, Tynan," she said. "You've made a place here. We'll get out of this, and then you'll have a story you can be proud of. How you helped stop one of the most powerful and sadistic terrorist groups in human history."

He gave a short laugh—the idea that he was somehow a hero in this, or that they would come out alive, was absurd.

She squeezed his hand "I'm serious," she said. "We're going to be fine. We've got the best strike teams in the galaxy, and Armstrong isn't going to lose the *Avalon* without a fight. Mill and

Rhodes and the rest are on their way back. We'll have the upper hand again soon."

"I hope you're right," he said.

She brought her other hand to his face now, tilting it so she could look into his eyes.

"I'm always right," she said, a smile on her lips.

33

Though it looked as serene from the exterior as always, Jaya imagined she could see the conflict within the *Avalon*. Its surface was darker than usual, though perhaps that was the darkness of the red dwarf. The ship looked strangely fragile hanging there in the black of space, and fear seized at her chest.

Zamya piloted the stolen ship as fast as she could, though the small vessel strained at the unusual mass of its cargo. They had packed the remainder of the strike team into the small vessel. There was hardly room for Jaya's chest to expand to take in a breath. But it was enough to get them out of the station's pull and hurtling back to the *Avalon*.

The shields were down, and the nareian slowed the ship just enough to pass through the force field keeping the manufactured atmosphere inside the *Avalon*, skid across the shuttle bay floor, and come to a full stop a few meters from the wall. She pressed a button on the console and the doors opened.

Jaya didn't even have to give the order—her strike team poured out the door, following the strategy they had laid out on the short ride.

Jaya stopped briefly and looked back at the ship. The nareian stood in the entryway, already pressing the command to close the gate. Jaya nodded to her, and to her surprise, Zamya paused, her hand a breath away from the control panel. She nodded once as well, then pressed the button.

As Jaya sprinted up ahead, she heard the sound of the engines engaging again, then the shuttle breaking through the seal and into the vacuum of space. Then all she could hear were the boots of her team clanging on the floor behind her.

She stopped before rounding a corner and held up her hand. Her palm drive's scans told her there were hostile forces around the bend. They were in the corridor near the training gym, and Jaya watched the small dots on her schematic as they fought. A scant three of the dots had Union Navy identifiers, against seven hostiles. Jaya could hear every scuffle of feet on the floor, every whine of a recharging weapon, and every heavy breath of exertion as if it were occurring inside her own head. Their people were losing.

On her mark, Jaya's team took aim and fired. Four of the Sons of Priam dropped immediately, and the other three looked over their shoulders. Before they had a chance to readjust and find cover, the three marines that had been losing just moments before began advancing.

Another Son dropped, and Jaya leapt forward, taking the other two down with a simultaneous EMP pulse from her palm drive. She stood over the two stunned men, her gun in her hand without a thought. She leveled it at the head of one of them, then she paused.

"Is a path clear to the brig?" she asked.

"Yes," said one of the crew members—a new recruit.

Her name came foggily to Jaya's mind. Bareilles.

"Most of them are in engineering or the bridge," Bareilles continued. "We drew this group away from engineering, but there are more."

"Take these two men to the brig, then," Jaya said. "Use your EMP pulse if they start to wake up."

"Yes, Lieutenant Commander," Bareilles replied.

She and another marine scooped up the two stunned men and dragged them away.

Jaya turned her attention back to her team. "Rhodes, you take Thompson, Pathak, Werner, and Roberts to engineering. The rest of you, you're with me. We're going to the bridge."

Rhodes nodded, and his team split off.

For a brief moment, Jaya let herself watch them, their backs retreating into certain gunfire. She turned back to the four faces that were watching her now. Sal's frown tugged at something inside of her, and she stood taller.

"Follow me," she said.

Jaya and her small team made their way toward the bridge. As they drew closer, the scream of heavy fire quickly outstripped the pounding of their own boots on the steel floors.

The entrance to the bridge was thronging with Sons of Priam and Union officers. Jaya shot one Son of Priam as she entered the corridor. Shock registered on the man's face as he fell to the floor. The Union officers were outnumbered, entrenched behind weakened portable shields as particle beams turned the corridor into a death trap. Jaya flattened herself against a low wall next to one of the officers who had stayed behind on the *Avalon*.

"What's the situation?" she asked, the whine of the particle beams muffling her voice.

"They've held the bridge since a little after they got here," he said. "Armstrong is in there with their leader."

Jaya closed her eyes for a moment, feeling the movement of the battle ripple through the air like an electrical current. The only door into the bridge was blocked by two men, and at least a dozen more had fanned out along the wall and were shooting at the Union forces. She could sense them inside, too, half a dozen or so, moving around the bridge.

"Do you have a flashbang?" she asked, opening her eyes again.

He reached down and produced one, holding it out to her on the flat of his hand.

She pulled up a display on her palm drive; its holographic screen glowed blue against the dark of her armor. She accessed the *Avalon*'s communications systems and logged in with her password. The controls for the bridge door were near the top of the list, and she paused when she reached them.

"On my mark," she said. "I need you to throw it. Right at the door."

"You're not going to try to get through," he said in disbelief.

"Just do it," she said. "On three."

As she counted, she adjusted her pose, her muscles tensing into a squat, ready to jump. *One.* She tightened her grip around her gun. *Two.* She focused on the door in her mind, feeling its location only meters away. *Three.*

Jaya tapped a symbol on the holographic screen, and the doors swung open. He threw the flashbang, watching its trajectory on his own screen and detonating it as it landed at the base of the door.

She leapt up and sprinted through the corridor, which was briefly silenced as the disoriented Sons of Priam blinked in vain, their vision temporarily stolen. She broke through them, stunning the two by the door with her EMP and bursting into the bridge.

She ducked immediately as a shot rang out over her head.

"Stop! Stop shooting now!" Kier's voice registered powerfully across the room, and the enemy forces stilled at the sound of it.

She looked up.

Armstrong was ahead, kneeling on the ground. And Kier stood over him, his gun coolly pointed at Armstrong's temple, free hand raised, ceasing the fire from his men. Behind Kier stood Tully, flanked by a dozen Sons of Priam. Jaya trained her gun on Kier and slowly moved closer.

"We have company," Tully said, his voice chillingly casual.

Kier kept his hand raised, and the Sons of Priam held their fire, though their guns remained at the ready.

Jaya could hear the wheeze in Armstrong's erratic breathing. The sour bite of blood clung to her nasal passages.

"Let him go," Jaya said.

"I can't do that," Kier replied, his voice still alarmingly neutral, rational. He had turned his attention back to Armstrong, resting his free hand on his hip. "Your world is so simple," he went on, almost sighing. "You're blind. And in your blindness you trample on the worthy. You yield to evil. You stand in the way of peace."

"You call this peace?" Jaya asked.

Before his team could even raise their weapons, Kier had waved his hand to stop them.

"Did he tell you what he knows?" Kier asked. "Who else has he told? Jaya, you can help me."

"Kier, you're better than this," Jaya said.

"You're letting them slow you down," Kier said, his voice a prayer. His eyes were wide, the hazel irises bright with unshed tears. He blinked, and the glimmer was gone. Then he hoisted Armstrong up from the floor with one arm, imprisoning the older man against himself with a firm grasp.

Armstrong's eyes met Jaya's.

"Don't you see?" Kier continued. "You're the one who could be so much more than you have chosen to be. We're different, Jaya. We could have everything. We have a chance to make a difference in this galaxy and change things for the better."

"You've killed millions of people, Kier," she said. "How is that changing things for the better?"

"Violence is the language of the galaxy. Once we have won, it will no longer be necessary. We can invent a new language. A new world, Jaya. Full of good. Why can't you see it?"

Jaya didn't reply. She kept her eyes locked on Kier's and her gun pointed at him. He stared down the sleek lines of the particle beam weapon, his gaze suddenly sad. Out of the corner of her eye, Jaya's sharp vision caught Armstrong's arm.

Slowly, he was loosening it from Kier's grasp.

"Jaya," Kier whispered. "Little bear…"

"Kier, please," she said, echoing his frantic whisper. Her throat was thick, the sound straining to pass through it. "Let him go. Let it all go. It's not over for you."

Behind Kier, framed in the observation windows, there was a bright flash, and then black. The station was gone. Jaya felt a tiny release—despite the terrible turn this night had taken, at least they had accomplished their objective. Tully took a few steps toward the window, as if looking closer would make the station come back. Then he swore and looked accusingly at Jaya.

"I checked the nukes when we realized we had an inside man," she said, looking at Kier, her explanation a plea. *Don't take this out on him. Don't do something you can't walk back from.*

Kier made a sound not unlike a hiss.

"I defended you," he shouted, his posture suddenly stiff with rage. "I told him you would help us. I believed in you, Jaya."

"Defended me to who, Kier?"

"I know he is only testing me. I am the first—the one who will stand by his side. I've been with him from the start, and I'll be there at the end. You can't stand in my way anymore."

The line of his jaw was sharp as he spoke, his teeth bared with every word. He looked at her with a mixture of hatred and longing in his eyes. The little boy Jaya had seen in him before had vanished.

"I wanted to bring you to him," he said, the words slow and dreamlike. "But I see now that the only way to prove myself is to let you go."

Kier raised his own gun at Jaya. They stood facing each other, each training their weapon at the other's head.

Jaya saw the message in Armstrong's eyes as his free hand worked its way toward his gun.

"Kier," she said. "Big bear, please."

"No!" he shouted, staggering forward.

Armstrong, jostled by the sudden movement, stumbled, knocking his gun from its holster.

Kier watched it clatter to the ground—then he saw Jaya's expression. "Him," Kier said, his voice shaking. "He's the one who poisoned you against me."

"No, Kier," she said. "That's not how it is."

Kier lowered his weapon, then pressed the barrel against Armstrong's temple. Jaya's finger touched her trigger, didn't compress it. The moment seemed to stretch into a lifetime. She saw the fire in Kier's eyes, the resolve in Armstrong's. She couldn't move.

Kier squeezed the trigger.

The sound of a gunshot followed, cacophonous, percussive, and terrible. Jaya opened her mouth, felt her legs begin to move toward the two as Armstrong crumpled in Kier's grip. Another gunshot, and Kier staggered back. Jaya saw him turn and run, then she heard Sal's voice, a rough shout.

The Sons of Priam reacted, particle beams lighting up the room.

Muscle memory sent her diving behind the nearest console. She felt the impact of the blasts against the console and the loss in the same instant, searing through her gut and freezing her to her spot behind cover.

Tremors ran down her arms and legs, and her stomach roiled. For what felt like an eternity, she couldn't move, pinned to her spot in shock. Then, she stood. She heard her voice rise above the noise that was growing her own head, but she could not make out the words. She was moving, closing the distance between herself and Tully and the remaining Sons of Priam, her gun trembling with each shot she fired. One by one, they fell, and Jaya felt a presence seep into the space behind her. Her friends, her team. The flashes of their weapons joined hers. The outcry of their boots on the ground and their particle beams filled what little space was not occupied in her head by her own screaming mind.

And then it was over.

She was lowering her gun.

Tully remained, his weapon useless on the floor, his wounded legs preventing him from reaching it.

Jaya stared at him. His face was suddenly foreign to her. It scowled at her.

"A shuttle just pulled away," Rhodes said. "At least one of them escaped."

Tully's face twisted into a pained smirk. *Kier.* The knowledge settled on her, heavy and cold. She had lost sight of him in the chaos, and that had been enough.

"The brig," she said simply to the group that now stood at her side. "Make sure the doctor sees him."

She sensed Rhodes nod, though she didn't see it. There was no hesitation in the crew as they moved to lock away their former first officer. Sal's presence grew closer, and she felt his hand on her shoulder. He asked her a question, and while she didn't hear the words, she heard the message.

"He's gone," she said.

Sal's arms closed around her. She smelled the sweat in his hair, and she felt her free arm return the gesture and her head lean against his. Her other hand still grasped the gun, her grip as solid as the weapon's heavy barrel. Heat radiated up her arm, but her grip remained tight against the steel.

"He's gone," she said again, and the words burned in her mouth.

She loosened herself from Sal's embrace and walked out of the bridge, the acrid smell of fire and death following her into the hall.

It was quiet now. The remaining Sons of Priam had been killed or taken to the brig. A sparse crew stared up at her, eyes weary, faces smeared with blood and sweat.

"Mill to engineering," she said into her comm link, surprised at the steadiness of her own voice. "What's your status?"

The response was prompt: "We lost three. Two wounded on the med bay's security team. Systems damage was minimal."

"I want a full report as soon as possible. Doctor Choi," she said, switching her link to the med bay, "What's the situation down there?"

It was a moment before Sunny replied, and her voice was strained. "It's crowded. We've got a lot of wounded. We could use more hands."

"Understood," Jaya said. She switched her link to broadcast to the entire ship. "All available crew members on lower deck, report to the med bay and take your orders from Doctor Choi."

Down the hall, she caught a glimpse of Rhodes, returning from the brig. He saw her look and gave her a solemn nod, which she returned.

She took the lift up to the captain's quarters.

The room was quiet and tidy. She took a seat at Armstrong's desk, her hand hovering over the all-ship comm link. Tully was in the brig, and Armstrong was gone. She knew the chain of command —she was the second officer. In light of Tully's treachery, she inherited his responsibilities. And then with the death of Armstrong...

Jaya depressed the button, and let the words flow out of her to the rest of the ship.

"Crew of the *Avalon*," she began. "Today, we have experienced losses that I hope none of you have seen before or will see again. Our executive officer has chosen to place his loyalties elsewhere. Many of you witnessed his betrayal of the *Avalon*."

She paused, the evenness of her voice beginning to falter. She swallowed hard and clenched her fists so tightly that her short fingernails began to dig into the flesh of her palm.

"And I regret to inform you of the loss of Captain Armstrong." She swallowed again, willing her voice to remain divorced from the heavy ache in her chest. "He fought to the last. Until the Union installs a new captain, as second officer aboard this ship, I am acting captain. We will return to Argos and await instructions there."

She ended the announcement, and felt the silence in the ship as acutely as the silence in the captain's quarters. Though she could not see into the other levels, she knew the stillness that would fall over the narrow corridors of the *Avalon.* The ship was in mourning.

Jaya didn't know how long she had been sitting in silence in Armstrong's chair before the message came through on her palm drive. It was marked urgent priority, and the chime in her earpiece alerted her to its presence. She connected her palm drive to the console on Armstrong's—*her*—desk, and the text flashed up on the screen.

Lieutenant Commander Mill, it read. *If you have received this message, then I am dead. I only wish I could leave you better prepared.*

You are the only person I trust directly with this information. While I have no reason to doubt the rest of the crew, you are the one whose instincts I have faith will lead them in the right direction. And the information I have uncovered threatens to reach to the deepest levels. In the past few months, I have grown suspicious of the activity of those at the highest echelons of the Union.

I have attached my own personal notes on the investigation into the Sons of Priam. I don't know if I am right in my line of inquiry, but I trust you to carry on my work.

I have always tried to be the commanding officer that my crew needed. I know I have not done a perfect job, but I have done my best. There are many things I have left unsaid—we must always expect to lose those we love, in our line of work, and it has always been easier for me to send you into danger when I only filled the role of captain. But there is no place anymore for formality. If I had a daughter, I would hope she was half the woman you are.

I am proud of you, Jaya.

- Peter Armstrong

The surreal composure she had managed to keep since the explosion on the bridge began to crack. She opened the files he had attached, but found the words blurred by the sharp sting of tears in her eyes. She surrendered, letting her head drop to the desk, her arms folding up and around herself as grief shuddered through her. All the aches in her muscles and bones from the intense battle they had fought seemed to melt away against the pain in her chest and the war that raged inside her head. The world she wanted to believe could still exist had been ripped away.

She had lost a father once—a distant scientist who had been little more than a faint presence in her childhood. The loss of Armstrong bore no resemblance to the loss of her father. With this loss, the security of his presence and guidance was torn violently from her, and the pain was as real and as deep as the loss of her mother.

And Kier.

She had lost him once before, and perhaps he had in a sense died twenty-three years ago. He had become someone else, and this someone else had cost her one of the precious few left she could call family.

Anger rose up, and she felt as though her tears began to boil. The salt and heat stung the damp, sweaty skin of her face, burning trails down to her chin, where they dropped onto the table below. And after anger, determination flooded her. She stood, saving the message from Armstrong and its accompanying files to a secure, password-protected folder in her palm drive and deleting the message from the console.

She scanned his notes. He had been tracking connections between the Sons of Priam and TA Tech. Distant subsidiaries and shell corporations connected by misty threads of money and rumor. They shared subcontractors. They might share more than that. Armstrong had been concerned enough to write it down, to keep it hidden. He may have even died for it.

Indigo Onyema. Jaya recalled the woman that the szacante doctor told her about. The one who had tried to help him. She had worked with whomever purchased Tynan's research out from under him.

She had been an early investor in TA Tech, too. Jaya added her name to Armstrong's notes.

Although he was gone, she would not let his mission die with him.

34

Sunny moved with such focus and precision amidst the carnage in the med bay that, as much as Tynan wished to be helpful, he felt like little more than a hindrance. Still, when she would call for a supply, he was ready to reach for the proper item. This sort of hands-on biology was something he had never trained for, never studied. His work was meant to be done in petri dishes and on computer screens, not on living and breathing bodies whose continued life and breath depended on his quick action.

"I need the regen tool," she called as she examined the blackened, charred skin on one soldier's leg.

He scrambled to sort through the pile of equipment on the table and retrieved the tool, placing it in Sunny's outstretched hand.

Somehow, she found the time to send him a smile over her shoulder—and though it was only a microsecond, he registered it and replied with one of his own. She returned her focus to the patient, taking a small biopsy from their skin. After a moment, the tool beeped, and she applied a thin layer of its contents to the injured soldier.

"Stem cells?" Tynan asked when she had finished and handed the tool back to him.

"Yes," she replied. "The skin should regenerate within a day or two."

Tynan nodded. Though szacante biology was different, they had adapted some comparable technologies. He had simply never seen them applied in this manner. He had never had to.

She was smiling at him again.

"What?" he asked.

"You're thinking," she replied.

"Of course," he said, somewhat befuddled.

She only chuckled. "Everyone's been seen to. Now I just need to clean up."

He began to gather up the wrappings that had once covered sterilized surgical tools and bandages, cast aside in the frenzied rush earlier. Sunny drew the curtains that separated the hospital beds from the front office, moving rolling cabinets out of the way and securing them back against the wall and locking them in place for transit.

After a moment, Tynan stopped, still clutching plastic and paper against his chest. "Hey," he said, and she turned to look at him. His words died in his chest.

Your heart rate is unusually high, Min said in his private earpiece. *You have been under a lot of stress, Tynan. Perhaps you should sit down.*

He wished he could gesture at her or shoot her a meaningful look, but in her non-manifested form, the only way to respond was to speak to her.

"I'm fine, Min," he muttered, as quietly as he could manage.

Sunny raised her eyebrows in an expression he had learned meant *curiosity.*

"What?" she asked.

"I just," he began, the words rising up again. "I just wanted to say that I've never really…"

Her lips were curving up again—he had seen that expression often on her. It was strangely sly.

"I've never really understood what it felt like before I got involved in all this," he stammered. "To know that you were about to die."

Her eyebrows knit together at that, and she stepped closer and took the bundle of wrappers from his arms, dropping them onto a nearby cabinet. She held his hands gently in hers.

"I guess I just want to tell you that you made it easier," he said.

He had never let his guard down with another person in his adult life. He'd always had Min, and Min always understood. But Min didn't think about death the way a living, breathing being did. At least, he didn't think she did. They'd never really had occasion to discuss it.

But before, when his heart squeezed tighter with every distant blast, and his hands trembled so fiercely he had to sit on them to hide it, having the warm, solid reassurance of Sunny at his side had tethered him somehow.

"Thank you," he said. "I've just not had many near-death experiences and well—I'm glad I didn't have to do it alone."

Her smile was wide and easy, and she squeezed his hands before releasing them. "I'll try not to make it a pattern," she said. "I get the feeling you're not quite ready to try a new line of work."

He chuckled at that. "No, you're right. I'm not."

Tynan still wasn't entirely sure what to tell Jaya when she walked through the door of the medical bay. She took a seat in his tiny office as he closed the door behind her. When he looked back, she was staring at him, her face serious. Her eyes were rimmed with red, but she held his gaze calmly. He sat on the other side of his desk.

"You are very unusual, Lieutenant Commander Mill," he said.

"Jaya," she corrected. "What did you find?"

Her voice was sharp and her words short. But Tynan thought he was beginning to understand human expressions, and the look she was giving him wasn't one of anger. He had the strange feeling this conversation wasn't going to surprise her as much as he had been expecting.

"I've found a significant amount of synthetic material in your blood and tissue," he said.

She frowned. "The military tests for nanotech. It's illegal in the Union. Wouldn't they have caught something like that?"

"Not this technology," he said. "The first run returned no unusual results. It wasn't until I refined my search and looked closer that I began to see unusual behavior. I wouldn't have found it at all if you hadn't told me your concerns. If I hadn't been looking for something specific."

Her hands, clasped in her lap, moved to her knees, as though she were bracing herself for an impact. "So what is this technology? What does it do?"

"I don't actually know," he said. "I would need more samples, and time to study it. It's like nothing I've ever seen before. It seems to behave like a virus, but it's not natural. It's a synthetic virus of some sort. It works not just with the cells in your body, but seems to function on its own, as if they were cells themselves, supplementing the biological structure you inherited from your parents with something else…"

He could not read the look she was giving him now. The silence pressed in on him.

"Have you always been like this?" he asked. "You never noticed an abrupt change in your physical stamina, strength, or anything?"

She shook her head, and he nodded.

"What does that mean?" she asked.

"It means this was done to you very young. Perhaps in infancy, perhaps even before birth. You are likely a result of a carefully crafted design," he said. "Probably the culmination of years of work and practice. There may have been earlier models with varying degrees of success."

"Earlier models?"

"Yes. And later ones as well. Any project requires multiple iterations, a progression toward the final step. But your design is nearly perfect—indistinguishable from the human body except at the smallest of levels, and from what you've told me, it has enhanced your abilities beyond that of ordinary humans."

She said nothing, only continued to give him that look that he could not understand. His reaction tempered a bit, diminished by her unnatural stillness. There was more. He wanted to say it, but he had no proof. And he knew the damage he could cause by making an unsupported claim, by tying her in with the very thing she was fighting to destroy. He needed more data, if he was going to determine whether her enhancements were the same ones the Sons of Priam had just succeeded in perfecting in adults.

"I'd like to run more tests," he said. "With your permission, of course. And obviously, this remains between the two of us. You came to me in confidence."

She still watched him with an unreadable expression, her eyes narrowed slightly but focused intently on him. He suddenly realized how his words must sound to her. Too late, he wished he could say it all differently.

She stood abruptly.

"I need to think," she said. "Thank you, doctor."

And with that, she was gone. The door closed behind her, leaving him with only his racing thoughts and hundreds of questions.

The metal box on his desk called his attention. He had never determined what happened to that man who had died so suddenly. The autopsy report had indicated a perfectly healthy heart, until it had stopped working. Some signs of acute strain. It was like he had been frightened to death.

Tynan opened the box, lifted the small vials out, and held them in his palm. The stream of questions was starting to narrow, his thoughts coalescing into something tangible. A hypothesis. A place to start.

35

Mara couldn't get the image of Yanu's corpse out of her head.

Yanu, who had first pried Mara from her mother's grip. Yanu, whose beauty had frozen a younger Mara in awe, whose attention had flattered and flustered and filled Mara's head with the deep fog of first love. Yanu, who had seduced Mara away from her family.

Who, for much longer than she was Mara's lover, had been her enemy.

All these years, Mara thought that closing herself up, locking her heart away deep behind her knives and her guns and her refusal to show mercy—she thought it was all for the better. That she would come out of it on the other side, and the reward for all her bloody work would be peace.

But when she had been bleeding out in Onyema's ship, she had been ready to go. When she had faced Yanu one last time in that blood-spattered laboratory on a terrorist's space station, she had been ready to go. Maybe she was just tired. Maybe she had just been in this game for too long. But she had felt that lick of peace at the edges of her consciousness, and she had been willing to go.

The tightness in her chest loosened, the pressure behind it ready to burst out. The thing she had not wanted to understand was there now. It was inside her, in the force that radiated out from her core.

She had lost the very reason she had begun this work. And she had found peace at the brink of death because she knew it in her heart: she had no place anymore in this galaxy. There was nothing for her.

The dam broke. Her whole body shook with rage and fear and the deep, inexhaustible sadness that had inhabited her since Tai's death.

Mara cried until she was wrung out. Her chest ached and her face stung with the irritation of tears. And then she raised her head. She went back to Yanu's room and pulled out the simplest clothing she could find from Yanu's closet.

She showered, scrubbing the brown and crumbling blood from her skin and prying dried clumps of it from her mane. She put on Yanu's clothes and went to the small medical bay and injected the wound in her side with the strongest antibiotic she could find. Followed it with another painkiller chaser. She would need a real doctor at some point to look at her haphazard stitching. No matter what, it would heal ugly.

That was okay. Scars, like her tattoos, told stories. And she didn't want to forget the lessons these stories held for her. Onyema's face swum before her: cool, dark eyes; hair fanning out in the reduced gravity. The strange calm, the flicker of regret. Mara blinked. What had Onyema said to her? *Richard sent you.*

Who was Richard? She hadn't cared at the time. Hadn't wanted to know how the job she was working tangled into some larger, messier web. She shouldn't care now.

Perhaps her first mistake was thinking she could run away from the mess of the galaxy's wars and struggles. The galaxy had a way of drawing her right back to the center of the web. She had thought before that the monster at the center of the web was her family, but now she wondered how many more creatures lay tangled together in the darkness.

An incoming communication chimed at her from the control panel. She returned to the captain's chair and watched the signal.

Mara accepted the call, and the pale and freckled face of the man who had imprisoned her appeared before her. His eyes were raw and his face haggard, and anger flashed across his face the moment he saw her.

He was expecting Yanu.

He snarled. "What do you think you're doing?"

She cocked her head at his question, a calm that she had not expected suffusing her body.

"I'm going far away," she replied. "And if you know what's good for you, you will leave me and my family out of your coup."

"I will do nothing of the sort."

"Yanu was a fool," Mara said.

"I knew she was a fool," he snapped.

"So you'll have a contingency plan?"

A nasty smile spread across his face.

She nodded. It wasn't over yet, was it?

"Thank your sister for her help, by the way," Mara said. "At least, I assume it was your sister who killed Yanu and who I brought back to the *Avalon.* She looked just like you."

He cut the feed, the holographic image vanishing into the darkened control room.

The next move was his. And Mara knew what card he had left to play.

Mara sifted through Yanu's messages. She had been working with the Sons of Priam since shortly before Mara's run-in with Balei. Her net had not been strong enough until these powerful new allies stepped in. They promised her Mara. She promised them a Nareian Empire which would turn a blind eye. Which would turn its attention to the conflict inside its heart while the Sons of Priam took the Union's government hostage and purged the Union Navy.

This purge was imminent. The gears were already in motion. Lieutenant Commander Jaya Mill would return home only to be swept away by those loyal to the Sons of Priam.

Richard... Richard Emory. The Union's newest Chancellor. Onyema had been an early investor in his company. He had repaid her by sending an assassin.

What exactly did Onyema know about him? If she had known his associations with the Sons of Priam, why not just turn him in to the Union's government? It was an easy solution—an elegant one— and this cunning woman had chosen not to take it.

I should have spoken when I had the chance.

So something had changed. Something that meant Onyema could not rely on that solution. And Onyema had regretted it.

Mara's stomach soured, and she gulped water from her bulb, swishing it to wash away the bitter taste.

Mara was still a monster. She felt her own darkness eating away at her, but she also felt something nagging at her. The center of that web. The dark enclave of power that harbored and sheltered a select few individuals in this gods-forsaken bloody galaxy. It had reached out to her, had twisted a knife into her. And sometimes it took a monster to fight a monster.

The speed with which the broadcast went out confirmed that the Sons of Priam had been prepared for Yanu to fail.

It was a short video, but it made its point. One minute of spliced-together images of Mara from her time on Argos hunting Onyema, and a short announcement:

This is the lost princess of Narei. She is our agent.

The Fox was not happy to receive her call. Rage etched the pointed lines of his face and turned his cheeks red. He spat his words, hissing and furious. Behind him stood Ahmad, eyes blazing and body tightly coiled.

Mara was sure that if she had been standing before him, he would have shot her in the heart without a second thought.

Mara let the Fox boil his rage out until he was empty. Ahmad's eyes remained filled with hatred. She looked at him when she spoke.

"I need to talk to her."

That set the Fox off again, and she waited for his sputtering choler to cease again. His friend rested a hand on his shoulder, and the Fox shrugged him off and walked away. Ahmad stepped forward, scrutinizing Mara.

"Why should we even consider what you have to say?" His voice was as cold and dangerous as the vacuum of space.

"Because I have something you need," she said. "I have information that will help you take down Richard Emory."

The silence stretched. Ahmad cocked an eyebrow, thick and dark over eyes that still brimmed with desire for vengeance. Mara understood him, she thought. A similar desire rose up as her blood thickened again, as her health returned.

Finally, he nodded.

With Mara's face broadcast on every frequency across the galaxy, there was no chance of her docking on Argos and waltzing off her ship without every security agent and bounty hunter on the station immediately pouncing on her.

So Ahmad and the Fox agreed to meet her off the grid.

She approached the coordinates they had sent her, waiting for Yanu's ship to pick up anything in the darkness of space. She supposed she might be walking into an ambush. She also supposed she deserved it.

Then her sensors picked it up: another ship, waiting quietly in the dark. She cut her main engines, let the drift carry her closer. Then she used maneuvering thrusters to match their vector, pulling up alongside them.

She sent them a short communication burst. *I'm here.*

They lit up their own thrusters, brought their ship up against hers, and locked their stabilizers to her hull.

Mara opened her airlock and waited. After a delay long enough to make her think that they must have changed their minds, their airlock spiraled open.

The Fox was no longer spitting with rage, but his expression said *just give me a reason.*

She looked from him to Ahmad, who leaned slightly against the airlock's aperture, watching her with a calculating look in his dark eyes. He folded his arms at his chest as though he were waiting for her to speak. Based on his expression, she imagined he had some questions. She didn't have time for that.

"Where is she?" Mara asked.

"She's recovering from a very serious wound." Ahmad's words were carefully aimed. They hit their mark. "Make your case to us."

"I need her help," Mara said. "I need access to military records. Need to find out when a Union ship called the *Avalon* got back to Argos and where the crew is staying."

Ahmad's expression betrayed little—he raised his eyebrows in a mild gesture of surprise, but his eyes remained just as calculating.

"I know she has contacts in the military," Mara continued. "Hell, I'm sure now that you all do. Someone with enough access to find out what I need to know." Ahmad opened his mouth and Mara held up her hand to silence him. "I also know there is going to be a purge."

"A purge?" The Fox was leaning forward again.

"How do you know this?" Ahmad asked.

"You already know I was hired to kill Onyema," Mara said. "You also know I failed."

Lightning flashed across the face of the darker man. Onyema might not be dead, but two of his friends were.

She lifted her shirt to show the mess of a wound on her abdomen. It wasn't enough, but the gesture, the hint of vulnerability, seemed to soften him.

"The man who hired me wanted to use me for something else when I finished that job," she said. "Regardless of whether I succeeded. He wanted to trade me to my family's chief political rivals for their silence as he cleansed the Union of those who weren't loyal to him. With the elections over, they're making their move now. Mass arrests. Court martials. Executions."

The Fox exchanged a glance with Ahmad.

"I have a list," Mara said. "It's a big one. I can show it to you, let you see if your friends in the Navy are on it. But I need you to help me too."

"And if you're full of shit?" The Fox's hands were fists now.

Mara shrugged. "You can take that chance. But I don't think you want to."

Ahmad uncrossed his arms and took a step toward Mara. "What do you want with a Union ship?"

"I owe someone a favor on that ship," Mara said.

"Bullshit," the Fox said. "That's not a good reason."

"Okay. I think this person has a chance to destroy the man who tried to destroy me. Who's trying to control my people. I'm willing to give her the tools she needs to get it done."

That seemed to satisfy the Fox, because he didn't ask any

follow-up questions. Ahmad still considered her, his eyes narrowed slightly.

She saw the strength in his shoulders as he sized her up. For the first time, she realized how young he would have been when he served under Onyema.

She couldn't confirm that the Fox had been a part of that team as well, but the longer this conversation continued, the more certain she was that he had also served with Onyema. He had slipped right into this negotiation with no hesitation, seeming to understand the rules the moment the game had begun. His craggy face was shaped into a sour expression, his mouth a little frown, as though he was about to reprimand her.

The two men continued to watch her. Ahmad's look imposed silence on both of them—he may have been the baby of the group at the beginning, but it seemed he was calling the shots these days.

She didn't have time for mind games.

"Well?" she asked. "Are you in or out?"

"Show us something," Ahmad said. "One piece of evidence."

"Oh, for fuck's sake." But she supposed she would have asked for the same thing. She sighed and headed to the console of Yanu's ship, beckoning them to follow. They did, and she pulled up a message that referenced the upcoming purge. Ahmad leaned over the console, a tendril of hair falling into his face from his loose ponytail. He whistled under his breath.

"It's worse than she thought," the Fox said.

"We didn't move early enough," Ahmad replied.

"We didn't know. She didn't either."

"We knew enough." Ahmad's voice was hard. He stood, tucking the hair behind his ears, and turned to Mara. "We'll help."

Mara smiled. "It's about fucking time."

36

Their return trip to Argos felt longer than any Jaya had ever experienced. She had contacted HQ—the call had been brief and perfunctory. They agreed with the decision to return immediately, and they arranged for Tully to be turned over to Union authorities at the dock. Jaya avoided the brig. She could not look into that man's eyes and hold her temper.

She sat tensely in the captain's chair as the silver-hued Argos grew in the bridge's viewing screen.

"Lieutenant Commander Rhodes," she said. "Please assemble a security team and escort our prisoner to the main door. We'll be arriving shortly."

Rhodes nodded and left the bridge. Sal exchanged a look with Jaya, his eyebrows raised in a question.

She sent him a half-hearted smile back.

"We have permission to dock," Lupo announced.

"Bring us in," Jaya said.

They coasted slowly through the large entrance to Argos's military docking bay, passing gently through the magnetic field separating artificial atmosphere from empty space. Lupo set them down easily at the awaiting pier and ran through the shut-down protocols.

The ship switched over to low-power settings, the hum of the engines quieting and the lights dimming.

They had arrived.

Jaya headed down a level to the short corridor that led to the main entrance. The door was opening to Argos's docking bay, its blue-tinged artificial daylight cutting into the dimness of the hall. At the end stood Rhodes with Tully and a small group of guards. As she neared the group and the light began to creep across Tully's face, she saw that he was smiling.

It was an unpleasant smile. A meaningful one. And he caught her eye, making sure that she saw the pleasure in his expression. Her extremities went cold, and she looked up at Rhodes. His expression was dark but set—he had either not noticed Tully's unusually good mood or was ignoring it.

"Everything okay, Rhodes?" she asked.

He nodded, moving closer to her and out of Tully's earshot. "All good. Just can't wait to be rid of the rat bastard." He paused, then added, "Captain."

She waved that off. Before she'd had a chance to ask him anything more, the doors opened, and their greeting party was stepping onto the *Avalon.*

Jaya stepped up to the group, led by Admiral Reid. She saluted crisply. "Admiral Reid. Acting Captain Jaya Mill turning over—"

The party that flanked Reid raised their guns, pointing them at Jaya and her crew in a simultaneous movement. Jaya raised her hands above her head and saw Rhodes do the same. She met Reid's chilly gaze.

"That will not be necessary, *Lieutenant Commander* Mill," Reid said.

She kept her hands raised, but her mind was absorbing every piece of information it could. Twelve people in Reid's attaché, all IRC from the look of them. Their weapons were standard military-issue particle rifles, and she saw the rounded shapes of gas grenades in their utility belts. They stood tensely, their muscles on a hair-trigger. There was no path around them, no matter how quickly she might be able to move. And then there was the matter of her crew.

Reid gestured to an officer behind him, who then approached Jaya. Before that sinking feeling in her stomach could turn into a coherent thought, the officer had grabbed her arms and twisted her around, cuffing her hands behind her back. Other officers were doing the same to Rhodes and the security contingent. Reid waved his hand, and a security team charged down the corridor into the *Avalon*.

"What's going on?" Jaya demanded.

She knew she could overpower the officer who was now guiding her off the *Avalon*, and perhaps even run fast enough to escape the remaining guards, but as she watched her officers escorted in cuffs off the ship, she stilled. She allowed herself to be led away, only struggling enough to throw her question back at Reid, who was unlocking the cuffs that bound Tully.

"Lieutenant Commander Mill," he replied, "you and your crew are under arrest."

"What charges?" she shouted.

His mouth pursed in contempt: "Mutiny."

The military prison on Argos was pushing its capacity, with every officer of the *Avalon* in their own cell. Jaya sat cross-legged on the ground in her cell, her head resting against the wall behind her.

"This is bullshit," Sal fumed from across the way.

They had been there for hours—how many, Jaya was not sure. They had been brought food and water, but it lay untouched in every cell. Every member of the *Avalon*'s company knew too well what tactics the Navy might use to loosen their lips. After all, they had all been trained in the same methods. Tynan had not received the same training, and so he had jumped about two feet in the air when he had reached for his water only to be shouted at by a dozen marines in unison. Now he crouched in his cell, eyeing his glass of water with a bug-eyed suspicion that would have made Jaya laugh if she weren't so preoccupied.

"We just have to wait it out," Jaya said, with a calm she didn't really feel. "See what they want from us."

The doors opened suddenly, and two guards entered. It seemed they had tired of waiting as well. The guards went straight for her cell, and she stood to face the door. The taller of the two jabbed his gun toward her, a scowl on his flat face.

"Turn around. Hands on your head."

She obeyed, and heard the door open behind her. Two hands grabbed her own, securing them behind her lower back with strong handcuffs.

"Where are you taking her?" Sal asked.

The guards pretended not to hear him, but Jaya shot him a wry smile. He returned it with an anxious grin, tension etched into his jaw.

They led her out of the jail cell and down the hall. They didn't bother to cover her eyes. She knew these halls well after all—they were mapped out in her head. A turn to the left, another to the right, and they were opening to the door to one of the interrogation rooms.

Three chairs, one table. Her legs shifted automatically as if to carry her to the side where she usually sat, but the guards tugged her toward the opposite one and shoved her into the chair. They removed one cuff and connected the other to the table.

Not one word was exchanged, which was fine with Jaya. They left the room. She wondered if they would try to use the same techniques on her that they usually used on terrorists, knowing the years she'd spent training in those very techniques. How exactly does one interrogate a counterterrorism agent? She wasn't excited to find out. She chewed on the side of her mouth, trying to wet her dry throat.

The door opened again after only a moment. So perhaps they were throwing out the rulebook on this one. Two agents took a seat across from her. She knew one of them—Taylor, a promising new recruit. As he settled into his chair, leaning forward and resting his weight on his forearms, she immediately recognized the tack he would take.

"Do you understand how serious these charges against you are?" Taylor asked. His tone was friendly, as if he considered himself an ally. Someone there to help her out of this tough jam she'd gotten herself into.

Jaya knew better than to think he was rooting for her. She didn't respond to his question, simply met his eyes with as much outward calm as she could muster.

He blinked, gray eyes revealing nothing. "Lieutenant Commander," he tried again. "Tell me what happened on the *Avalon*. What made you and your crew turn on Commander Coolidge? If this is just a misunderstanding, I'm sure we can find a way to fix it."

Jaya glanced at his companion and noted the steely look and the harsh line of his uniformed shoulders. His jaw worked. Despite Taylor's poise, they still viewed her as the enemy. She was surprised this one hadn't spit on her yet; the disgust in his face was that strong. He wasn't as good as Taylor.

"Lieutenant, my official report is accurate," she said calmly. "I have nothing to add."

Taylor crossed his arms. He furrowed his forehead, his eyebrows knit together in a perfect expression of concern.

"Mill." His voice was pleading. "Don't make this harder on yourself. Your report is just words—a story you told. Commander Coolidge tells a very different one, and you have no evidence to support yours."

Jaya held her posture stiff, but kept the muscles of her face relaxed and smooth.

"I don't know what you think you'll gain by silence," he said.

"We already have you for mutiny, but I can tell you that top brass is pushing for more than that. They're pushing for murder."

He caught her involuntary blink, or perhaps it was her pupils dilating that gave away her surprise, but either way, he leaned forward. His face eased a little, and a smile hinted at the corners of his mouth. "You thought they wouldn't ask questions about Captain Armstrong's death?"

Now a smirk clearly emerged, and his carefully constructed sympathy began to fall away. Jaya's fists clenched as she tried to control the increase in her heartbeat. The sick, acidic feeling of anger and regret poisoned her gut, and the memory of ash and blood and smoke tainted the air.

"What good would it do?" Taylor continued. "Why would a terrorist want to kill the captain of your ship? Why not just destroy the entire vessel? Or capture the crew?"

He paused, and she kept herself as still as she could. The blood throbbed in the veins of her fingers, and the beat of her pulse surged through her forearms and into her chest. The quiet sounds of the room—the hum of the air vents and the shifting fabric of the two officers' uniforms—crescendoed in her senses, even as she tried to quiet her mind.

Taylor seemed to expect an outburst, and when she remained silent, tightly coiled in her chair, he sat back. Disappointment flickered across his face as his frown returned.

"We'll let you think about it a while," he said.

Jaya didn't watch as they left the room, the sound of their footsteps vanishing with the finality of the slammed door. And then silence. She hadn't figured out their game yet. This wasn't a typical interrogation—she could sense that much—and she hadn't begun to perceive their intentions.

A sudden weakness struck her. Her muscles relaxed without her permission, like they could no longer sustain her. She leaned forward, bracing herself against the table, and tried to collect her thoughts again. She needed to understand what they were trying to do. She needed to be able to fight them.

Nausea rose up in her and she began to shiver. She had never felt like this before, like every last drop of blood had turned to liquid lead. Heavy. Tired.

She hadn't eaten or drank anything—had she somehow been poisoned?

Harsh, discordant noise pierced through her thoughts. The strident tones filled the space of the room, and Jaya flinched, covering her ears as best she could with one hand cuffed to the table. The components of the sound screeched and fought with each other, the noise so jumbled that she could not make out instruments or tunes. It was the sound of shredding and tearing. The sound of destruction ripped through the delicate nerves in her ears. She sensed a vibration through her eardrums and into her brain, creating a tinny whine that rose slowly with the din.

And then, silence so sudden that its relief was a pang in itself. Her heart still thumped, the sweat on her face suddenly too cool in the dry air of the room. She took a deep breath and willed the ringing in her ears to subside.

"You aren't as trusting of your own kind as you appear."

She hadn't heard him come in. It was Richard Emory, now slowly closing the distance between them. Approaching the table as if it were a social meeting, a break from a busy day. He removed two plugs from his ears, set them on the table, and took a seat. A droplet of sweat trickled down the side of Jaya's face as she tilted her head, watching his motions out of the corner of her eyes, but not looking directly at his face.

"You've always had one foot out the door, haven't you?" he asked. "Always felt like your time was borrowed. You were never one of them. You never trusted them. I saw it in your face when I offered you a job. Why didn't you accept?"

Jaya silenced the words of reply that rose up in her. The invisible enemy that had haunted her past—the people that had taken away her family and her childhood—had always lurked in her awareness. But the faces that rose to her mind now were faces she trusted. The sharp blue of Armstrong's eyes softening in a smile. Sal's warm hands grasping hers as she helped him up. Rhodes's determined nod when they parted ways on a mission. Vargas's quick grin when she landed a solid blow in training.

And she pictured Luka's earnest face, the way his eyes lit up when she started to play. How he looked at her like he understood all the complexity of her, despite the way she had split up and compartmentalized those pieces of herself for so long.

"You haven't eaten anything since you were brought in," Emory said. "Or even had a sip of water. You know they would take away your will if they could. Take away even your ability to decide what to share with them, and what to hold back. And that is the ultimate danger, isn't it?"

She resisted the urge to look up at him, keeping her face calm even though every muscle trembled with the effort of holding herself upright. Any reaction from her would give him a piece of information, the value of which she couldn't determine yet. She heard him lean back in his chair.

"I told you I've been watching you," he said then. "You were a rising star in your field, remarkable despite your best attempts to blend in. But then, I know what to look for. I know excellence when I see it. And I know what hiding looks like. I know who you really are."

That's not something you lose.

Those pieces of herself had never been gone. Just buried. She met Emory's eyes. "I know who you really are, too."

He chuckled at that, his perfectly constructed face barely giving against the cold smile. There were no creases at the corners of his hazel eyes, not the way there had always been around Armstrong's blue ones.

"You know who I am?" he asked lightly. "I don't think you do."

She returned his icy smile, meaning something much less friendly by it. Despite her outward calm, she was cold with dread. There was something unsettling in those eyes and the way they seemed to know her—to see something in her she did not quite see herself.

"You're a remarkable soldier," he said, "and you think on your feet. You could go far. But not if you're convicted of treason."

"It's a little premature to be talking of convictions," she said. "The court-martial hasn't even been convened."

"Is it premature?" His tone was mild.

She didn't reply, knowing the truth in his implication. Court-martials operated in secrecy, closed to the public and even most of the Union's military. The Chancellor held great influence over the proceedings. And while they had been created as a system to weigh evidence and arrive at truth, they bore little resemblance to that ideal anymore.

Power and influence won out. And she had neither of those.

Emory seemed to watch these thoughts play across her face. She struggled to project confidence, her body betraying her, trying to drag her down.

"You are a threat to the Union," he added. "They will always be watching a little closer now. Even if you are acquitted—and with Commander Coolidge's testimony, I find that unlikely—they will still keep their eyes on you. And I know as well as you that there are things about your life that you would rather keep hidden."

Of course he knew about Kier. He was only confirming what was in Armstrong's notes: that Richard Emory and TA Tech, and now the very highest level of the Union government, were closely tied with the Sons of Priam. Emory was only making her clarity of mind stronger, and tying her loyalty closer to where it had always belonged: not with the Union government but with the people it was meant to serve. The people she fought with daily and for whom she would die as quickly as they would die for her.

"Think about your future, Jaya," Emory said, and the way he spoke her name tugged at something powerful and primitive inside her.

She searched his face, as unreadable as it was.

"I see potential in you," he continued, standing and pushing his chair back into the table. "You could do great things working for me. But I need your complete commitment to my cause. I intend to clean up the mess that hundreds of years of corruption left in its wake."

"You can't fight darkness with more darkness," she said.

He stepped back, and for a moment, she thought she saw genuine regret cross his features. And then it was gone, his expression as cool as his eyes.

"I'm sorry you disapprove of my methods."

Every word was carefully spoken, deliberate and controlled. She stared back at him with a look equally collected and distant. Her muscles were beginning to shake at the effort of appearing strong, but she clenched her jaw.

And then he turned and left, the door slamming behind him, leaving the room in silence.

She shivered violently in her chair, her arms and legs growing heavier by the moment. Intense nausea rose up in her and she fought the urge to vomit, clinging to the cold metal table with her hands. She could not keep her head up; this sudden fatigue had robbed her of all her strength.

Then the sound started again. That horrifying discordance that sound like the rending of her own flesh. She slid down, the chair clattering to the floor beside her, its back coming down hard on her ankle, but she didn't even have the strength to shout. Jaya tried to bury her ears in her arms, to block out the sound by pressing her arms against the side of her head. The cuffs dug into her left wrist—it was the only thing keeping her partially upright.

Silence. Her ears rang. And she was tired, so tired. She wondered if she would ever have the strength to lift herself up again, and instead she pressed herself against the legs of the table, willing them to hold her up.

As the echoing in her ears began to subside, Jaya did as Emory said. She thought about her future, and the future of her colleagues and friends. The future of the Union, and even the entire galaxy.

Emory had just confirmed Armstrong's suspicions. And she knew what needed to be done.

37

The Fox and Ahmad smuggled Mara back into Argos in a container of antiques—statues of bronze and ceramic and iron, their edges uncomfortable against her aching body. They brought her thick costume makeup to alter her facial features, and she wore long pants and sleeves to her wrists. It was not quite enough, but if she kept to the shadows, it would do.

The Fox remained in his warehouse, while Ahmad took Mara to meet his contact in a dingy motel in one of the poorer neighborhoods of Argos. The contact was sitting in the room at a small metal table when they arrived. She wore simple civilian clothing, and the only sign of her military association was the tight bun of dark hair at the nape of her neck. When they entered the room, she stood, her expression bleak.

"I can't believe it," the contact whispered. Ahmad opened his arms and she embraced him. When she pulled away, she brushed tears from her eyes.

"Thank you for meeting us," Ahmad said, gesturing toward Mara.

"Your message was sufficiently concerning," the woman said, raising a delicately arched black eyebrow at Mara. "What can I do?"

"I need information about a ship called the *Avalon,*" Mara said. "I need to contact one of the crew."

Her pale face blanched even more, and her mouth set in a grim line. "That's going to be difficult. The *Avalon*'s company was all arrested for mutiny not three hours ago."

"What?" Mara snarled. "That's impossible."

"Who was your contact?" the woman asked.

"One of the officers," Mara replied. "Jaya Mill."

"What?"

Mara was startled at the reaction from Ahmad. Until this moment, she might have believed that nothing could really surprise him, but he was staring at her now, his dark eyes wide. His friends watched him, the confusion on their faces mirroring her own.

"You know her?" Mara asked.

He swore and turned away, running his anxious hands through his hair. "What happened to them?"

The woman began to type on her data pad, her head down and her eyes narrowed at the screen. Mara watched Ahmad, who sat on a chair and leaned his elbows on his knees. He watched his friend with the same intense focus she directed at her work, deliberately ignoring Mara's searching gaze.

After a moment, the woman spoke. "They're being held here on Argos. It says the investigation is ongoing, and I don't have more than that in official records. But they've called in some of the intelligence specialists to question them."

No fucking way she was going to be able to break into a Union military prison to get this woman out.

"Is there anything we can do?" Ahmad asked. "Any way in?"

The woman chewed on her lower lip thoughtfully, brown eyes still narrowed in focus. "It says here that their captain was killed and their first officer is the only one of the company not arrested, but I doubt he's going to be interested in breaking them out of jail since he's the one accusing them. I can look for anyone who left the

Avalon before the mutiny. Maybe one of them will want to help, but it's a long shot."

Ahmad crossed his arms, his expression determined. "Do it."

She began to type again, and Ahmad looked over at Mara, who was still watching him closely. He had formed his features back into that composed expression again, but his eyes still burned with intensity. Mara recognized that look. She didn't even have to give him the list of targets if she didn't want to—he was all in. But giving him the list had been part of her plan all along.

She was starting to understand that she needed other people on her side.

"Their doctor retired a few months ago," the woman finally said. "And they had a marine recently hospitalized on Argos. She's outpatient now, but still on a physical therapy regime at the military hospital. I've got both their addresses for you."

She pulled out a small tube and removed its lid. She began to write on the surface of the table—two names, two addresses. Mara and Ahmad both leaned over the table, copying the information into their own palm drives. Then the contact used the long sleeve of her black shirt to rub away the words on the table. Some sort of grease pencil, then. Mara hadn't seen one of those in a long time.

Then she looked up at Mara, her expression a question.

Mara took a small drive from her belt. "I made a copy," she said. "Of everything I found. It's yours."

She tossed the drive to Ahmad, who caught it and immediately began to sync it with his palm drive. He sat down next to his friend, and they bent their heads together and sorted through the files. Ahmad glanced at Mara from time to time, until she finally sat on the bed across the room where it would be easier for him to see her in his periphery. She wasn't here for them. No point in antagonizing her new allies.

After a moment, she saw them both exhale in relief.

The woman closed her eyes, dark lashes casting shadows in the dim light against her sharp cheekbones. Ahmad squeezed her shoulder, and she opened her eyes and looked at Mara.

"Thank you," she said.

"Not on the list, then?" Mara asked.

She smiled. "No. And I can do a lot of good with this information. Save some people, even."

"Good," Mara said. "Maybe the scales are a little more balanced now." Even she was surprised at how tired she sounded. "Better act fast. And so should we. I vote we try the marine first. She's probably itching for a fight."

"I think you're right," Ahmad replied slowly. "She's more likely to still have people on the *Avalon* that she's close with."

"Glad we agree," Mara said. "Let's go talk to her."

The woman was named Jordan Vargas. She had been aboard the *Avalon* until a leg injury forced her into rehab on Argos a few weeks ago. They were betting on the year she had spent on the ship, in close quarters with lots of other people. They were betting that she still cared about some of them.

In Mara's experience, that was usually a pretty good bet.

Ahmad stood quietly beside her, his face focused and calm. He had his arms folded again, but this time the posture was relaxed and graceful as he leaned against the wall of the corridor. With his shirt loose at the neck and the sleeves rolled up to his elbows, he looked like he had no cares in the world. Just a man waiting for a friend to meet him for dinner.

"So Kai Ahmad's not really your name, is it?" she asked.

"No," he replied. "But I'm guessing you knew that."

She shrugged. "We're not in the business of using our real names, are we?"

"No, we're not. But I know yours now."

Irritation surged through Mara, but Ahmad fixed his eyes on her and she remained silent.

"If you think I'm ready to forgive you," he said slowly, softly, but with a tremble in his voice, "for killing two people I love, then you're a lot more naive than you seem."

Their faces flashed before her again: The blonde woman dropping, her blood soaking the grass below her. The clean line drawn through the throat of the man. Suddenly, their namelessness was a dark void in her mind.

"I'm sorry," she said. "Though I know my apology is worth nothing."

He worked his jaw and looked away from her. "Maybe someday it will be."

"Who were they?" she asked.

He held up a hand, his eyes fixed on the hospital door. "That's her."

Mara looked at the woman he meant—a short, muscular woman leaning on a cane. Black textured curls spilled over her face, which was set, though she didn't really seem to be in pain. No, that was just the face of someone who had a bone to pick with the world. They could work with that.

"Corporal Vargas?" Ahmad said as he approached the woman. He smiled and tucked his dark hair behind his ears in a gesture so casual and relaxed it almost put Mara at ease. At least he was good at this.

Vargas stopped at her name and frowned. "Yeah?"

"Lieutenant Commander Mill sent me. She needs your help with something."

"My help? You notice how helpful I am right now?" She gestured to her leg.

"Just give me a few minutes to deliver her message," he said. "We'll go to a public place. I'm not armed, but I'm sure you are."

Mara saw fire flash in the woman's eyes. Well, that was a confirmation on the weaponry.

Vargas considered Ahmad for a moment, brown eyes narrowed. Her hand went to her jacket, rested comfortably on something inside.

"Okay," she said. "There's a café around the corner. Buy me a coffee. You have until I finish it."

"Deal," he said with a warm smile.

Vargas just raised an eyebrow at him. Good thing he had more than charm going for him, because he was clearly not her type.

As he walked alongside Vargas toward the café, Ahmad sent Mara a cautioning look. She stayed a safe distance behind them and waited for them to be seated at a table near the door before she entered and sat at the table next to them. She pulled out her data pad and pretended to read as they ordered their drinks.

"Okay," Vargas said. "What do you have?"

"You don't know what's happened to the *Avalon*, do you?" he asked.

She cocked an eyebrow. "The fuck are you talking about?"

"Captain Armstrong has been killed," he said. "And the rest of the ship arrested for mutiny. All except for the XO."

"No way," she said. "No fucking way. Who are you saying killed Armstrong and committed mutiny? Mill?"

Their coffee came, and they stopped speaking until the waiter had left.

"No fucking way," Vargas repeated when the waiter was out of earshot. "Jaya would never do something like that."

"Your instincts are right," Ahmad said. "I have a source. She has proof, but I need you to trust me enough to talk to her. There's something else going on here, and the company of the *Avalon* is being framed."

Vargas didn't reply for a moment, and Ahmad took a sip from

his drink in that easy way he had. Mara saw Vargas's shoulders relax a little. She was softening.

"Who's your source?" Vargas asked.

Ahmad looked up at Mara then, and jerked his head toward the seat beside him. Mara joined them at the table and sat across from Vargas, whose eyes widened.

She recovered quickly. "I'm supposed to believe some nareian knows something about the Union Navy that I don't?" But her gaze returned to Mara's face and she frowned. "Wait, have we met or something? You look—"

"It's a long story," Mara said. "I'll tell it later." Vargas sat back and brough her coffee to her lips, taking a large gulp. Mara sighed and told the fastest version she could. "I'm a bounty hunter. I took a job that went to shit and ended up on a space station. Turns out, that station belongs to this Augustus asshole you guys are trying so hard to kill."

Vargas choked on her coffee. Mara waited for her to stop coughing, then continued.

"And we've never met. I just have one of those faces. Sort of. Anyway, I found this when I was on the station."

She opened the files on her palm drive and projected them onto the table. She angled her shoulders to obscure the writing from the tables beside them, and Ahmad shifted to do the same on his side. She watched Vargas read the words, her mouth forming around the phrase that ended the communiqué: *Fortune befriends the bold.*

Vargas looked from Ahmad to Mara and back again. "This is legit. I still don't understand how you got this."

"Does it matter?" Mara asked. The seconds were ticking by, and she was irritated. "Read the next one."

Vargas cast her eyes down again, the message about the upcoming purge glowing dimly against the surface of the table. She clenched her fists.

"Who's on the list?" she asked.

"We have a full list of military personnel they're targeting," Ahmad said. "Captain Armstrong was on it, and I would guess that his loyal crew has been upgraded to high priority since they've been arrested."

"When were they arrested?" Vargas asked.

"Yesterday afternoon," Ahmad said. "They've been interrogated, but not released. The charges are not just mutiny, but treason."

"They can't execute everyone." Vargas was staring at a space between them, her eyes distant. Her fists grew tighter.

"Can't they?" Mara asked. Vargas just kept staring at her. Mara bit back a growl. "Look, there's about to be a massive purge by the same group you got injured trying to stop. And now all your friends are caught up in it. If there's anyone on that ship that you give a fuck about, you'll want to help us."

Vargas dropped her head into her hands then, the curls peeking through her fingers. Her shoulders shook once as she took a deep, uncertain breath. Then she raised her head. "I was never going to be able to get back on the *Avalon*."

Mara wasn't sure what she was talking about, but Ahmad leaned forward, sympathy in his eyes.

Vargas kept talking. "I got hurt too bad. I could work somewhere else for the Navy, but my only shot at IRC is over. I'm too big of a risk. I was happy there. I had someone."

Ahmad nodded slightly, and Vargas took another deep breath.

"Fuck it," she said. "How do we do this?"

"Well," Mara said. "That requires a little more information about why you recognized my face. And before I tell that story, we need to go somewhere a little more private."

38

Even in the jail, screens stretched across the walls, broadcasting news, advertisements, and entertainment. Tynan held his head in his hands—external stimulus was never a welcome intrusion into the already busy world in his mind. In the cell across the narrow corridor, Sal was pacing. His motion was almost as distracting as the flashing and noise of the screens.

On nearly every screen, the headlining story was the election of the new Union Chancellor, Richard Emory. His face splashed across the wall, white teeth bared in a smile.

Tynan was not familiar with human standards of attractiveness, but he could tell that the look of this Emory was smooth and polished. As the announcer went on, the screen continued to show footage of Emory. Publicity images provided from his company, TA Tech; video of him interacting with fans as he campaigned; visits with foreign dignitaries.

A flash of an image drew Tynan up, his eyes fixed on the screens, hoping to see it again. Richard Emory with Kujei Oszca at some large meeting, their heads bowed together in deep discussion. Tynan clenched his fists, a turmoil of mixed anger and guilt confusing his thoughts. If only he had learned a thing or two from his parents about politics. Regret brought a bitter taste to his mouth. His own stubbornness had closed the way to him—Kujei had taken every advantage he had been given and then created a few more advantages for himself. And what had Tynan's purism gotten him?

The glass of the cell around him answered his silent question with more silence. He continued to stare at the screen until his eyes burned, but the image never resurfaced.

After a while, the programs tired of showing pictures of their newly elected leader and switched instead to grainy security footage of a nareian.

"Well, look at that." Rhodes moved to the front of his cell, gaping at the screen.

Shea followed his gaze, and their eyes widened. "Hey Azima, you were so excited about meeting a duchess you didn't even realize you were talking to actual royalty."

"No one knew she was royalty, genius," Sal said, glancing up at the screen. He sat down hard on the floor and put his head in his knees. "That's why they call her the lost princess."

Shea rolled their eyes.

The doors to the cell block opened then, and two officers walked in, dragging someone behind them. Sal was on his feet instantly. It was Jaya, Tynan realized with a jolt. Although he had never seen her like this. Her head lolled forward; half of her hair had escaped from its braid and fell wildly across her face. Her feet slid along the floor as the two guards hoisted her up, their arms hooked under her armpits.

Suddenly, Tynan wondered if his own assumptions about the behavior of her blood and tissue were false. She looked weak, broken. Not like someone whose body had an extra special repair system in place.

They opened the door to her cell and nudged her inside. She stumbled, throwing her hands against the wall to catch herself.

The guards closed the door and left, and she sank slowly to her knees.

When the door closed behind the guards, there was a clamor of voices. Jaya held one hand up in protest.

"One at a time," she groaned.

"Are you okay?" Sal asked.

Jaya grimaced and lay down on the floor, rolling slowly onto her back. "I'll make it," she replied. She took a deep, shaky breath. "We just need to find a way out of here."

"Right," Sal scoffed. "Piece of cake."

"Let me think," Jaya protested.

Everyone watched her. Tynan realized the trust he had developed in her was near-universal among the *Avalon*'s company. Rhodes's face remained dark and angular, his eyes narrowed and his arms crossed as he watched his colleague in concern. Sal sat heavily on the floor again and grabbed onto his own hair as though he could physically pull a solution out of his head.

Tynan found it difficult to keep himself calm. Normally, enclosed spaces didn't bother him, but there was something about a jail cell that was not quite as soothing as his little closet-turned-office on the *Avalon*. And Jaya's cryptic replies and clear physical distress weren't helping him find reasons to relax. He closed his eyes and tried deep breathing to slow his heart rate, Min's soothing voice in his ear, tracking his respiration, pulse, and blood pressure.

"How are you?"

He opened his eyes. Sunny was looking across the narrow aisle at him.

"I've been better," he said.

"We'll be okay," she said, repeating the words she'd spoken to him back on the *Avalon* in the heat of the ambush.

This time, he couldn't bring himself to respond.

Jaya sat up slowly. Color was returning to her face, though she still leaned against the wall.

"I don't know what to do," she confessed. No one replied. The silence held them tightly. Jaya sighed and began to rub her face. She hoisted herself up and leaned against the wall.

"Don't push yourself," Sunny cautioned, her hands reaching out, although she couldn't help Jaya from her own cell. Jaya waved away her concern, her eyes less glassy, more focused. Perhaps he had been too quick to doubt his own work—she was bouncing back very quickly.

A noise outside the door drew their attention. The door opened, and another guard entered, her face obscured by the shadow of a tall nareian whose arm she grasped.

A chill ran through Tynan at the sheer size of the being. He was not looking forward to sharing a space with that.

"The fuck?" Sal exclaimed. He was staring at the nareian.

In fact, so was Rhodes. And all of the marines. Tynan looked over at Jaya, who was also watching the nareian, her eyes narrowed in concentration. Her eyes flickered to the screen and then widened in surprise. Tynan followed her gaze. The nareian—it was the very princess they had all been talking about.

Then Jaya looked at the guard and smiled. She turned her gaze back to the nareian.

"You're kind of a big deal, huh?" she asked the nareian.

"Didn't believe me, did you?" the nareian retorted. "How is it being the captain of your own ship?"

"It's complicated." Jaya gave a surprised laugh. "Never thought I'd see you again."

The door closed behind the guard, and the nareian moved suddenly. Her walk was ragged, like one of her legs was heavier than the other. The guard released the nareian and unlocked her handcuffs, then crossed to Jaya's cell and grinned widely.

"I got you, boss," the guard said. "Even if you did get yourself into one hell of a mess."

Jaya laughed again, her eyes bright. "Glad to have you on my team, Vargas."

The guard opened Jaya's cell and then began to open the rest one by one. The last one she opened was Lupo's, and the tiny pilot wrapped her arms around their rescuer in a fierce embrace.

The mechanical whirring of the doors opening caught Tynan's attention, as well as Jaya's. Guards surged in, and then, with loud, rhythmic bursts, they dropped one by one at Jaya's feet. Tynan closed his eyes instinctively, flinching against the noise and the violence, and when he opened them a second later, the sound of particle beam fire and bodies thudding to the floor had ceased.

Jaya grasped a gun in her hand, but it was not raised. Instead, she was looking behind her with incredulity. The nareian stood coolly, hands freed and wielding two particle beam pistols.

"I'll give this to you, Mill," she said. "You've got skill, and you've got brains. What you haven't got is finesse. Keep their attention elsewhere, and someone like you could walk out of this place carrying its most deeply guarded secrets without even a glance from a security guard."

There was a brief silence, in which Tynan heard a small scoff from Sal. Then, Jaya holstered the gun she had picked up.

"Thanks for the help," she replied. "Marantos, is it?"

"I prefer Mara. Now let's not waste time."

The officers of the *Avalon* emptied into the aisle, picking over the guards with precision and passing guns down the line to each other. Sal held one out to Tynan, who hesitated.

"You'll want it, I promise," Sal said, thrusting it into Tynan's hand and closing his long fingers around it.

"We need to split up," Jaya said. "Two teams. Sal, I need you to deactivate the trackers in everyone's palm drives. We should do this on the move—they'll see us splitting up and then disappear. Once everyone's off the grid, we rendezvous in the civilian wards."

"What's the RP?" Rhodes asked.

"There's a shop on the third floor of the Sol quarter where I do a lot of business," Mara said. "It's thanks to the owner and his friend I was able to get you lot out. They're waiting for us there." She tapped something into her palm drive, and Jaya and Rhodes both checked their devices and gave a thumbs up.

"Do what you can to blend in until we're all there," Jaya said. "Absolute radio silence. No exceptions."

"Understood," replied Rhodes.

Jaya and Rhodes divided everyone into two groups. Sunny slipped her hand into Tynan's and gave a slight squeeze.

"See?" she whispered. "I told you we'd be fine."

But Tynan knew that their fates were not decided just yet.

Tynan's lungs were constricted with fear, and he tried not to gasp his breaths loudly. His alien features stood out here. There were some szacante on Argos, conducting business or as diplomatic officials, but he knew his very presence would draw attention, even without the potential that at any moment their escape could be noticed and their faces broadcast on every screen in Argos.

Jaya moved them quickly down the halls, darting in and out of alleys. Tynan was grateful for the urgency and for the silence of the abandoned corridors she chose. A creeping tickle of anxiety moved up his spine as though he were trapped in a slowly rising tide.

He still did not fully understand why they were running, except that the *Avalon*'s officers had been arrested and seemingly betrayed by their own people. This, too, he did not understand—he had barely been among them long enough to understand their most basic of customs, let alone the apparently intricate and fragile system of relations between government and people. But Jaya had always shown him that he belonged, and he had seen her strength. Of all the humans to trust, she seemed the best investment.

And after all, he had been arrested along with Jaya and her officers. He had been designated a part of their group. He had picked a
side when he'd left with the humans back on Dresha, and he would
have to see it through.

"You going to be okay with that weapon there, doc?"

Sal was staring at him with a look that Tynan could not work
out. He had dropped back slightly and was standing close now, his
eyes moving from Tynan's face to the gun in his hands. Tynan
suddenly realized his hands were shaking.

"I don't know," he said, surprising himself with his own candor.
But then, he wouldn't have known what else to say.

That pulled a sigh from the human, who glanced ahead at
Jaya and the other soldier. Jaya had paused and she threw a
look back at them. Sal flashed her a quick hand signal and she
responded with her own. The awareness of Tynan's foreignness
plunged down into his stomach. He was just as lost now as he
had been the first day he had spent with the humans,
suspended in the darkness of utter incomprehension with barely
even a foothold. Sunny had become his translator and his
teacher, slowly digging away at the rubble of his cultural
confusion and exposing him to human ways in little doses. He
thought he had come to understand them, but he found himself
now surrounded by inscrutable faces and a language that
wasn't even words.

A sudden and powerful urge to hold Sunny's hand pushed its
way into Tynan's mind. He set aside the childish thought, but still
felt the wish settle into his chest and fix itself there, deep below
where his conscious mind could chase it away.

Sal was looking at him again, a crease etched into the place
between his eyebrows.

"Just stick close to me," he said. "Whenever possible, stay
behind cover. Walls, desks, chairs—whatever you're closest to. And
once we're in there and the fighting starts, if someone who is not

one of us ends up behind that cover with you, just shoot. Until they stop moving."

"Okay," Tynan said, and winced at the way his voice came out weak and strained. He thought he heard Sal mutter one last thing under his breath as he turned away:

And pray.

But it could have been his own subconscious talking.

39

It wasn't until they were safely outside of the Diplomatic Level that Jaya allowed them to take a moment to deactivate their trackers. She took a moment to breathe deeply and stretch her limbs out. The strong pulse of life that thrummed through her again seemed strangely alien after whatever they had done to her in that interrogation room. After whatever Emory had done to her. She relished the feeling of strength again.

She had led them down winding backstreets in the opposite direction of the RP, and she checked the Argos map on her palm drive now as they waited in silence. Mara continued ahead as Sal worked on the team's palm drives, and Jaya tapped out a message to Rhodes. The information Armstrong had given her was too important to hold on her own. And if there was anyone she could trust in this galaxy, it was the people who had broken out of the Navy's prison with her. She sent the message off.

Sal finished with a drive and moved toward Jaya. He leaned in close as he worked on hers.

"Why do I have the feeling we're not going straight to the rendezvous point?" Sal asked.

Jaya gave him a grim smile. "Because we're not. I have a stop to make—it could pay off."

"Where are we going?"

"The Chancellor's home," she replied.

Even in the dark, she could see Sal's grin. "Sounds exciting."

Her tracker went offline with a quiet beep, and Sal switched to his own. Jaya checked the pistol she had taken from the guard. It was regulation—small and solid, but light on charge and power. She holstered it in her belt and a silent breath escaped her. She hadn't realized until then just how much tension she had been holding in. Until they were aboard the *Avalon* and traveling at FTL speeds away from Argos, she knew a part of her would feel as though she were suspended in air, her feet never quite resting solidly on the ground.

Barely more than twenty people—the officers, enlisted sailors, and marines that had been arrested with her and Doctor Vasuda—were all that remained of the crew Armstrong had once commanded. Their window was a small one, only open while the administrative details of the *Avalon*'s duties were sorted out, and while she knew the ship would be guarded, this was their best chance, as it would also be empty.

What they would do once they had the *Avalon* back, she hadn't figured out.

"Can we trust her?" Sal asked suddenly, lowering his voice.

Jaya followed his gaze to Mara, who was returning toward them silently through the shadows. "She came back. She didn't have to."

Sal's tracker beeped once and silenced.

"Okay," he said. "We're good to go."

Jaya and Sal crept forward and met Mara ahead.

"We're not far," Jaya said. "Sal, there's likely to be high security —I need you to feel it out for me."

"You got it," he replied.

They rounded the corner, and Jaya stopped. Sal scurried up ahead, already tapped into his palm drive, typing furiously. She addressed the people who were following her.

"I want you to go ahead with Mara. She'll take you to the RP, but we're making a short detour here first. Sal and I will meet up with you at the RP. If we're not there in fifteen minutes, leave without us."

"Hell, no." Thompson's whisper was fierce. "We're not leaving you."

"I have intel that Armstrong passed on to me," she said. "I've passed it along in turn to Rhodes. This is bigger than just us. And I need more information before we go. This is the last chance to get it, but the fewer of us involved the safer it will be. You understand?"

Thompson wrinkled his face up in disapproval, but he nodded. "I understand."

"Good," she said. "Now go. We'll catch up."

She watched them disappear silently into the darkness of Argos's midnight. Was this how Armstrong had felt? The uncertainty gnawed at her, but she didn't hear any trace of it in her own voice. Sal appeared back at her side.

"The encryption is military," he reported. "The same code we use at HQ. They must not know we're out yet."

Jaya frowned. "It's hard to believe they haven't noticed."

"I can take the system down," Sal continued, "and they may not notice for a while. But the moment they realize what's happened they'll change the encryption and we'll be fucked in under five minutes. You still want to do this?"

"Yes." She wished she could do this alone, but she met Sal's eyes in the dark and she knew that he would never let her shake him on a job like this. Thompson was stubborn, but he had nothing on Sal. So she sighed and put her hand on his shoulder. "Bring it down."

It didn't take long, and soon she and Sal were creeping into the home of Richard Emory himself. He lived alone, and Jaya's heat scans confirmed he was not home tonight. She suspected he was still with those members of the Union Navy who had sold their loyalty to him, fortuitously leaving her and Sal to explore his home in peace.

She paused in front of the painting, its agonized figures like tormented ghosts in the dark. Back when she had met with Emory in his home, this painting felt like a point of contact. Something that drew them both in. Now, she wondered.

They tiptoed past the kitchen and its state-of-the-art appliances and found a door on the right. Jaya nudged it open with her shoulder.

Offices for high-ranking officials still held many of the outdated touches of their predecessors. The trappings of power—accumulated rare items and aesthetic draws—were on display, regardless of their utility. At the center of this office was a real antique desk—wood from the long-destroyed forests of Earth, in a symbolic gesture. The paintings that hung on the wall were actual oil on canvas. Their smell permeated the room, foreign and ancient.

And there were books—real books, bound in paper or cardboard or leather, their covers ranging from brightly painted to simple earthy brown. An intricately carved shelf behind the desk boasted dozens of titles. With everything available at the blink of an eye on a palm drive, books were reserved for those with money to burn and space to fill. Or old romantics. Jaya's childhood residence had housed exactly one paper book—the old collection of sheet music that her father had bought for her mother as a wedding present. Everything else had been housed in the library of a data pad, since even they couldn't afford real books in money or in space.

"Look around," she told Sal. "Anything out of the ordinary could be relevant. Anything to tie him to the Sons of Priam."

Though Sal raised an eyebrow, she saw by his smirk that he had known why they were searching Emory's office. He had always been able to read her. Sometimes it felt as if her hunches were his as well.

He took a seat at the desk and woke the console, his fingers immediately flying over the keys, coaxing out information. Jaya rifled through the desk's drawers, drawing them stiffly out of their frames. Most of them were empty—once used to store paper and office supplies that the modern world had no need for, they now served as empty caverns that held little more than stale air.

"Got something," Sal said. "Looks like an encrypted message. There's a quote at the end, something in Latin: *tu ne cede malis.*"

"Do not yield to evil," Jaya translated, the words too familiar by now on her tongue. She finished the phrase from memory. "But advance boldly against it. It's from the *Aeneid.*"

Sal nodded. "I'm copying all his messages over."

"Good," Jaya said. "We don't know how far this reaches."

As Sal continued to copy data from Emory's console, Jaya stood back and looked around the room again.

The décor was carefully generic, although it dripped wealth. It was meant more to be representative of the man Emory projected to the world than a personal statement. This was a place he would bring powerful people to woo them to his cause, and he would be very careful with the message it sent. Jaya had already experienced that once, but he had kept their meeting out of his office, so she filtered her observations through that lens now.

No personal photographs, she realized right away. A few token shots with foreign diplomats and high-ranking members of the Union, but nothing indicating family or friends. She picked one of the photographs from the bookshelf, looking more closely. Emory stood beside a szacante she didn't recognize, smiling his supernova smile, every hair in place. It was perfectly superficial.

She replaced the photo on the shelf and picked up a book that had been beside it. Even as she touched it, her heart dropped into her stomach. Her every sense recalled this book—the smell of the old paper, the faded ink of the cover, the texture of the leather.

For a moment, she froze, the book suddenly heavy in her hands. Her pulse raced through her fingers, beating against the cover. She opened it, gently folding the first page back. Her heart was reciting the words before her eyes were reading them.

For bringing music into my life—I love you.

She understood now why Emory's voice sent subtle chills through her. That voice didn't belong in that polished new face. Behind the plastic surgery was a face that was not too different from Jaya's own.

The architect behind this all—the man who had recruited Kier and had tried to recruit her, the self-made billionaire who had captured the vote of the Union's citizens—was the father she had long thought was dead. Burned with his research.

Like Kier, he had escaped. This whole time, he had been building a new life, rising to the top. While Jaya lived in poverty and fear.

"Jaya?"

Sal's voice pulled her back to the present. She glanced over her shoulder at him.

"I've got it," he said, holding up a small data drive. "Everything from his console."

"That's good," she said, though she barely felt the words form in her throat.

"What's that?" Sal asked, gesturing to the book in her hand.

She looked down at it, not sure how to answer his question. For a moment, she considered tucking the small book under her arm and bringing it back to the *Avalon* with her. She swallowed the lump in her throat.

"It's the only sentimental thing he has in this office," she said. The words were true, even if they didn't mean much to Sal. She let out a slow breath.

"Useful?" Sal asked.

Her fingers lingered as she slowly replaced it on the shelf. "No." She looked back up, taking in Sal's expectant face.

"Let's go," she said. "We don't have much time."

By the time they reached the rendezvous point, Jaya had grown unnerved by the silence on Argos. It was late, and few people were walking the corridor of the station, but they stayed in the dark and quiet alleys, winding their way through empty streets until they arrived in front of the shop that Mara had sent them to.

The door opened and Mara ushered them in quickly. The lighting was dim, but still brighter than the black night on the street. Jaya blinked as she adjusted to the light. Rhodes stood waiting with his team behind him. His arms were crossed over his chest, a shadow in the dark. Tynan was sitting in a chair, picking at his sleeve with one hand. The gun Sal had given him lay on the table next to him, discarded, but the doctor cast it anxious looks. Vargas had a cane now, and she leaned heavily on it, but she still managed a smile, which Jaya returned.

And behind Vargas stood another person. Tall and lean, his dark hair sweeping across his cheekbones and shadowing his eyes. Jaya blinked at him, not certain her eyes had fully adjusted. But he was still there.

"Luka?"

He smiled, the expression rueful. "I haven't *entirely* escaped my past," he half-explained. He watched her with those dark eyes, intense and focused, and she didn't know how to respond.

Mara snorted. Jaya broke the eye contact and looked at the nareian, who shrugged.

"He got a lot keener on helping me when he found out it would help you," Mara said.

"Wait, is this your antiques salesman?" Sal asked in a low voice. "No wonder you were always up there."

She jabbed him with her elbow.

"Is anyone going to explain what's going on?" asked the *Avalon*'s engineer, Fisher.

Jaya turned toward her. "Emory's involved with the Sons of Priam. He's got someone in the Navy under his thumb."

"More than one," Luka said, his voice calm. "There's been a purge. My contact confirmed it."

Jaya's chest constricted and she drew a shallow breath. No wonder not a single person had tried to stop them. They were all too busy killing or being killed to be concerned about a bunch of prisoners supposedly safe in a cell. She wondered how many of those carrying out orders from above knew who they were really working for.

"I'm supposed to believe that?" Fisher asked.

"Emory was sending messages filled with Sons of Priam codewords," Sal said. "We don't know exactly what his role is, but he's definitely connected."

Fisher swallowed. "Fucking hell."

"Amen," said Thompson. "We're in deep shit."

"We can't stay here long," Jaya said. "They must know we're gone by now."

"Where exactly do we go," Sal asked dryly, "when the leader of our entire government wants us dead?"

"Dresha," Jaya offered. "The government there had a close relationship with Chancellor Lavelle—we can claim political asylum. We've been working with one of their own—who was threatened by Emory and the Sons of Priam before their coup."

"They won't be sympathetic."

Jaya turned toward the voice that had spoken—Tynan's voice. The scientist was still in the chair, still picking at his sleeve, but he had raised his head to meet her eyes.

"Why not?" she asked.

He sighed, his hands pausing in their nervous movement. "The Arbiter's closest advisor," he said. "Kujei Oszca. He's got some connection to Emory, and he's been influencing the Arbiter for a while now. I think he may even have been behind the takeover of my research."

Jaya's heart dropped. "What kind of connection to Emory?"

"I don't have proof," the szacante confessed. "I just saw a picture of them together, at some conference. It doesn't necessarily mean anything. But Kujei was pursuing work along the lines of..." He paused, then, and shot a wary glance around the room. "He was talking about doing the same kind of enhancement work we spoke about. He always argued the humans were doing it, too. He wanted access to my research, and I think he has it now, thanks to Emory." He took a deep breath. "I don't like to operate on hunches. But I also don't think the Szacante Federation is safe for us. Not now."

Tynan fixed his pale green eyes on her. His shoulders were still slumped, his body conveying a message of utter misery and defeat. But his face was set, his eyes glinting in the low light of the room.

"He's probably right." Luka spoke up. "Emory's been working with szacante scientists for a while now. And after his attempts to manipulate the Nareian Empress, I think we can assume he's been looking for ways into Dresha as well. And likely found them."

She looked at Rhodes, whose steady gaze was already on her. "The colonies," he suggested. "Somewhere remote."

"We'll have to stay moving," she countered. "Even on the outskirts of the Union, we'll be hard to hide."

"Good thing we're the best reconnaissance team the galaxy." He smiled as he said it.

"The *Avalon*, then," she said. "Getting the *Avalon* back is our best chance."

Heads nodded around them. Agreement.

"We're short on guns," she continued, meaning not just the limited capacity of the guard weapons they had stolen, but also the muscle of their team.

Mara was powerful, but unpredictable. Most of these officers had field training, but many of them were used to administrative or technological duties. Vargas was still hurting. For each person experienced in combat, she had a more vulnerable support member to worry about. That was not a ratio she liked, especially considering the odds they faced.

"We'll have to rely on stealth," she added. "Move quietly and quickly."

Mara scoffed and Jaya snapped her attention to the nareian's catlike eyes.

"You have something to say?" Jaya asked.

"If all it takes is speed and silence for twenty people to capture a human military ship, how did my people not smear you across the galaxy in the war?" Mara said.

"You have something *helpful* to say?" Sal amended.

"I told you before," Mara said. "It's about innovation. Creativity. Don't think the way they expect you to. You're trained for infiltrations in a certain way, right? You're trained to sneak. So don't do that—you'll play right into their hands."

"The security offices," Jaya said. She turned to Sal, her mind clicking all the pieces of the plan into place even as she spoke it. "Sal, you know Union naval code inside and out. How easy would it be for you to rewrite the programs that govern the dock's defenses?"

He shrugged. "Possible, if I had time to actually do it. How exactly are we going to get quality time with the security office's computers?"

"I have an idea," Jaya said. "We split into two teams. One of us goes in the front door—we take on the security office. The other team goes to the docks and waits. When we drop the defenses, they go in and take care of the rest. We'll have to time it carefully." She leaned forward as she spoke, her team fixed in her attention. "Sal, Thompson, Shea, and Tynan, you're with me. We're going to the security offices. Rhodes, you lead a team to the *Avalon* with the rest of the crew."

"Any chance I could catch a ride?" Mara said. "I'm not really keen on being smuggled back out of here. Blasting out on a stolen ship is more my style."

Jaya nodded. "You can go with Rhodes."

Vargas met her eyes, her expression uncertain.

"Boss, I know I'm not in shape," she said, letting the thought drop there. She leaned on her cane and looked away. Lupo took her free hand in hers.

"Go with the dock team, too," Jaya said. "Make sure you're the first one onboard, and help Lupo and Fisher with whatever they need to get the *Avalon* ready to go."

Vargas nodded, her eyes bright. "Yes, Commander."

"Our number one objective is to get off this station," Jaya said. "The less time we spend engaging them, the better off we'll be."

Luka was watching her closely. She met his eyes and held the look for a moment. There was no time now, no way to get all her questions answered. No way to say all the things she had a sudden urge to say. But he seemed to read one of her questions in her eyes.

"I have things I need to do here," he said. "The resistance needs a foothold."

It wasn't a surprise, but the confirmation settled cold in her chest. His eyes were bleak, scanning over her face like he wanted to memorize it. Like he might never see her again.

"Teams, you have your assignments," Jaya said, not taking her eyes off Luka. "We're moving out."

Luka's mouth quirked up in a sad smile. She blinked, tearing herself reluctantly away.

Rhodes led Lupo and the rest out first. Mara exchanged a quiet word with Luka, then followed them with her head ducked down to keep her face in shadows. Sal put a comforting hand on Jaya's shoulder.

A terrible awareness seized Jaya and she stopped short.

"Wait," she said. "My uncles. He knows about them. Knows

where they live and how to find them. He knows he could use them to get to me."

From behind her, Luka answered, "I'll take care of it."

She spun to face him, and Sal moved away, steering the rest of their team to the door to wait.

"I have somewhere I can take them," Luka added. "Somewhere I know is safe. Will they trust me?"

Jaya closed her eyes, searching for some way to send them a message that Emory could not intercept. Some way to tell them that Luka was safe, that Jaya had sent him. When she opened her eyes again, it was to look into his. She held out a hand to him, and he took it.

"Ask them if they remember the song my mother wrote for them," she said.

"Do I know this one?" His voice was hushed, as if listening to a memory of the music.

She brought the melody into her mind and hummed it, the vibration traveling down her sternum, reverberating in her chest and releasing the music into the air.

Luka's face broke into a smile, but his eyes still watched her heavily. He squeezed her hand tightly and gathered up her other hand as well.

"Can you remember it?" she asked.

"Yes," he said. "Of course."

He released her hands then, and she turned back to where Sal had herded the others. Sal was watching her with an eyebrow quirked up.

Jaya sent her uncles' coordinates to Luka, closing her eyes and wishing them safety. Praying it wasn't too late.

They left, and the door closed quietly behind them.

40

An open lobby—peaceful and simply decorated, with the furniture neatly arranged around the central reception desk—stood between Jaya's team and the security office. Jaya flattened herself against the wall and edged as far out as she could without being seen. The room appeared in her periphery, and she took in what details she could from the corner of her eye.

This late, the lights were dim, and every chair was empty. The lights on the reception desk were off, and a small display screen broadcast the morning's opening hours. She noted immediately the guard standing in the security office doorway. His hands rested on his hips and he moved slightly. His eyes flicked from screen to screen, but without the heightened urgency she would have expected from Argos police when a security concern of this level was loose in the station. Another guard approached from inside the office and followed his companion's gaze up to the screens.

"Anything?"

"Not yet," the first one replied.

They stood in silence a moment longer, both waiting for news. Finally the second one made an exasperated sound.

"Let me know if anything interesting happens," he said, disappearing back into the security office.

Jaya took the opportunity as the first one looked away, distracted briefly while watching his companion leave. She stole out from behind the wall, replacing its cover with the shadow of one of the chairs. Thompson, Sal, and Shea stayed back with Tynan.

Sal had cast many furtive glances back at their alien companion, and she saw the frown crease his forehead. Tynan's nerves were palpable, and Jaya couldn't help but feel the same concern Sal did. This mission had more liabilities than any she had ever conducted. She was certain that Tynan had absolutely no experience with weaponry of any kind, and while she knew his gifted mind would be quick to grasp the details of the gun's functionality, there was much more to combat than knowing how to make the gun work.

She just hoped she could keep him out of the way and safe without compromising the focus of the rest of her team.

She tapped out a quick message on her palm drive to her team: *Two guards that I know of. Probably more within.*

Their time was limited, but Jaya knew that rushing in without thinking was bound to end in too much blood. The element of surprise could only take them so far. She tried to settle her thoughts and focused on just listening instead.

There were at least two security guards, and within the interior room there were bound to be a few military officers. These offices handled the security for the naval docks, so they were run by naval personnel. The sound of feet shuffling inside reached her sensitive ears. Fingers tapped on a console. There were three, maybe four inside. Her palm drive scanned the room, confirming four heat signatures.

She moved back to where the rest waited, her steps silent.

"Four inside—at least one is security—and one security guard at the door," she confirmed.

"We can take a number like that," Thompson whispered.

Jaya nodded, her mind still on the people in the office. "The biggest concern is them calling for backup. But five is a number we can handle." Her voice was calm, but unease constricted her chest.

"This feels different," Shea said. They looked at Jaya, a question in their brown eyes.

"It is," Jaya replied.

"How?" Tynan spoke for the first time, his voice wavering.

Thompson said what the rest of them were thinking. "They're Union. Like us."

"The Union locked us up," Jaya said. "The Union is working with the Sons of Priam. We don't belong here anymore."

But still. They were all uncomfortable with what that change meant.

"If we can keep them from calling for help, we can do this without loss of life," Jaya said. She turned to Sal. "Can you scramble their palm drives?"

"Not without taking down our own."

"How about a timed scramble? Thirty seconds, to distract them and disrupt their communications while we take them down."

Sal grinned. "Just tell me when."

"Okay," Jaya said. "On my mark, Sal will scramble all the palm drives in the area for thirty seconds. That means ours, too. We have to move quickly and take them down while they're distracted. Wound, disarm, restrain. But if this becomes kill or be killed, I want every one of you coming out of here alive. Understood?"

All four nodded their agreement.

They got into position, creeping closer to the office. Jaya motioned for Thompson to move to a location closer to the door and she did the same, stealing over to the reception desk as the security guard looked away momentarily. Jaya looked back—everyone was ready, crouched in the shadows. It was time.

She held up three fingers in their view and slowly, deliberately ticked down to two, then one. With a forward thrust of her finger, she propelled herself up, sensing the others following her.

Thirty. Twenty-nine. Twenty-eight.

She kept a running count in her head, feeling the rhythm of each second in her chest, and even though her heart should have been racing, it kept the beat. Everything appeared slow around her, like she had shifted just slightly in time, able to cut corners in the fourth dimension that no one else could. The security guard saw her and raised his weapon. Jaya threw herself forward into a roll, ducking the shot and sweeping his legs out from under him.

She found her feet quickly and pressed a heel to the man's throat as he lay heaving on the ground. Thompson wrenched the gun from the guard's hand, holstering his own. Footsteps behind her reminded her of the others' approach.

Twenty-one. Twenty. Nineteen.

She paused in the doorway just long enough to check that no one was coming through the door just yet. She could sense the presences inside the room agitated and moving. Cut off from communications and sensors, they would be disoriented and unmoored. She took advantage of that, ducking her head out just long enough to line up a shot.

She compressed the trigger, her shot blowing out a knee. The man she hit shouted and fell hard. Her eyes registered four figures, including the technician who was sprawled on the ground now, moaning. There was a security guard and two other officials. They were shouting now. *Fifteen. Fourteen. Thirteen.*

One of the officers moved toward the emergency call button to alert security headquarters. She pressed in, shooting the officer in the shoulder as he raised his arm. The guard swiveled around to take aim at her, and she aimed another precise shot, hitting his weapon arm. His shot went wide as he fell back, dropping his gun. Jaya ducked behind a desk. Thompson and Shea pressed into the room. Spurts of gunfire, and Sal and Tynan followed.

Jaya motioned to Tynan to hide behind the desk. She stayed just long enough to see him duck out of view, then rolled to her feet again.

Eight. Seven. Six. The security guard was on the ground, his weapon still skittering away along the floor. The other two were crouched and firing on Thompson and Sal, who took cover as best they could behind narrow consoles. Jaya leveled her gun, the beam searing one of the officer's sleeves as he dodged.

He was too distracted to see Sal raise his own pistol, and then he went down, the shoulder of his light armor seared. Thompson, Shea, and Sal focused fire on the remaining officer, wounding him.

Four. Three. The security guard was pulling himself up with his good arm, reaching toward his gun. Jaya launched herself over a console and rushed toward him. Her gun was already returning to its holster as she closed the small gap between them.

The guard was reaching for his weapon, fingers brushing the handle.

Two. He grasped the gun, his torso rotating to bring him up to face Jaya.

She was on top of him before he could aim.

One.

Zero.

Her hand pressed flat on his chest as her palm drive came back online, the EMP pulse surging into the armor and the muscle beneath. She saw his features freeze as the blast went through his nerves. And then he fell back, gun dangling from limp fingers.

Jaya took a breath.

A shout from across the room grabbed her attention. One of the officers was back up, clutching his wounded shoulder with one arm and Shea's leg with the other. Shea went down, but kept a grip on their pistol. The man moved fast, his bloody hand releasing his wound and clutching at Shea's gun, wrenching it from their hands, raising it, aiming it at the young corporal's head.

Jaya didn't hesitate. She shot him, the beam punching a clean hole through his temple. He collapsed.

In the silence that hung in the air afterward, she looked back at Sal and Thompson, who returned her look with grim faces. Shea was breathing heavily, still on the ground, and Jaya crossed the room and knelt beside them. They sat up, unharmed.

"I'm okay," Shea said.

Jaya held out a hand and helped them stand. She bent down, prying the gun that had nearly just ended Shea's life from the hand of the dead officer and wiping it clean. She handed it back to Shea, who took it and holstered it.

Jaya knelt next to the dead officer. His rank insignia were brand new, shiny on the collar of his bloodied uniform. He was young—barely twenty—fresh out of the academy. This assignment was likely his first. She lowered her head, blinking back tears, swallowing the burning lump in her throat.

Sal slid into a chair at one of the consoles and began to type. It wouldn't be long before he was done reprogramming the security protocol, and then they would need to move quickly. Jaya moved back to the security guard, releasing the catch of his helmet and gently removing it, along with his light-armor vest. Thompson and Shea began to pick through the others, restraining them with cuffs from the office's security locker and removing whatever pieces of armor or protective gear were still useful.

Jaya slipped into the protective vest and tucked the helmet under her arm. She continued to dig through the room, focusing her attention on each small motion, trying to quell the dark churn in her stomach.

Outside, the *Avalon* waited.

The chaos of the docks threatened to penetrate Jaya's precision focus.

Rhodes had led his team onto the *Avalon* and was firing the ship's powerful guns. Mara lurked in the ship's airlock and took a more precise approach to the covering fire. Debris scattered with each powerful discharge from the *Avalon*, and Union marines who were able to pull their focus away from the ship had trained it all on the little spot where Jaya and Thompson crouched.

Jaya's team had outfitted themselves with armor and supplies from the officers in the security rooms. Their supplies were sparse, but she was grateful for the helmet and the single frag grenade that dangled from her belt.

Shea, Sal, and Tynan had pushed farther ahead. Jaya was drawing the fire away from them and toward herself and Thompson. Despite the brave face he was trying to wear, she knew Tynan's ability to handle combat was limited at best. He had contained his shaking, but she could still read the fear in his eyes. That look crossed the species gap.

The *Avalon*'s engines started with a deep bellow, and she could feel the ripple of air against her, even through the stolen armor. Their time was growing limited. She needed to get everyone on the *Avalon*.

"Go!" she called over the comms to Sal, popping up over her cover to fire into the nearest group.

They focused everything on her in response, and she dropped back down, firing blindly around the edge of the overturned supply cart she was hiding behind. She saw Tynan and Sal disappear into the *Avalon* with Shea trailing just behind them, and a little of the knot in her stomach released. Now it was just the two of them. She rolled to hide behind a small transport a few feet away.

"Thompson," she spoke into the comms, "I'm going to draw their fire again. When I do, you get to the ship, or as close as you can get. We need to get on board, and we need to do it now."

"Understood, Captain," he replied.

She raised herself up again, taking down one of the marines before they noticed her, then dropped back down. Their particle beams heated up the metal she was leaning against. It cast a warm glow that might have been comforting in any other scenario.

Thompson ducked out from cover, keeping himself low to the ground as he traveled closer to the *Avalon*. Then he crumpled and fell, and Jaya's heart sank.

"Thompson!" she shouted. "You okay?"

"I'm hit," he replied, his voice strained, but calm.

"I'm joining you." Jaya pulled the grenade from her belt and released the pin.

She threw the grenade out in front of her, and the blast erupted. The flash and the noise provided a second of distraction that she used to launch herself up and over her hiding place, then she sprinted to where Thompson sat.

As she slid in beside him, she could already see the blood spreading across the ground beneath him. It clung to the leg of her pants and soaked its way in. She thought she could smell it through the acrid scent of destruction that already hung in the air.

"It's not good," Thompson said, and Jaya cringed at the note of apology in his voice.

"I've seen worse," she said.

It wasn't exactly a lie, but the rapidly spreading pool beneath Thompson was enough to elevate her heart rate.

The *Avalon* was hovering now, its smaller precision thrusters balancing it away from the docks, keeping the furious Union marines and their malfunctioning security equipment from boarding easily. Shea and Sal were at the edge of the entrance now. They crouched behind the open doors, firing on the attempted boarders.

Jaya carried the bleeding Thompson behind a security console, shielding them both from oncoming blasts. The *Avalon* was still distressingly far from them. She could see the tension in Sal and

Shea, and she knew that Lupo could only keep the ship in space travel limbo for so long before she would be forced to land or leave them behind.

"I'll cover you," Thompson said, and though Jaya could tell he was putting all his energy into it, his voice was low and weak, the air thin in his throat.

"No," Jaya said. "We're both getting on that ship."

The Union forces were weakening, bowed by the powerful guns of the *Avalon*, but they were in the most heavily armed human station, the headquarters of the military. Any moment now, fresh boots would be on the ground and bursting through the doors of the docks. Even in the midst of a purge, this would be a priority. Every second was precious, and they were bleeding time.

Behind Jaya, they were clear. Most of the remaining firepower came from one side of the room, and if she made a break for the *Avalon*, that firepower would all be coming from her left. She could shield Thompson with her own body, but the *Avalon* was still a difficult jump away. A jump that most members of her team could barely make on fresh legs, not fatigued ones, and certainly not with the added hundred kilos of a well-fed marine. But she had to try. She had spent fifteen years controlling herself, trying to look like her skills put her at the top of the class, but not high enough to be exceptional. She had never pushed herself beyond that—never tested her own capabilities, too afraid of what she might discover. What she had discovered only the other day.

Now didn't seem like the most convenient time to test Vasuda's theory. But it might be the only chance she and Thompson had.

"Mill to *Avalon*," she said over her comm. "Cover us."

With a quick but sincere apology to Thompson, she heaved him over her shoulder. He was heavy and torpid, his limbs slick with blood, and Jaya angled her body to keep his head and chest from the onslaught of particle beam fire. She secured her own helmet and eased herself up onto the balls of her feet, feeling the slow rise of heat to the muscles in her legs as they worked to keep her steady. And then, as soon as she heard the click that preceded the firing of the *Avalon*'s main guns, she burst forward.

She managed three large steps, with Thompson's crushing weight across her shoulder, before the first sear of particle beam tore into her leg.

She kept going, picking up speed, every muscle in her core working to keep her on balance as her body reacted to the shock and pain of the injury. A few hundred feet to go, and she lowered her head and shoulders, driving herself toward the ship. Another burst ripped through the armor of her left shoulder. She could smell the melting alloys and feel the metal fuse with burning flesh.

Just a few more hell-bent steps and the ledge was upon her. She couldn't afford the time to think—she jumped.

It was not until after she watched the docks dwindling as the *Avalon* pulled away that Jaya's feet stumbled beneath her. The floor was slippery as she lugged Thompson down the hall.

Sal, Tynan, and Sunny approached, their footsteps quick and urgent on the floor and the rattle of the gurneys' wheels an insistent undercurrent. Sunny and Tynan gently pried Thompson from Jaya's arms and laid him on one of the gurneys. Sal caught her arm around his shoulder, and despite her protestations, pulled her toward the other gurney. His response reached her muffled and muddy—a strange collection of syllables.

She realized then that she could not focus her eyes. And as they wheeled her away, it dawned on her that the floor's slick red coating was her own blood.

Unconsciousness teased at the edges of her mind, searing away at her focus, but she held on to the image of the *Avalon*'s smooth-paneled ceilings as they approached the med bay. The pain was sharp and insistent, but it was pushed back by the feeling that was now making a smile spread across her face.

"What's wrong with you?" Sal asked, his brown eyes locking onto the dopey, toothy grin she couldn't help.

She almost laughed at the way bewilderment and concern struggled with each other to dominate his expression.

Sal gripped the handholds in the corridor with one white-knuckled hand as he helped move the gurney along the hall, struggling to stay upright as the ship accelerated.

"We did it," she whispered, feeling inertia tug at her.

"You've lost a lot of blood," Sal said, and Jaya could see that concern was winning the battle.

"I'm okay." Despite the way her head felt light and her limbs felt heavy, she found strength in her voice.

Sunny had a needle in her arm and a blood transfusion started before the med bay doors had even shut behind her. Her fingertips fluttered across Jaya's eyelids and neck, her eyes sharp with focus, before she thrust a gadget into Tynan's hands.

"She's stable," Sunny said. "Suture those wounds and run a complete scan, and let me know when it's done." She waved Sal over as she rushed to Thompson's side. "I need every extra pair of hands over here."

As Tynan passed the scanner over her body, small electromagnetic pulses searching for internal damage, Jaya heard Sunny continue to shout orders, the doctor's usual sweet demeanor sharpened by urgency and focus. Jaya felt the world retreat as the blood transfusion replenished her and the painkillers began to reach her nervous system.

The jolt of the crash cart frequently broke through Jaya's drugged, distant state as they struggled to stabilize Thompson. When there was finally quiet, the background tune of murmuring and beeping machines slowly rose into her awareness.

41

Tynan gasped for air as the *Avalon* heaved beneath his feet. Adrenaline swam through his head, a buzzing swarm of chemicals that made him feel terrified, powerful, and a little drunk all at once.

He was waiting for Sunny to answer his question.

"Tynan, you should sit," Min cautioned him yet again. Her voice had been in his ears all night and he had pushed it away like just more of the buzzing.

Sunny had secured a safety harness around his chest, designed for mid-combat triage, and strapped a similar one around her own torso. Between them, Thompson lay motionless, his skin starkly white against the dark spatters of his own blood. Machines whined, their droning tone invading Tynan's mind, pushing rational thoughts aside.

"What do you need?" Tynan asked again. His voice was ragged.

Sunny dashed the back of her wrists against her eyes and shook her head. "Nothing," she said quietly. "We can't do anything more."

The machine continued to blare.

Tynan looked back down at the man strapped tightly to the gurney, secured against the same jostling that made the straps of Tynan's harness bite into his shoulders.

"What?" he asked.

Sunny sniffed loudly and looked away, reaching across Thompson's body to switch the machine off. Even with the noise of the *Avalon*'s engines dragging them out of Argos as fast as possible, the room seemed to fall silent.

The *Avalon* pulled to the side, and despite the firm hold of the safety straps, Tynan reached out to steady himself. He opened his mouth, but found himself without words.

When the pull of the sharp turn eased, Sunny reached forward and drew a blanket over Thompson, tucking it neatly under his shoulders and head. Methodically, she switched the other machines off, her grief only indicated by the way her shoulders rose and fell unevenly. She cleaned her hands with sterile wipes and then reached for Tynan's hands.

He let her scour the pads of his fingers, the creases in his palms. The material was rough and abrasive, and soon his hands were clean and the cloths a bloody red. Sunny disposed of them and wiped the tears from her face. Tynan stared at his hands still, and she grasped them again until he looked at her.

Behind Sunny, Jaya lay peaceful, her chest rising and falling slowly, but with surprising power. Tubes carried clear liquids and garnet-red blood into her arms, and her eyelids fluttered slightly as though trying to wake despite the drugs keeping her at rest.

"Does it get easier?" Tynan asked.

Sunny shrugged with one shoulder, the movement a plea, as if to say, *It does and it doesn't. It is what it is.*

Tynan had a much harder time with that than Sunny did. He could not make that shrug of dispassion, of synthesizing two entirely incompatible feelings into some state of *everything will be okay, even when it's not.* He had a much harder time going on.

He knew it was how he had gotten himself here in the first place. Why he had fought so hard to take back something that had been placed out of his reach by powers much larger than himself. It was why he now felt like something about the universe was broken, if someone could go so suddenly from alive to dead. Even though he had barely known Thompson and been far from liking him.

Tynan was fine with death. As a concept. Facing it straight on was another thing entirely.

The announcement came over the comms to brace for the FTL transition. Sunny squeezed his hands tighter, but they remained standing there in their harnesses as the ship made the jump. The surgical instruments rattled slightly in their magnetic box, but stayed fixed in place.

And then there was only the smoothness of superluminal transit. Sunny stowed the emergency harnesses and her equipment, and Tynan did his best to clean the surfaces, pulling wipes from the sterile box until his hands were full of red-stained cloths and the only other place that blood remained was where it had soaked into the absorbent material of the gurney.

Min had gone quiet. Tynan wasn't remembering his breathing, but he was somehow breathing nonetheless. He sat down heavily, finally heeding her advice.

"Are you okay?" Min asked cautiously.

He nodded. She didn't ask again. Sunny sat down beside him and he sought out her hand again. He knew he liked that now. He knew he wanted her hand in his. Even if it didn't change anything about the world, it somehow made it all *feel* different. Less cold.

"She's strong," Sunny said, nodding toward Jaya. "The captain. She should have been in much worse shape than Thompson and yet I was able to control the bleeding right away."

A sudden rush of adrenaline sent heat to Tynan's face and chest. *She's strong.*

"It's a good thing," he said. "Or none of us would be here right now."

He sensed the frown on her face more than saw it, knew how she would be looking at him right now. Her statement had been a question—a probe. But it wasn't his place to answer that question. It was Jaya's. He had promised her that much.

She would want to know, when she woke, what he had found after they had spoken that last time on the *Avalon*. There hadn't been the time until now. But what he had discovered in her cells made him reconsider the autopsy she had asked him to investigate. He had looked at the samples taken from the dead man. And he had found something.

It was not quite the same thing he had found in Jaya's cells. Not the same strength and resilience. Not the same virtual indestructibility. But there was evidence of the same construction, or at least alteration.

Sunny accepted his silence. She kept his hand in hers. And after they had sat there for a while in quiet companionship, Jaya began to stir.

She blinked back into full alertness, taking a deep but shaky breath. Sunny got up and typed an order into the machine regulating Jaya's medication before turning back to her.

"How are you feeling?" Sunny asked, but despite her smile, her voice was edged with tension. The corners of her eyes were tight, and this was perhaps the first time Tynan had seen her smile not reach her eyes.

"Thompson?" Jaya asked.

Sunny's tentative smile melted into a firm line. She let out a heavy sigh. "Gone."

Jaya tried to push herself up, and Sunny pressed her back gently with a firm hand on her shoulder. She pressed a button that raised the back of the bed so Jaya could sit upright.

Jaya squeezed her eyes shut and swallowed hard. She drew another shaky breath and brushed a tear from the corner of her eye. "If we can get near Yangtze, we should—" Her voice broke and she swallowed again.

"Of course." Sunny pulled a chair up to the side of her bed.

"And my prognosis?" She asked the question flatly, already knowing the answer.

Sunny arched an eyebrow. "You took a lot of damage out there," she said. "I'm not sure how you're even stable or awake right now. You're in much better condition than you should be. Better than I've ever seen coming out of a fight like that."

Jaya looked at Tynan. Every muscle went tense and stiff, like his body couldn't possibly determine the right response, and so it had chosen none at all. Jaya gestured for him to come over and join them.

"Sometimes in medicine," Sunny continued, "things happen you can't explain. The body does amazing things, but this..." Sunny paused. "This kind of trauma does not heal this quickly."

Her voice carried a flat undertone, a note of skepticism that suggested that despite her outward optimism and good cheer, Sunny was not someone who subscribed to the idea of miracles. There was a question in her expression, in the way one corner of her lips tweaked up a little, and in the way she already seemed to be looking for the answer on Jaya's face.

"Something has been made clear to me recently," Jaya began. "We've taken on a huge task, and it will take a lot if we have any hope of achieving it." She cleared her throat, closing her eyes for a moment. Then she continued. "And it will require complete honesty from me. I asked Tynan to look into something for me before... well, before all this. He can probably tell you more than I can."

Sunny turned her questioning look on Tynan, whose chest seemed to empty of air at her gaze.

He blinked and swallowed. "I ran some tests, at Jaya's—Captain Mill's—request. She asked me to keep the results to myself, but with her permission, I can give all my data to you. She's been altered in some way. I don't know when, but I suspect in early childhood. It's some combination of organic material and synthetic technology more advanced than cybernetics or any medical nanotech I've ever seen. I think it's the same technology the Sons of Priam were working on."

Sunny stared at him as if his translator had stopped functioning.

"I no longer work for the Union," Jaya said to Sunny, turning the doctor's attention back to her, "and neither do you. If I'm going to be your captain, and if you're going to choose to follow me, we need to trust each other. I am willing to submit to any tests you wish to do. Whatever this is, I need to understand it."

There was a slow, measured pause as Sunny contemplated first Jaya, and then Tynan.

"Of course," she said finally. "If I'm going to be able to treat you, I'll need to know the appropriate way to do that."

Jaya held out her hand, and Sunny took it in a firm grip.

"So," Jaya said, the hint of a grin flickering in her eyes, "when will I be able to leave?"

"At the rate you're healing, I wouldn't be surprised if the answer was any minute." Sunny's voice turned firm, then, and she fixed Jaya with a strict look. "But I will monitor you and let you know when I think you are in a condition to stand."

"Of course, doc." Jaya smiled for real this time. "Whatever you say."

Sunny shook her head in bewilderment. "Whatever this mystery is, it saved your life."

Jaya spoke the words the very moment they crossed Tynan's mind. "And could be our key to stopping the Sons of Priam."

Tynan met her eyes, and understood what she meant. "I'll figure out what I can."

He would get started right away.

42

The dust kicked up by the *Avalon* still hung in the air as Mara disembarked into the bright daylight. She closed her eyes, and for a moment, she felt the hot desert winds of Uduak in the grit and the flush of sun on her skin.

But she was not going back to Uduak.

Half a dozen others followed her off the ship. They were the few who had chosen not to stay with Jaya and her crew, who had chosen to make this stop on a remote colony their last with their new captain. Mara didn't envy that choice: stay and fight alongside the newly minted enemy of everything they had once served, or try to fade into the same poverty and misery that most of them had come from.

Mara looked back at the ship. Jaya made her way down the gangplank, stepping cautiously but intentionally unassisted, flanked by Rhodes and Azima. The wind picked up loose strands of her hair, teasing more from her braid and whipping them about her face. Mara waited as Jaya approached her.

"You know where you're going next?" Jaya asked.

Mara squinted up into the pale wash of sky. "After Yangtze system, you mean."

Jaya nodded. "Yes."

The purse on Mara's belt hung full enough. She had been surprised when Ahmad—Luka, as she now knew he was really called—had thrust it in her hand as they left the Fox's store, and even more surprised when she had found a collection of antique jewelry within it. The kind of pieces wealthy nareians loved to show off, which could easily be fenced.

Make it right, he had said.

Mara had split the jewels with the *Avalon*. It would give them all a place to start, and Mara felt certain she would find a way to survive. The company of the *Avalon* had gifted her a small ground shuttle in exchange for the promise to find a final resting place for the ashes of their fallen friend in his home system.

"I'll figure it out," she replied. "I know where the lost people of the galaxy live. Figured I'd start there."

"Well," Jaya said, the gold in her eyes sparkling in the sunlight, "I imagine you'll be able to find us, when it's time."

Mara smiled. "It's what I do."

She shook the woman's hand and climbed into the small all-terrain vehicle. A metal box was already packed into the footwell of the passenger side.

The humans began to disperse, and Jaya and her crew returned to the *Avalon*.

Mara started the ATV up and accelerated, kicking up dust behind her.

She waited to make the call. Until she had made it to the next town and bartered her land vehicle and a significant amount of her cash for an old-model passenger ship, barely large enough for two people. Until she had dusted off its captain's chair and rewired the faulty control panel. Until she was halfway to Yangtze.

The Fox's face appeared scowling over her control panel. "All is well?"

"As well as it can be," she replied. "Is your friend enjoying my gift?"

"The *Nasdenika* got him where he needed to go without suspicion. New name and new paperwork now, though."

"I would expect no less. Names are important after all. You both know mine now, and I know his. Somehow only you escaped with your anonymity."

"I imagine that will change," he said, a shadow crossing over his face. "It's only a matter of time."

"You better get back to your friend. He's got a chip on his shoulder and I'm pretty sure he's ready to take the Union down all by himself."

"Luka can handle himself," the Fox said. "But I'll be damned if I let him start a rebellion without me."

He closed the connection and Mara settled back into her seat. One stop, to put a soul to rest. Properly, for a change.

There had been a lot of changes, and Mara only foresaw more ahead. But she would start with what she knew. There were a lot of lost people in the galaxy. People cast off from their homes, their societies. People who had never belonged in the first place. Some of them might be looking for the long-missing nareian princess. Some of them even for the right reasons.

Mara would start with the lost ones. After all, she had until very recently been one of them.

43

They had broken free of Argos and the Union's grip. They had departed the quiet colony where they had left those who chose not to join the fight. Now Jaya sat at the desk in the captain's quarters, her closest friends seated across from her.

Rhodes held the responsibility of executive officer with the gravitas she had come to rely on. Tynan fidgeted in the seat next to him, his eyes alight with the ideas that never seemed to cease swirling in his mind. And Sal leaned back, one ankle balanced on the other knee with careless grace, his confidence ready to bolster her when she needed it most.

Her crew was now formally reduced to only eighteen. Even with their sparse membership, she had a deep conviction in her crew. She would rather have a few that she trusted than a horde of unknowns. Still, she knew they had to build an army if they were to stand a chance.

These three were the keepers of all the information they had compiled so far. Sal had not yet sorted through all the messages he'd pulled from Emory's console, but Jaya presented Armstrong's theory to her top three ranking officers. And she told them of her own connections to the Sons of Priam: her father, her brother, and her own strange physiology. The lone desk lamp illuminated their serious faces staring back at her in the gloom of the ship's artificial night. Above them, the cabin window provided a cool, neutral cast of starlight.

"I know who we're up against," she concluded. "And as the most trusted members of my crew, you should know, too. Armstrong found Emory's connection to the Sons of Priam, but when he traced his identity back, he could only follow it for a few years. Emory did everything he could to erase the man he was before TA Tech. But there was one loose end he didn't manage to tie up: his family."

Sal's dark eyes glittered in the starlight, his face set in firm lines. Rhodes managed a soft smile, his shoulders straight and confident, as though he were preparing to carry the load quite literally on his back. And even Tynan, whose expressions were still foreign to her, conveyed a strange sense of peace at this new role. She had sensed his frustration under the Union when he had been relegated to a closet and deprived of information. He was eager to help, and his pale skin shone silver in the dim light. Although she knew it was just the starlight on his alien complexion, Jaya couldn't suppress the sense that he was renewed by this mission.

She connected her palm drive to the console and brought up her password-protected folder. The first message from Kier, news articles from years past, old family pictures, and every other scrap of data she had pulled together in the fifteen-year search for her brother filled this folder. She added it to the data from Armstrong— the file that she would give to Tynan, Sal, and Rhodes.

She paused, letting out the breath that had been heavy in her chest. The silence was knitted into the very air, and as Jaya watched the faces of the three friends across from her, she read a multitude of emotions in their shifting expressions.

It was Sal who broke the silence.

"What's the plan, Captain?" he asked, the rare words of defer-
ence countered by the emergence of a sly smile.

"We plant the seeds of a rebellion," Jaya said, feeling a smile
soften the lines of her own face. "We gather intelligence, we recruit
an army of spies and of specialists. We fight, but we fight smart. We
take every step that brings us closer to my father, and we stop him.
Whatever it takes."

Deep into the artificial night, they talked. The starlight never
dimmed, the ever-changing pattern of lights in the window keeping
them company until reveille. The new day was beginning, and
Jaya's companions rose stiff-legged from their chairs to their duties.
The lack of sleep held little power; four sets of eyes were bright
with the potential of the future.

As Rhodes and Tynan left, Jaya held Sal back. He was the only
one who had ever come near this revelation about her past.

"Sal," she said, her voice sounding softer than she had intended.
"Thank you."

"For what?"

"Trusting me."

"Jaya." The smile had returned, all brash confidence. "You've
never given me a reason not to."

He reached out, clasping her hand in a gentle squeeze, and then
he let go and touched the blade of his hand to his forehead in a brisk
salute. There was a genuine straightness to his spine, and a truth in
the reverence of his pose that stirred a hope in her.

She returned the salute, letting herself believe that the sting in
her eyes was from the dry air and the long night.

"On your way, Lieutenant Commander Azima," she said,
releasing her salute and her second officer in one motion.

The door closed on Sal's heels, and Jaya sat down, the stiffness
in her rapidly healing wounds protesting modestly at the stretch.
She looked beyond the desk to where her mother's violin rested in
its case, leaning against the wall. She had not expected to find it still

safely on the *Avalon*, and its presence brought a swift rush of emotion. Anger. She hadn't been willing to see what had been in front of her the whole time. Kier. Her father. And it had cost them so much. *She* had cost them so much.

Was there time to make it right?

She stood and picked up the case, its edges ragged from the years, and locked it away inside one of the storage spaces of the captain's quarters. The ambient lighting had risen in the cabin to early morning levels, and the artificial sunlight infused the energy of a new day into her. She looked up at the window and the deep pockets of stars in the blackness of space.

When she strode onto the bridge a few minutes later and took her seat in the captain's chair, the same unfathomable depth gazed back at her. The galaxy was as diverse as it was vast. It was a scattering of worlds, of peoples, and of ideas. It was full of empty swaths of space and places to hide. And it was full of potential.

Together, they had settled on a new name for the ship. The *Avalon* had belonged to the Union, and this ship had a new life. They called it the *First Light*, in hopes that the night would soon be over. For the first time, she found herself believing her own words. There would come a day when their struggle would end, when truth would prevail, and even if she were not there to see their victory, she knew it would be etched in the stars, its light reaching out to distant worlds to tell their tale.

ALSO IN THE SERIES

FIRST LIGHT

URSA MAJOR

DARK STARS

Looking for more great Science Fiction?

Titan's rebellion is coming. Only one man can stop it.

GET BOOK ONE OF THE CHILDREN OF TITAN NOW!

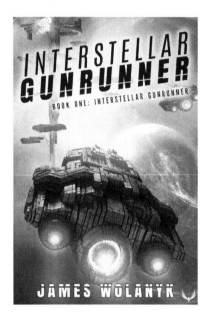

Nolan Garrett is Cerberus. A government assassin, tasked with fixing the galaxy's darkest, ugliest problems.

GET INTERSTELLAR GUNRUNNER NOW!

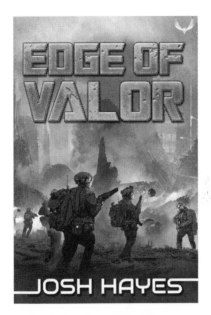

When their mission fails, his begins.

GET EDGE OF VALOR TODAY!

"Aliens, agents, and espionage abound in this Cold War-era alternate history adventure... A wild ride!" — Dennis E. Taylor, bestselling author of We Are Legion (We Are Bob)

GET THE LUNA MISSILE CRISIS NOW!

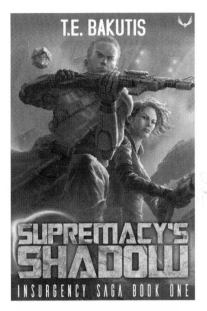

Someone betrayed him. He'll probably die finding out who.

GET SUPREMACY'S SHADOW NOW!

For all our Sci-Fi books, visit our website.